A DRAUGHT
✦⟺ *for a* ⟺✦
DEAD MAN

Caroline Roe

BERKLEY PRIME CRIME, NEW YORK

For Harry, with love

A DRAUGHT FOR A DEAD MAN

A Berkley Prime Crime Book / published by arrangement with the author

PRINTING HISTORY

Berkley Prime Crime hardcover edition / November 2002
Berkley Prime Crime mass-market edition / November 2003

Copyright © 2002 by Medora Sale.
Cover art by Jeff Barson.
Cover design by Judith Murello.
Text design by Kristin del Rosario.

For information address: The Berkley Publishing Group,
a division of Penguin Group (USA) Inc.,
375 Hudson Street, New York, New York 10014.

ISBN: 0-425-19308-X

Berkley Prime Crime Books are published
by The Berkley Publishing Group,
a division of Penguin Group (USA) Inc.,
375 Hudson Street, New York, New York 10014.
The name BERKLEY PRIME CRIME and the BERKLEY PRIME CRIME
design are trademarks belonging to Penguin Group (USA) Inc.

PRINTED IN THE UNITED STATES OF AMERICA

10 9 8 7 6 5 4 3 2 1

continued . . .

CURE FOR A CHARLATAN

"Caroline Roe is the real deal . . . The story is filled with detail and action that paints a panorama of medieval Spain, especially the Jewish quarter. The medical mystery is absolutely awesome, but it is the depth to all the characters that turns this into one of the best historical mystery entries . . . the Chronicles of Isaac are first-rate reads."
—*Painted Rock Reviews*

"A rich tale of ethnicity and superstition. I was entranced by the plot and the colorful cast of characters. A definite winner."
—*Rendezvous*

REMEDY FOR TREASON

AN ANTHONY FINALIST FOR BEST PAPERBACK ORIGINAL
NOMINATED FOR THE ARTHUR ELLIS AWARD FOR BEST NOVEL

"Intelligent, beautifully written, and superbly researched . . . Roe gives us genuinely interesting characters, chief of whom is her detective, Blind Isaac."
—*The Toronto Globe and Mail*

"Isaac of Girona, a good man in a bad time, should delight readers in this tale of court intrigue and religious tension in medieval Spain—a rich, spicy paella of a book."
—Bruce Alexander, author of *Blind Justice*

"Not only a good mystery, it is a window into a time and place not usually approached by anyone but the dedicated scholar."
—*The Washington Times*

"Blind Isaac and Yusuf are a delightfully incongruous pair . . . A deliciously nasty brew of fanatics and scheming royals."
—Candace Robb, author of *The King's Bishop*

"A clever mystery, unusual setting, and lashings of historical and social detail."
—*The Toronto Star*

LIST OF CHARACTERS

From Girona:

ISAAC, physician of Girona
JUDITH, his wife
RAQUEL, his daughter
LEAH, their maid
DANIEL, Raquel's suitor
ASTRUCH AFAMAN, a wealthy banker
DURAN, his son
BONAFILLA, his daughter
ESTER, her maid

BERENGUER DE CRUÏLLES, Bishop of Girona

From Perpignan:

ARNAU MARÇA
JOHANA MARÇA, his wife
JORDI, their servant
FELICITAT, Arnau's nurse
FELIP CASSA, a man of business
FATHER MIRÓ, a Dominican

Syndicate:
    PERE VIDAL
    PERE PEYRO
    DON RAMON JULIÀ
    MARTIN, agent to an unnamed viscount

The *call*:
    JACOB BONJUHES, a physician
    DAVID, his brother
    RUTH, Jacob's wife
    ABRAM DAYOT, Jacob's apprentice
    MORDECAI, Jacob's houseman
    JACINTA, their servant

The palace:
    PRINCESS CONSTANÇA, daughter of Pedro of Aragon
    LADY MARGARIDA, one of her ladies-in-waiting
    HUGUET, procurator during the King's absence
    BERNARD BONSHOM, Lord Puigbalador

Outcasts:
    GARCIA DE L'ALMUNYA, jailer
    ESCLARMONDA, a prostitute
    Porters: EL GROS, AHMED, ROGER, THE ENGLISHMAN

On the road:

    BENIAMIN, a Figueres businessman
    JOHAN CERVIAN, a convert to Christianity
    FRANCESCA, his wife

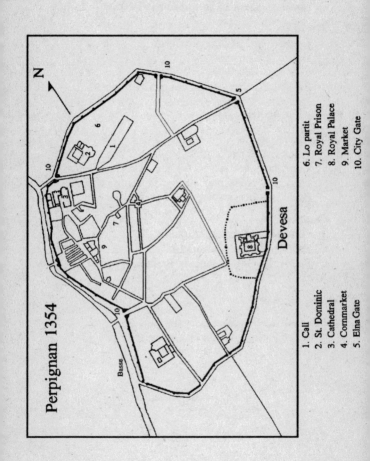

Perpignan 1354

N

1. Call
2. St. Dominic
3. Cathedral
4. Cornmarket
5. Elna Gate
6. Lo partit
7. Royal Prison
8. Royal Palace
9. Market
10. City Gate

Basse

Devesa

HISTORICAL NOTE

AT the time this novel takes place, the territories belonging to the crown of Aragon extended from the kingdom of Aragon at its western border to various islands in the Mediterranean at its eastern limits; from Valencia in the south, to the counties of Roussillon and Cerdagne. The lands that the kings of Aragon ruled now form part of Spain (Aragon, Catalonia, Valencia, and the Balearic Islands), Italy (Sardinia), and France (Roussillon, Cerdagne, and the area around Montpellier).

Jaume, or James, I of Aragon (1213–1276), known as the Conqueror, had sons by both his wives. He was persuaded by his second wife, who wished to see her children rule their own kingdoms, to divide up his lands among his sons. In the end, only two survived to inherit: Pere, or Peter, and his younger brother, Jaume. Pere was given the territories of Catalonia, Aragon, and Valencia, and Jaume received the Balearic Islands of Mallorca, Menorca, and Ibiza, along with the counties of Roussillon and Cerdagne, and the district of Montpellier. Young Jaume was named

Jaume II of Mallorca, and given his lands to hold as a separate and independent unit within the Aragonese Empire. Jaume the Conqueror's gift fueled almost a century of bitter conflicts and war between the descendents of the two branches of the ruling house.

Well before his father's death, Jaume II of Mallorca started construction on a magnificent, strongly fortified palace on a hill to the south of the city of Perpignan in the county of Roussillon, now in present-day France. He moved into it in 1275, when he married Esclarmonda, a year before he became King. When the Conqueror died, in 1276, his son, bypassing other prominent candidates for the honor, made this city the capital of his realm, thus ensuring its prosperity and its undying affection for him.

MORE than sixty years later, when Pere the Ceremonious, count-king of Aragon, succeeded to the kingdom his great-grandfather had divided up, the bitterness between cousins had not yet subsided. Jaume III was King of Mallorca. He was a popular monarch in Roussillon, Cerdagne, and Mont-pellier, but resented in the Mediterranean islands, which felt burdened by the king's heavy taxes. Taking advantage of the islanders' discontent, Pere raised an army, set sail with his fleet, and took Mallorca in 1343. Roussillon and Cerdagne fell to him in 1344 and Jaume III was forced to hand over his stronghold in Perpignan.

Captured and held prisoner in Vilafranca de Conflent, Jaume III arranged his escape, determined to regain his ter-ritories. He fled northward, where he sold Montpellier—his birthplace—to the French in order to raise an army. He died in Mallorca in 1347 during an attempt to retake the island.

Now part of a kingdom that contained Saragossa, Va-lencia, Barcelona, and other rich and important cities, Per-pignan abruptly suffered a loss of relative importance. Well aware that he would be resented, Pere went to considerable effort to woo the populace of the city, mingling with the people, and holding popular entertainments and dances at the palace for them. His children spent considerable time there, as did he and his Queens, Maria (died 1347) and Eleanora. His heir, the Infant Johan, was born in Perpignan in 1350.

His efforts were only partially successful. In his constant travels around his kingdom, Pere visited Perpignan frequently, often staying for long periods of time, but the palace had become a military garrison as much as a royal court. It was an enclosed society, not answerable to local authorities, and inhabited by "foreigners" born outside of Roussillon. The soldiers were single or had left wives behind; they were well paid in comparison with the locals. Like any army encamped in a mildly hostile but safe territory, the men grew bored and troublesome. In addition to pursuing women and gambling to pass the time, they were accused of running up huge unpaid bills, embezzlement, and theft.

The King dealt with the problems of public vice by instituting controls and checks, which were alternately ignored or rigorously enforced. Prostitution, although legal, was contained and severely restricted; gambling was forbidden, with heavy penalties for both players and organizers of games. Both activities thrived.

At the time of the events of this book, the King and Queen were in Sardinia, fighting a war; in spite of its various problems, Perpignan remained a center of trade and commerce. That year, a syndicate raised the money to charter a ship called the *Santa Maria Nunciada*. She set out for the eastern Mediterranean with a cargo of high-quality goods made in Roussillon or imported into the county for expert finishing there. Investments of this magnitude were common in a port like Barcelona, where large capital sums were easier to raise. Such an enterprise was more difficult to carry out in Perpignan, especially in Their Majesties' absence, during a time when loyalties remained shaky even in the palace.

PROLOGUE

Girona, Wednesday, September 17, 1354

"Who was that at the gate?" asked the physician's wife. She was sitting under the trees in the garden, a pile of fine linen in her lap and a needle in her hand, looking off into the distance over the rooftops.

"A messenger, Mama. He said he was from Perpignan with a letter for Papa," added her daughter.

"Then fetch him, Raquel, my dear," said her mother.

"He has fetched himself, Judith," said her husband. "I could not help hearing the clamor of the bell. What do you have for me from Perpignan?"

Raquel broke the seal and opened the letter. "It is from a Master Jacob Bonjuhes, Papa."

"Jacob," said Isaac the physician. "Poor little Jacob. We were students together. How many years it has been since we met. I was always fond of him—such a sad, solemn boy he was then. Please, my dear, tell me what he says."

Raquel sat down by her mother and began to read. "It is dated the tenth day of September, and he says:

My dear Master Isaac,

It has been some time since we have been able to speak together, but you are always in my thoughts. I pray that you and your family are well. I have had much conversation about you in recent days, and it has given me a strong desire to see you again.

I would like with all my heart to invite you to the wedding celebration of my younger brother, David, and Bonafilla, the daughter of Astruch Afaman of Girona. The match will take place in Perpignan on Tuesday, the fourteenth day of October as the King counts the days.

My brother, David, has been like a son to me since my parents died when he was seven, and left him, a lonely and unhappy little boy, in my care. I have tried to look after him as you looked after me, when my parents decided to send me to study with our revered teacher, Master Vidal. I too was just seven, and as lonely and bewildered as David was. I remember clearly how you comforted and guided me— and I have tried to do for him what you did for me. He is now a fine man and it would please me very much if you could be here to witness his marriage.

I have a few interesting patients right now. I am eager to lay out before you my diagnoses and treatments of them and to hear your comments. Your skill was ever much greater than mine, especially in diagnosing complaints and in compounding remedies. The learned master from Granada at whose feet you sat before you came to Master Vidal taught you more than I can ever hope to know. Astruch assures me that your loss of sight has not hampered you, for you are assisted by your skilled daughter and a clever apprentice.

You could travel with Astruch, who intends to start his journey back to Perpignan the last Monday in the month. He has business in Figueres and in Collioure, and should be arriving on Wednesday evening or Thursday morning.

My wife heartily joins me in this invitation, and hopes

that your estimable wife, Judith, and your daughter Raquel
will be able to come with you, as well as your apprentice.

"Old friend or not, Isaac, I am not traveling to Perpignan. Not right now," said Judith.

"Why not, Mama?" asked Raquel. "It is not far. Not nearly as far as Tarragona. We would be on the road only two or three nights. And staying with friends or acquaintances, not in inns."

"Finish the letter, Raquel. You may discuss your mother's reluctance to travel later," said her father.

"Yes, Papa," said Raquel. "But I should think I had more reasons to object to going away. Daniel has only just come home."

"Finish the letter."

"There is not much more. He goes on to say, 'The messenger will be returning to Perpignan. Please let us know your answer by him.' And indeed, Papa, I forgot to say that the messenger promised to come back early tomorrow for your answer."

"You had best have Raquel write your excuses now," said Judith. "Then the letter will be ready when the messenger comes."

"I will take him some of my newer compounds," said her husband. "And a vial of our potent remedy for pain. But we do not have enough on hand to give any of it away right now. We will set to work on it early tomorrow, Raquel. I must send Yusuf out at dawn to gather more herbs."

"You can't mean to go all the way to Perpignan," said Judith. "What of His Excellency? What if something happened to us?"

"His Excellency is in excellent health," said Isaac. "And what is more to the point, so are you. We will leave the first Monday in the month, the wedding is the following Tuesday, and we will set out for home the next day at sunrise. If Astruch Afaman wishes to remain longer to see his daughter well settled, we will return on our own. Either way, we shall be home on Friday, well before Sabbath. We will be away no more than eleven days at most, my dear."

"Why should Mama not be in excellent health?" asked Raquel with a frown. "She is never ill. Although you do seem not quite yourself these days, Mama. I certainly won't leave you if you are not well."

"There is nothing wrong with me, Raquel," said her mother sharply. "Except that I am . . ." Her daughter's eyes were fixed on her, and Judith suddenly colored. She picked up her sewing and bent over it to hide her face. "I am with child," she said.

"At your age?" said Raquel, startled.

"What do you mean, my age? I'm not that old, Raquel. I was fifteen when I wed your father, and Rebecca—I mean, you were born three years later. Do I look that old?"

"Certainly not, Mama," said Raquel hastily. "You look more like my sister than my mother. Everyone says so. But since I'm about to marry, it seems odd, that's all. Even if it does happen all the time. After Hannah married, her mother had two babies . . ." Her voice trailed away in amazement.

"You had better accustom yourself to it, then," said her mother.

"How are you feeling?"

"Very well. A little sick at moments, and rather tired at others, but very well. That does not mean that I am willing to sit on a mule bouncing all the way to Perpignan and back."

"Her Majesty does," said Raquel. "She seems to be with child half the time and rides all over the kingdom."

"She no doubt has a better mule than I will ever ride on," said Judith tartly. "And a snail can outrun those royal processions from city to city."

"Well, between my wedding and your baby, there will be much sewing to do. Miriam had better start improving her needlework," said Raquel briskly. "I can't do it all. And distill compounds for Papa."

"We will need another servant," said Judith in a threatening voice.

"I have suggested that for some time," said Isaac. "We will find one when we get back from Perpignan. Forgive me for leaving you, my dear, but I am looking forward to visiting young Jacob. I want to know why he thinks I was such a friend to him."

"First, you had better go to see the Bishop. He may not permit you to leave him," said Judith.

"Very true, my dear. I will do that as soon as someone can locate Yusuf."

"I'M not going to Perpignan, Mama," said Raquel. "I have too much to do, and I am not putting off my wedding again. Daniel will think I don't want to marry him."

"Nonsense," said her mother. "He knows you want to get married."

"And I don't want to leave you here alone."

"I'm not ill, Raquel. And I have Naomi to look after me. Go with your father."

"Daniel's been away for months and he's only now come back. It's cruel that I should have to leave so soon."

"You'll have a whole lifetime together, my dear," said her mother. "And answer the door, please. If we have to wait for Ibrahim to think of it, our visitors will have given up long since."

"Yes, Mama," said Raquel mutinously.

STANDING at the gate was a tall, willowy creature dressed in a dark gown and so swathed in veils that she was scarcely visible. Behind her was a bored-looking maid whose veil, in contrast, clung precariously to the top of her head by a pin thrust into a knot of hair. "*Hola,* Raquel," said the veiled creature. "It is Bonafilla, Astruch's daughter."

"Bonafilla," said Raquel, startled. "Welcome to our house. How delightful to see you. And may I be the first in our family to wish you great joy."

"You've heard," whispered Bonafilla, sliding like a cat through the gate as it opened.

Judith set aside her work, rose, and came over to add her good wishes to those of her daughter. "If you will excuse me for a little while, Raquel will entertain you. I have a few things to do before my husband returns."

Raquel opened her mouth to speak, but Judith's ferocious look cut off whatever objection she might have made. She urged their guest over to a seat beneath the trees and sat down. "Don't do too much, Mama," she said. "It's hot. My mother has no idea when she should slow down and rest," she added in explanation, and waited for Bonafilla to say something.

There was silence except for small chirping sounds from the birds in the trees and the purring of Feliu, the cat, who had jumped on Raquel's lap.

"Are you excited?" asked Raquel finally. "I know I was terribly excited at first and a little nervous as well."

"I'm terrified." The words were scarcely audible under the heavy wrapping.

"Bonafilla, loosen your veil," said Raquel. "Please. How can I talk to you if I can't see you or hear you. You must be terribly hot."

The young woman unwrapped the outer veil that covered her completely from head to hips and dropped it onto the bench. Under it another one shielded her hair and part of her face from view.

"Why did you start veiling yourself like that?"

"I don't like being stared at by strangers when I go out."

"In the *call*? But everyone here knows you already," said Raquel.

"They still stare at me as if there were something terrible wrong with me," she whispered.

"But that's foolish, Bonafilla," said Raquel. "I promise you that no one will stare at you here."

She loosened her second veil and let it drop onto her shoulders.

"That's better," said Raquel. "I'm glad to see by your face that it really is you. Did you say you were frightened?" she asked her. "Why?"

"Wouldn't you be frightened?" she asked. "I'm supposed to marry him and I haven't even met him yet. They sent me a likeness of David, but a likeness doesn't tell you anything. My father decided ages ago that we should marry."

"Are you in love with someone else, Bonafilla?" asked Raquel.

"Someone else? No," she said vehemently. "I just don't want to get married to a stranger in a faraway city. I sometimes wish I were a Christian, Raquel, because then I could be a nun and not have to marry."

"I think Christian girls whose parents have made up good marriages for them have a hard time going into convents," observed Raquel. "After all, their dowries go with them."

"I didn't think of that," said Bonafilla vaguely. "Papa and I are to ride to Perpignan next week, all alone, except for my useless brother and Ester, my maid, who is as much comfort as a lump of ice on a winter's day." She nodded in the direction of the maid, who was gossiping with Leah on the other side of the courtyard. Suddenly she grasped Raquel's hand. "And if I get there and meet him and we hate each other, as I know we shall, there'll be no one to help me tell Papa that I can't marry him. My brother won't. Duran just keeps saying the only respectable men here are either already married or my cousins." Tears began to fill her eyes; she let go of Raquel and covered her face with her hands.

Raquel waited until she raised her head again and dabbed at her eyes with a silk square. "What about your stepmother?" she asked.

"Preciosa? She's no use. She doesn't want to leave her wonderful babies with the nursery-maid."

"I don't suppose she does," said Raquel.

"Could you come with me?" said Bonafilla. "Please? I know your papa is coming because David's brother is an old friend, but my papa says you won't come because you're so happy about your wedding and busy preparing for it. He said that to make me feel how wrong I am," she added, and began to cry again.

"Bonafilla, please, stop crying," said Raquel, looking desperately over her shoulder at the staircase in hopes that her mother might be coming back to the courtyard.

"I can't," she said, blowing her nose and mopping her eyes as if in preparation for a fresh onslaught. "I need someone with me I can trust. Someone strong to help me with Papa. And someone closer to my own age."

When at last Judith came down the stairs into the courtyard, a smiling Bonafilla rose to meet her. "Mistress Judith," she said, "Raquel has so kindly offered to come with me to Perpignan if she has your permission to go."

"Has she?" said Judith. "That is kind of her. She has my permission. I would think it is Daniel's permission that might be difficult to obtain," she added teasingly. "But I am sure that we can deal with that."

＊━━＝ ━━＝＋

BERENGUER de Cruïlles, Bishop of Girona, looked up as his physician was ushered into his private study, and then glowered at his attendant. "Master Isaac," he said, attempting to disguise his impatience. "Which of these incompetent wretches I surround myself with has sent for you? I must be looking pale and unwell today."

"No one has sent for me, Your Excellency," said his personal physician. "I am disturbing your peace on my own account, for which I apologize."

"Then it is for a reason, my friend," said the Bishop. "There is always a reason for your actions, I have learned. But I cannot promise to give you much time today. I dine with a pack of tedious visitors. Perhaps one brief game of chess?"

"As tempting as that sounds, Your Excellency," said the physician, "I am here to ask a favor."

"Then ask it quickly," said Berenguer with a slight frown, "so that after it, if the request is not too outrageous, we will have time for chess still."

"And if it is?"

"I will be in no mood to play chess. What do you ask of me?"

"To grant me leave to go to Perpignan on Monday, the seventh day of October, Your Excellency, and be away for eleven or twelve days. It is to attend a wedding between Astruch's daughter and David Bonjuhes, the brother of an old friend."

"Which Astruch?"

"He who is known as Afaman," said Isaac.

"A man of substance," noted the Bishop. "And if I fall ill?"

"It should be within Your Excellency's power to remain in good health for twelve days. I will leave ample supplies of gout medication and other remedies with your attendant, who is a most careful man, and perhaps some instructions with your cook on how you should be fed."

"Do not threaten me with that, Master Isaac," said Berenguer, laughing. "Promise not to speak to the cook and you have my leave to travel to Perpignan for the wedding. Will you ride with Master Astruch?"

"Indeed. Master Astruch, his daughter, his son, and their attendants."

"Does your family travel with you?"

"Only Yusuf and Raquel. The bride has been most earnest in her request that Raquel accompany us."

"She will be company for her," said Berenguer. "From what I know of them, women cling together."

"They do, Your Excellency, especially at times like these."

"Bernat will have a letter of permission drawn up giving you and your party license to travel to Perpignan and back, as well as freedom from dress and other restrictions for three weeks, in case you are delayed. That should protect you from officious fools. Do not consider that license to stay long away from us. And for your own safety, Isaac, dress discreetly. There have been rumors of trouble on that road. I do not wish to lose my physician over a wedding."

"I assure you, Your Excellency, that we will travel circumspectly and with great caution, and I thank you for your kindness in allowing us to leave."

But instead of calling for refreshment, or the chessboard, or even bidding farewell to Isaac, Berenguer pushed his chair back a little and studied the blind physician. "And so your business takes you to Perpignan," he said. "There have been rumors coming out of the city lately, Isaac. Today I received a letter from the noble Vidal de Blanes in which he asks me if I have heard anything of interest from there. He speaks, he pointed out, as abbot of Sant Feliu, not as His Majesty's procurator during the war in Sardinia."

"Does that distinction matter?"

"Since one of the rumors involves Huguet, the procurator royal in Perpignan, it does matter."

"A delicate situation."

"It is. Other names, of wealthy citizens and of nobles, have been mentioned, my friend. They include my lord of Puigbalador, Bernard Bonshom."

"Surely men of rank attract much malicious gossip," observed Isaac. "Especially in a city that has changed rulers recently."

"I would not call it a recent change. It was at least ten years ago. I remember," said Berenguer nostalgically, "the day Jaume of Mallorca ordered his castellan to turn over the keys of the palace to Felip de Castres. De Castres was acting for His Majesty at the time. And later His Majesty rode through the streets of the city, exchanging pleasant conversation and merry jests with the populace—knowing how much they might resent the loss of their old king and becoming part of the kingdom of Aragon."

"It was eleven years," said Isaac.

"Ten or eleven," said Berenguer impatiently. "Then Don Pedro spent much time and effort in the following months winning over the people of the city, inviting them to celebrations and entertainments at the palace. It was generally believed that his efforts were successful."

"Perhaps they were. Let us hope that these present tales are no more than malicious gossip," said Isaac.

"My friend, if the abbot of Sant Feliu foresees trouble, there will be trouble. He can smell it as a dog smells carrion. It will be a useful skill in his next appointment, Master Isaac. Vidal de Blanes will be an archbishop soon."

"Responsible for the city of Perpignan?"

Berenguer laughed. "Not precisely. I suspect the question about Perpignan came originally from His Majesty. When His Majesty hears rumors of problems, he prefers to know the opinions of observant bystanders first. Then he will listen to the voices of those who are involved."

"Sensible," said Isaac, "since the person involved is almost certainly going to lie to him. What sorts of problems? Or do you have leave to tell me?"

"They are but rumors . . ." Berenguer paused. "But why should you not know? The moment you reach the city you will hear about them. They say that false coinage is being minted in or near the city, and that the procurator either permits it through his silence, or profits from it, or perhaps is even actively involved in it. In addition, the behavior of the lord of Puigbalador becomes more outrageous by the day, they say, so much so that many of his trusted servants have fled his service."

"That would be easy to verify," said Isaac. "Of course, outrageous behavior can mean anything from a life of total debauchery to an extra cup of wine over supper. These things become sadly distorted in the telling."

"That is what I hope for," said the Bishop. "But I am preparing letters to two or three men in Perpignan, Isaac, which I would prefer not to send through our usual couriers. If I hand them to you, perhaps you could arrange to have them delivered promptly and discreetly, without occasioning any comment."

"Where must they go?"

"To the royal palace and the cathedral."

"I shall do my utmost to have them delivered discreetly," said Isaac.

"And cautiously, my friend. If these rumors are true, there are some who might consider your life to be less important than their schemes. And don't let young Yusuf run free all over the city either. His Majesty has enemies there—still."

"Active after all this time, in spite of His Majesty's efforts? Did you not insist a moment ago that the populace had forgotten old grievances?"

"And had nothing but loyal and contented leaders? That was a nostalgic dream, my friend," said Berenguer firmly. "Those who had great power under the kings of Mallorca and have lost it are likely to have long memories and a great many allies."

ONE

Outside Perpignan, Wednesday, September 17, 1354

IN the evening of that same day, two men strolled through the garden of a large country house. The approach of evening was at last beginning to moderate the heat of the day. A breeze ruffled the still air, and above the horizon to the west, the sun hung low in the sky, a globe of molten gold, that turned the stones of the house, the dried grasses in the fields, and the fruit on the trees into its own substance.

"I fear I must leave now," said the younger of the two men. He was staring off in the distance, watching a heavily-laden donkey trudge along a path, urged on by a small boy.

"My dear Don Ramon, how can you? There is a magnificent supper in preparation, and some charming companions have arrived. I am sure they will ease your suffering and, perhaps, even cast a charm or two upon the dice and cards."

"Why?" said Ramon, transferring his gaze to the ground under his foot. "I cannot stake myself to so much as one hand of cards. Until I have the right to sell what is mine,

I cannot even sit down at the table. And unfortunately, my father seems determined to live forever," he added dryly.

"Then you must get yourself some money," said the other, raising an eyebrow in astonishment.

"How?" asked Don Ramon, turning to his host.

"Surely your circumstances cannot be that desperate," said the other.

"They are more than desperate."

"Can you raise four thousand sous, my young friend?"

"Four thousand! Impossible. I cannot raise half that sum."

"Then go to the Jews. Borrow it."

"Do you think I have not thought of that already? I assure you that they too wish to know how I will pay it back."

"Paying it back will be the least of your problems. Don Ramon, listen to me. I know someone who is desperate to sell his share in a shipping venture. It is worth more than five thousand sous. Possibly much more. He will gladly sell it for four thousand."

"How am I to get four thousand? I am having trouble finding four sous," said Don Ramon.

"The castle is worth more than that."

"My good lord, you forget. I do not own the castle."

"I will say it again. Go to the Jews. You can borrow it."

"Without security?"

"I will take you myself to a friend in the *call*, Don Ramon. This evening if you like. I will offer him my word to back you. You will give him as security your share in this venture of which I speak. Add to that what every man knows, that you are heir to lands and property worth at least ten times more than the sum you wish to borrow, and you will not have to worry. He will lend you four thousand."

"On what terms?"

"What is legal and not a penny more. Twenty percent.

And I guarantee that this venture will return to you at least four times what you invest in it—or to be more exact, what my friend the moneylender invests in it, for you will not have to put down a penny of your own money. In fact, he might advance you a few sous extra to join us at the tables tonight. Or whenever you wish."

"You must give me some time to think about this. It is a monstrous sum of money. And whatever you may say, I know well that I am the man who will have to bear the risk."

"Doña Violant—"

"Which Doña Violant?" asked young Ramon, his eyes losing their gloom for a moment. "The viscount's daughter? Don Francesc's wife?"

"What other Doña Violant worth naming is there? She has expressed an interest in riding out here to see you play. If she can be sure that you will be here."

"To watch me play at cards?" The young man seemed stupefied.

"Or whatever you and Doña Violant care to play at. The house, as you can see if you take the trouble to look behind you, is large enough for all kinds of play."

Perpignan, Thursday, October 2, 1354

"YOUR lady wife is in the city, señor." The head jailer's words were sufficiently respectful, but his probing voice, quivering with curiosity, filled the cell. For all his schooling in self-control, Arnau Marça felt a powerful jolt in his belly at the words.

"You yourself have seen her?" he asked casually, addressing the jailer as if he were a servant.

"No, Don Arnau."

"Then why do you conclude that she is here, my good Garcia?"

"The food your servant brought is of better quality today. I made bold to assume that the affectionate touch of a wife lies behind the fare."

"Bold indeed," said the knight coldly, turning away. For in spite of all the malice in the jailer's sly remarks, he knew exactly where Johana was, and his knowledge armed him against Garcia's petty torments. Arnau Marça's first act on being arrested had been to send a message to his wife instructing her to bar the castle doors and stay within. In any case, she knew better than to travel right now, for fearless as she was, she trembled at the possibility of losing this baby.

Garcia de l'Almunya closed the door to Arnau's cell and leaned against it, brooding. He wanted his little revenge on Arnau Marça, who treated him as if he were a man of no importance. His present exalted position had not been easy to achieve. He had fought off many other contenders for the post of Keeper of the Royal Prison. It was a pleasant life. The Keeper's duties were light, the salary excellent, the additional revenues from the prisoners useful, and among his usual associates, the Keeper's prestige was high. It made him almost a gentleman, and all his acquaintances acknowledged it. He particularly enjoyed entertaining the occasional member of the nobility or the gentry in his establishment. They were elegant and open-handed, even if they were sometimes proud and overbearing, like Arnau Marça. And they were at his mercy.

He brooded on it until the arrival of his prisoner's dinner interrupted his train of thought and he shrugged. There was no point. He wasn't the one who would be beheaded for treason as soon as they brought him to trial. Tomorrow, they said, and then off to Malloles with him, to Puig Johan, for an appointment with the headsman. Then where would his sneers and arrogance be? He opened the door a crack. "Well, señor," he said, "They've come at last. I'll have your meal brought in."

This time the jailer pushed the door wide open. An assistant entered carrying a small table heavily laden with covered dishes. A young girl followed clutching a jug of wine in her small hands. The table was set down by the room's only chair, the child put the jug on the floor, picked up the prisoner's cup, and set it on the table.

Arnau reached into his purse, took out two pennies, and gave one to each of the miserable-looking subordinates. "I thank you," he said gravely, "for your kind attentions."

"Thank you, sir," said the girl, stuffing the coin into her ragged gown. "And I'm to bring you more wine if you like," she added in a very soft voice, "or anything else." At that she ran, avoiding the two men with practiced skill, off to hide the precious coin in some dark recess of the building.

WHEN he was alone again, Arnau Marça glanced at the laden table with distaste. Odd, he thought wryly, how the imminent approach of death takes away one's appetite. But curious about the wretched Garcia's insolent comments, he removed the linen covers from the dishes. A shaft of sunlight that penetrated his little cage at this hour in the afternoon edged over and lit up a bowl of braised lamb and vegetables. In the gloom beside it were a plate of grilled sardines and a spit-roasted chicken—dainty fare indeed for a good-as-condemned man. And without a doubt Johana's hand was in it. The dishes were ones she delighted in, as if she had been planning to share his dinner in this tiny cell. For an instant tears burnt in his eyes; to distract himself from such thoughts, he picked up the half-loaf of bread that sat beside the chicken.

He grasped the end of the loaf to tear off a piece and dropped it again. His meal no longer seemed inviting, no more than a venomous snake seems friendly, or a poisonous mushroom appetizing.

A portion of the soft crumb had been pulled out and set

back inside with great care. Surely no one expected him to miss that clumsy device. Could his enemy—whoever he was—not have waited for the headsman? Since the outcome of his trial was all but certain, his premature death would only invite unwelcome questions. Or was the outcome perhaps not certain? A flicker of hope twisted his gut for the first time since his arrest two days before. He pushed that thought away and turned back to the bread. He pulled out the loosened piece and inspected it with care in the shaft of golden sunlight. No odor, no change of color, no suspicious dampness or powder. Wrapping a linen cloth around the loaf, he held it up to the light as well.

No further attempt had been made to hide the pale gray-brown square packet inside. Slowly and carefully, he extracted a tightly folded piece of parchment, unfolded it, and discovered, not some bizarre instrument of death, but a message in the neat, familiar hand of one who had been schooled by the Sisters. "Tonight I shall hold you in my arms. Do not despair. J."

He considered the message. It was a more tempting subject than his impending death. Lost in thought, he ate all the sardines and half the chicken without noticing. Perhaps she meant that she would spend tonight praying for him, and dreaming of holding him in her arms once more. No. If she had meant that, she would have said it. One of Johana's many endearing qualities was that she said exactly what she meant. Therefore, tonight, for some reason, she was convinced that they would be together. Had she contacted the procurator so quickly? It seemed improbable. But now he was certain that the jailer was right. She was in the city.

He poured himself a cup of wine and waited patiently for the little girl to return. He sipped it as slowly as if it were the last wine on earth, and by the time she returned, he had not finished even half the cup. He had no desire to cloud his mind with drink. "Can you fetch a pen and some ink?" he asked her.

"Oh, yes, sir," she said. "It's common for those as can write to want pen and ink. But I'd better bring you something to write on if you can pay for it, or they'll think it's odd."

"Then all three, by all means," said Arnau. A smile flickered on his lips. "We wouldn't want them to think it odd."

"And more wine. They'll expect you to drink heavy tonight, seeing as you'll know what's supposed to happen tomorrow."

"And a priest?"

"You'll not need a priest," she whispered with assurance. "That would only be after the trial, you see. But there's another thing—you're to ask for the comfortable room. It costs a lot, but she said you'd have enough money for it. It's important. You must move into it."

"Do you arrange that as well?"

"No, señor. They do. I'll tell them after I fetch the parchment and the extra wine. Do you want that dinner?" she asked suddenly, pointing at the lamb and remaining chicken.

"I've had enough," said Arnau. "The rest is yours."

"I'll share it with Pep. No one brings him food. He's very hungry."

"And the wine too."

"There are three poor souls who are to be hanged in the morning," she said. "I'll give it to them."

┼══ ══┼

A few hours later, Arnau Marça lay on a real bed in a room large enough for furniture. On a table nearby was a cup of wine—"They'll expect it"—and across the room stood the little girl.

"Why this room?" asked Arnau softly.

"See this wall?" she said, pointing to the one beside her.

"Yes," he said. "Of course I see it. It's a wall. A plastered stone wall."

"It's the wall of the shop next door to the prison."

"*That* is the shop wall?" said Arnau, pointing.

The little girl nodded.

"The prison doesn't have its own walls?" asked Arnau.

"Not on this side. And it's not stone, just wood plastered with clay," she said.

"The only obstacle between the royal prison and a common shop is a wood and mud wall? I can't believe it."

She nodded again. "Everyone knows about it."

"If that is so, why doesn't everyone leave?" asked Arnau.

"They would," said the child, "but it costs a lot. The shopkeeper expects gold to let people break through her wall—she's worried she'll be thrown out if too many escape that way—and then there's all that money you had to give my master."

"You mean Garcia knows?"

"Not exactly," she said. "Except that he charges a lot to sleep in this room. Usually it's his. When someone else has it, he sleeps on the other side of the building, where he can't hear anything. There," she said, cocking her head to listen. "Hear them, señor? They're in."

And for endless hours, it seemed, he lay on the bed, listening to the soft thud of hammer and chisel eating away at the wall that divided his despair from his hope while the child listened at the door. For some reason, his rescuers had started work while people still roamed the streets and jailers wandered up and down the corridors, talking, laughing, sharing bottles of wine. Once, when the footsteps came too close, she glided over to the wall and rapped sharply. The chiseling stopped. The assistant jailer looked in. "What are you doing here?" he asked the little girl.

"The prisoner wanted someone to talk to," she said.

"He could have made a better choice," muttered the other, and left.

She rapped on the wall. The hammer and chisel started once more.

Arnau was drifting off into a light sleep when a chunk of plaster hit the floor. He sat up with a start and saw the beginnings of an opening in the connecting wall. He set a chair in front of the breach and then sat on it. After several falls of dried mud, plaster, and pebbles, the hole was big enough even for his broad shoulders and sturdy frame. He took out his leather purse, glanced inside, extracted a few coins, and handed the rest, purse and all, to the child. "Hide that well and use it when you need it," he said. "You have saved my life. Thank you."

"Not yet, señor," she whispered. "Go now. This is the dangerous part."

❧ ⸻ ❧

BY the light of a candle flickering in a lantern, Arnau could see Jordi, his servant, and behind him, Johana, his wife. "Quickly," she murmured. "We must get away."

He caught her in a tight embrace, swelling belly and all. "I told you to stay at the castle," he said, still holding her.

"Had I done that, you would have kept your appointment with the headsman tomorrow," she said. "There will be time for this later," she added. "You must not be found here."

"Quickly, señor," murmured Jordi. "We bribed many people. If only one of them has talked, we are lost."

Jordi opened the door cautiously, looking up and down the street. He beckoned to them. The warm October night was full of voices in the dark, calling out, here and there, followed by shouts and laughter. "Harvest celebrations are starting early this year," whispered Jordi. "That is good for us, señor—it gives us a reason to be out."

❧ ⸻ ❧

THEY climbed slowly up the dark, hilly streets, following Jordi. "Where are we going?" asked Arnau.

"I know a quiet garden that is tended by a friend," said Jordi. "Near the street of the Templars. His master, who is old and deaf, sleeps well and the gate will be unlocked. Inside are three old cloaks for warmth and cushions for comfort. We may rest in the garden until the crowds come through the gates for the markets, when we can leave the city unremarked. If her ladyship does not object, we will return to the castle on a market cart."

"I do not mind how we return," said Lady Johana, "if we return safely."

Suddenly a shout went up behind them. "There he is. Up ahead. Death to the traitor." The voice boomed and echoed between the tall houses on either side of them. It was joined by the sound of running feet.

Jordi turned. "Four," he said, "armed with cudgels. Señor, my lady, run. I will hold them off."

"Come along, you idiot," said Arnau, grabbing him and pulling.

"I am too slow," said Johana. "Go. They won't hurt me."

"Nonsense," said Arnau. He reached for his sword and found nothing by his side. He looked around, saw a chunk of wood by a doorway, and picked it up.

Johana slipped into the darkness of a narrow alley between two buildings.

The two men stood shoulder to shoulder, Jordi armed with a knife and a hammer and Arnau with a piece of wood. One of their opponents melted into a doorway; the others moved steadily toward them. Before the first blows landed, Arnau and Jordi split apart, ducking, dodging, and confusing their attackers. But quick as they were, they could not hope to hold off three brawny men with cudgels for long. One blow connected with a sickening crack; Jordi's knife dropped and his arm dangled uselessly.

Jordi's opponent snatched up the knife and lunged. Jordi

turned, taking the blow on his right shoulder as he planted his hammer with his left hand on the other's head. He dropped to the ground and lay where he had fallen, quite still. The attackers were down to two men, the defenders to one and a half.

Dizzy with pain and shock, Jordi stumbled and fell, leaving Arnau to fend off two cudgels with his log. A swinging blow hit his wrist. His numbed fingers dropped the wood, a heavy object caught the back of his head, and he felt nothing more.

"SEÑOR, you must help me," said Johana.

"I am always ready to help a pretty woman," said the big man leaning against the arches, grinning.

"Four men—" she said, panting, holding her swelling belly, "attacking my husband and his servant. Please. Another man on his side might frighten them away. I will pay you. Help me, please."

"Are you in difficulties, señora?" asked a loud voice behind her. "If so, you are asking the wrong man for help."

She turned toward a black shape holding a torch in front of him, dazzling her. "Please, señor," she said, pouring out her brief tale again.

"Of course I'll help," said the first man, picking up a heavy wooden staff. "What use is a priest against four villains? Which way?"

Johana pointed.

"And I will come to protect you," said the priest, raising his torch high and striding along behind the first man.

"As long as the guard don't turn up," said the first man. "Then I can't stay. I'm a porter, see? At night I'm supposed to sleep peacefully, getting ready to work in the morning. Down there?" he asked, turning in the direction of the noise without waiting for an answer.

They could hear fists and wood thudding against human

flesh. "Quickly," said Johana. "Before they kill him."

Both men, priest and porter, were tall and heavyset. "Stop that," roared the priest in a voice that could fill the biggest cathedral in Christendom. The man in the doorway stepped farther back into the darkness and disappeared.

The porter picked up the fallen man's cudgel and addressed himself to the two men who were kicking the injured gentleman and his servant as they lay on the cobbles. A few rapid blows, another roar from the priest, and they too made good their escape. Johana knelt beside her husband.

"I fear all this noise will draw the guard on watch," said the porter. "It would be wise for me to go before they can ask why portering at night brings me such excellent profits."

"A common thief," said the priest in disgust.

"No, Father," said the porter. "Never a thief. An uncommonly good gambler." And he strolled off.

"Is your husband . . ."

"He is alive, Father," said Johana. "They are both alive. But I must get them away from here."

Jordi stirred and raised himself unsteadily to a sitting position. "I will help, my lady," he said, "if you would do me the kindness to tie up my injured arm. I am fine otherwise."

"Will you be able to get your husband to friends?" asked the priest uneasily. "Nearby? For I am summoned to a deathbed, and I would be loath to arrive after the poor soul has fled."

"Go, Father, with my thanks for your aid," said Lady Johana as she fashioned a sling for Jordi's injured arm with her kerchief. "We will soon be in safe hands."

"MAY I ask whose safe hands, my lady?" asked Jordi, bending over his fallen master. "My master was unwilling to trust any of his friends in the city."

"Nor should we," said Johana briskly. "But we had to get rid of the priest before he wondered who we were."

"Where shall we go, then?" asked the servant helplessly.

Johana shook her head. "We cannot hide my lord overnight in a stranger's garden and then wait for a farm cart to bring him to the castle. We must find him a physician."

"I agree, my lady. There are excellent physicians in the city . . ."

"There are, but those whose skills I trust would recognize your master at once. I think we are safer remaining nameless."

"I agree, my lady."

"Do you know anyone who would take him in? I can stay with a friend at the royal palace, and find you a bed there, but I can scarcely take Arnau with us tonight. Think, Jordi," she said desperately, sitting down in the dust and dirt of a step.

Jordi seemed not to have heard her. He was staring to the south in the direction of the palace, walled and impenetrable. "Of course we cannot take his lordship to the palace, my lady," he said, shaking his head and looking over toward the east. "I have only one idea, and your ladyship will no doubt find it distasteful, but I know a discreet and reliable woman who might take us in. Does your ladyship have money still?"

"I do, Jordi. Gold was necessary to get him out of prison, and I knew that even more would be needed to keep him out until my plea can reach the procurator. And so I brought gold. What is wrong with your discreet and reliable woman?"

"She lives in Lo Partit, my lady."

"A whore?"

"Yes, my lady. For which I apologize. At least no one would expect your ladyship to take her husband to Esclarmonda."

"She calls herself after the old queen?"

"She does. It is her fancy. But after her own fashion, she is honest, and she knows what it is to have the world turn upon you like a pack of dogs."

Johana laid a hand on her husband's forehead. He stirred and groaned, then lay still once more. "Since we have few choices, let us throw ourselves on her mercy. As well, I like the sound of this queenly woman. Help me pick him up, Jordi, and we will carry him to her."

"I can walk," said a faint voice.

"Excellent, my love," said Johana. "You are awake. Put your arms around our shoulders. Jordi, stand on your master's right side and put your good arm around his waist. I will do the same on the left."

"And what do we say when someone comes by?" asked Jordi.

"Nothing," said the woman. "We sing and stagger like all the other drunks in the city. Off to Lo Partit!"

And in spite of his size and weight, they raised Arnau to his feet. He leaned on their backs and shoulders, with his arms clutching them weakly. At his first step he gasped and swore. "I fear that leg is injured," he said apologetically. "It will not bear my weight."

"Then drag it," said Johana. "Drag it, or you are a dead man, and by all the saints in heaven I won't have that."

THEY made their way toward the east, an agonizing walk up the hill past the Jewish Quarter and down toward the canal at the foot of the ramparts. They sang lustily, were cursed by the inhabitants, and staggered convincingly under Arnau's weight; he lapsed more and more frequently into merciful unconsciousness. At last the stench of sewage farms and knackers' yards gave them notice that they had reached the district where the prostitutes lived and carried on their trade. They fell silent, concentrating on finding their way and carrying Arnau without further damage to his already battered body.

"Clarmon," said Jordi softly at the door of a small hut. "Are you busy?"

"Never too busy to see you," said a voice from within. "Whoever you are." She opened the door a crack. "Jordi. With friends. Friends are extra and only if they look trust-worthy," she added suspiciously.

"Money is no problem," said Johana quietly. "Mistress Esclarmonda, we need your help. We'll pay generously for it and for your silence."

"For him?" Johana nodded. "Sick or injured?"

"Injured."

"How generously?"

"With gold."

"Bring him in," said Esclarmonda, opening the door wider to accommodate them. "The gentleman certainly looks in need of help. Set him down on the bed." She lit an extra candle and held it up to look first at him and then at his wife. "He will have a pretty assortment of bruises, I see."

"And a broken limb or two on the right side," said Johana. "He needs a bonesetter or a surgeon."

"Well, my lady, what I can do, I will, and without unnecessary explanations. I don't chatter about my clients."

"And different clothes. Some not so—"

"Suitable for one of his rank?" asked Esclarmonda.

"Yes. He has enemies. And there are other reasons, strong reasons, for keeping him out of sight."

"I can change his appearance and keep him for a day or two. I will send for the surgeon tonight to look at them both, for I see that my friend Jordi was in the fight as well. But your husband, my lady, should be under the care of a good physician. Why not take him to Master Pere Vila instead of Esclarmonda?"

"Master Pere would recognize him, and I do not know if we can trust him to keep silent."

"I see. Then leave him with me. I will find him someplace safe to stay where he will be well cared for. Not here. Word spreads like the plague in this place—in three or four days there will be someone at the door wondering who is living with me, why he's here, and whether anyone in the city will pay for the information. There are many here who would betray their grandfathers for a penny."

"But he will be safe for a day or two?"

"Yes. Travelers with a bit of money often spend two days with me before starting off again. No one thinks anything of it."

"Well, mistress, I have no choice but to believe you," said Johana. "You will contact me when you have made arrangements?"

"I will. Where can I find you?"

Johana took the candle from Esclarmonda's hand and held it up. Her rescuer was taller than most women, with a high, broad forehead, large, clear dark eyes, and a mouth that twitched in amusement at the close examination. Esclarmonda pushed her dark hair back from her face to give her visitor a better view, and it tumbled back in place in a mass of lively curls. Arnau's troubled wife took a deep breath and placed their lives in her hands. "At the palace. The Lady Johana Marça."

Esclarmonda nodded in comprehension. "I assure you, my lady," she said quietly, "the headsman will not get him while I have charge of his safety."

"This is for you," said Johana, handing her a leather purse. "If you need more, you have only to ask. Be true to us and we will be your very good friends and allies."

"You can't ask fairer than that," said Esclarmonda, looking in the purse. "Dear God in heaven, my lady," she said. "This is not generous. It is a fortune."

"Spend what is needed on surgeons, clothing, physicians,

medicines. The rest is for you. If it costs you more than half, I will replenish the purse."

"I will send for the surgeon now," she said, and pulled aside a piece of leather that hung to form a door at the back of the room. "Robert," she said. "Go quickly and fetch the surgeon. And be careful."

She turned back to Lady Johana. "Robert is very quick. He will have the surgeon here in a few moments. Then he will take you to the palace, my lady, while I stay with your husband. He will make sure that you arrive safely. You can trust him." A boy who looked to be twelve came out from the back room, smiled shyly, and left the tiny house.

"I thank you. Is that Robert?"

"Yes, my lady. He is the son of a neighbor. He sleeps here when necessary. Do you wish me to send my guest's clothing with him to the palace as well?"

"No, my good Esclarmonda. Perhaps your neighbor's son could find some use for it. But it is in need of cleaning and mending."

"You are a generous woman, my lady," murmured Esclarmonda. "I shall do my best for your husband."

━┼╼━ ╾━┼━

"Is he dead?" In spite of the warmth of the night, the man in the private room of the inn was sitting close to the fire. He spoke with nervous rapidity in an accent that irritated his rough-spoken listeners.

"No, sir," said one of the two men in the doorway. "I fear he isn't. Hurt bad, though, sir. Like to die. But not dead."

"Hurt bad, as you put it, is not enough," said the man by the fire. "Nor is like to die. Come in and close the door, for God's sake. We don't want our private business to become the buzz of the inn. What went wrong?"

"Mistress Blanca, who holds the lease of the shop, vowed she never whispered a word about the escape, but I reckon he found out there'd be a trap, and so he left earlier."

"How could he know? Didn't you stay with the woman all day?"

"Yes, sir, I did. And into the evening. She never told anyone, I swear. But that servant, he must have been suspicious. I think he went to work on the wall the minute the shop closed. When we came along they were well away from the prison."

"I know they were," said the man by the fire. "I was there."

"If there had only been the two of them, and if we'd been able to surprise them in the shop . . ."

"But there weren't only two, and you didn't. May they rot in hell and you bumbling idiots with them. Get out of here before I call someone to throw you out."

"But sir, you still owe us—"

"Out!" screamed the man by the fire.

The two men by the door turned and fled.

THE next morning, just before midday, a small group of men sat around a polished table in a dimly lit room. Two menservants and a boy came in carrying wine, bowls of fresh and dried fruit, and other delectables. The man at the head of the table waved irritably at them. "Leave us," he said.

They set their plates and bowls down in disarray on the sideboard and fled.

"You have heard what has happened?" the same man asked.

"Yes, Vidal, we have heard," said an elegant young man, splendid in velvet and soft leather. He yawned. "Will you need us for long?" he added fretfully. "I had scarcely gone to bed when your message dragged me from it."

"I apologize for disturbing you, Don Ramon," said Master Pere Vidal with great deference. "But in your own interests I felt you would want to be here. A great deal of money is at stake."

"But it always has been, hasn't it?" asked Don Ramon Julià, and yawned again. "Is there no one to pour the wine?"

Pere Vidal hastened to supply his guest with a silver goblet filled with wine.

The man sitting across from Don Ramon leaned forward. "I would be sorry to slow down the meeting, but why are we here? I seem to be the only person at the table who does not know what has happened or how it affects our interests. Could you explain it to me, sir?" he said, turning to Pere Vidal.

A fourth man, who until this point had been listening silently, turned to the questioner. "Allow me, Martin," he said. "My unfortunate friend here is so distressed that he cannot put one sensible word after another. It could take him until the dinner hour before you understood him. Is that not so, Pere?"

"It is, Pere," said the man at the head of the table. For the two men, Pere Vidal and Pere Peyro, had known each other for many years, and had exchanged this tired jest many times before.

"To put it briefly," said Pere Peyro, "someone—probably his wife, who is cleverer than he is—arranged Don Arnau's escape from prison last night. Our problems would have ceased, one way or another, if he had been tried this morning as he was supposed to be. He would have been acquitted on the charges or executed for treason. We had planned for either of those verdicts yesterday, if you will remember. We did not plan for his disappearing like the morning mist into the air."

"Where is he?" asked Ramon Julià.

"We do not know, Don Ramon," said Vidal. "That is the problem."

"I expect he has left Roussillon by now," said Peyro.

"I don't see the difficulty," said Don Ramon. "We can divide up his share between us."

"The difficulty lies in what happens to us, my lord. The trial would have settled whether a crime was committed," said Peyro with the air of someone who has already tried to explain this point several times. "And if it was, whether the rest of us might be considered involved."

"My lord the viscount, whom I represent, will not tolerate any imputation of wrongdoing to touch him," said Martin firmly.

"No one here wishes that for his lordship the viscount or any of the rest of us," said Vidal. "It would be disastrous. After all our work . . ." He glanced despairingly at Don Ramon.

"It is disastrous. And the only way that we will survive this disaster," said Pere Peyro, "is to stand by each other. If one of us goes, so will all the rest."

"Not his lordship the viscount," said Martin stubbornly.

"Perhaps not. But his man of business will," said Vidal with a flick of malice.

"It is time for us to discuss what we know freely and openly among ourselves," said Peyro, "and to keep silent in front of the rest of the world."

"You never kept silent about anything in your life, Pere, my friend," said Vidal.

"That may be," said Peyro. "I was not in danger of losing my head before. First of all, does anyone know exactly everything that is on board that ship?"

They looked at each other. No one spoke.

"I know there was a great deal of talk of various things," said Martin, uneasily. "But actually knowing . . ."

"Who is supervising the loading?" asked Martin.

"Don Arnau and his man of business were going to do it, or so I was told," said Peyro.

"And when does she sail?" Martin lifted his hand from the note he was making to dip his pen in the inkwell.

"Yes—when does the ship sail?" asked Don Ramon, looking up with interest. "I'd like to see that."

"She was supposed to sail as soon as her cargo was loaded and the wind was favorable," said Pere Vidal. "It might have been yesterday, or more likely, today or tomorrow. But now that this has happened—I do not know."

"That brings us back to Master Pere Peyro's first question," said Martin. "Who knows what is on board?"

"If no one here knows, then only Arnau and the master of the vessel," said Peyro.

"What about his man of business?" asked Peyro. "He was handling the details."

"Cassa?" asked Martin. "I saw him yesterday. He was in a terrible state. He told me he had been dismissed just after the ship came into port. Don Arnau took over the arrangements."

"Dismissed? By Arnau? How very strange," said Peyro. "Well, Cassa cannot know much, then. Arnau is far from Roussillon by now, I suppose, but the ship's master should be in the city. He was to testify at the trial. Someone should try to find him."

There was a pause. "I will," said Vidal.

"And I will go to Collioure and try to discover what is going on," said Peyro.

"I must report to his lordship the viscount and request further instructions," said Martin in worried tones. "He will not be pleased."

Don Ramon Julià yawned.

Pere Vidal ushered his noble guest, Don Ramon, into the main hallway, where a manservant stood ready to fling open the door. Pere Peyro and Martin followed after, engaged in desultory conversation. "If you will excuse the impertinence of the question, Master Pere," said Martin, "why is Master Pere Vidal so concerned about the opinions of a raw boy who, as I understand it, cannot possibly bring him a pennyworth of profit?"

"Do you mean Don Ramon Julià?" asked Pere Peyro.
"Cast your eye quickly up the staircase, Martin, and you
will see a young woman clad in enough silk to fit out the
royal court."

"I see her," said Martin.

"That is his daughter. Pere Vidal has dreams, Martin.
Grandiose dreams of hearing the world address his daughter as 'my lady,' and of seeing her presented at court. That
impoverished twig of a noble house, with his mind fixed
on cards and dice, easy women, and fine clothes, can be
purchased if the price be high enough. Or so Vidal believes."

"But Don Ramon's debts are enormous," said Martin. "I
know little about the city, having arrived so recently, but
even I have heard that."

"It will cost Vidal a fortune," agreed Peyro. "But he
thinks it is worth it."

TWO

Saturday, October 4

DOÑA Johana Marça was seated by the window in a small sitting room beside her chamber. The late morning sun streamed in, lighting up the pallor of her face and the dark circles under her eyes. She was bent over her sewing, working with a ferocious intensity at a infant's dress. Footsteps on the stone floors of the hall warned her of someone's approach, but she neither stirred nor raised her eyes from her work. The door opened and a pleasant-looking woman in a simple gown of elegant cut stood in the doorway, looking at her.

"They told me you would be in here," the woman said at last. "They said you never move from this room."

"Margarida!" said Johana, setting down her work. "No one told me you were expected."

"That is because I wasn't," said Margarida. "But the Princess Constança, tiring of listening to me, sent me here to prepare for her arrival."

"When does the Princess arrive?"

"Soon. Perhaps tomorrow, perhaps in a week, perhaps in

three or four," said Margarida. "While Their Majesties are away in Sardinia, Her Royal Highness no longer has to worry about time. But I am more concerned about you, my dearest Johana."

"It is comforting to hear that, but I assure you I do very well."

"That is not what I hear. They tell me you avoid everyone. You cannot be drawn into conversation, you refuse to walk with the others, or bring your needlework into the courtyard or even listen to Lady Angelica reading."

"That is because it is Lady Angelica. If it were you, Margarida, perhaps I could listen for hours."

"You flatter me. Now I know you are unwell. They fear you will fade away from grief before your child is born, Johana, and from the look of you, their fears are justified."

"I cannot bear their sympathy or their curiosity, Margarida," said Johana, clenching her hands until the knuckles whitened. "They have heard so many wild stories of our troubles that they circle me like a pack of stray dogs, wanting every detail of all that I know and feel."

"You cannot blame them. I can occupy myself quite happily when I am here with my needle and my books, but it is a dull life for most of them while Their Majesties are away. It's more like a military garrison than a royal court."

"I hardly notice the soldiers, Margarida."

"That is because you never leave this room, Johana. You would have horrified my old nurse."

"Why?" asked Johana vaguely. "Sit down, Margarida, and talk to me. It might do me good. Tell me about your old nurse."

"It is too hot and close in here," said Margarida. "Come out into the gallery where there is more air. If you wish, we can slip through the private passage over to His Majesty's chamber. There we can talk to our hearts' content in very pleasant—and private—surroundings."

"I'd be stuck in the middle if I tried to get through that

passage," said Johana. "It's very narrow and I am much too great a size. But tell me about your nurse. You used to listen to my selfish complaints for hours and never spoke of where you came from. Some wild place far to the north, they used to say."

"Come out, first," she said, holding out her hand.

Johana rose from her chair, straightened her gown, and, arm in arm with Margarida, went out to the stone-flagged open gallery that overlooked the palace's smaller courtyard.

"I come from Scotland," continued Margarida. "It is not as wild, or far, or cold as they say, but I confess that it is not like this. Every day, in sunshine or pelting rain, or when winds howled through the keep bringing snow and ice, my nurse dragged me out to walk." Margarida leaned on the balustrade, studying the neatly trimmed trees and shrubs in the sunny courtyard.

"Scotland was not like this at all," she said again with a wave of her hand that took in the courtyard, the trees, the sun, and the warm, almost still air. "But my nurse used to say that fresh winds made sturdy children. 'You must walk every day, Mary,' she would say, taking me by the hand and dragging me out, shivering, in my little cloak."

"Mary?" said Johana, stumbling a bit over the unfamiliar sounds.

"Yes. Didn't I tell you that at home they call me Mary? It is not a difficult name. But our late Queen was like you, my dear Johana, and couldn't get her tongue around it either. And so she changed my name."

"But why not to Maria?"

"Queen Maria said there were enough Marias at court already, and she didn't want another one. Since it is one of my names, she chose to call me Margarida. Now I'm used to it. Come along," she said, taking her by the hand.

The galleries on which they were standing and the chambers opening onto it were royal apartments, set aside for Her Majesty, the Queen, and the King's daughters with their attendants. They overlooked Her Majesty's courtyard; the chamber windows to the south side overlooked Her Majesty's orchard. This arrangement spared the royal ladies from having their activities overlooked by the bored and often rowdy young officers who garrisoned the palace.

The officers were left to amuse themselves in the great courtyard with games of cards or dice, or up on the walls at their own form of archery practice, shooting at rabbits foolish enough to emerge from the royal *devesa*, the hunting preserve to the south of the palace.

"It has been a great relief to talk of something other than my troubles, Margarida," said Johana, trying to smile. "But I think I will go back to my chamber now."

"Certainly not. You must come down to Her Majesty's courtyard with me. I have ordered refreshments set out for us there, under the trees. We will sit, eat a little, and talk. I have hardly spoken to you since the day you left the tutelage of the Sisters. I missed you, Johana. Come. You are not too big to walk down to the courtyard."

"I still walk," said Johana. "I go out early. That is how I escape the rude stares of the officers and the sympathy of the ladies. But if you insist, Margarida, I have not the strength to resist any longer." She meekly followed her friend to the staircase. They sat in the shade of a lemon tree; between them a servant set a small table with fruit, cold meats, olives, and nuts laid out temptingly.

"You must eat," said Margarida. "They tell me you eat almost nothing."

"I can't," she replied. "A single olive would choke me now."

"For the sake of the child you carry, you must eat," she repeated. She picked up a ripe pear and cut a slice of it for Johana, who smiled helplessly and ate it slowly.

"I don't know how you can order me about like a small child. No one else could do it, Margarida. Not even my father."

"It is time that someone did," replied Margarida, cutting her another slice of pear.

"When did you return to court?" asked Johana, setting the second piece of pear to one side. "You told me that you had decided to leave all such frivolities behind you. I thought you would have taken your vows by now."

"Not long after you left to be married. One of my husband's relations sought my present post for me, and shortly after that I returned to the court as lady to the Princess Constança."

"Why did you change your mind?"

"Because of you, in a way. When you left, taking all your liveliness and energy with you, the convent seemed like a living death. Suddenly I wanted company again, and to have the chance to talk to others like you."

"But you were happy with the Sisters," said Johana, looking at her with a puzzled frown. "Or at least, happier than I was."

"Not really," said Margarida. "My husband was dead; my boys had been sent away to learn to be men. Having no place in the Scottish court and no one to find me a Scottish marriage, I decided that I could not go home. I fled to the Sisters, intending to die peacefully in their care. But then you arrived, looking like a lost sparrow blown in by a storm and needing comfort. In helping you I found I was enjoying life again. You saved my life, Johana, and I propose to do the same for you, whether you agree or not. But speaking of lost sparrows, you are looking particularly sparrow-like today for one who is such a good size. Is something wrong? I mean, more than I have already heard."

"Nothing unexpected," said Johana, all the life draining from her voice again.

"What is it?"

"Today the procurator sent me a letter, saying that he has looked with care into the charges against my husband

and regrets that he is unable to intervene in the course of justice."

"That man is a beast," said Margarida. "I could tell you tales of him—but I won't. Not now. What are you going to do?"

"What can I do, Margarida?" she asked. "I have done everything and none of it has helped."

"You cannot give up now. Where is your courage, sparrow? I will help if I can, but first you must confide a little in me." Margarida lowered her voice. "We are alone here, and if we keep our voices low, we cannot be overheard. Now tell me, what has happened to Arnau? Where is he?"

Johana shook her head. "Somewhere safe, I hope. I am not even sure that he is alive."

"You truly do not know where he is?"

"Margarida, if I knew where he was, I would go to him and sit by his side until he recovered or died in my arms. But if I went to him . . ." She stopped. "At present, I am a source of danger for him. I cannot slip away from here without being noticed."

"I heard that he had been imprisoned," said Margarida soberly. "And, I suspect, most unjustly." She looked narrowly at her friend. "I also heard that some bold soul organized his escape from prison."

"That is true," said Johana, cautiously.

"Do not worry, little sparrow," said Margarida. "I won't talk about to this to others. I do not know who arranged his escape, but I know only one woman who has the courage to do it and the shrewdness to do it well. What went wrong?"

"I was not able to organize everything myself," said Johana resignedly. "I was forced, under the circumstances, to rely on trusted servants. Someone talked. Arnau was set upon on his way out of the city."

"And badly injured, they say."

"They speak true this time."

"How many servants did you take into your confidence? Many?"

Johana shook her head. "Two. One I would trust with my life. If he betrayed Arnau, then the world has no truth or honesty left in it. As for the other—Arnau places great reliance on him. I have no reason to doubt him, but I am less sure of him. Of course, one of the jailers that we bribed might have been bribed once more to betray us."

"But who hates Don Arnau enough to bribe the jailer? Because I suspect that you had already paid him very well, and perhaps promised him much more if he had stayed true to his word. And you are still accounted a rich woman. Are you not, Johana?"

Ignoring the final question, Johana shook her head. "Yes, he was well paid, with promises of more should the escape be successful. And I do not know who his enemy is," she said wearily. "All I know is that my husband is as good as dead. If he does recover he will be discovered, tried, and executed before I can get him away from the country. I pleaded with the procurator, Margarida. And knowing as well as you do what he is like, I offered him gold—a great deal of gold. Clearly he is deaf to my voice."

"Your voice I can believe. Our noble procurator, Huguet, is always deaf to women's voices. But your gold—that astonishes me. Gold speaks to him like a mother to her babe. There is little that he and his friends would not do, I think, to enrich themselves further. He must believe that there is more profit in rejecting your plea than in listening to it."

"You mean that someone has outbid me?"

"Can you think of another reason for him turning down your plea and your gold? You'll have to go elsewhere for help."

"Who else can I apply to? His Majesty's uncle, Prince Pere? He does not know me and, I fear, does not trust Arnau."

"I shall write to Her Majesty," said Margarida. "And when the Princess Constança arrives, she will write to her royal papa."

"I fear that will be too late, Margarida. My husband might as well be dead."

"We shall see about that," said Doña Margarida firmly.

AFTER dinner, which she took in her room, Johana wandered out once more. Although she could not bear the empty frivolity of the conversation of the ladies still in residence at the palace, she could bear her loneliness no better. Seeing Margarida had awakened in her a hunger for someone to talk to. But Margarida was nowhere to be found. Johana sat down in the little courtyard; the heat of the afternoon and nights of wakefulness combined to make her sleepy. She closed her eyes and tried to forget for a brief moment all that life had taken from her.

"You look quiet and peaceful, Lady Johana," said a male voice. "From everything that I had heard said, I expected to find you enshrouded in grief, unable to speak."

"Did you, my lord?" said Johana, raising an eyebrow. "Why is that?"

"More fool I for believing in the professions of a widow's grief," said Bernard Bonshom, Lord Puigbalador.

"I have not yet been informed that I am a widow, my lord," she said. "When that moment comes, if it comes, I shall no doubt express my grief."

"True," said Puigbalador. "But a man whose beloved wife is on the point of death mourns as fiercely as one who has already lost his. I had not thought that women were so different."

"Perhaps we are not," said Johana, yawning sleepily. "But you, my lord, who I had thought had no cares, are looking somewhat heated in temper."

"I have many cares, Lady Johana," said Bonshom. "Not

serious ones, that is true, but a tangle of small ridiculous ones. I have just dined with Master Pere Vidal, a ridiculous man, who spent two hours pouring out a litany of complaints into me along with his wine. It was enough to set anyone's temper out of order."

"What has Master Pere Vidal to complain of?" said Johana.

"I understand your ire," said Bonshom. "Compared to your husband's situation, his is near perfection. But he is an ambitious man, my lady, very ambitious. So ambitious that he would part with some of his gold to marry his daughter to a title. But he was complaining that the venture he was in with your husband might very well sink in this great tempest."

"Tempest?"

"The one that has brought you so low, I am sorry to say. If it does, then how could he give the child a dowry large enough to buy a lord with?"

"What did he expect you to do, my lord?"

"He thought I could make the whole problem disappear with a word whispered in the right ear."

"And could you, my lord?"

"If I were asked by the right person, I might be able to," he said, bowing over her hand and brushing it with his lips.

"Before we delve into that question, my lord, I believe that you are being summoned."

He turned his head to look. A servant in royal livery was crossing the courtyard toward them. "Again? This is my objection to my service here, Lady Johana. It has its compensations, but one is always at the mercy of others. There are so few places to hide. But perhaps it is you he seeks, Lady Johana."

It was not. The servant walked up to Bonshom and murmured politely.

"Are you sure, man?" he snapped.

"Yes, my lord," said the servant. "He waits near the stair to the great courtyard. Do you wish me to attend you?"

"I can find him myself," he said. "Insolent dog," he added to Johana. "But I fear I must go."

"My lord, I excuse you from further attendance on me," said Lady Johana and closed her eyes once more.

"I thank you, my lady," said the noble Bonshom.

BONSHOM walked quickly out of the peace of the small courtyard to the noise and bustle of the large one. "I told you not to disturb me here," he said. "Too many people know you, and I might find that inconvenient someday."

"I regret that very much, my lord, but I did not wish to entrust my report to writing, nor to give it to a messenger to deliver, no matter how indefinitely worded."

"Come to the point, man," he said. "Quickly."

"Yes, my lord," he murmured. "Here?"

"What better place? Who can hear us?"

And, indeed, between those who were working, noisily calling back and forth, and those who were passing the time at gambling games, you could scarcely hear the chink of coins hitting the paving stones, much less the murmur of soft-voiced conversation.

"I am sorry, my lord, but I have not as yet found what you were looking for. I have tried all the places that you suggested, my lord, as well as several more, and it is nowhere. It has, apparently, disappeared without a trace."

"What about the woman?"

"She doesn't have it, no matter what we were told. I swear. I've looked myself. Not a trace of it. My informant now says she didn't know the woman had it, she only thought she might. I have no doubt that she believed she would not be paid unless she gave us something clear and definite."

"I hope you took back whatever you paid her," said Bonshom viciously. "I want that piece of property. It's worth a great deal."

"Shall I keep looking?" asked the man.

"Try the estate," said Bonshom. "Ask around there."

"Yes, my lord."

"But don't spend a month on it. Time is important."

"Do you wish me to carry on to the manor house at Elna?"

"It's unlikely to be there. And I myself will take care of that. You know where to contact me after today if you hear anything."

"Yes, my lord."

"I will be returning here this day next week."

"Very good, my lord."

THREE

Girona, Sunday, October 5

THE physician's household had been in a ferment for the entire day. There were tunics to be brushed and folded and laid in a box, then covered with clean linen shifts and shirts. The box had to be sealed up, ready to be loaded. Clothes for traveling had to be set out for donning in the early morning. All was done, and Judith was putting together small bundles for each of the three of them for the road, when someone rang at the front gate.

"Leah," she said impatiently, "go and see who that is."

"I have my own things to look to, mistress," the maid complained. "Let Ibrahim go."

"Ibrahim is taking the box over to Master Astruch's house," said Raquel from her chamber on the floor above.

Judith tied up the last bundle, Yusuf's, and went down to the courtyard. A dusty, weary-looking man stood at the gate. "I have a message, urgent, for Isaac the physician," he said, taking a folded paper from a leather pouch by his side.

"From whom?" asked Judith.

"From Master Jacob Bonjuhes in Perpignan. I have ridden since before dawn with it. He was most anxious that it arrive today."

"Come in, good man," said Judith. "And take some refreshment while I send someone for my husband. Naomi," she called. "Some wine and other refreshment for the messenger."

While Naomi was looking after the messenger, Raquel ran down from her chamber, and Ibrahim came in at the gate. Judith looked around. "Where are your papa and Yusuf, Raquel?"

"I was to tell you, mistress," said Ibrahim, "that they are with Master Astruch. They will not be long."

"When were you to tell me that?" said Judith.

"As soon as I could," said Ibrahim, looking toward his small room off the courtyard with longing.

"When did your master say that?"

"Before we left, mistress," said Ibrahim under his breath. "Look, mistress. There he is."

And while the messenger slaked his thirst with wine mixed with water and satisfied his hunger with bread, cheese, and fruit, everyone sat around the big table in the courtyard waiting for Raquel to break the seal on the paper. "It is dated this morning, Papa," said Raquel. "And it is very short. 'My dear Isaac,' he says, 'I beg you for some assistance. I am at the moment treating a patient who is staying in my house until he dies or has recovered enough to be moved. He is in pain beyond bearing. None of my poor and ineffectual medications can touch his agony. Could I beg you to bring some of yours? Nothing that I have mixed from the juice of the poppy is as efficacious against pain as that which you gave me the last time we met. My patient will be happy to pay a suitable price for whatever you choose to bring.' And then it is signed with his name, Papa."

"I wonder what disease induces such pain in him," said

Isaac. "Jacob seems to believe that the pain will not be eased through death or recovery before we arrive. I can think of only a few ailments, but perhaps we should put together something for them as well. Come, Raquel. I will need your help if this is to be done before supper."

◆━◆ ◆━◆

"IT will rain," said Judith to her husband as she opened the shutters and gazed out the window of their chamber the next morning. The sky was gray and threatening. Clouds were gathering against the hills and the wind was sharp and chill for early October.

"Then it is fortunate that you are not coming with us, for I would not wish you to fall ill," replied Isaac, who was beginning his morning ablutions.

"I wish you would stay home," she said, not for the first time since Jacob Bonjuhes's first letter had arrived, but with uncharacteristic gentle wistfulness. Then she shook back her long and heavy hair and returned to her usual sharpness. "I do not see why this Jacob cannot marry off his brother to Bonafilla without your presence. And Raquel's. She has much to do with her own wedding."

"Put on your gown, my love," said Isaac, drying his face and beard, "and help Naomi prepare us a good breakfast before the journey. I promise you we will stay dry, travel as carefully as possible, and bring you back some special delight from the city."

"Isaac, I am not Miriam or Nathan to be soothed with promises of sweetmeats or even silk gowns because their papa is going away for two weeks."

"I know that, Judith. You are my most-beloved wife, the keeper of my conscience, and the mother of my children. I will come back to you, I promise it." He moved expertly in the direction of her voice, laid a hand on her cheek, caught her around the waist, and drew her to him.

"Isaac," she murmured. "You must hurry or you will be late."

"A moment ago," he said, "you would have me stay. Now you are sending me away."

"I had better go and help Naomi," said the physician's wife, with tears in her eyes as she pulled away. She fastened her gown, pushed her hair into place, tied a veil over it, and hurried off to the kitchen.

TWO hours later, with much bustle, noise, and cheerful farewells, the party set off. In the lead were Astruch and his son Duran, mounted on mules; following them were Astruch's daughter, Bonafilla, Isaac, Raquel, and Yusuf, Isaac's apprentice, who carried his own letter of permission to travel freely throughout the kingdom of Aragon, as page and ward of His Majesty. He rode his mare and was armed with a sword that he was becoming adept at using. Ester and Leah, the maids, rode in the first cart with the travelers' bundles and boxes. The second cart was piled high with the bride's possessions: a feather bed, boxes filled with linens and clothing, some valuable small pieces of furniture, and a chest designed for the safekeeping of gold. In addition to two menservants, one to drive each cart, Astruch had brought two armed men, who rode at the rear of the procession for protection. A light rain washed over the countryside as they headed north and east, but the sky was brightening. Since none were walking, they moved ahead at a moderately lively pace.

When a mile or two had passed, Astruch dropped back until he was beside Raquel, who was holding the leading rein of her father's mule. "There is much that I would talk to your father about, Mistress Raquel," he said. "If you would allow me to take the lead you could perhaps talk to my foolish daughter. Cheer her a little. Reassure her."

And so, with considerable reluctance, Raquel handed

over the rein and urged her mount forward to talk to Bonafilla.

"You see what's in that small black chest?" said Bonafilla.

"I'm afraid I can't, Bonafilla," said Raquel. "It's closed and it's on the cart behind us."

"Well, of course it's closed," she said. "It's filled with gold. Papa is buying me a husband as far away from Girona as he can find one, and paying a fortune for him."

"That's your dowry, Bonafilla," said Raquel in a whisper. "And I wouldn't talk about it out here on the road. You know perfectly well it's for you and your children, so that you can live in safety and comfort. If it's big, that's because your papa loves you enough to sacrifice that much for you."

"Then why is he sending me so far away?"

"Perpignan isn't far," said Yusuf, who was unashamedly listening in. At twelve, or perhaps thirteen, he still availed himself when it suited him of the privileges of childhood—especially to free access to women. "Valencia is much farther. You have to ride to Barcelona and then sail down there."

"Who lives in the *call* in Girona whom you would rather marry?" said Raquel. "Between the ages of thirteen and sixty."

"I cannot think of one right now," said Bonafilla, in confusion.

"The Ravaya brothers?" asked Raquel. "Or how about Salomó de Mestre?"

"He's so shy he can't speak to a girl without turning as red as a poppy," said Bonafilla with contempt. "And he's in love with Master Vidal's daughter."

"That's a problem. And the Ravaya brothers?"

"They're thirteen and fifteen," said Bonafilla. "What would I do with them?"

"How about a widower, then? Bonastruch Bonafet?"

"But he's old," said Bonafilla. "And his belly jiggles when he walks."

"And when he sees me he pulls at my veil and says, 'Who's the pretty girl under this?'" said Raquel. "But he's still a fine vigorous man, in truth."

"Of course," said Bonafilla, dropping her voice to a whisper, "I'd be a widow sooner with someone like that. How about Master Mahir? They say he can hardly stir from the house. Think how little trouble he'd be." At that Bonafilla began to giggle. "All I'd have to do would be to feed him his soup. Like another baby in the house." The giggle grew into a laugh, a laugh with more cruelty than humor in it.

Raquel looked at her uneasily. "It is not kind to laugh at old age, Bonafilla. Master Mahir is a good and learned man."

Bonafilla tossed her head under its veil. "I had rather be going to Barcelona to marry a fabulously rich man the way Dalia did," she said sulkily. "Instead of being shunted off to the north to marry a physician's brother."

+‑==‑ ‑==‑+

"I did not think ever to hear my daughter laugh again, Isaac," said Astruch. "She behaves as if I am bearing her off to be beheaded, not married to a handsome, prosperous young man."

"Does she love someone closer to home?" asked Isaac.

"How is that possible?" asked her father. "If you could see her, Isaac. So young, so shy, and so carefully guarded. She is never alone."

"It is my experience that no matter how young, how shy, how innocent, and how carefully guarded, daughters fall in love. And sometimes with very odd men."

"When she leaves the house, she is so heavily veiled—and by her own choice—that even I cannot recognize her unless she speaks, Isaac. She is always accompanied by her maid and a member of the family. The only young men she sees, I swear, are her brothers."

"Is she close to her brothers?"

"Of course," said her father automatically. "Well—not that close, I suppose. They are out, helping me with business affairs or amusing themselves most of the time, and whenever they speak to her, it seems, they are chiding her for her sulky behavior. They prefer to talk to their stepmother, who is a cheerful and sensible woman. I wish she could be more like Preciosa."

"Mistress Preciosa has noticed no signs that young Mistress Bonafilla has given her heart to someone, no matter how unsuitable?"

"No. And she has been on guard. Bonafilla is so unhappy about this marriage that frankly it will be a relief to have her away from the house. The sun is out, Master Isaac," said Astruch with his normal cheerfulness. "We should arrive in Figueres in time to dine."

"Do you have much business to transact there?"

"Who said I had business?"

"Why else would a man as lively as you, Master Astruch, not carry on for a few more hours in order to reach his destination all the sooner?"

"I do, with our host and one or two others. I hope it is not too wearisome for the rest of our party."

"MY lord Puigbalador is back," said Margarida. They were sitting in Her Majesty's orchard, a walled garden of great peace and beauty that sheltered against the south face of the palace; Johana and Margarida were at their needles. A small tortoiseshell cat, the great-granddaughter of the cat Margarida had brought with her from her remote Scottish home, having grown tired of tangling up silk thread, jumped into Margarida's lap and fell suddenly asleep.

"Is he?" said Johana. "I had not noticed that he had gone."

"How fortunate you are," said Margarida. "I always notice when he goes. There is a most agreeable absence of an odor in the upper rooms of the palace when he rides out the gates."

"What kind of odor?" said Johana, laughing in spite of herself.

"A sort of base masculinity, I suppose, mixed with a sandalwood scent that he affects. Myself, I prefer the smell of my mule on a hot day before she has been groomed."

"Margarida, you are good for me. It seems so long since I have even smiled. But I must confess that I have not even noticed Bonshom's comings and goings."

"I would, if I were you, sparrow. He is entirely too curious about you. He now wants to know exactly how much money you will have when—"

"When Arnau dies disgraced and all his goods are seized?"

"Precisely."

"What did you tell him?"

"The truth, as I knew it," said Margarida. "I thought it would be useful to know how he reacts." She sniffed the air. "I think we are about to discover."

"The smell of sandalwood and base masculinity?" asked Johana.

"That very smell."

Margarida gathered up her needlework, tucked her cat in the crook of her arm, and took herself over to another bench under a fig tree, just as Bernard Bonshom, Lord Puigbalador, approached seeking a few moments' speech with Lady Johana.

"My lady," said Bonshom, picking up Johana's hand and pressing it to his lips. "You have been much in my thoughts since our brief conversation of Saturday. Is it too much to hope that I have been in yours, at least for a moment or two?"

"Certainly for a moment or two," said Johana.

"I could have wished for more," he said, "but I am grateful for that. You do not ask me why I thought of you."

"I thought it wiser to remain silent, my lord," she said.

"Wise indeed," said Bonshom. "I have been concerned with your welfare. Whatever you may tell yourself, my lady, from what I hear, your husband lies near death."

"You amaze me, my lord," said Johana, with an air of indifference. "You appear to hear more than I do. From whom do you get your intelligence?"

"I have no certain knowledge, of course. But it is known that he was badly injured, is it not? And few recover from such injuries. Thus, most assume that he is near death. When that sad day comes, everything that he possesses, except for your dowry, will be seized. You will be destitute. You must face that."

"Surely that depends on what you believe destitute to be. It is, as you know, quite different for a cobbler or a tailor, and for a great lord like yourself. If a cobbler has enough to pay his rent, feed his wife and children, and buy lengths of cloth from time to time for their clothes, he considers himself rich. A great lord like yourself feels poor if he cannot maintain several houses and a lordly manor."

"And you?" he asked softly, dropping into the familiar form.

"I am somewhere in between, my lord. Neither a lord nor a cobbler in my desires."

"With a strong and influential man to pursue your complaint," said Puigbalador, "it is very possible that your husband's estates would be returned to you."

"You mean, someone as strong and influential even as you, my lord?"

"I mean just that," said Puigbalador. "When you have a moment free for thoughts of me, consider that."

As soon as an excellent dinner was done justice to and the table cleared, Astruch and Beniamin, their host, retreated to the small study, leaving the others to rest or enjoy the shade of the trees in the courtyard. Raquel sat on a low bench and took out a pile of fine white linen that she was working on. If she had to be on this trip, she thought fiercely, at least she would use as much of her time as she could in useful endeavors.

Bonafilla, her hands empty, sat down beside her.

"Does your father plan to transact much business on this trip?" asked Raquel.

"I don't know," said Bonafilla. "Why?"

"I wondered whether to unpack another length of cloth to work on," she said. "But it is in our box, which would have to be undone, and right at the bottom. I wouldn't bother unless I knew the journey was going to be very slow."

"We didn't talk about it," said Bonafilla. "But I will ask him if you like." She stood up.

"Not now, when he's busy, Bonafilla. Ask him when he is at leisure." She held up the work in her hands and looked critically at it. "If it will only be a day or two, I won't touch the box until we arrive. I have enough to keep me occupied until then."

"Why do you work all the time?" asked Bonafilla, sitting down again.

"Because I dislike being bored," said Raquel. "Why don't you work when there is nothing else to do?"

Bonafilla looked at Raquel curiously. "I don't like working. Do you miss Daniel?"

"How could she have time to miss Daniel?" said a lazy voice from just behind Bonafilla.

Bonafilla jumped with a small shriek. "Who's that?" she said breathlessly and turned around. Stretched out on the warm paving tiles beside her, leaning against the trunk of a pear tree, was Yusuf, his eyes closed.

"She said farewell to him at breakfast and waved good-bye at the bridge. Didn't you see him?" he continued.

"I didn't notice," said Bonafilla.

"I thought you were going to look at the town," said Raquel accusingly.

"I already did," said Yusuf. "It has few walls. How do they protect themselves when trouble comes?"

"Perhaps trouble doesn't come here," said Bonafilla.

"Trouble always comes," said Yusuf.

+>===—===<+

THE cool evening air, scented with fruit and flowers, drew everyone out to the courtyard, one by one. The last to appear were Astruch and Beniamin, both looking amicable and pleased with themselves. "I am afraid we are a great trouble to you and your household, Master Beniamin," said Isaac, as they gathered together around the newly set-up board.

"Not at all," said their host. "I cannot think how many times I have enjoyed the hospitality of friends in Girona. And so I say that, if this is trouble, may it always come in so pleasant a form," he added, pouring some wine into the physician's cup.

"Do you expect trouble?" asked Yusuf, and then hastily excused himself for interrupting.

"Not especially," said Beniamin, looking shrewdly at the boy from Granada. "Why should you ask?"

"It seemed to me there was an air of uneasiness in the city," said Yusuf tentatively. "I am probably wrong. It is only my ignorance that speaks," he added.

"Perceptive ignorance," said his host. "People are uneasy. Our small community is especially uneasy, having little extra protection here aside from that which we provide for ourselves."

Everyone glanced at the solid walls and stout gates surrounding the courtyard. "Why now?" asked Raquel.

"His Majesty is away; the kingdom is in the hands of many different people," said Beniamin. "And when he is gone, we worry."

"Why?" asked Raquel.

"We all know His Majesty—what he requires and expects and what we can expect from him," added Astruch. "Unlike some rulers, he does not waver back and forth in his judgments. Also, the expenses of the war are heavy—"

"The expenses of all wars are heavy," interrupted Beniamin.

"Very true," said Astruch. "In Girona, there is now an extra tax on bread, wine, and meat to pay for the loans the city took out for the war. That tax is resented, and when there is resentment, we suffer," he added grimly. "I would not be happy, living outside the stout walls of our *call* and our city, Beniamin. When the farmers and peasants are bitter they take their anger out on the city and on us. Fortunately we are protected by double walls, and now the King promises to extend the city walls to enclose all those on the outskirts."

"An expensive undertaking," said Beniamin. "I wonder that he considers it."

"But what if armies come down once more from the north?" said Astruch. "Those people would be helpless."

"They'll attack us in Figueres first," said Beniamin. "And give the citizens of Sant Feliu time to get inside the walls of Girona. Speaking of all this, where do you stay tomorrow?"

"I had thought we could stay with a cousin of the Cresques, who is married to my cousin," said Astruch. "He has a farm near the coast. I dispatched a letter to him when I was first working out this journey."

"Let us go into my study and talk about your route."

"Come, Bonafilla," said Raquel briskly. "We'll go for a walk. Where are Leah and Ester? Yusuf?"

"You sound exactly like Mistress Judith," muttered Yusuf, as he stood up from the table.

THE sun was hovering above the horizon, shining directly into their eyes, when the travelers from Girona left Figueres. Astruch's plans involved a somewhat longer journey on the second day, through countryside that, although fertile and pleasant, was not of any particular importance to him. "The sun is in my eyes," said Bonafilla to Raquel, who was now permanently assigned to accompanying her, rather than riding by her father, with whom she could always carry on a conversation.

"Turn your head to one side," said Raquel. "The mule can see the road—you don't have to look ahead."

"We wouldn't have had to make this journey at all if Papa hadn't insisted on marrying me to someone in Perpignan," she continued, paying no attention to Raquel. "I'm stiff and sore from riding all day yesterday."

"You'll be stiffer and sorer tomorrow," said Raquel unsympathetically. "But you'll get over it. Do you know how far your papa expects to travel today?"

"Why would I know?" said Bonafilla crossly. "He doesn't talk to me. He tells me to do this or do that and don't ask why. I'll be glad to get away from them all," she said, her voice trembling. She drew a deep breath and looked around her at the fields, woods, vineyards, and orchards on both sides of the road. "Where will we have dinner? There is nothing around us but fields."

"Are you hungry?" asked Raquel, who had watched Bonafilla picking unhappily at her breakfast.

"No," she said. "I just wondered."

"I expect we'll eat by the side of the road. Your papa knows this road well. He'll know a place where we can stop. It should have water and grass for the animals and trees for shade to sit under."

The road was snaking its way across the broad coastal plains toward the sea, and the day was getting hotter by the minute. Bonafilla's questions and complaints rippled like a stream past Raquel's ear, and like the music of a stream, became so familiar she ceased to hear them. Aside from suggesting that she throw aside her outer veil and loosen her inner one for the sake of catching the slight breeze on her face, she paid no attention to her, lost in her own thoughts.

They paused briefly at a clear river sometime between the bells for terce and those for sext to water the sweating animals and set off again. Even Yusuf's mare slowed as they traversed the gentle hills in the heat. At last a cooler, livelier breeze touched their faces. Yusuf sniffed the air. "That's the sea," he said. "It can't be very far."

"As soon as we find another resting place we will stop for dinner," said Astruch.

"When is that, Papa?" asked Bonafilla. "I would be glad to stop for a while."

"In an hour or two," he said. "Most of the streams along here are brackish—we have to get farther up the coast."

Raquel urged her mule up beside Astruch and her father, who were talking of a variety of things.

"Master Astruch," she said. "Where do we spend the night? It is a matter of lively conjecture between your daughter and me."

"It is? I told Bonafilla several days ago what our route would be, but then, she rarely listens to her papa. There is a farm," said Astruch, "a few miles in from the coast, perhaps four hours from here. I stayed there a few times, years ago, when the old couple who held the lease were alive. They were not well off, but lived comfortably, and were always glad of visitors. They had a splendid orchard, and vines, as well as olive trees and some goats," he added. "Their son, Mosse, will be managing it now."

THE casual life at the palace in Perpignan had been completely overturned in a moment that midday by the arrival of the Princess Constança and her retinue. An extra troop of soldiers and their officers had to be accommodated, a bevy of ladies-in-waiting settled, and everyone's pathways from here to there altered to safeguard the privacy of the young Princess.

At the sound of the distant trumpet, the cooks had hastily revised the menu for dinner, adding several courses, and taking away some others to conform to the Princess's likes and dislikes. "What idiot said she would not be here until next week at the earliest?" said the head cook in the middle of a rapid flow of instructions. "Those fish you brought me I wouldn't feed to her dog," he snarled at the sous-chef. Then he stopped for a moment to pour himself a cupful of wine to steady his nerves.

No one had the courage to reply.

As soon as they had set aside their traveling clothes and washed away the dust of the road, the Princess and her ladies came down into the small courtyard. Johana, on Margarida's instructions, had already seated herself where she could greet the royal party, and rose, curtsying as deeply as she could.

"Lady Johana," said the Princess, acknowledging her with a nod of the head and a smile. "It gives me great pleasure to see you again. It has been too long since I have had the pleasure of your company."

"I am overjoyed to greet Your Highness once more," said Johana, her head bowed low still. "And very grateful to have been allowed to stay here at the palace."

"Come and sit by me, Lady Johana," said Constança.

Johana rose and took the proffered chair.

"Now, tell me what has happened," she said in a soft voice. "I have heard so many reports, some of them too bizarre to be true. But, even so, it sounds most grave." In spite of the gentleness of her manner, she was regarding Lady Johana with eyes as shrewd and probing as her royal father's.

Johana recounted the story—the ship, the investors, the accusation of contraband, which she knew was not true, and the arrest. At every point in the tale, the Princess stopped her, with questions and requests for clarification of details.

"Lady Margarida told me how you rescued him," said Constança, her eyes sparkling with interest now that the matters of law and trade had been dealt with. "It sounded like a tale one reads in a book. But she also said that he was severely injured, for which I am very sorry. They tell me you married him for love," she added in her clear, almost childish voice. "That must be a wonderful thing," she said wistfully, and suddenly Johana felt a deep surge of pity for her.

At that moment, a door opened and closed somewhere above them, and a frenzied, high-pitched barking resounded through the courtyard. "Who has let out Morena?" asked Constança, with a frown to equal her royal father's.

In the middle of a flurry of replies and exculpations a small brown spaniel with a white patch on her face came scrambling down the staircase, raced across the courtyard, and took a great leap into the Princess's lap. "Poor little Morena," she said to Johana, cradling the dog in her arms. "She thought we were traveling again, and had forgotten her."

"She is a charming and most loyal little creature," said Johana.

"She is," said the Princess, with a smile that spoke of

real joy. "Even though she muddies my best gowns with her paws. I have one more question, Lady Johana. On your honor, did Arnau Marça do that which he has been accused of?" she asked. "For I would not expect my papa to pardon a man who plotted against him. Although I confess he has done so, when he felt circumstances warranted it."

"Oh, no, Your Highness," said Johana. "On my honor, my husband has not plotted against His Highness. He is as loyal a subject as can be found in the kingdom. At a meeting one of the investors suggested that they could all make a greater profit if contraband were concealed under the proper cargo. Arnau refused absolutely. It would be illegal, disloyal, and dangerous, he said. He also argued that there was no need to smuggle contraband, for the profit with a legal cargo would be sufficient."

"You heard this?"

"Yes, Your Highness. I heard it. And I swear on my soul, that is what he said. And again I swear, as I hope for salvation, that my husband is an honest and loyal man."

"That is a solemn oath, Lady Johana."

"I would swear it again, with my hand on the cross before the altar, Your Highness."

"Then I will write to His Majesty, for whether Don Arnau recovers or not, Lady Margarida tells me you wish his name to be cleared of the imputation of treachery. And that is understandable."

"I do, Your Highness, with all my heart. And I am most grateful for your intervention."

AT about that time, a young serving girl arrived at the gates of the palace. "I carry an urgent message for the Lady Johana," she said to the guard at the gate.

"And who are you?" asked the guard.

"My name is Jacinta, sir," she said firmly.

"Give me the message and I will take it to her," said the guard.

"I may not do that," said the girl. "I was to tell it in her ear alone. No one else's."

"You'll tell me or leave here at once," said the guard softly, grabbing her arm and squeezing it menacingly.

"I will not tell you," said the girl, raising her high-pitched voice until it filled the courtyard. "It is for the Lady Johana and no one else!" An officer, a captain, turned quickly at the sound.

"Here, guard," said the captain. "What is this all about?"

"This girl wants to see Lady Johana with a message."

"I will take her to the Lady Johana," said the captain, his eyes sharp with curiosity. "Come along." He took Jacinta by the other arm, jerked her away from the guard, and pulled her toward the sweeping staircase that led to the royal apartments and reception rooms. "Now, what do you wish to tell her? Perhaps you should say it to me, so I can prepare her. She is very near her time, you know. You wouldn't want to harm her."

"What I have to say is for her alone," said the girl, stubbornly. "Otherwise I don't get paid."

"Who gave you the message?"

"A priest," said the girl. "One of those Dominicans. He said he'd come to the palace to check I did it right."

By now, word had flown throughout the palace, and Lady Margarida came out to the steps leading down to the main courtyard. "I hear there is a message for Lady Johana," she called down to the captain. "Is this the girl who brought it?"

"I am, mistress," said the girl.

"Come up here and I'll take you to her. Let her go, captain."

"Do you want me to stay?" said the captain. "She's a shifty-looking creature, likely to do anything."

"No. Send her up." The captain, still looking up at Margarida, kept a tight hold on Jacinta's arm. "And do it at once, Captain, or I'll fetch the Princess." The captain bowed and went back down the long stone staircase.

"Lady Johana is sitting in the inner courtyard, my child," said Margarida. She pointed down.

Johana rose at Margarida's signal, curtsied to the Princess Constança, and walked over to the foot of the inner stairs. Margarida watched the child run quickly down the staircase, and standing on her tiptoes, speak to Johana, whose head was bent down to listen. She saw Johana giving her a coin and a pat on the head, and then summoning one of the servants to see the child safely out of the palace. As soon as Jacinta left the courtyard Margarida hurried down the stairs.

Johana turned and fell into Margarida's arms. "He's gone, Margarida," she said dully. "He's gone." She pushed herself upright and walked heavily over to the Princess. She lowered herself down on her knees and murmured something that even the sharpest-eared of the ladies could not hear.

"Of course you must go," said the Princess. She set down her spaniel and drew herself up with regal bearing, in spite of her fourteen years. "And after, we will be most content to have you return here to live with us in safety. Do not linger at the castle, Lady Johana, but return at once. I will send a guard with you."

Johana rose to her feet, curtsied as best she could, and made her way back to her chamber.

THE road to Perpignan turned northeast to follow the coast, bringing some relief to the travelers from Girona. The midday sun was now at their backs and a cooling wind was blowing in from the sea. But even so, the road climbed over a multitude of small hills and crossed a discouraging number of dried-up streams and rivers too murky or salty for man or beast to drink. "When do you think we will stop?" asked Bonafilla after a long period of exhausted silence.

Raquel shook her head. "Soon, I hope," she said, too tired, hungry, and thirsty to say anything more. Then her mule pricked up her ears and shook her head until her bridle jangled.

"Look at those trees to our left," said Yusuf. "Behind that hill."

"We are coming to another river," said Isaac to Astruch. "I think I can hear it. And my mule certainly smells it."

"We have reached the place that I have been looking for," said Astruch.

They crested the hill. In front of them the road veered sharply to the left, angling across a steep slope down to the water. Just ahead of them, a stream crossed the road and then raced off to lose itself in the sand and mud of a salt marsh on the edge of the sea. They had reached the stopping place.

The steep rocky ground above them and to their left supported sizable trees that clustered about the fast-moving stream. The water tumbled over a stony bed and coarse grass grew in profusion in clumps between the rocks. As they climbed up toward it, the breeze played with Raquel's veil, threatening to snatch it off and carry it away. "This spot seems pleasantly cool," she said.

"It is. There is nothing like it on this stretch of road," said Astruch, looking around with great satisfaction. "And thanks to Master Beniamin's housekeeper and our own resources, we have an abundant, if cold, dinner. We can rest here long enough to eat and drink our fill, but then we must carry on if we are to reach our destination before dark."

Leah and Ester climbed stiffly down from the cart and began to unpack a variety of dishes: bread, olives, salted fish cooked in oil and herbs, braised beef, and a roasted chicken, along with fruit, almonds, and a cask of excellent wine.

Bonafilla dismounted and went over to the stream. She knelt by the water, took off her slightly heavier outer veil, dropping it on the ground beside the stream, and pushed back the lighter one. Her face was red with heat and wet with perspiration. She bent over the cold, clear water as far as she could and splashed it over her face and hair. "I like this place you found, Papa," she said, with more good humor than anyone had heard from her on the journey so far. Just as she spoke, however, a gust of wind snatched her veil up from the bank of the stream. She reached out for it and missed. "My veil," she shrieked, pointing at the flimsy piece of cloth.

The first gust took it far above their heads. Once up there, it floated high over the valley next to them and onto the next hill, where it was stopped by a stand of trees, caught in the topmost branches of a tall oak. "We have no time to go chasing after a veil," said Astruch. "We'll find you another one in Perpignan," said her father. "You don't need two anyway."

The animals were loosed to graze and drink as they wished, watched over by the two menservants in turn, and the travelers fell on their dinner with considerable enthusiasm. Each member of the party found himself a comfortable place to sit and eat. Astruch and Duran went off to a shady group of pines, the servants collected near the carts, Bonafilla stretched out on a thick patch of grass, and Raquel, Isaac, and Yusuf sat by the stream with their backs resting on chunks of rock. They had set out before sunrise; they had ridden many miles that morning and it had been many, many hours since they had breakfasted. Everyone was weary. There was nothing to disturb them in their perch above the sea except for the murmur of the stream, and the distant sound of the waves hitting the shore.

Within minutes of finishing the last of their meals, each one of them was fast asleep.

Isaac woke first, uncertain whether he had been disturbed by a noise or simply by the sense of time passing. He nudged Raquel and Yusuf awake and began to prepare himself to continue.

"Look where the sun is, Yusuf," said Raquel, and hastened over to find Astruch Afaman.

"Come, come, everyone," he called. "If we are to sleep under a roof tonight, we must set out at once."

WHILE the party from Girona was packing up again, splashing more cold water from the stream on their faces to wake themselves, and generally making ready for the road, the same four investors in the syndicate to charter the *Santa Maria Nunciada* gathered once more in Pere Vidal's dining room to mull over their problems.

"I called everyone together this afternoon," said Pere Vidal, "because of a disturbing piece of news that has been brought to me."

"I hope it won't take too long to tell," said Ramon Julià. "I must ride out to—I must go out of the city before sundown. I am expected somewhere."

"We will be through long before sundown, Don Ramon," said Pere Vidal in his most soothing voice.

"What news?" asked Pere Peyro.

"I have it on excellent authority that Don Arnau Marça died this morning. His body has just been taken from the city in greatest secrecy to be entombed at the castle with his ancestors."

"Are you sure?" asked Peyro.

"I am," said Vidal. "I had it from someone at the palace. Doña Johana is staying there with the Princess. She has just left to accompany her husband on his last journey."

"How does this change things?" asked Martin sharply.

"Or does it? After all, Marça in France or Marça in his tomb—aren't they all the same as far as we are concerned?"

"Except that Marça in his tomb is not likely to testify at our trials, Martin," said Peyro.

"We must petition for judgment against him," said Vidal. "After all, didn't he supervise the loading of cargo?"

"Don Arnau?" said Peyro. "That depends on the exact moment that he dismissed his man of business. But it seems likely that he did, with the help of the captain of the ship."

"I have been told that Cassa has already given his sworn evidence to the court to be used in Arnau's trial," said Vidal.

"It is a pity that we did not get to speak to him," said Peyro. "I would like to know what that evidence was."

"I saw him," said Ramon Julià, looking up. "Last night." He frowned in concentration. "Or was it the night before?"

"Where?" asked Peyro.

"I was having a game of cards," said Don Ramon. "Had I known you wished to speak to him, I would have addressed him myself."

"What was he doing out there?"

"Walking around," said Don Ramon. "Looking. If I think of it when I see him again, I'll speak to him."

"Thank you, Don Ramon," said Pere Vidal. "That will be helpful. Now let us consider the matter of a petition."

"We need more information before we can draft a petition to the court," said Peyro.

"I must write to his lordship the viscount and find out what he wishes me to do," said Martin.

"Yes. Write to his lordship," said Peyro. "I will ride down to Collioure in the morning. There are more questions to be asked."

❖——❖ ❖——❖

THE sun was a reddish glow on the horizon when Astruch finally said, "There. That's the road up to the farm. It's not far now."

"Every time Master Astruch says something is not far," said Yusuf softly to Raquel, "I know we are in for a long, long ride."

And Yusuf was not far wrong. The blue of the western sky had silvered over with approaching night when at last Astruch called out, "That's it. Isn't it a delightful farm?"

"I don't know how you can see it in the dark," said Bonafilla.

"Put aside your veil and you'll see it. The house looks pleasant but rather small," said Raquel. "Do you think they can take us all in?"

"One way or another," said Astruch. "Straw makes a fine bed when you've traveled since daybreak."

They rode up the narrow track and caught sight of a man walking toward them from the back of the house. "Who are you?" he said, glancing around him. Fear blended with hostility in his voice, and Raquel nudged her mule closer to her father's.

"I am Astruch Afaman," said the merchant, "and you must be young Mosse. You've grown into a man since I saw you last."

"My name is Johan," said the young man.

"But are you not the son of Abram Cresques? I am sorry if I am mistaken, but you look—"

"Ssh." He raised his hand for silence. "Bring those animals and the carts around to the back," he said in a low, urgent voice. "As quickly as you can. And quietly. Behind the barn. I will see you there. Go."

They moved quickly enough, but nine mules, three horses, and two carts with rattling wheels cannot be silent. Just as the last cart disappeared around the side of the house, making for the barn, the door opened.

"Who is it, Johan?" called a woman's voice from a window in the upper floor of the house.

"No one, Francesca," said the farmer loudly. "A messenger. He was looking for old Roger."

"He'll have a time finding the rascal." A big hearty-looking man stepped out of the house. "Unless he's willing to go off to Purgatory and start searching." Apparently finding this extremely witty, the big man began to laugh, turned and waved good-bye to someone in the house, and headed down the lane, still laughing. "Off to Purgatory," he said. "Or maybe even Hell. I wouldn't be surprised to hear he was down there cheating the very devils themselves."

THE travelers stood behind the barn, uneasy in the dwindling twilight. A breeze sprang up and the odor of the manure pile battled for supremacy with the sweet scent of ripe grass. After what seemed an unconscionably long time, Johan appeared around the corner.

"I am sorry," he said, his voice and manner stiff, "but a neighbor was in our house when you arrived—a man who is too interested in our affairs and too free with his tongue. Your arrival would have been the talk of the tavern this evening. My father was Abram Cresques, sir, and I remember you from your last visit here. I was only a boy then."

"I was warned that you might not be able to take us in, Johan," said Astruch, with a certain emphasis on the name. "I was not told why."

"I will not turn you from my door, Master Astruch," said the young man. "It is almost dark and the moon will not rise high enough to light your road for many hours. You would have a long, difficult ride to reach other accommodation for the night."

"We spent last night in Figueres," said Astruch, by way of explanation. "I usually ride straight through Figueres from Girona and nightfall catches me elsewhere."

"You are welcome to whatever we have and to spend the night," said Johan. "Between the loft and the house, we can find places for you all to sleep. But I ask you to be very quiet."

━┿━ ━┿━

JOHAN'S wife, Francesca, came down the narrow stairs from the upper story where she had been putting the children to bed, and laid plates piled with olives, cold meat, nuts, and fruit on the table, along with a massive loaf of bread and a pot of soup. After the assembled company had eaten their fill, the menservants went out to make themselves as comfortable as they could in the loft of the barn. Francesca excused herself to see to beds in the house. After a glare from Raquel, the two maids took their bundles and slipped upstairs after Johan's wife to help and to see what sort of accommodation they could find for themselves.

"I will make myself a bed out in the loft as well," said Duran. "There will be more room for the rest that way."

"Move quietly," said his father. "Don't create a disturbance."

"Indeed, I beg you, don't make any noise," said Johan. The young man nodded, took his bundle, and left the big kitchen quietly. "You have an excellent son, Master Astruch," Johan added. "I can only hope that mine grow up as fine as yours."

"With such parents," said Astruch gently, "I am sure that they will."

"It was for them as much as for us that we converted," said Johan defensively. "We were going to be driven off our land one way or another if we did not. This is not a city, with a community to help us and walls to protect us, nor do I have other skills with which to earn my bread."

"But you have prosperous kin in several cities, all of

whom would help you," said Astruch. "As would your friends and your parents' friends."

"I have always lived on this land," said Johan stubbornly. "My grandfather planted those olives," he said. "And to-night we ate the pears my father planted. I can remember when he set out the seedlings that became those trees."

"It is a well-tended and prosperous farm," murmured Astruch.

"It has been in our family for more generations than I can count. But the only other Jewish family in the district was burnt out, forcibly converted, and driven away to live in misery and deprivation. They have left the kingdom."

"Where did they go?" asked Raquel.

"I don't know," said Johan. "But that was enough for us. I went to the noble Francesch de Cervian, who knew my uncle well in the way of business and is a fair and good-hearted man. He agreed to sponsor us as converts."

"And have you taken his name?" asked Isaac.

"With his permission we have. It is safer. I am Johan Cervian, and my Dolsa is Francesca Dolsa Cervian, but I try hard to call her Francesca. And that man you heard is the curse of our existence. He is a neighbor who hopes to pick up the lease to our land at a good price if he can prove that I have fallen back into the old ways. He turns up at all hours, prying, listening, trying to catch us out."

"We will leave before dawn breaks," said Astruch.

"It grieves me to turn my father's old friend from my house at such an hour," said Johan, "but I would be most grateful."

"How early must we get up?" said Bonafilla in alarm.

"Our neighbor is a man who drinks heartily in the evening," said Johan.

"Does he sleep late?" asked Isaac.

"Not always," said Johan, "but sometimes he has trouble getting himself from his bed before the bells ring for terce."

FOUR

IN the blackness before dawn, Raquel lay on her side at the edge of the narrow bed, listening to the small noises of someone moving quietly below them. She was sharing the tiny bed with Bonafilla, and had passed a long and unpleasant night of sleeplessness and strange dreams. Grateful that it was over, she slipped out of bed, opened the shutters, and put on her gown in the pale moonlight. She tidied her hair with her fingers as best she could, prodded Bonafilla awake, and went down the stairs. Francesca was in the kitchen, preparing food by candlelight.

Still suffering from the sense of choking oppression, Raquel fled the house, found her way to the little earth closet behind it, and then went into the courtyard to wash. The cold water of the well on her face, neck, and arms cleared her head. The cry of the owl had given way to the quarrels of the small birds that hide during the night, and suddenly the heady smell of bread baking in the outdoor oven filled the air and chased away the last terrors of the night.

When Raquel came in, Francesca smiled shyly and

handed her a piece of linen toweling. When she had dried herself and straightened her clothing again, Francesca set a small loaf of coarse country bread on the table in front of her, along with a large cheese of goat's milk and a basket filled with fruit. As Raquel ate, Francesca brought in more loaves from the oven, set them on the table for the others, and sat down across from her.

"Do you have no one to help you?" asked Raquel.

Francesca shook her head. "Only a girl of ten, and she is with her mother, who is ill. So many died in the Black Death that there are few left to be hired, and none at the wages we can pay. I do not mind for myself, but it is difficult for Johan to run the farm with only a few extra workers at harvest. But my eldest, Robert, is almost five and already knows how to do many things," she added with shy pride. "Soon he will be able to help his papa."

"I wish we could help," said Raquel.

Francesca smiled helplessly and said nothing.

The door opened and a crowd of men came in from the courtyard. "Thank you for that excellent breakfast, mistress," said Raquel. "I will return in a moment."

"Good morning, Mistress Francesca," said Astruch, looking appreciatively at the table. "What a welcome sight."

━►➤ ═ ◄━

"Papa," said Raquel, who came across her father as he was completing his morning prayers, "I would like to do something for Johan and his wife. They have a hard life here."

"What do you suggest?" asked her father.

"They could use some good cloth to cover themselves and those children," said Raquel. "I have some linen I was going to work, but I can buy a new length in Perpignan."

"Would it not be more useful to give her medication for the baby's cough? Leave plenty with her—they are taking great risks for us. And as for clothing, I shall speak to

Astruch," said Isaac. "He has brought a great deal of cloth
to show to the merchants and then to leave with his daughter. More than she needs. Go through the basket and see
what we have brought that a family such as theirs might
find they need."

THE waning moon was still high enough in the western
sky to light up the road when the party from Girona left
the farmhouse. Francesca stood in the doorway, clasping a
heavy bundle from Astruch. It contained fine linen for underclothes and wool for winter garments, and was more
cloth than she had ever dreamed of possessing at one time
in her life. On the kitchen shelf was a basket filled with a
variety of medications, all carefully labeled, with instructions, for Francesca knew her letters well enough to read
them. Johan, the guards, and the menservants had saddled
the horses and mules; they had hitched the baggage animals to the carts. All the beasts were led down the track
with soft murmurs of encouragement in a futile effort to
keep them quiet. Yusuf's mare whinnied impatiently and
shook her head. Her bridle jangled in the silence of the
morning. "Ssh," he said softly, to no avail.

"We should have tied straw to their hoofs," murmured
Astruch. Duran shrugged his shoulders and kept walking.
No one else responded.

When they reached the road, Astruch mounted and the
others followed suit. They set off in silence, enveloped in
their dark cloaks, with their eyes fixed to the ground, until
they were well past the neighbor's house.

"It's brightening fast to the east," said Astruch when
they neared the main road, and as if this were a signal,
everyone began talking at once.

"I have never been so frightened in my life," said Bonafilla.

"There was no need for you to be frightened," said

Duran. "We have travel documents from the Bishop and the King guaranteeing us safe passage free from harassment."

"Then why were we creeping about like that?" asked Bonafilla, astonished.

"For Johan's sake, you foolish girl. We were thinking of the safety of our host and his family if rumors get about that he consorts with Jews and is therefore not a good Christian. And since he has a malicious neighbor, this kind of thing can happen."

Before she could think of a reply, the sound of a horse galloping up behind them made everyone turn. It was a bay mare, who tossed her head, danced to a trot, and then a walk, slowing down right beside Raquel. "Yusuf," said Raquel. "Where have you been? I thought you were with us."

"She needed some exercise," said the boy. "And I wanted to see what happened after everyone else had gone by."

"Was anyone stirring at that farm?" asked Raquel.

"A boy came out to the well to get water as I rode by. I waved at him and he waved back," said Yusuf. "The rest of the house seemed very quiet."

"Excellent," said Astruch. "I hope that Johan Cervian may be safe. And I regret the loss of the place to stay. I shall never be able to go back there."

+>===<+

WHEN the sun was well above the treetops, people began pouring onto the road—some walking, in groups or alone, and some leading donkeys and mules laden with goods of all kinds. Farmworkers, highly prized in those days of labor shortages, strolled to their next jobs, talking, laughing and singing, passing wineskins back and forth. They passed another group of merchants, serious-looking and well guarded, heading toward Barcelona with a string of baggage mules laden with boxes and bundles. They exchanged courteous greetings. Official couriers on their sturdy, efficient mounts rode by at an easy gallop, with barely a nod of acknowledgment. Even though October was well under way, the heat of summer lingered on, and the sun, although lower in the sky, was bright and warm, turning the countryside into a Midas's kingdom of gold.

"Perhaps I should warn you, my friend," said Astruch to Isaac, "that I am not sure where we will sleep tonight."

"We have our cloaks," said Isaac. "Unless the rains return we can sleep dry enough in a field. It won't disturb me."

"The situation is not that dire," said Astruch, laughing. "We will either stay with a friend in Collioure or with Jacob in Perpignan. But I have serious business to take care of in Collioure."

"When do you think we will reach the town?" asked Isaac.

"In no time at all," said Astruch cheerfully.

Yusuf looked over at Raquel and raised an eyebrow.

"We will certainly be there in time for dinner," he added. "And most likely well before. If all goes well, I can take care of my business concerns at once. Then we will leave after dinner and arrive in Perpignan by sunset. Or perhaps slightly after."

"It would be helpful to arrive before the city gates are closed," said Isaac.

"True," said Astruch.

"Is your business in Collioure complex?" asked Isaac.

"Not particularly, I hope. I undertake it only partly for myself. It is mainly for Guillem de Castell."

"In Collioure?"

"Yes. He has invested in a ship's cargo that is heading for the East. I advanced a good part of the sum required to buy in, so it is in my interest to make sure that all goes well with the venture."

"I have always thought Don Guillem to be a prosperous

and honest man," said Isaac. "I would not have thought that any loan to him would be a problem."

"One would think not," said Astruch. "And if the voyage is successful it is certain not to be a problem. He has purchased a minor share—a sixteenth—of a trading voyage of a cargo ship called the *Santa Maria Nunciada*. She is at anchor, I believe, at Collioure, and due to leave soon. He has asked me to have a word with the ship's master and the majority owner, Arnau Marça, and to find out how preparations are going. They should both be in Collioure right now. If, as I expect, everything is proceeding normally, my inquiries will be very brief."

"Then tonight we sleep in Perpignan no doubt," said Isaac courteously.

"But since it is Master Astruch who speaks," murmured Yusuf to Raquel, "tonight we will actually sleep in Collioure. I hope this friend has ampler accommodations than the last one."

FIVE

THE harbor at Collioure was filled with boats at anchor:
a splendid galley, two broad-beamed cargo ships, and a host
of fishing boats from the tiniest shell to multi-oared substantial vessels with all the variations in between. Astruch
had settled Raquel and Bonafilla with their maids at the
house of his friend and then, filled with restless energy, had
urged his son, along with Isaac and Yusuf, to come down
with him to the harbor. "I wonder if one of those is the
Santa Maria?" said Astruch, pointing at the cargo ships.

"It is possible," said his son Duran, amiably.

"It is possible," said a weather-beaten man with gnarled
hands and a deeply bronzed lined face who was sitting
nearby on an outcrop of rock. "They're both cargo ships.
But that one isn't the *Santa Maria*."

"Why do you say that, old man?"

"Because the *Santa Maria Nunciada* raised anchor and
sailed at daybreak last Thursday," he said. "I saw her. And
since I can't see her anymore, I suspect she's well on her
way by now," he added.

"Do you know if she took on all her cargo?" asked Astruch.

"I don't know about cargo and things like that," he said vaguely. "I see them come in and anchor and then I see them raise anchor and go out again. When you're too old and stiff to work in the boats anymore, watching their comings and goings is something to do. It fills in the hours between breakfast and dinner."

"Do you know anyone who would know about her cargo?"

"The harbor master ought to know. Except of course he's ridden off to Perpignan because of the fuss." The old man rose stiffly from the rock and began to walk slowly up toward the town. "I'm off to my dinner," he added.

"Thank you, old man," said Astruch, pressing a coin into his hand. "Have a cup of wine for me. You have been of help."

"Don't know how," he said, his hand curling tightly around the coin as he continued on his way. When he was some ten or twenty strides farther along, he paused and turned back toward them. "Master Pere knows all about it. Pere Peyro. He comes from Perpignan. You'll find him down there, I expect, if he hasn't gone elsewhere for his dinner."

"DOWN there" turned out to be one of the town's taverns. The landlord nodded in the direction of Pere Peyro, who was seated in a corner, in earnest contemplation of a jug of wine. He raised his head in some surprise at discovering himself the center of interest of three grown men and a boy. "Have you business with me, gentlemen?" he asked, pleasantly enough to encourage conversation.

"We are from Girona," said Astruch with a bow. "Stopping in Collioure on our way to Perpignan. My name is Astruch. Astruch Afaman, most men call me. This is Master Isaac, a physician, my son Duran, and Master Isaac's student," he added, pointing at Yusuf.

Master Pere rose from his seat. He was of medium size, slim, and modishly dressed in a yellow tunic slashed with black velvet. His hose were yellow as well, and on his neat foot was a boot elegant enough to make a leather merchant sigh in appreciation. He bowed to Astruch and again, inclusively, to the other men. "You were looking for me?" he asked. "I am Pere Peyro. What is it I can do for you?"

"I am here on behalf of Guillem de Castell," said Astruch.

"I know him well. He is a partner in a venture that I am involved in."

"If this venture that you refer to is the voyage of the *Santa Maria Nunciada*," said Astruch, "then I have come to the right place. Don Guillem asked me to inquire into the state of things. He did not realize," added Astruch with delicacy, "that the ship would be sailing so soon."

"Nor did any of us," said Peyro. "Please, gentlemen, be seated and take a cup of wine with me. I myself arrived last night expecting to see her before she left."

"Do you have any news of her that I can carry back to Don Guillem?" asked Astruch.

"I don't like to seem suspicious," said Peyro, "but how do I know that you are acting on his behalf?"

"That should be called prudence rather than suspicion, Master Pere," said Astruch approvingly. He took his leather purse from inside his richly sober dark brown tunic, loosened the strings, and drew out a piece of parchment. He unfolded it and spread it out in front of the merchant.

Peyro read it carefully, his finger following along the line of writing, and then looked up and smiled. "Excellent. And you are a physician, sir?"

"Physician to His Excellency, the Bishop of Girona," said Astruch. "And, I am fortunate to be able to say, mine as well. Duran is in business with me."

"And the student?"

"Yusuf," said Isaac. "Yusuf ibn Hasan, ward to His Majesty, learning the rudiments of medicine at my side."

"I have heard of you, Yusuf," said Peyro. "Good. I like to know the people I am talking to. Now, as for the *Santa Maria Nunciada*, there is no need to tell you, obviously, that she has sailed. And you may also have heard that there were certain problems . . ."

"What kind of problems?" asked Astruch quickly.

"Almost every kind of problem that a cargo ship can run into while riding at anchor in a safe port," said Peyro in wry tones. "Problems with manning the ship, with loading cargo, with the various duties to be paid, and with export permissions. Pick whichever ones you prefer. We had them all."

"This is not reassuring," said Astruch.

"Perhaps not. But the ship is manned, the crew is experienced, and all the cargo that we purchased has been loaded. Or so I have been told. I have also been told that there is no extra cargo on board, as has been alleged. I do not know whether to believe that or not."

"Extra cargo?" said Astruch, his look of painful inquiry intensifying.

"Goods that we did not know were to be shipped."

"What kind of goods?" said Astruch, with a sort of horrified fascination.

"I will tell you what I know and what I have heard," said Peyro. "A charge has been laid that several documents—export permissions—were forged. That—the charge, that is—is certain. The forgeries, if they exist, were for goods essential to the safety of the kingdom in time of war."

"Weapons," said Astruch in a hollow voice.

"And armor, along with other necessary goods," added Peyro. "I see that I do not need to explain how serious this is."

"How could that have happened? Surely this is a very bad time to be carrying contraband, no matter how high the profits," said Astruch. "And I was assured that there was no question of doubtful cargo being on board."

"You asked him about it?" Peyro seemed surprised.

"Certainly, Master Pere. The presence of contraband raises the risk. But Don Guillem assured me that the owners had agreed that it was too risky in time of war to allow contraband on board."

"True enough," said Peyro vaguely. "But something seems to have gone wrong and I'm trying to find out what it was."

"Have you?" asked Astruch sharply.

"It's very difficult. The worst problem is the death of the majority shareholder, Arnau Marça. He was overseeing all of these things, and that means that his man of business, Felip Cassa, was responsible for having the goods transported here, and obtaining export permits."

"Arnau Marça is dead?"

"Yes. And in the most unfortunate, not to say scandalous, circumstances. He was arrested a week ago over this question of export permits."

"Arrested?" said Astruch, shocked.

"Yes. It seems that he was seriously injured in an attempt to break out of prison and has recently died of his injuries. His widow has taken his body in greatest secrecy to bury it with his ancestors at the castle."

"Surely his man of business would be the person to ask about the matters that concern you," said Isaac. "When a man of noble family becomes involved in such ventures, he rarely deals with these things himself."

"It seems that Don Arnau dismissed his man of business during the loading of the *Santa Maria*. Cassa said that Marça took the lists and documents from him, saying that he would deal with it all himself."

"Is this generally known?" asked Astruch.

"No," said Peyro. "Cassa has not spoken much of it, and we have been concerned to keep the gossips quiet."

"Yet we are talking about it in a tavern?" said Isaac.

"Only his partners know of his death," explained Peyro. "And very few people more of Cassa's dismissal."

"And now us," said Isaac. "And anyone else who is listening to us."

"No one around here would be bothered to listen," said Peyro. "And you are acting for a partner, aren't you?" He smiled at everyone around the table and pushed aside his wine cup. "But let us return to Arnau Marça. At the moment, I believe that once she buries him his wife is hoping to clear him of the charge of treachery. Of course, that is in order to protect herself and her unborn child."

"Don Arnau's death comes as a great shock," said Astruch, picking his words with care. "I had hoped to talk at length with him about the voyage. That is why we are here."

"Then I'm afraid you came a little late," said Peyro, looking around. Several more people were crowding in and shouting orders to the innkeeper. "May I suggest, gentlemen, that we walk down by the harbor to find an appetite for dinner? I assure you that this tavern, although not the most inviting-looking of places, has the most acceptable food in town. Shall we order our dinners before we take our walk, gentlemen?"

EARLIER that morning, a half-day's ride away, some forty or fifty retainers, villagers, and two or three curious neighbors gathered in the chapel of the *castell* for a funeral mass. They had come to see the body of Arnau Marça, wrapped in its shroud, carried to the vault beneath the chapel, where it was to join Arnau's noble, and in some cases, not quite so noble, ancestors. His widow, veiled and heavy with child, loosened the linen from the face and brushed the cold forehead with her lips. Then she turned and beckoned to an olive-skinned, attractive woman of forty or more years, who was standing shyly at the door.

"Felicitat, come stand here by me. You were closer to him than anyone else when he was a child," she said in a clear voice to the woman walking toward her. "It is fitting that you say farewell to him." She took her by the arm and drew her close to her side. "Prepare yourself," she said softly.

Felicitat looked down at the marble-like face and cried out in distress.

"Be brave," murmured Lady Johana. "For him, for all he did, and for all of us, be brave."

Felicitat drew a deep, shuddering breath. "I will, my lady," she said. "It was the shock of seeing him like this." She bent over and kissed him, murmuring a prayer in her own tongue, and shrouded his face again. When she straightened up, her face was covered with tears.

"Whatever they say," said one of the neighbors, as they moved away into the sunlight, "he must have been a good man. Look how stricken the serving woman is at his death."

"She was his nurse, I believe," said another.

"It is possible," said someone else. "A nurse will forgive any sort of evil behavior in one of her own fostering."

But in the crowd, Arnau Marça's wife took Felicitat's arm and drew her closer once more. "Please, come with me," said Lady Johana. "Help me to my chamber."

"Of course, my lady."

ONCE the door to Lady Johana's chamber was closed, she turned to the serving woman and shook her head. "I am so sorry," she said. "But I wanted you to say farewell to him."

"How did he die, my lady?"

"From wounds which he received fighting. Felicitat, I

saw them fight against heavy odds. No man could have been braver or more ferocious," said Lady Johana. "He was both courageous and clever," she added. "He will be sorely missed. No matter what anyone might say, he deserves to lie with the noble lords of Marça."

"The family tomb is where he belongs, my lady. You were right to bring him back."

"We must take comfort in the thought that he brought nothing but honor to his ancestors," said Johana. "Felicitat, tomorrow I must return to Perpignan. Can you help me? Come with me?"

"My lady, in your condition much travel surely is not wise."

"Not returning to the city to ensure that justice is accomplished would be even more foolish."

"Whatever I can do, my lady, I will."

"Excellent. Would you send for Felip Cassa now? I wish to speak to him before we leave."

"You have not heard, my lady?" said Felicitat. "He returned a few days ago to pack up his belongings, saying that his lordship had dismissed him. He told someone he was returning to the city."

"When was this?"

"He arrived the day after my lord's arrest."

"Before news of the escape?"

"Yes, my lady. The talk in the village is that he has gone to see his old master, in hopes of regaining his position with him."

"Then I must put someone else in charge until our return. Can you be ready to leave tomorrow at dawn?"

"I can, my lady."

AT Collioure, Astruch and his son, Pere Peyro, Isaac, and Yusuf strolled out onto a rocky point, where any approach, by land or water, would be noticed well in advance. "It is best," said Peyro, although perhaps somewhat tardily, "that we not spread out our troubles for everyone in the town."

"Are we safe from eavesdropping here?" asked Isaac, turning his head to listen. All he could perceive, though, was the water against the shore and the wind as it passed by.

"As safe as we can be," said Peyro.

"What more is there to say?" asked Astruch. "I would have thought that you had told us the worst."

"Not by any means," said Peyro in tones of deep gloom. "More legal difficulties turned up after the ship set sail. In my opinion the best way to deal with them would be to recall the ship for inspection of the cargo."

"Why?" asked Duran. "It's already been inspected, hasn't it?"

"Not carefully enough to prove that we are not shipping contraband, it seems," said Peyro. "But the master has his orders, you see, and unless we can intercept him . . ."

"That sounds most difficult," said Isaac.

"A fast galley could reach him," pointed out Yusuf, suddenly, having had some experience with such vessels earlier in the year.

"And very expensive," said Astruch in alarm. "A galley, on top of the cost of chartering the ship . . ." His voice trailed away as he made some calculations.

"Now that Marça is dead," said Peyro, "rumors are flying that the master was given a change in destination that would allow the cargo to be offered to other purchasers. Ones who would be willing to pay a great deal more for it."

"We are talking here of a possible cargo of arms?" asked Isaac.

"Yes," said Peyro, still sunk in gloom. "Arms that could be sold to enemies of the realm. That would implicate all of the owners in treasonable activity."

"Implicate?" said Astruch. "It would do more than implicate. Do you realize that every one of you is subject to the confiscation of all you own?"

"In the worst case," said Peyro. "Yes. We know. It would be most uncomfortable for our unfortunate families. What concerns me more than losing everything we own, I must confess, is that His Majesty would want our heads as well."

"Leaving me without my money," said Astruch.

"And poor Don Guillem without his life," said Isaac.

"How far has this gone?" said Astruch. "Beyond speculation and rumors, I mean?"

"Before his death, Arnau Marça was charged with attempting to smuggle out of the county of Roussillon weapons of war essential to the kingdom, under cover of an innocent shipment of cloth and foodstuffs."

"An uncomfortable accusation in time of war," murmured Isaac.

"The charge does not name any partners, and it is possible that the judges will decide that the rest of us are not involved. I confess that I would be very glad to hear that."

"Was there a trial?"

"No. And now he's dead. If he hadn't died, whether he had been found guilty or not, at least the judges would have come to some sort of decision about the whole venture. Now, with the King away, and Marça not having come to trial, and with Perpignan out of the line of sight of those looking after things for the moment, it could be years before the ownership of the cargo is cleared up."

"But what proof have you, has anyone, that the ship is carrying contraband?" asked Isaac.

"Proof? How can I have any proof?" said Peyro. "The ship is on its way to Egypt." He shook his head. "Whether it's carrying contraband, or simply the goods that it's supposed to be carrying, I do not know. What I do know, however, is that a galley, flying the royal standard, left from here early this morning."

"Where was it headed?" asked Astruch.

"No one knows. The master received his orders last night, they say, but no one is sure of that either. It may be off to His Majesty in Sardinia with the whole story."

"Or it may be chasing after the *Santa Maria*," said Astruch.

"Not likely," said Peyro. "It's a big sea. If it wants to catch up with it, it will have to meet it in Egypt." He stopped and looked gloomily out over the water, as if he were calculating the size of the sea. "If that ship is noticed pulling into any other harbor and offloading its cargo, we are in deep trouble. I came down here to find out if contrary orders have been dispatched. Come, gentlemen, I will join you for dinner and we can discuss this further."

+≈— —≈+

THE conversation carried on in the same circles of gloomy speculation throughout a badly cooked dinner of boiled greens, fish, and bread. Finally, Master Pere bade them farewell and took his gloomy way out of the tavern.

Astruch rose a few moments later. "Let us leave this place," he said. "It is no more convivial than its food is good."

"Are we returning to the others, Papa?" asked Duran. "If not, I think I will walk around the harbor once more."

"Do as you please," said Astruch, with a dismissive gesture of the hand. "I do not know what news I can take back to Don Guillem now," he continued. "Prepare him for disgrace and death? Warn him to pack up his valuables and flee?"

"If the ship's master had received contrary orders that had been signed by a minority of the owners, would he obey them, do you think?" asked Isaac.

"I doubt it very much," said Astruch. "Not without trying to confirm them. But all this talk is foolish, my friend. Surely nothing can be done until the ship returns, judgment is passed on Marça, and his will is proved."

"I agree, Master Astruch."

"If he is declared innocent, his heirs will make the decisions. If he is confirmed as guilty, the cargo belongs to His Majesty. Either way, it will be a while before I see my money, but I am prepared for that. But this too is speculation. I will put the case before my friend here, who knows much more about the laws concerning shipping than I do."

"We shall not leave for Perpignan tonight, I suspect," said Isaac.

"The sun is already low in the sky, lord," said Yusuf quietly.

"Then let us return at once to the women. My friend has offered most urgently to be our host for the night, but it is only courteous to tell him we are staying," said Astruch. "I shall seek his counsel and listen with great eagerness to his expounding of maritime law."

"For Castell or yourself?" asked Isaac.

"For both of us. If Castell is indicted, I shall not escape punishment, Isaac."

SIX

BEFORE the bells of the town rang for terce the next morning, the party from Girona was on its way, riding inland under blustery skies and occasional bursts of rain toward Perpignan.

"Had our host any words of comfort for you, Master Astruch?" asked Isaac, once he had ascertained that they were out of earshot of the rest of the party.

"He has heard rumors that two or three of the other owners were sending a fast galley to intercept the ship at its first port of call," said Astruch. "With new orders, they say."

"Does he credit these rumors?"

"No," said Astruch. "He does not believe that the ship can possibly carry cargo valuable enough to justify the expense of the galley."

"But if a galley were on its way to Egypt," said Isaac, "with its own cargo of passengers or valuable goods . . ."

"He suggested that. A galley lies at anchor now in Collioure port, preparing to sail. How much space does a new set of orders take?" asked Astruch gloomily.

"All this is speculation, Master Astruch," said Isaac. "We cannot know what a group of men might do. What Don Guillem needs to know is what illegal acts have been committed. Then he can dispute the charge that he was involved in them. If I am not mistaken, Jacob Bonjuhes will know which person in Perpignan we should approach with this difficulty. And if he does not know, one of his friends or his patients will. I believe the rain has stopped," he added. "I can feel the sun on my damp cheek. We cannot be very far from the city."

"Not far at all," said Astruch without looking up.

"Master Astruch, what town is that ahead with the church tower that stands so high?" called Yusuf from his place toward the rear of the group.

As Astruch peered ahead to see, a clump of shrubbery to their right apparently answered him in clear, definitely masculine tones. "It is the old cathedral at Elna, young man," it said.

Everyone turned to see a gray mare poking her head out from the edge of the shrubbery, and then starting toward them. A second or two later a man appeared, walking beside her with his hand on her withers. He was dressed for traveling with fashionable elegance; his manners matched his outer appearance. As soon as he came into view of the party, he bowed deeply, with an apologetic smile. Bonafilla, who had been riding almost bare-faced, gasped and pulled her veil across her mouth and chin, leaving only her eyes and forehead exposed.

"I apologize for startling you," he said. "I have been riding since before dawn and there is a quiet and comfortable place back there for man and beast to rest. But when I heard a question to which I knew so well the answer, I could not resist speaking out."

He set his foot in the stirrup and mounted with ease.

He urged his mare onto the road and forward until he was beside Astruch and not far ahead of Bonafilla. Then without asking leave, he slackened his pace to that of the party from Girona.

Under lowered eyelids, Raquel inspected the man carefully. He was too elegant and self-assured to be a servant. The tunic he wore was too good, too well made, and his voice was that of an educated man. And yet he was not a gentleman. Raquel was sure of that. A clerk, or perhaps even a secretary, to a rich man, or a head clerk to a merchant. He was handsome in a rather fierce kind of way, thin of cheek with prominent cheekbones and shrewd gray eyes, like a bird of prey. An interesting man, she thought, but not a comfortable one. She also thought that he knew he was being carefully assessed and that it amused him.

"I am called Felip," said the newcomer easily. "Heading home after some wearying business negotiations. I am from near Perpignan."

"And I am Astruch Afaman from Girona," said Astruch. "We ride to Perpignan for a wedding."

Felip looked around at the party and said, "And which of the two charming ladies is the bride? Surely one of them must be."

"My daughter," said Astruch, with a wave of his hand in the direction of Bonafilla. Bonafilla's response was to rearrange her veil so that now it covered all of her face.

"Such modesty and timidity become a bride very well," said Felip gravely. "Do you think that we will have more rain before we reach the city?" he asked, and with that, it seemed clear that he intended to make himself a part of their group.

+>==+ +==<+

"PAPA," said Raquel once they had passed through Elna and were well on their way to Perpignan, "we are riding by a most magnificent forest. It seems to go on forever."

"That explains why I no longer feel the sun on my face," said her father dryly. "Although it was clear to me from the sounds that we were in a forest."

"It does go on forever," said Felip. "It is His Majesty's *devesa,* his hunting preserve. No man ever saw so many fat deer and other game as live in that forest."

"What sort of game?" asked Yusuf, looking interested.

"Along with the deer beyond number," said the stranger, "there are boar. This forest is famous for its boar. And countless birds and other small game, of course. But there's no point in looking like that, young man," he said to Yusuf. "Only those close to His Majesty are allowed to hunt here. There are terrible punishments for trespassers and poachers on the King's hunting grounds."

"No doubt," said Yusuf easily. "But it is pleasant to look in from here and imagine what the preserve is like."

"But surely, Yusuf, if you wished to hunt in His Majesty's *devesa* it would not be a problem," said Astruch, smiling and turning to Felip. "Yusuf is His Majesty's ward and page. He could hunt in the royal preserve to his heart's content if he wished."

"Is he indeed?" said Felip with even more interest than Yusuf had shown in His Majesty's *devesa.*

"Yusuf," said Isaac before anyone could continue on the topic, "there is something I would say."

"Yes, lord," said the boy quickly, edging his mare closer.

"It would be well, perhaps," he said in a low voice, "not to speak of who you are to casual strangers."

"I have not, lord," said the boy. "It was—"

"I will speak to Master Astruch," said the physician. "There is a storm coming, I believe," he continued in louder tones.

As he spoke, the forest road, already shaded, darkened perceptibly. Somewhere a small animal squealed. The mules shook their harnesses uneasily and a rumble of thunder rolled off the mountains in the distance; scraps of blue sky that had been visible through the great arch of tree branches above them darkened and were replaced with black storm clouds.

"Yes, lord. I too feel a storm coming," said Yusuf. Moments later there was a blinding flash of lightning, followed rapidly by a crash of thunder, and the storm broke in all its fury. Rain pelted down in waves, bringing leaves, twigs, and small branches with it.

"Papa," said Raquel, "we must go off the road into the forest to find shelter before we are soaked to our skins." It needed only this to send everyone scrambling away from the relatively open spaces toward a thick stand of oaks.

Once under the trees, Raquel helped her father dismount and looked around for a relatively dry spot. "There is shelter over to our right and forward, Papa," she said. "Place your hand on my shoulder and stay close." Isaac moved over the strange territory more slowly than usual, feeling the way with his feet and trying to avoid rocks, roots, and stray branches hidden beneath the leaves. His staff, cumbersome to hold while riding, was on one of the carts, and without it, walking over uneven surfaces was difficult. Yusuf followed them, bringing their mounts.

When they reached the shelter Raquel had noticed, an outcropping of rock on the edge of a hollow, she stopped. "There is a slope down to the place, Papa," she said. "It is steep, but no longer than your arm. I shall go first." She turned to face it and slipped to the floor of the hollow.

"Are you down?" asked her father.

"Yes, Papa. By your right hand is a sapling. If you climb down facing the slope, the sapling will steady you.

"Yes, my dear. I know how to climb down a hill." He placed a hand on the sapling and sprang down with no difficulty. The hollow was open to the sky. "I thank you for your excellent directions," he added, "but I am getting wet."

"There is a crevice close by in some large rocks. It makes

a shallow cave that will shelter us from the heaviest downpour."

"Then let us hurry," said Isaac, "before we drown."

Yusuf left the animals under the trees and crowded in beside Isaac and Raquel. "You have chosen well, my dear," said Isaac. "This space is quite dry and comfortable."

"I hope the others are as well off," said Raquel.

"I hope so too," said Yusuf, "because there's no room in here for anything bigger than a mouse."

At the side of the road, Astruch and Duran, assisted by the terrified maids, were fussing over the baggage; the menservants had unhitched the mules and were leading them to shelter.

Instead of dismounting like the others, Bonafilla, panic-stricken, had spurred her mule toward the thickest patch of wood she could see. But the creature was as strong-willed as her mistress, and objected to squeezing between tree trunks and being caught in undergrowth. The mule balked and Bonafilla jumped down to find a safer place on foot. She passed the rocky outcrop where Isaac was sheltered with Raquel and Yusuf, noticing how well placed they were—and how crowded. Then her roving glance fell on the largest tree she had ever seen in her life. Its massive beginning had given rise over the years to three substantial subsidiary trunks. Two of them reached for the heavens, forming a broad protective canopy over the other, which started low and flattened out, growing almost parallel to the ground. Under it was a small hollow, a soft, dry space thick with freshly fallen leaves. She hurried over, knelt down on the ground, and crawled into it.

Wind, rain, thunder, and lightning increased their fury. The maids dropped what they were doing and scrambled under the carts, where they were joined by the menservants. Astruch and Duran, barely able to see through the pounding rain, checked that everyone seemed to be safely settled and headed for the shelter of a large tree.

Bonafilla had scarcely straightened her disarranged gown when that amused, elegant voice that had so startled her before said, "You seem to have found the only dry spot in His Majesty's forest." Before the words reached her ear, Felip had jumped down from his mare and slid under the branch into the hollow beside her. "Where have you left your mule?" he asked. "I hope you don't mind if I join you," he added.

"I do mind," she said. "And the wood is too thickly planted for my mule to pass. I left her back there."

"That's because you didn't follow the paths. If I hadn't caught a glimpse of saffron-colored silk through the trees, I would not have known where you were," said Felip. "But if my presence annoys you, mistress, I shall go back out to the road."

"If you go back out to the road," said Bonafilla impatiently, "you'll get soaking wet and I'll be blamed for it."

"Then what do you wish me to do?" he asked. "You must tell me. Do you wish me to stay?"

"No," said Bonafilla. "You mustn't stay."

"Do you wish me to ride on?"

"How can I wish you to ride on in this storm?"

"Then you must teach me how to disappear without leaving."

Bonafilla gave him a puzzled look and thought for a few moments. "I am to be married in five days," she said at last, as if this were an answer.

"I wish you much happiness," said Felip. "But that does not answer my question."

"I mean that my husband—"

"I beg your pardon, mistress, but you are not married now, are you?"

"Hardly," she said. "I've never met him. How could I possibly be married to him?"

"There are ways. But you don't seem terribly pleased

about the wedding," he observed, this time allowing a smile to play around his lips.

"Why should I be?" she said. "What if he's horrible? Besides, I would rather not marry." She tossed her head in the way that her family knew so well, and her veil fell away from her face.

As she reached for it, another bolt of lightning struck, this time so close to them that sound and blinding light came together. Bonafilla shrieked in real fear and turned to Felip. He put his arms around her and pulled her head down to his chest to shut out the storm. Gently, he patted her shoulder. Then, cautiously, he laid his cheek on her glossy hair and drew her closer in. All the while he kept his eyes open, alert, moving back and forth, searching the woods for the rest of the party. "Do not spoil your beauty with salty tears," he murmured, raising his head a little and stroking her hair. "If you would permit me the liberty, the only teardrops that would touch that lovely face would be those I showered over you, teardrops of gold and precious gems." He raised her chin and kissed her eyelids, mopping up her tears with a kerchief made of silk, but still his shrewd gray eyes continued to move back and forth, scanning the woods.

"Where's Bonafilla?" cried out her father's voice all of a sudden. "Bonafilla, where are you? Are you all right?"

"Here, Papa, safe and dry under a tree," she called. "You must go," she said softly. "This is wrong."

"It is not wrong at all, my beautiful Bonafilla," he said. "But still, I will go, since it would be wiser to do so. But I shall wait until the storm lets up a little."

"And if Papa comes looking for me?"

"Now that he knows you are safe, he too will wait for the storm to cease. Do you know the story of the beautiful Queen Dido, the great hero Aeneas, and the thunderstorm?"

"Who were they?"

"Shall I pass the time until the storm eases telling you their tale?" he asked softly.

But if anyone had been listening, they might have wondered that he omitted to include Dido's tragic fate in his somewhat shortened version of her history.

THE lightning and thunder eased off slightly, but the wind rose and the storm continued to rage. "I think I will go and find Bonafilla, Papa," said Duran. "And make sure she is all right." But as he crawled out from their shelter under another low-branched tree, a blast of wind ripped off a limb that came crashing down next to his head, knocking him over. He sat on the ground where he had fallen, looking dazed and rubbing his head where it had been struck by a branch.

"Come back at once," said his father angrily. "Bonafilla is not far away, and if I know my daughter, she's somewhere safe. I don't want you killed just to bring her closer. And if she says she's dry, then she's likely drier than we are." The wind howled furiously and Duran crawled back to his refuge.

And for almost an hour, high winds and pounding rain kept everyone in their places. Then the lightning and thunder moved off into the distance. The high winds, which had seemed set to continue forever, began to abate until they suddenly stopped altogether. With their absence, the pounding rain dwindled to a light shower.

"Papa," said Raquel, holding her hand out from under their rocky shelter. "The rain has stopped." She got up and stepped out into the hollow. "The clouds are breaking up," she added. "I can see a bit of blue sky."

Isaac raised his hand to check for hazards above his head and then he too stood up and came out. "It is good to have space again," he said. "Although I was most grateful for the shelter when we needed it."

"Where are the others?" asked Yusuf, who, it must be admitted, had fallen asleep as soon as he was dry and comfortable, and was now yawning himself awake.

"Not far away," said Raquel. "I heard Master Astruch and Bonafilla calling back and forth."

"I will check on the animals," said Yusuf. "They will likely need some grooming."

The sun was next to appear, then the servants, who set about collecting the mules, rubbing them down with handfuls of the straw that had been spread thickly on the carts to cushion riders and goods from the rigors of the road, while the maids laid out the wettest items of baggage to dry. Then Master Astruch and his son arrived at the road, along with the stranger, Felip, who immediately set to work on his gray mare.

"Where is Bonafilla?" asked Duran.

"I'm right here," said that familiar voice from somewhere nearby. "And I'm all muddy and rumpled from being huddled under a tree all that time. Where's Ester?"

"Here, mistress."

"Come and give me some help," she said impatiently.

But when, ten minutes later, the procession had straightened itself out and started on its way again, the maid Ester was looking at her mistress with a very thoughtful expression on her face.

JOHANA and Felicitat were almost at the palace gate when the storm unleashed its fury on Perpignan. By the time they had dismounted from their agitated mules and climbed the open stairs that led from the royal courtyard up to the Great Hall and the private apartments, their gowns were sodden, their veils drenched, and their hair was dripping onto the stones of the gallery. "My lady, you are soaked to the skin," said Felicitat, bustling her into her chamber and closing the door.

"If I am, Felicitat, then you must be as well," said Johana. "I am sorry to have taken you from your safe, dry house, but I cannot trust my maid the way I trust you. That is why I left her behind. Am I right? Would you betray me, Felicitat?"

"There is no fortune in this world that could tempt me to betray my lord's wife, my lady," said Felicitat calmly. "For if you are dead, then how am I, a poor slave, to seek vengeance for the suffering that I and mine have undergone?"

"You are free, Felicitat. You are no slave. Not any longer."

"That may be, but when powerful men look at me, they see a slave, without power or friends."

"Not as long as I live," said Johana. "Come, get me out of these wet garments and I will help you out of yours."

They were both in dry shifts and stockings and Felicitat was rubbing Johana's hair with a linen towel when they looked up to see Lady Margarida standing in the open doorway.

"Margarida," said Johana, "have you been here long?"

"No longer than it takes me to draw a breath," she said. "I am pleased to see that you have arrived safely, but I would have hoped that you had sense enough to shelter from the rain," she added, pointing at the heap of sodden clothing on the floor.

"We were only minutes from the palace gate when the storm broke and rain started to pour down," said Johana. "There was no shelter, and in the time it took us to reach cover, we were wet to our skins. But not for long." Suddenly the world turned a greenish white and thunder shook the heavy stone walls of the palace. The three women stood silent, waiting until the sound died away.

"I cannot stay," said Margarida when it was quiet enough for her to be heard. "I will return when the storm is over. The Princess is not fond of thunder, and likes to have her ladies about her. In some ways she is but a child still," she added, "although she bears herself like a queen."

"Return when you can," said Johana. "Not only have I spent much time in thought during these last days, but I have also brought Felicitat, who understands what has been happening at the castle. Much of what she speaks of I had never heard before."

"I promise you," said Margarida. "Stay warm, sparrow. Look after her, Felicitat."

+=——=+

SHE was true to her word. When the sun appeared, and the last rumble of thunder was almost too distant to be heard, Margarida came into the small sitting room. Johana was again seated by the window, sewing, with Felicitat nearby, also at her needle. "Tell me about these new thoughts," Margarida said directly, sitting down across from them.

"You asked me who could hate Arnau enough to spend great sums to destroy him and his family. I have thought and thought about that. He was not a man to make deadly enemies, Margarida. He wasn't quarrelsome, nor grasping, nor wildly ambitious. The fields are not littered with the corpses of his rivals, I swear. He won me through his wit and sweet disposition, and I have dealt with his money affairs since then. I would know."

"I am willing to believe you for now," said Margarida, "although I don't think any man—or his dearest friend—can judge who hates him."

"That may be, but I needed a starting point. I talked to Felicitat as we rode here—and a long ride it was, for I heeded your warning to move gently, and I swear that my mule was ambling at so slow a pace that two or three times she fell asleep in boredom."

"Did you come alone? Two women?"

"No. We brought Felicitat's son, a stout lad of sixteen,

who armed himself with a heavy staff. Right now, he is downstairs, doubtless learning much he should not know from the soldiers."

"What have you decided?"

"I will let Felicitat tell it," said Johana, nodding to the woman by her.

"My lady did not believe that it was fitting for her to take part in the meetings the gentlemen held about the ship," said Felicitat.

"That is true," said Johana. "My Arnau always welcomed my advice, but those others, I thought, would not have. I stayed far away when the syndicate visited."

"I reported all that I heard to my lady," said Felicitat. "Every time there was a messenger or a man of business arriving, and there were many, Lady Margarida, in the last month before his arrest, and of course, every time there was a meeting of the syndicate. My master, his lordship, in those hot days, frequently met them in the orchard."

"Very true," said Johana.

"I waited on them," said Felicitat, "at his request, when they met there, since he knew that he could trust me. Also he asked me to try to keep your ladyship from walking into the middle of some unpleasantness. They could be very quarrelsome."

"Foolish, foolish man," said Johana. "He spoke of occasional disagreements, that was all. He should have let me know. As if a little unpleasantness could disturb me."

"Who were these people?" asked Margarida.

"The members of the syndicate? They were part of the ship syndicate I told you of."

"What had they to quarrel over?" said Margarida. "How many sacks of barley to load into the ship?"

"No, Margarida. Contraband. It seems they quarreled over how much contraband they could safely hide under the bolts of cloth and sacks of barley."

"Arnau?"

"Oh, no, my lady," said Felicitat. "His lordship was against it from the first; some of the others seemed to feel that the only reason for chartering a boat was to fill it with contraband."

"You think that it was one of the syndicate?" asked Margarida.

"I do," said Johana. "Who else?"

"Who were they?" asked Margarida.

"We broke it into sixteen shares," said Johana. "I reckoned that we needed investors for ten of those shares at least. We would take the remaining shares. If the ship foundered and all was lost, we would risk the loss of only six shares in the venture."

"I have always been astonished that someone dressed in bright silks and laces like you, Johana, could have such a clear head for business matters."

"Arnau was not brought up to have a clear head for business matters, Margarida. He was trained to be brave, clever on the field of battle and in diplomacy, and a leader of men. His father and grandfather before him were too, and trusted their affairs to men of business. That may be why, when I met him, they were all as poor as church mice. But that is not important right now. We were fortunate enough to attract people who took twelve of the sixteen shares."

"Twelve people?"

"No. Some took more than one. The first three shares went to three friends of my father. They live in Barcelona and I think we need not concern ourselves with them unless we find reason to." Johana sat upright, her eyes bright and intense with concentration. "One of my father's friends recommended the venture to an important client of his, one Guillem de Castell, of Girona. Again, he has no connection with Arnau. He took another share."

"There are eight left, then," said Margarida.

"Yes. Four men from Roussillon took two shares each.

They feel that, because of the size of their investment, they should have control of the venture."

"Are they of one mind?" asked Margarida.

"Fortunately, no. But only Felicitat can attest to this."

Felicitat put down her sewing and looked steadily over at Margarida. "When the first of the meetings took place, my mistress was in her bed, unwell. Her maid stayed with her and I attended to the gentlemen. When I wasn't wanted, I waited nearby so that I could answer my lord's call the sooner, but their voices were loud enough that I could hear what they were saying most of the time. I knew that her ladyship would be interested, since everyone knows that she looks after such affairs in the house, and so I listened carefully. I have a good memory, my lady."

"She does," said Johana. "An excellent memory."

"What did they find to talk about?" asked Margarida.

"Prices of goods for the cargo and how much of each they should ship," said Felicitat. "But then things changed."

"I will explain this," said Johana. "Each of these men had two shares, as I said. Near the end of summer, two shareholders from Roussillon who had promised to make part of the syndicate were unable to raise the funds. They were replaced by Don Ramon and this Martin."

"And at the next meeting," said Felicitat, "the members quarreled, very loudly."

"What was the quarrel about?" asked Margarida.

"It was about making more money with contraband," said Felicitat. "Don Ramon Julià said first that he had put all his money into the ship because he expected to get six times as much back. Then he said that he spat on their talk of a modest profit. He didn't seem to think it was enough."

"He is a great gambler and a noted womanizer," explained Johana.

"Even my cat knows that," said Margarida. "He wears

out his welcome around here; he is as troublesome as Bernard Bonshom. Or almost as troublesome."

"And then," said Felicitat, "he said that there was only one way to make a handsome profit for all, and that was to conceal a substantial amount of contraband in with the cargo. Pere Vidal, who was also there, agreed with everything he had to say."

"And the others?"

"The other Master Pere, Pere Peyro, was against it, but for the danger only," said Felicitat. "I don't know if he concerned himself that it was not legal."

"Master Pere Vidal is such a careful man," said Johana. "I wonder that he joined in the syndicate. He usually invests in safer ventures, like houses."

"He has cloth warehouses and finishing workshops in the city, I know," said Margarida. "I think they are very profitable."

"Then what Lord Puigbalador said must be true," murmured Johana. "He is determined to amass a huge dowry for his daughter by any means, legal or illegal. Please, Felicitat, continue. I did not mean to disrupt your explanations."

"I am not sure who the fourth man is," said Felicitat. "He spoke softly and I could not hear much of what he said. I think that sometimes he agreed with Don Ramon and sometimes with Master Pere Peyro."

"Did you hear his name?"

"They called him Martin; I did not recognize him. From his speech I would say that he comes from the south. He was one of the new members," she added apologetically.

"Who chose the new investors? Arnau?" asked Margarida.

Johana paused. "Yes," she said. "Arnau."

"Then we must find out more about them," said Margarida.

"True," said Johana. "But how?"

"Don Ramon is a great friend to Bonshom, Johana. You must be as forthcoming as possible to the disgusting creature and find out what he can tell you."

"In my condition?"

"My lord Puigbalador will not concern himself with that."

FELIP left the party from Girona at the road that led westward near the gate to the city, thanking each one for their kindness in allowing him to travel with them. "I hope that I will meet all of you again. Since Mistress Bonafilla will be in the city, I trust she will draw you here often, señores. My business lies with someone at the royal palace," he added. "I promised I would be there in time to dine." He put spurs to his horse and rode off.

They all looked over in the direction he had taken, and there, standing in splendid isolation on a hill, was the royal palace. To its south, it overlooked the *devesa,* and to its north, the walled city of Perpignan, with its rivers and streams running down to the sea not so very far away. "No wonder His Majesty likes the palace and the city," said Yusuf. "It is so calm and beautiful."

The bells of the cathedral, followed quickly by the bells of the four parishes of the city, began to ring for sext. The sun, so fickle that morning, was now high in a cloudless sky, and mist rose from the animals, from clothing, and from the cobbled streets.

SEVEN

THE gate to the *call* was situated on the same square as the church and house of the Dominican fathers. The group from Girona, led by Astruch, picked its way through the hilly streets of the town and circled around to come into the square facing the church. "There is the *call*," said Astruch. "We are almost there."

"I am glad of that," said Raquel, for the last hour of their journey had been tedious and uncomfortable. Everyone was at least somewhat wet, and their spirits, which had seemed so high when they set out that morning, had been dampened as well by the storm.

For once, Astruch was right in his estimation. They passed through the gate, went a short way up the steep street ahead of them, and came to a halt in front of a tall house, large in comparison with its neighbors. It was not as imposing a building as the solid stone of Isaac's house in Girona, but then, few of the houses in the city were fashioned in that manner.

The door was opened at once by a pleasant-looking,

smiling man of about thirty, who stepped out onto the
pavement with his arms open in greeting. "Astruch,
Duran," he said, embracing them in turn, "we were
alarmed that it had taken you so long to come from Collioure."

"I am sorry, Jacob, to have caused you uneasiness. We
were caught by a most ferocious storm," said Astruch.

"We too had heavy rain," he said, and turned toward
the veiled figure standing behind her brother. "Mistress
Bonafilla," he said gently. "We are honored to have you at
our house."

Those duties accomplished, he strode quickly over to
where Isaac, Raquel, and Yusuf were standing. "Isaac," he
said, clasping him to his breast, "you cannot know what
great delight it gives me to see you." He stopped for a
moment. "I fear my eyes overflow with my emotion. And
this must be your daughter Raquel, of whom I have heard
so much." Raquel curtsied and smiled. "And your apprentice, Yusuf. We are truly honored. Ruth, my dearest, take
the ladies in so that they may recover from the rigors of
the journey. Gentlemen, this way."

A shadow, scarcely noticeable in the relative darkness of
the doorway, moved and turned into a woman, sweet-faced,
pretty, and with sharp, bright eyes. "You are most welcome," she said softly, and led Raquel and Bonafilla up the
staircase, followed by the maids.

"I am truly sorry that we cannot offer a room to each,"
said Jacob, "although if Duran should change his mind and
prefer to stay here, I am sure we can make shift to accommodate everyone. If you do not mind the small rooms under the roof . . ."

"I will be most comfortable at my cousin's house," said
Duran quickly. "He is a distant relation but a good friend.
We have stayed with him before."

"Then, my friends," said Jacob, "no doubt you would
like to wash away the dust of travel before dinner. Will

you dine with us, at least?" he added, turning to Astruch's son.

"I think I am expected at my cousin's house," said Duran.

"And I believe my son is most anxious to get there as soon as possible," said Astruch, and laughed heartily at his own words.

"Your cousin has a daughter, I believe," said Jacob. "Then we will not keep you. But now I understand why your son was so intent in fostering this marriage between my brother and your daughter, Astruch," he added, laughing as well.

"These distant cousins have a charming daughter?" asked Isaac. "More charming than the young women of Girona?"

"Only because Mistress Raquel is spoken for," said Duran gallantly. "I will return later in the day," he added, turned back, and walked toward the gate to the *call* in the direction of their distant cousin's house.

"I would like to scrape off the mud of travel if I could," said Astruch cheerfully once he had said a brief farewell to his son. "And I would welcome the opportunity to change into a dry tunic." And with much bustle and shifting of boxes and bundles, Astruch was accommodated in a generous chamber with means of washing and his dry clothing at hand.

"Now, Isaac," said Jacob, the bouncy cheer in his voice disappearing completely, "would you like to change as well?"

"I am perfectly dry," said Isaac. "And so, I believe, is Yusuf."

"I am, lord," said Yusuf, falling back into the form of address he always used when they were alone.

"If we could but wash our hands and faces, we can face the world."

Jacob called for water and a towel to fulfil their needs. "I am looking forward to much conversation, but now, I pray you, Isaac, bring your apprentice and come with me to examine my patient."

"Can you send for Raquel without disturbing the women?"

"I will go, lord," said Yusuf. "If Master Jacob will point the way. I am used to fetching Mistress Raquel," he added in explanation.

"Still lurking about the women's quarters?" said Jacob with amusement. "I warn you. A thumbsbreadth more height and the beginnings of a beard, and they will start chasing you from their door. But go up those stairs and turn to your right, then up the staircase to the left. Bring her down here."

"Does his condition improve since you wrote?" asked Isaac after Yusuf had left the room to fetch Raquel.

"It is difficult to say," said Jacob. "You will understand better when I take you to him. I will be most grateful if you could add your greater wisdom to my understanding of how to treat him."

"What I can do, I will do gladly," said Isaac. "Raquel and Yusuf will assist your apprentice in watching over your patient. He will no doubt welcome the relief."

"At the moment," said Jacob tightly, "I have no apprentice."

"My good Jacob, how have you been able to manage?"

"My Ruth helps me, as does her maid, who is a trustworthy soul. When the patient came in, I decided to send my apprentice back to his parents for a short while," he said, speaking with all the rapid insincerity of a much-repeated account. "With all the guests coming to the house, he seemed to be taking up more space than he was worth. He's a good lad, though, coming along well. His name is Abram, and his father is the most senior, skilled, and prosperous physician in the *call*, Master Baron Dayot Cohen. He has been proposed for one of our next counselors. I will present them to you at the wedding."

"Master Baron offers a proper compliment to your skills by placing his son with you," said Isaac. "And I hear Raquel coming down the stairs with Yusuf. Let us examine your patient."

THE patient's quarters were accessible by a staircase from the courtyard behind the main part of the house. The room was generous in proportions for a sleeping chamber, large enough to hold two beds, a table, two chairs, and a wardrobe. It had a window in each of two walls, and was probably bright and airy when they were open, but at the moment, both windows were shuttered tightly against both sun and wind. The housemaid sat with him; as soon as her master entered, she bobbed a small curtsy and hurried off to help her mistress.

Raquel began to murmur in her father's ear as soon as they came into the room. "The patient is dressed in his shirt, Papa, and there is a light sheet covering him. He is lying on his back. He is very pale and sunken-looking, as if he has not eaten or drunk in some time, but his eyes are clear. He holds himself very stiffly."

She also noticed that hanging on a peg on the outside of the wardrobe was a much mended tunic such as would be worn by a Jewish merchant of modest means. On one of the shelves of the same piece of furniture was a bundle no doubt containing whatever else he needed.

"My patient is a merchant from Carcassonne," said Jacob. "He fell ill while traveling near Perpignan and a kind-hearted stranger brought him to the *call*."

"A Christian found him and brought him here?"

"Yes," said Jacob.

"How far is Carcassonne from here?" asked Isaac, turning toward the bed to address the patient.

"Some twenty-five leagues through the mountains," said the man hoarsely. He stopped to catch a breath and carried on again, his voice growing fainter. "No more than three days at a moderate pace."

"Has he water?" asked Isaac.

"Here, Papa," said Raquel and held the cup to his lips. He drank a little and let his head drop back on the bedding.

"You fell ill?" asked Isaac.

"I suffer from the arthritis," said the patient.

"So young a man? I take it you are a young man," said Isaac.

"Twenty-five years," he said in a whisper. "I was heading for the hot baths, of which I had heard wonderful things."

"Before you continue, I would like to examine you. You will have noticed that I cannot see, but I can feel. Since what takes place inside the body can be seen by no one, I am not at such a disadvantage as you might suppose. My daughter and my apprentice are my eyes when needed. Raquel, loosen his shirt."

"Yes, Papa." With great care she untied the laces closing his shirt, noting with interest the fine quality of the linen. "His chest is covered with bruises, Papa. They are very marked."

"Can you take the shirt off?"

"I fear that in doing so I might hurt him badly."

"I have not ventured to remove the shirt," said Jacob. "For that very reason."

"Then we must work around it or cut it off, if needs be."

"It is only a shirt," growled the man in the bed.

"Indeed, sir, it is only a shirt," said Isaac, in a humoring tone, and with Raquel's guidance, placed his hands on the man's head. After examining the skull carefully, he started to work down, letting his fingers run with great delicacy over the chest and rib cage. His patient stiffened. "That is painful," said Isaac.

"It is," he gasped.

"There is a terrible bruise there, Papa, and swelling."

"I can feel the swelling. That rib is broken. I will agree that the arthritis can be a terrible condition, sir, but it does not often cause bones to break. What happened?"

"My condition worsened," he said with a gasp, "from traveling in the cold and damp of the mountains. I was so stiff on the second morning that I fell off my mule and injured myself badly."

"Did you?" said Isaac. "Raquel, take your scissors and cut the laces holding the sleeves of his shirt. Carefully."

Raquel took her scissors from her work bag, snipped the laces, and then gently pulled each sleeve away, revealing the man's bare arms. "There is a splint on the right arm," she said, "and much bruising on the left. The right arm is very swollen."

"We will leave them for later," said Isaac.

He pulled down the sheet and began to probe his patient's belly. "If you value your life, sir," said Isaac, "you must speak. You must tell me if I am hurting you."

"I value my life, my good physician," he said with emphasis. "You cannot know how much I value it."

"Excellent. The belly seems relatively unscathed," he murmured. "Which surprises me. But let us see the legs." He pulled the sheet back up and signaled to Raquel to raise the sheet from the foot of the bed to uncover his patient's legs.

"Papa, his right leg is horribly bruised and swollen out of shape from the knee to the foot."

"Is there bone showing?"

"None that I can see."

"The other leg?"

"It appears to be fine."

"Is that true, sir? Only one leg injured?"

"Only one," said the patient.

Starting at the knee, Isaac probed with his fingers, gently and cautiously at first, and then with greater force. Then his hands moved down to the foot and ankle, following each bone and sinew with his sensitive fingers. The man on the bed was rigid and gray-faced with pain. When Isaac's fingers pressed against the bone along his shin, his whole body shuddered from the pain and suddenly relaxed as he slid into unconsciousness. "Now I know," said the physician. "There is much heat and damage to the flesh, and under the swelling I feel a break in the bone, here. But it is not much displaced. I hope it will not present a great problem," he said.

"Yes, Papa," said his daughter.

"Now, show me that arm, Raquel."

"Undo the bandages and take away the splint?"

"Yes. And then see if you can revive him."

Once that had been done, Isaac did the same with the arm that he had with the leg. "How drunk was the bone-setter who treated you?" he asked casually as he continued probing.

"Very drunk," said the patient, speaking with difficulty. "But he was the best she could find."

Isaac returned to the wrist and hand; the patient gasped and was silent.

"He has fainted again, Papa."

"Then prepare a potion for him. My friend," he said to Jacob, "do you have a half-cup of wine mixed with water that we might give him?"

"A half-cup in total? Or a half-cup of each, mixed?"

"In total."

Jacob took a jug from the shelf in the wardrobe, poured out the wine, added the water, and handed the cup to Raquel.

"It was that quality about him, even when he was a child, that made me prize him," said Isaac. "A precision that boded well."

"And a lack of imagination that boded ill, as you once told me," said Jacob.

"Did I? Three drops, Raquel," said her father. "And see if a little water on his brow will revive him long enough to drink it."

The patient opened his eyes. "I am awake."

Raquel lifted his head and held the cup to his lips. "It is bitter," she said, "but you must drink it all as quickly as you can."

"And if my stomach cannot tolerate it?"

"You will not allow that to happen," she said firmly. "You will drink it and not spew it up again. Do you understand? After a few moments you will feel much better. Drink."

The patient drank, swallowing with difficulty the bitter potion, and then panting with the effort of self-control required to keep it down. Gradually that particular agony eased. "I no longer feel sick," he said.

"Excellent. And soon the pain will recede," said Isaac. "Do not fight against it, but have faith that the pain will recede, because it will. Is it going?"

"I think so," said the patient, his voice thickening.

"Good. We will wait a little longer."

Isaac drew Jacob and Yusuf over to the other side of the room, leaving Raquel to watch the patient. "Why did you not give him that earlier?" asked Jacob. "Since it is clear that you can feel the damage within his body, surely you did not need his reactions as well."

"I cannot feel everything. I had to know the full extent of his injuries, and his pain helped tell me that as it helps you. You have made no attempt to reset the bones, Jacob?"

"No, I have not," he said. "I am no bonesetter, I confess. I feared that in trying to improve matters several days after the injuries, I would cause even more harm to him. And for reasons I cannot explain right now, I could not call in a bonesetter or a surgeon to help. Would I have done better . . ." He stopped to think what to say.

"He is still alive, and I will do my best to set the bones

aright. Fortunately they have not begun to knit as yet. Now we will need a great many bandages and several splints, I fear, my friend."

"I will go and arrange that. I will be back shortly," said Jacob, and hastened from the room.

"He is asleep, Papa," said Raquel.

"Excellent. Have you made any other observations that I should know? Especially now that Jacob is away?"

"Only that the patient is not a humble merchant from Carcassonne, Papa. His tunic which hangs on the clothespress behind you is worn and well-mended, suitable for that station in life, but his shirt is of the finest linen and almost new. And, Papa, he is not Jewish. I can swear to that."

"As can I, lord," said Yusuf. "When you uncovered him—"

"I suspected as much, but it is best to have it confirmed. It is always good to know one's patient," said Isaac. "We will need to move the bed out far enough so that we can stand on either side and move back and forth easily. Jacob will help me set the bones, but a pair of sturdy servants to move the bed would be useful right now."

"I will get them," said Yusuf.

"From where?" said Raquel, as the boy disappeared.

"I do not question his ways, Raquel, but I am sure that he will return with two stout men."

THEY started with the arm and wrist. Isaac began the process, pulling on the hand to free the pieces of bone from their awkward placement and then turning the task of holding steady pressure on it to Jacob. With both hands working quickly, Isaac nudged the bones back into their proper places as closely as could be done. Without slowing his pace, he began to wrap the splints in place to hold the bones where they belonged. "It would have been easier to do this a week ago," he said. "There is much swelling to contend with. Raquel, place another layer of bandage over all and tie it closely. But not too tightly."

"Yes, Papa."

"And now the leg."

"Are you not going to bind the rib, Papa?"

"I want to deal with that leg before I touch the rest of his body."

And so, while Raquel wrapped and tied up the lower arm, Jacob and Isaac worked with as much speed as possible to set the leg bone in its place. "Pull, my friend," said Isaac. "Yusuf, hold the knee steady." And with all the strength in his powerful hands he edged the bone over and then probed deeply to make sure that it was sitting true. "It was a clean break, I think," he said. "But with all these injuries, I am surprised that he has stayed alive in the— how many is it?—seven? eight? days since the attack. He is a very determined man."

"Attack?" said Jacob Bonjuhes cautiously.

"What else could reasonably cause these injuries and no others?" said Isaac, splinting the injured leg. "Most men, if they had suffered a fall bad enough to make these breaks, would have broken many more bones, on all parts of the body, and died. Consider, Jacob, how odd is the pattern of injuries. One arm, his chest, and one leg are badly affected, but not his head or his belly. Imagine a man lying on the ground, shielding his head with his arms and protecting his belly by pulling his legs up. He could not have defended himself that way for long, and so I suspect his attackers were interrupted before they finished with him."

"What you say makes much sense, Isaac," said his host in guarded tones. "But perhaps it is best not to speak of it just yet."

"As you wish, my friend. Not just yet."

When the arm and leg were firmly wrapped, Isaac bound the rib cage to protect the broken rib and pronounced himself finished. "Now he only needs to recover from what we have just done to him," said Isaac. "That will take some care."

"I think he has fallen back into sleep, Papa. I will sit with him for now," said Raquel.

"But it is time for dinner," said Jacob.

"Have them put something on a plate for me," said Raquel, "and I will eat it here."

+≻=≺+

THE patient slept for several hours, deeply at first, and then very restlessly. He awoke, Raquel gave him a little water, and he slipped back into his restless doze. When Isaac returned the patient seemed to be half-awake, muttering and moaning softly. He signaled to his daughter to stay quiet and sat down beside him. "Are you awake, señor?" he asked.

"I may be," said the patient vaguely.

"Are you in much pain?"

"I am," he said, "but it is very far away. So far away I can hardly feel it."

"We have set your limbs," said Isaac. "They should now heal and you should be able to use them again."

"It matters not how much pain there is," he said, "I must not die. Not yet." And he slept again.

+≻=≺+

THE next time he awoke his eyes and speech were clear and Raquel sent for her father. "Hola, señor," the patient said. "You must be the physician."

"I am, señor, indeed. I have just set your limbs."

"I remember someone said that to me not long ago," he said. "But I have spoken to you before," he added.

"When I first came in. Jacob Bonjuhes tells me you are a Jewish merchant. And then you told me that you were from Carcassonne and suffered from the arthritis. I am happy to be able to tell you that the shock of your injuries has cured your arthritis. Your joints feel perfectly sound and supple. It has also changed your religion."

"Very well, señor, I admit to not being Jewish."

"That was abundantly clear as soon as the sheets no longer covered your body, señor," said Isaac.

"Master Jacob feared . . ."

"I know well what Master Jacob feared, but he did not need to fear it from me. It is easier to treat a man if I know who he is and what he is."

"I cannot see why that should be. Is not a broken bone the same for Christian or Jew? Rich man or poor man? Lord or peasant?"

"Not at all, señor, for many reasons that I will gladly dispute with you when you are stronger."

"Very well. Until then I am willing to believe you. My background is commonplace enough. I come from an ancient family of high repute, or so they have always told me. Its fortunes have been ruined by bad times, the plague, and no small measure of greed and stupidity on the part of my forebears. They lost money on every bad venture in the county of Roussillon."

"It is often true that those who feel they are losing their wealth and power do foolish things to try to regain it," said Isaac.

"Indeed," said the patient. "You describe my grandfather and my father with great precision. But not being as proud or as stupid as my ancestors, I took the advice of a servant, and married a merchant's daughter. I am therefore rich enough to pay your fee and that of Master Jacob. I have also found life pleasant enough in my new state to wish to continue it."

"Then, señor, you must fight to stay alive. My daughter Raquel, and my apprentice, Yusuf, will stay with you. You will do what they say. If you need me, they will fetch me."

"And you are?"

"Isaac, physician of Girona."

"Of whom many wondrous tales are told. I am honored, Master Isaac." And the patient slipped back into sleep.

RAQUEL sat by the patient's side until just before sundown. In his brief intervals of wakefulness, she coaxed him into drinking some broth and a cool drink of mint and bitter orange, gave him one drop of pain medication, and watched him fall into an exhausted sleep. She moved about restlessly, feeling hot and sticky, her eyes heavy with sleep. At last she sat down and dozed on the uncomfortable chair until Yusuf arrived.

"How is he?" whispered the boy.

"Sleeping," said Raquel. "If he wakes up again, try to get him to take some more broth and cool drinks."

"You had better hurry," said Yusuf. "The family and guests are gathering in the courtyard."

"Have you eaten?" asked Raquel.

"Of course," said Yusuf. "In the kitchen before I came up here."

"And took the best of everything, no doubt," said Raquel, and headed off toward the other side of the house, calculating that she still had time to wash off the sweat and dust of travel, change her muddy gown for a clean one, rest for a while, and join the others for supper.

When she found the chamber she was to share with Bonafilla, the bride was still there, lying on the bed in her shift, staring up at the ceiling. "Everyone is gathering in the courtyard, Bonafilla," she said as brightly as she could. "It is a pleasant evening." There was no response from the bed. "Perhaps we could go for a walk with some of the family," Raquel added. "We need to get out. It would be interesting to see something of the town, don't you think?"

"I don't want to go for a walk with the family," said

Bonafilla, goaded into speech at last. "I can't face any of them right now."

"What do you mean, face them?" said Raquel impatiently. "They are not monsters or assassins, to be faced."

"I can't, Raquel. Couldn't you ask Papa to excuse me? Tell him I don't want any supper."

"No, I can't, Bonafilla. What will David think if you refuse to come down?"

"He may think as he likes," said Bonafilla. "It won't trouble me," she said, and began to cry again.

"Why are you . . ." Raquel began and gave up.

"Did you ask me something?" said Bonafilla out of the depths of her misery and self-absorption. "I couldn't quite hear you."

Since the unspoken end of her question had been, "behaving like an irritating fool," Raquel said the first random thing that came to her head. "I was only going to ask if he was like his brother. If he is," she added, "he must be pleasant and good-looking."

"I don't know. I haven't seen him yet. I couldn't eat dinner and so I stayed up here."

Raquel sighed in exasperation. "Really, Bonafilla, I don't understand what you are trying to do to everyone. You have to go down. You haven't eaten since breakfast and you're being most discourteous to his family. You must at least meet David. You cannot refuse to marry him—if that is what you want to do—if you have never seen or spoken to him. It won't make any sense to them." Or to me, she thought.

"But, Raquel, I have no choice. Now I have to marry him," she wailed.

"What do you mean?"

"After what's happened—I mean—we've come all this way and they've made preparations. I can't refuse now. I have to."

"I don't see why you can't refuse him now," said Raquel.

"It would be awkward and unpleasant, but not impossible. But you have to meet him first."

"If I go down, will you promise to stay with me?"

"When I can, Bonafilla. Remember there's a very sick man staying here, and I am helping Papa to look after him."

"I wondered where you were. I wanted to talk to you earlier. What's wrong with him? Oh, and call Ester, will you? I need her to help me dress."

SUPPER was set out in the courtyard, on a long board covered with embroidered linen cloths and piled high with dishes of festive food. Raquel glanced at their hostess and decided that the effort of entertaining such a crowd of people with only a few to help her was too great a task. Ruth was pale and miserable-looking; Raquel ached for her. The cook, looking harassed, brought out the last dishes and jugs of wine, with the dubious assistance of a lad of ten and a twelve-year-old under-housemaid. Raquel moved quietly up to her hostess. "Can I help you in any way?" she said. "There are so many of us, we must stretch your kitchen's resources."

The young woman jumped, startled, and colored. "I am not used to much company," she said. "I have always lived rather quietly. But I am enjoying this," she added, lying bravely. "All would have been well, especially with you helping by looking after the patient, except that my maid, Eva, has fallen ill. It is the unexpected that makes life difficult."

"Your maid is sick? And you have all of us to look after? I'm sorry I didn't know earlier. You may have Leah. She isn't a lady's maid, you know—she can do anything, even help in the kitchen. My mother sent her with me not to dress my hair or mend my gowns but because she did not wish me to travel without an attendant on our return."

"If she's quick to learn, that would help a great deal," said Mistress Ruth. "Can she look after the baby for me?"

"Certainly. She has looked after my twin brother and sister since they were born. I will tell her that she is a nursemaid again. As for me, I can share Mistress Bonafilla's maid, who has precious little to do, it seems to me."

"Mistress Bonafilla seems rather shy," said Ruth.

"Don't believe it," said Raquel. "She's nervous and in a mood. But she'll come out of it, I hope. She's at a difficult age."

Mistress Ruth sighed and shook her head. "A difficult age?" she said. "That is something to look forward to. What's she nervous about? Marriage?"

"I don't know," said Raquel. "I suppose that must be it. I hope she comes down for supper. If not, I'll go up and fetch her. She hasn't left that bed since she arrived here, and I assure you, she's perfectly well."

"Oh, no, Mistress Raquel. She certainly didn't come down to dinner, but she and her maid went out for a walk in the quiet of the afternoon. Or so my cook tells me, for she saw them slipping out of the house when everyone else had gone up to rest. Journeys take some people strangely, of course."

Before Raquel had a chance to wonder at Bonafilla's sudden desire for exercise, Bonafilla herself came out into the courtyard, dressed in a tawny yellow gown that set off her dark hair and eyes to great advantage. Her veil of the same color was fastened on top of her head, and for once only partially covered her face. Raquel realized she was the target of a furious gaze for having abandoned the bride, who then gave a toss to her head and moved over to stand near her father and Jacob Bonjuhes. Ester remained in the doorway, watching her intently.

Jacob turned and beckoned to a young man who was clearly his brother. The young man nodded, walked over with a firm step, and bowed, first to Astruch and then to

Bonafilla. Bonafilla responded with a deep curtsy, giving him her hand. He led her to the table and sat down beside her.

"He's certainly handsome and sure of himself," said Raquel to Ruth. "Like a young lord."

"Oh, he is," said Ruth. "She'll have a hard task bringing him to heel if that is what she has in mind. But he was very impressed with her beauty—he saw a likeness of her—and has always wanted sufficient wealth to be independent of Jacob."

"She has that," said Raquel. "She truly comes to him wrapped in gold."

"Their parents left a generous younger son's portion to David," said Ruth. "Even without her he'd never have been poor, but he enjoyed the idea of all that loveliness and all that money together." She stopped, raising her hand to her mouth, and looking in great distress at Raquel. "I don't know why I'm telling you this. It's not very kind of me at all. I don't usually speak so . . ."

"Openly?" added Raquel. "It's that sort of day, Mistress Ruth. When you are so tired that you actually say the truth aloud." And Raquel reflected that Jacob Bonjuhes had done better in his choice of wife than his brother. "Bonafilla could learn much by observing you," she said.

"I think not," she said. "I am a shy, rather wretched creature in company. I have none of her grace. But come, let us sit down at the table."

As Raquel walked over to the table with Ruth Bonjuhes, she noticed two things. Ruth was having another child, and Bonafilla was laughing, a low, intimate laugh, at something David Bonjuhes had said.

THE first sign of trouble came to the physician's house the next morning. It was reported by the cook. She had been off at dawn to the fish market, and then to the poul-

terers' and butchers' stalls, to have a chance at the fattest
fish, the choicest poultry, and the newest gossip to fortify
her for a day of nonstop cooking.

"It's what they're saying, mistress. Not in the big markets, thank the Lord for that, but here in the *call*."

"Are you sure?" said Ruth, setting down a great bundle
of fresh greens in surprise. She had come into the kitchen
to look over what the cook and the kitchen lad had carried
back from the market.

"One of those Cathars, they say he is. And that's trouble.
Is he, mistress?"

"Certainly not," said Ruth. "He a merchant from Carcassonne and he's a Jew, like everyone else around here.
Well, almost everyone else," she added, since there were
houses owned and lived in by Christians in the *call*, as there
were houses outside the *call* owned and lived in by Jews.
"But anyway, he's not one of those."

"Yes, my love, they are saying it," said Jacob Bonjuhes
to his wife, who had sent him out to investigate.

"But there haven't been any Cathars for years and years—
not in the lifetime of anyone around here. How could they
tell?"

"People have always said there were some still in the
mountains, you know," said Jacob. "It's unfortunate that
we told people he was from Carcassonne. We should have
said Valencia."

"Then they would have thought he was a Moor," said
Ruth. "You know what people are like."

"I think we should talk this over with David," said her
husband. "And I would like Isaac here. He is most discreet
and very wise in his advice. And perhaps Bonafilla, since
she—"

"I don't think it wise to trouble her with our problems
at this time," said Ruth calmly. "She has enough to think

about. Perhaps Raquel could make her go out for a while. I am sure she would like to visit some shops. Perhaps the cloth-makers and the glove-makers. There is so much here to delight an elegant young lady like Bonafilla."

And so Yusuf was sent to watch over the patient, a surprised Raquel was sent to drag the reluctant Bonafilla off to districts where the famous fabric industry of the city had its shops, and the rest of the family gathered in the courtyard to consider the problem.

"Do you believe that anyone will take this rumor to the authorities?" asked Isaac. "That is more important than whether the rumor exists or not."

"No," said David firmly. Everyone turned to look at him with surprise. "I too have been out this morning and heard what people were saying. It seems to have started last evening, among a few people having a cup of wine after stopping work. Now, of course, everyone has heard it. But what they all say is that no one is to breathe a word of it, or the Christians of the town will tear the *call* apart and drag us all before the Inquisitors. The laws against harboring heretics are very harsh."

"That is a small comfort. What do we do?" said Jacob.

"Get rid of him," said David. "I'm sorry, Jacob, but it is the only wise thing to do."

"It won't help, you know," said Isaac. "Unless you take him yourself to the authorities, saying you have just discovered what is being said, and chance the investigation. For you will be accused of the act of hiding a heretic anyway, and your change of heart will be put down to the rumors. They will say you refused to keep him out of fear of being caught—cowardice rather than virtue."

"He's right, you know, David. And it would be murder to move him right now. I am willing to bend a rule, but not to kill a man—a patient—in cold blood. But to say he is a Cathar!" he said. "As far as we're concerned, that's much, much worse than admitting that he is a Christian. If anyone were concerned that we were treating a Christian in our house in the *call*, which is unlikely, at most we would be fined."

While they were looking silently at one another, the cook appeared in the doorway. "Excuse me, mistress," she said crossly, "but with no one answering the door and all, I left what I was doing to see if it was important."

"Yes, cook. Is there a problem?"

"I don't know if it's a problem, but there's someone here says she has to see you. She has a letter or some such thing."

"Thank you, cook. I'll see that the door is tended from now on," said Ruth. "Send her in."

The someone was a girl of about nine or ten years of age, clean and neat in her dress and person. She curtsied and held out a sealed letter. "Mistress Ruth?" she asked in a quiet voice.

"Let us go into the other room," said Ruth, directing her away from the table with a firm hand on her shoulder.

THE letter was short and clear. Ruth began reading it and then grasped the child by her arm, ushering her back into the courtyard. "Jacob," she said, "you must help me deal with this," and handed him the piece of paper.

He read it to himself, and then aloud. " 'Mistress Ruth,' " he said, " 'I believe that at the moment you could use the services of my neighbor's daughter, Jacinta. She is nine, hardworking, and honest. For private reasons, it would be good for her to be in a house such as yours. If she does not suit, send her home at once or after your guests have left.' "

Jacob looked up from the paper. "It is signed with an E, only."

"Mama's friend's name is Esclarmonda," said Jacinta. "She sent me."

"What reason did she give you for sending you?" asked Isaac.

"Esclarmonda sent the sick man," said the child. "She knows that he needs much care. Then she heard that you had a wedding in the house and guests as well. She thought you needed help, señora, and I am used to helping. I helped her look after the sick man when he was at her house."

"This is truly all we need," said David. "Not only do we have a Christian patient, rumored to be a Cathar, but now we appear to have a Christian servant, as well. How many more laws are we going to break before I am married?"

"That is not so," said Jacinta, shaking her head gravely. "I too am a Jew. My mother says so."

"Is your mother?" asked Isaac.

"Yes. She is."

"And your father?" asked David.

The child shrugged her shoulders.

"That would explain why she wanted her to come here," said Ruth.

"Where does your mother live?" asked Jacob.

"In Lo Partit," said the girl. "It's not far from here."

EIGHT

RAQUEL was not in a pleasant mood when she took Bonafilla by the elbow and set out on their forced exploration of the city of Perpignan. She was armed with careful directions to guide her through the maze of streets to the west and north of the *call* and dire warnings of the consequences of straying off her path. She was assisted by the houseboy, who had been sent along to keep the two women from losing their way, and with all the might of ten years of age, to protect them if they did. He looked as if the responsibility hung heavily on his shoulders.

Raquel dragged Bonafilla through the morning shopping crowds into five different shops. Behind each of them was a busy workroom producing the beautifully finished cloth for which Perpignan was famous. Five times they looked at bolts of silk and of fine wool and bought nothing. In five shops Bonafilla asked the assistants to carry the heavy bolts out to the street so that she could see them in daylight; five times they took them back inside and put them away.

Tired of watching this parade, Raquel pushed her companion toward a glover's shop. "Let's go in here," she said. "I want to look at something." It was quiet inside, filled with the smell of new leather, and dimly lit by two small windows. A man wearing a leather apron and a look of pleasant prosperity entered from the back of the shop, setting a pair of gloves down on the counter as he went by.

One quick glance at them and Raquel realized that the gloves were unlike any she had seen before. Intrigued, she smiled at the shopkeeper and picked up one of them. "May I look at it?" she asked.

"Of course, madam," said the glover.

Raquel examined the glove carefully, from the stitching of the fingers to the finishing at the wrist. Diamond-shaped pieces of fine leather, each one an inch or slightly more in length, had been stitched together to form the back of the glove. The decoration on the back of the hand was made up of tiny beads set in a swirling pattern on the four central diamonds. The rest were plain. The design was ornate and complex, yet had an air of restraint. It was the work of a master craftsman. "I have just finished those," said the man behind the counter. "The last stitch went into them as you were entering the shop."

"They are beautiful," said Raquel. "The design is intricate and most pleasing to the eye. And those diamond-shaped pieces must put many small trimmings of fine leather to use economically as well," she added wryly.

"Madam knows something about making gloves," said the owner of the shop, with another smile. "But if they are carefully stitched together, those diamonds can also create a perfect fit. These were made for a lady who was very particular about the fit of her gloves. I devised that pattern for her. Slip the glove on, mistress, and you will see how it caresses the hand."

The glove was a little too big for her, but it was indeed as comfortable as its creator had promised. "Bonafilla," she said, "come and look at this." There was no answer. "Bonafilla," she repeated, turning around. There was no one behind her. She was alone in the shop with the shopkeeper.

"The young mistress slipped out the door a moment ago, no doubt for some air," said that tactful gentleman. "Pere, fetch the lady in the green-and-black gown."

A youthful apprentice came through from the back of the shop and went out, returning shortly afterward with Bonafilla.

"What do you think of these?" asked Raquel, holding up her hand with the glove on it.

"They're too big for you," said Bonafilla, staring at the shop windows, where her attention seemed to be fixed on a tabby cat sitting in a patch of sun and washing.

"I know that, Bonafilla. Otherwise, what do you think? They're beautifully made. You might want to order a pair of gloves here."

"I'm sure I will, Raquel," she said with a distracted glance in their direction, "but not now. I think I'll go out again. I find it warm in here."

Raquel watched her leave with a puzzled frown on her face. The morning sun was just penetrating the glover's small windows, but in spite of its best efforts, the shop was definitely chilly. She herself was shivering a little, and it seemed impossible that Bonafilla would be too warm. To cool herself, she was standing in the sun just outside the door, turned so that she could observe everyone passing by on either of the intersecting streets. The most unobservant of companions could see that she was looking for someone. Raquel sighed in exasperation. She had not expected to have to play the role of chaperon and jailer, as well as companion.

"Is the young lady unwell?" asked the shopkeeper. "May I be of any assistance?"

"There is nothing wrong," said Raquel, smiling as unconcernedly as possible, "except that we are newly arrived in Perpignan. My friend is about to marry and settle here. She wished to spend the morning looking through the shops, but the unfamiliar surroundings have made her somewhat nervous and distracted."

"Indeed. Most understandable," said the shopkeeper, eyeing Bonafilla's rich apparel through the window with an increase in interest.

"I stay only for the wedding," said Raquel, "or I would be tempted to order a pair of gloves like these for myself. But it is clear that such fine work cannot be done in a day or two."

"That is very true. They are time-consuming to fashion. If madam did not have such slender hands, she could purchase these," said the shopkeeper. "Before they were even finished, the lady who ordered them was unable to take them."

"Dead?" said Raquel.

He nodded with a suitably stricken look. "So unexpectedly as well. She too was purchasing wedding clothes, and now leaves both her guardian and her betrothed in despair . . ."

"And you with a pair of gloves that are beautiful but singular in design," said Raquel sympathetically. "And not paid for, I would guess. It's not everyone who wants designs that are out of the ordinary."

"Very true, mistress. I cannot tell you how many hours of work went into this pair. It would shock you to hear it."

"I am sure it would," said Raquel. "How much would you ask for them? I know they do not fit me, but they should fit my cousin. And we have glove-makers in Girona who could make small alterations in them, should it be necessary."

"Twelve sous," said the shopkeeper smartly.

"That's a high price for gloves you can't sell that might not fit my—"

"Eleven," he said with a quick glance at her. Raquel looked back without a flicker of interest in her clear, dark eyes. "But since you appreciate fine gloves more than most of the ladies who come into my shop, ten sous, mistress."

Raquel's response was to untie her purse strings and count out ten heavy silver coins. The shopkeeper wrapped the gloves in a piece of silk to protect them and she slipped the tiny package into her purse just as Bonafilla came back in.

"Why did you buy the gloves?" asked Bonafilla as they walked out of the glover's shop. "They don't fit you."

"I bought them for Daniel," said Raquel. "He is always looking for new designs, and this pair uses a different sort of cut from gloves at home. He'll be interested. After he's studied them he can alter them to fit me. Why did you keep running outside? Are you not feeling well?"

"It's not that. I am very well. It's just that . . ." She turned and began to hurry up the street.

"Bonafilla," said Raquel, catching up to her and taking her by the arm. "What is going on?"

"Nothing," said Bonafilla, moving faster. "I wish you would not pester me with questions. I cannot bear it any more."

"It's clear that something is wrong," said Raquel. "What is it? And who were you looking for?"

"No one. I swear it. I was looking for no one."

"Very well," said Raquel. "Then let us return to Master Jacob's house."

They walked in silence for a time. When they reached a stretch of road that was quieter than the rest, Bonafilla halted and turned to the physician's daughter. "Raquel," she said tentatively, "I have heard that those you treat for illness can tell you anything, and you never repeat it. Is that true?"

"I would never repeat something a patient told me in confidence," said Raquel.

"If I were to tell you something, would you promise not to tell Papa or David?"

"I might," said Raquel, cautiously, "although it depends on what it is." She refrained from pointing out that Bonafilla was not her patient.

Bonafilla tossed her head irritably, loosening her veil. A breeze pulled it over onto her shoulders, revealing her face completely. "Yesterday, I went out."

"So I heard," said Raquel.

"How? How can anyone have heard?"

"Easily. The cook saw you creep out with Ester while everyone was resting."

"The cook! What was she doing spying on me?"

"She wasn't. But if you are going to start taking furtive walks in the afternoon, you have to remember that in most houses the cook and the kitchen maid are the last to go off to their rooms. Why did you go out?"

"I was restless," said Bonafilla. "I couldn't stand being locked up in that house."

"Locked up?"

"That's how I feel there, so I took Ester and went out. And we went to the gate of the *call* and then down toward the river Basse. While we were walking through the streets where the city buildings and the courts and all those things are, who do you think I saw?"

"Felip?" asked Raquel.

Bonafilla went pale, but whether with shock or surprise was difficult to judge. "How did you know?"

"It was a guess, but not a difficult one, Bonafilla. How many people do we both know in Perpignan?" asked Raquel. "Our new acquaintance from the road and David's family. You may have met your cousins, but I haven't."

"Only my brother and my father know them," said Bonafilla.

"So it wouldn't have been them. And we would have heard if any of our friends or neighbors from Girona had come here recently. Therefore it would have been very strange if it had been anyone else."

"I suppose," said Bonafilla. "I didn't think of it that way."

"You saw Felip. What happened?"

"Nothing," said Bonafilla vaguely. "We talked."

"That was all?" asked Raquel. "You saw Felip and you talked to him. Why are you worried about secrecy? You go out with a female companion, meet a slight acquaintance by chance, and exchange a few words. I would think you could tell anyone that."

"Yes," said Bonafilla hesitantly. "But it wasn't just that."

"Bonafilla, either tell me what happened, and quickly enough so that you are finished by the time we reach the *call,* or let me walk up the hill in peace."

"He kept asking me about the wedding. When was it and had I signed the contracts yet? And jesting about the size of my dowry and why David wanted to marry me."

"And?"

Bonafilla lowered her voice and drew closer to her companion. "Then he said that we should run off together to the south with my dowry and start a new life, but when he said it he was laughing, so I couldn't tell if he meant it or not. It disturbed me, Raquel."

"Is that what you want to do? Run off with a stranger you've met only once for a brief moment and have spoken only a few words to?"

"No!" said Bonafilla. "That would be terrible. Except that. . . ."

"Except what?"

"Nothing."

"Do you like David?"

"He's very handsome. I hadn't expected him to have so pleasing a face and manner. And he's clever and witty. He makes me laugh. But . . ."

"Bonafilla," said Raquel, stopping, "where the hill flattens out up there is the square where the gate to the *call* is. I shall count to ten and then I am walking up. If you want to tell me what is bothering you, you have to do it now."

"Do you really think he is just marrying me for my dowry?" said Bonafilla, walking ahead slowly.

Raquel looked at her. "Bonafilla, don't be foolish. David has just met you. You can't expect him to be passionately in love with you, or at least, not yet. He wanted to marry you because he had seen a likeness of you, he had met your father and your brothers, who are very pleasant men, and had heard words of praise in your favor. And, no doubt, because your dowry met his needs. He thinks you are a woman he can love. But he is not a poor young man who seeks to mend his fortune through marriage. Is that what has been troubling you all this time?"

Bonafilla took Raquel's arm as they crossed the square and pulled her closer as if to speak in her ear.

"Mistress Bonafilla! Mistress Raquel!" called a voice from behind them. "Wait a moment and we will walk together."

They turned to see their hostess, her marketing basket filled, breathlessly making her way across the square as well.

As soon as they entered the house, Bonafilla fled up the stairs toward their chamber, leaving Raquel to help Ruth take the heavy shopping basket to the kitchen.

"No one can be spared to run errands outside the house right now," said Ruth, smiling. "And so the mistress, as the least important, goes on these commissions."

"You would not want to send the cook," said Raquel, stepping into the kitchen. "Such an excellent craftswoman should be allowed to stay in her kitchen as long as she needs."

The cook nodded curtly to acknowledge the compliment

but instead of turning to see what they had brought her, said, "Jacinta. See to the basket."

To Raquel's surprise, a little girl came away from the fire and wrested her burden from her. "Thank you, mistress," she said composedly, setting the basket on a table to unpack it.

"Who is she?" asked Raquel, as they walked back into the courtyard. "I didn't see her yesterday."

"She arrived this morning while you were out."

"How fortunate for you."

"Perhaps so," said Ruth. "I am not sure. The Lord knows how badly I need another pair of hands right now," she added in explanation. "But how can I take in such a child?"

"What is wrong with her?" asked Raquel. "She seemed pleasant and helpful. And much cleaner than most."

"But Mistress Raquel, her mother is a prostitute, and as far as I can make out, she grew up in a tiny room just next to where the mother—"

"Aside from that, though," said Raquel quickly, "how is she as a servant?"

"Fine," said Ruth distractedly. "The cook is very pleased with her quickness in picking things up, and it seems she hasn't stopped working since she arrived. But as soon as my Eva comes back and the wedding is over, I won't need her. For one thing, Bonafilla wants to keep her Ester, and in this house Ester will have more to do than arranging her mistress's hair. But to have someone like Jacinta cooking or looking after the children!"

"Think of all the people who have trusted servants whose mothers were slaves. It is close to the same thing."

"It seems different somehow," said Ruth. "Slave girls have no choice."

"Anyway, this is no time to make a decision," said Raquel. "Wait until after the wedding."

"You're right," she said thankfully. "I don't have to make a decision yet. Please excuse me for a moment. I must go in and get my work. I have had no time to finish mending the baby's smock."

◄►═══ ═══◄►

OUTSIDE the city walls, three men on horseback, coming from three separate starting points, converged on a pleasant grove and stopped. Two of them dismounted at once and walked over to the mounted man. One of those on his feet was a tall, good-looking, rugged sort; the other was a slight, agile man, who picked his way over the rough ground with nervous grace, like a deer. The stand of trees grew beside a rough track, far from the traffic of the major high roads; it was as quiet and private a place to idle away an hour as one was likely to find close to the city.

The mounted man had pulled his hood down over his forehead, and held a silk kerchief to his mouth, as a man would who had the toothache. "Why have you summoned me from my duties?" he asked. He looked down at them, his anger visible in his narrowed eyes, his pale cheeks, and his fingers, which were playing impatiently with the reins.

"I have stumbled upon a piece of luck, I think, señor," said the tall man.

The slight man remained silent, listening attentively.

"What is it?" asked the one in the hood.

"On my way into the city yesterday morning, I happened upon a group of travelers coming from Girona for a wedding. I won't waste your time, señor, explaining how it happened, but I chanced to spend considerable time with the bride."

"I will not be kept from my dinner to listen to you boast of your conquests," said the hooded man coldly.

"Certainly not, señor," the tall man replied quickly. "She chattered, as women do, and at one point she complained that they were having to carry medicine to a very sick man staying at the house—she felt that having a sick man around was not a good omen for a wedding or some such woman's foolishness, and believed that he should find another physician until she was safely wed. I thought nothing of it. But she is a lovely thing and I arranged to meet her yesterday afternoon should she be able to slip away. She did."

"I hope this is worth all this telling."

"I believe so, señor. I don't know why I asked whether she thought the sick man was still a bad omen now that she had met him, but I did, and she said that his presence in the house was a deathly secret. No one is allowed to see him; no one is allowed to mention him. Apparently that makes him an even worse omen." He stopped and looked at his two companions to assess their reactions.

There was a long pause, in which the chirp of a bird and the rustle of leaves in the slight breeze were the only sounds. "But it cannot be," said the hooded man at last. "He's dead."

"Perhaps it is someone else," suggested the slight man.

"It probably is, but we must know. We must move quickly to look into the matter—but carefully. Where is this house? Who is the doctor?"

"In the Jewish Quarter. His name is Jacob Bonjuhes."

"You will find out all you can about him," said the hooded man to the slight one.

"I will try."

"And then we will talk about how to smoke out the patient," he said. "And you, see what else you can discover from that woman," he added to the tall man.

"I will, señor."

"And now, ride back to the city before anyone discovers that you are missing." Before the last word was out of his mouth, he had wheeled his horse around and galloped off as if a pack of demons from Hell pursued him.

His two companions walked over to fetch their mounts in silence. "We had better not return together," said the slight man as he gathered up the reins. "I'll go round to the San Martin gate."

"Then I'll go east," said the other.

ANOTHER hour passed before Ruth hastened out to the courtyard again. The sun had warmed the city once more and most of her guests were sitting peacefully in the shade. Raquel had taken up her needlework; her father was deep in discussion with Jacob Bonjuhes; Astruch and David were talking in low murmurs apart from the others. Duran was not expected to join them before this evening's *seder*.

Raquel rose to her feet in an effort to convince Ruth to take her comfortable place in the shade. "No, no," said Ruth. "I only came out to see that everyone was contented. I will get Jacinta to bring out a little something to nibble on while we wait for dinner." She glanced up at the sky to see how far the sun had traveled above the roof of her house. "But first," she said in alarm, "I must get her to take some broth to our patient."

"Excellent," said Isaac. "Ask her to beat an egg into it, if she can, and take some bread to him to go with it."

"Do you think he is well enough?" asked Jacob.

"Let us find out," said Isaac. "I myself have never had a patient so intent upon getting well. I envy you. But without nourishment it is impossible."

"He is indeed a strong and determined man," said Jacob.

ISAAC accompanied the little maid up to the sick man's chamber, where Yusuf sat by the window, looking idly out at the rooftops. "How are things with him?" said the physician.

"Mostly he sleeps, lord," said Yusuf. "I wish I had thought to bring a book with me. I could have spent this time in useful study, since he rarely seems to need me."

"I suggest that you go down to Master Jacob and ask him if you might borrow one of his books. I shall sit with the patient while he has a little to eat. Can you help him, Jacinta?"

"I did before, Master Isaac," said the child.

"Shall I wake him before I go, lord?" asked Yusuf, looking curiously at Jacinta.

"Gently, Yusuf."

"There is no need," said a voice from the bed. "I am awake. *Hola,* Jacinta. Where did you appear from?"

"My mama sent me," said Jacinta. "To help Mistress Ruth."

"This is a remarkably resourceful and clever child, Master Isaac," said the patient. "They are fortunate to have her by them. What have you brought me?"

"Broth, señor," she said, "with an egg in and bread as a sop for it."

"Hold the cup near my lips," he said, "and I will try this bread in broth with egg." Awkwardly, he dipped the piece of bread with his left hand into the hot broth, scooping up the bits of egg, and eating hungrily.

While Isaac waited calmly, the sick man finished most of it and then pushed it away. The serving maid took the cup, curtsied, and returned to the kitchen. The physician turned at last to his patient. "You seem much better than yesterday," he said.

"I am hungrier," he replied, "and confoundedly sore everywhere, but not quite enough to keep me from eating and sleeping."

"Does it hurt you to breathe?"

"It does, but I continue to do so, preferring it to the alternative."

"If you can jest, señor, you are better than yesterday. But now I would like you to tell me how you came to be in such a state. But spare me the tale of the mule and the path through the mountains, please, señor. I will not accept it. Perhaps you can start by telling me how you came to be a follower of the Cathars."

"The Cathars," said the sick man in astonishment. "Me? How did you come to that conclusion, Master Isaac? I do not believe I have ever met a Cathar. I remember my grandfather speaking of them—of a priest who was a Cathar, and also a merchant he knew well. But that was many years ago. There are not many around here anymore. Nor have there been for a long time."

"Is that not what a Cathar would say?"

"It is also what a good Christian—or a good Jew, as well, I suspect—would say. It is the truth."

"It is generally believed around here that you are a Cathar, come down from the mountains for some sinister purpose."

"If it were not so dangerous," said the patient, "it would be most amusing. But as God is my witness, Master Isaac, I swear that I am not a Cathar. It is even possible that I could find witnesses to support my denial."

"We will not trouble you with that. But it would help to know the truth. Or some of it. If not a Cathar, then who are you?"

"Do you believe that I have lied to you, Master Isaac?"

"I believe that you have neglected to tell me what I need to know."

"Are you willing to believe that I have enemies?" he asked. "And that my silence springs from that?" He paused to catch a short, shallow breath. "There is water on a table close to your right hand, Master Isaac. I cannot reach it without great pain and effort."

Isaac found the table and brushed his fingers delicately over it until he found the cup. He carried it in the direction of his patient's voice.

"I have it now," said the man, and drank. He passed it back to the physician's waiting hand and continued.

"I had not thought that a friend had done that to you," said Isaac.

"If you are content with some of my story, then I shall tell you some of it. I am too weary to unveil it all right now."

"I am content to hear some of the truth. Let us begin with your shirt, señor. I am curious about that."

"My shirt, Master Isaac? Why are you curious about my shirt?"

"It is, according to my daughter, sorely at odds with the rest of your apparel and belongings."

"Did I tell you that, although poor myself, I am married to a rich woman? It is because of that that I have enemies."

"And your wife provides you with shirts of fine linen, but otherwise dresses you in worn and mended clothes."

"It is my way of fending off envy," said the patient. "I am most weary, my good physician. I must sleep."

Yusuf opened the door to the chamber. "They call for you, lord, to come for your dinner."

"And your patient needs to rest. I have taxed his strength enough for now."

NINE

THE next day, the house had settled into its Sabbath calm. A spoonful of baked custard had been added to the sick man's diet of egg and broth; he slept a little less and spoke more to his three younger attendants, but never of anything that touched on his past or his injuries.

After Yusuf had turned over the task of sitting with the patient to Raquel, he sought out the physician. "If I am not wanted, lord," he said, "I had thought to explore the town." For on the Sabbath he was accustomed to leave the house and wander free, making what friends he wished and satisfying his curiosity about everything that surrounded him.

"Certainly," said Isaac. "Enjoy the peace while it lasts."

BUT it was not peace that Yusuf was after. He put on his old tunic, tucked a purse with a few pennies in it under his sash, and headed down the broad central street—wide enough to bring a cart along—toward the gates of the *call*.

As he stepped outside the heavy gate, he walked into a whirlwind of noise and people racing in all directions. He was immediately caught between two sturdy women, and allowed himself to be pushed westward down a hill toward the central part of the city. Halfway down, he darted into a narrow cluttered alley and came out on a busier street in an area where the silversmiths and jewelers had set up shop. Their discreet premises were of little interest to him; he turned to the first person he saw, a man in a moderately shabby tunic, and laid his hand on his arm. "What's that up there?" he asked, pointing to his right.

"The royal prison," said the man in the tunic, "and from the look of you, young rascal, that's where you belong. Take your hand from my sleeve."

"I thank you for your courtesy," said Yusuf, bowing low. He turned left. He followed the noise and the smells from that direction straight to the sprawling open market. All the fruit, fish, fowl, and meat had been thoroughly picked over, but the market was still crowded with desperate housewives tardily filling their baskets with what remained. He bought himself a small loaf and some grilled meat to stuff into it, and then wandered farther along.

The old clothes stalls on the far side of the marketplace held his interest for a few moments; he inspected a torn and dirty tunic with interest. It would keep him from standing out amongst the hucksters and thieves who thronged the area. His coins were limited, however, and he passed on. He came to another street that appeared to be of consequence, turned left, in the direction of the *call,* and emerged back on the street of the silversmiths and the jewelers, only this time to the south of the royal prison. More bustle farther south piqued his curiosity and he continued on.

Ahead were the arches of the first ramparts to the city. He had arrived at the Corn Market, where the carts that rolled into the city every morning brought grain and flour for sale to the public. Wheat, rye, oats, barley, millet, and rice were heaped up in sacks and bins—a beautiful sight to many, no doubt, but of no interest to him. Under the arches, though, where they would be protected from sun and rain, groups of men sat about in roughly shaped circles, some on the ground, some on old casks, or crates, or pieces of wood. He drifted over near one group in time to see a tall, broad-shouldered type throwing dice into the center of the group. "Ha!" he said, in a guttural accent. "To me, Roger."

"No, you don't, Gros," said the man next to him. "It's still mine. Isn't it, lad?" he said, suddenly turning to Yusuf.

"I didn't see your throw," said Yusuf truthfully.

"The boy lies to save his friend," said a slender man with darkish skin and hair. He spoke to his neighbor in a language Yusuf knew well, but apparently none of the others did.

"As did your mother," replied Yusuf in the elegant diction of the Arabic he had learned at home from his parents, and had been striving to retain in the past few years. *"And he is no friend of mine."*

"Not rich enough for you, pretty lad?" asked the slender olive-skinned man.

"I came to throw the dice, not . . ." And while he searched for a way of expressing what he wanted to say out of his small horde of bawdy words in Arabic, he was rescued by an interruption.

"What are you two talking about?" asked the one called Gros, a fitting name for someone of his breadth and height.

"Pretty boy wants to gamble," said the slender man. "What's your name, pretty boy?"

"Yusuf. What's yours, ugly man?"

There was a hoot of laughter from the Arabic speaker. "Ahmed," he said.

"Aren't you afraid you'll be arrested, gambling out here

in the open where everyone can see you?" asked Yusuf.

"We're not gambling," said the big man, with an air of sweet innocence. "We're working. We're porters. They need us here, don't they? What if someone has something that has to be carried? They call me el Gros," he added with a grin, "because there isn't a bigger man in the city."

"El Gros hasn't carried anything on his back but his clothes in all the time I've known him," said Roger.

"Not true, Roger. I carried a cask of bad wine for someone and he gave me a skinful of it instead of paying. That must have been four winters ago. I learned my lesson then."

"You be wary, Yusuf," said Roger. "El Gros makes his living stripping boys like you of every penny they have."

"Boys, maybe," said Yusuf. "But not like me."

"That may be," said el Gros. "But when there's nothing to carry, we get bored, don't we? And if we're bored maybe we'll go find other work. And so everyone pretends we aren't gambling."

"As long as we put down the dice while the bells for Mass are ringing," said Roger. "Come and sit down, boy."

"And we stop for the night when vespers are rung," added el Gros.

"Oh, yes," said Roger. "We always stop for the night at vespers, don't we?" He winked.

"For at least an hour," said Ahmed.

"A man has to eat sometime," said el Gros.

"Are you from Perpignan?" asked Yusuf.

"Where have you been all your life?" asked Roger. "Nobody here comes from here, do we? That's why they can't touch us."

"They could," said Ahmed, "but they don't think it's worth their while."

"That's true," said Roger.

"Even Ahmed is from somewhere," said el Gros. "But he doesn't like to say where."

"Ahmed no remember," said a big, raw-boned man who

was sitting next to Yusuf. He spoke with great hesitation.

"Well done," said Roger with an approving smile.

"Who's he?" asked Yusuf.

"He's a Norman. That's why he speaks so badly. Don't ask me his name. No one can pronounce it."

"He's not a Norman," said Ahmed. "He's a soldier from England. We look after him. He can't work because he wounded his leg fighting."

"Who for?" asked Yusuf.

"Who were you fighting for?" asked el Gros.

The Englishman looked blankly around, and tried to repeat the words to himself in a low mutter. He shook his head in confusion.

"He begs for a living," said Roger. "Except for that leg he's very strong. Strong," repeated Roger loudly, pointing at the Englishman.

"Yes," said the Englishman. "Strong." And to illustrate, he reached over, grasped Yusuf around the waist with his huge hands, and lifted him up above his head. He set him down very gently and said "Strong" again, with a huge grin on his face.

"It's one of the words he knows," said el Gros. "He's very proud of it."

Yusuf took his bread stuffed with grilled meat out of his leather pouch, tore it in half, and gave half to the Englishman. "Bread. Meat. For you," he said. "Because you are so strong."

"Thank you," said the Englishman. "I am hungry. Thank you."

"Those are the other words he knows," said el Gros. "Come on, lad. Risk a penny for a throw of the dice with us."

And reckoning that as entertainment it was worth more than the penny he knew he would lose, Yusuf took out the coin and set it in front of him.

The penny lost, and el Gros grinning, Yusuf got up. "I must go back," he said. "May I return?"

"Thank you," said the Englishman.

"We look forward with pleasure to seeing you," said Ahmed.

"We're always here, except when the bells ring for Mass," said Roger.

"Next time I might let you win back your penny," said el Gros.

WHEN Yusuf returned to the courtyard, the scene had changed. Little Jacinta was in a shady corner, by the wall, playing with the baby. Bonafilla was sitting under a tree, alone, watching Jacinta and the little boy. Isaac, Jacob, Astruch, and David were seated at the table, engaged in a discussion over dinner of current problems caused by the war in Sardinia. No one else was there. The table was spread with cold dishes: chicken, baked fish, chickpeas dressed with herbs in oil and vinegar, lentils, fruits, and breads. He helped himself to some fish and a bit of chicken on a chunk of bread.

Weary of play, the baby crawled into Jacinta's lap and fell asleep. Leah appeared from the kitchen, picked him up, and carried him off to bed. Jacinta looked around to see who might be watching her and slipped out of the courtyard. After a few moments spent staring at the top of the garden wall, David rose as well and walked over to where Bonafilla was sitting.

Yusuf carried off his bread and chicken to a quiet spot behind some shrubs and sat down to eat it undisturbed. His peace did not last long.

"I had thought you were avoiding me, Master David," he heard Mistress Bonafilla say. Her voice sounded high-pitched and nervous to him, and yet oddly flirtatious.

"Would I be here if that were true?" replied David lightly.

"Perhaps, if you only came over because your brother said you must."

"How could you possibly believe that anyone would avoid you, Mistress Bonafilla?" said David. "Your beauty would attract stone and iron."

"Do you really think me beautiful?" asked Bonafilla. She had dropped her affected manner of speech and sounded hesitant and painfully sincere. "Were you not disappointed when you saw me?"

"Truthfully, I was not," said David. "I was greatly surprised when I saw you. I had assumed that the painter who took your likeness had lied but, I hoped, not outrageously."

"Is that the truth you speak?" she said. "Or your habitual gallantry? For I have observed that you are always polite and gallant."

"The truth," he said in a matter-of-fact tone. "Everyone praised your virtue and your modesty—they did not surprise me. And your timidity, which your brother had complained of before the match was made, seemed to me to be an addition to your virtues. But I had not believed they would be combined with such beauty. You are everything that they said of you," he said in a voice so low that Yusuf, now interested, could scarcely hear.

Yusuf heard a gasp, and then a rustle of clothing.

"Bonafilla, what is wrong?" said David. "Where are you going?"

When Yusuf turned his head he saw the hem of Bonafilla's gown drag across the stones as she stood up. Then the rest of her came into his line of vision—including her tear-drenched face—as she ran across the courtyard, up the steps, and into the house.

"What the devil is this all about?" he heard David say in puzzled tones.

＋＞━ ━＜＋

IN that same drowsy afternoon, Lady Johana had sought
the peace of Her Majesty's orchard, where she sat with her
needlework on her lap, watching Margarida's tortoiseshell
cat stalking a leaf under the shrubbery. A familiar voice
interrupted her idleness. "Lady Johana, I had not expected
to find you here. The whole world is sleeping the heat of
the afternoon away."

Johana picked up her work and glanced over. "My lord
Puigbalador," said Johana. "I sought only a cooling breeze
when I came down to the orchard. I had not expected to
find anything else here—not even you."

"Her Royal Highness is occupied elsewhere and so I
dared to seek you in this fastness," said Bonshom. "But is
that all you think me to be? Am I reduced to an anything
else?"

"I believe you are considered to be more than that," said
Johana. "And I think you deserve to be called amusing
company. Although I don't know you well enough to be
sure that one could trust you——"

"Trust me?" he said sharply.

"To glitter all the time as a source of amusement. I'm
sure that, like most, you have your dull moments."

"Never," he said.

"In January, when it rains, and you are suffering with a
cold, and the ground is too wet and dirty for hunting?"

"Then I have the fire built up, hot spiced wine brought
in, and tell merry tales," he said.

"How tiring you must find it," said Johana.

"When I wish to be dull and ill-tempered," said Bonshom, "I leave my friends and inflict my temper on a few
selected servants whom I pay well to endure it."

"I must remember that," said Johana.

"But I forget myself, my lady. It is unforgivable to jest

in a house of mourning. Fate has dealt you a cruel blow. Do you wish me to leave you in peace?"

"No, my lord," said Lady Johana. "For a few moments you have given me respite from sad thoughts. I am grateful."

"I wonder that you do not retreat to your country estate to escape the thoughtless conversation of such as I," said Bonshom.

"Her Royal Highness was most insistent that I return to her," said Johana. "She felt that, under the circumstances, it would be better."

"Princess Constança is the most gracious of ladies," said Bonshom.

"And even though it is very close on my lord's death . . ." Johana paused. "She speaks already of various matches for me. She fears that alone I could be in difficulties. Someone pleasant, she says, who could safeguard my interests."

"You will remember that I suggested that very thing," said Bonshom.

"Indeed, my lord. You did. Then I had hoped it would not be necessary. But now," she said, with troubled eyes, "truly I cannot think what is best to do."

"That is why others wish to think for you. Listen to them, my lady."

Johana leaned forward and looked directly into Bonshom's eyes. "But tell me, my lord, how I can choose a husband from Perpignan? Each time someone suggests a name, I fear he must be the man who hunted my lord to his death."

"Do you believe that?"

"I fear it. Tell me, what do you know of Don Ramon Julià?"

"I know what everyone knows," said Bonshom carefully.

"Tell me," said Johana. "And not a gentleman's polite lies, my lord, but the truth."

"That is more difficult. I can tell you that he is a man desperate for money right now."

"Would he kill for it?"

"If he thought he could do so without any danger to himself. He is not a particularly brave man, but his passion in life, my lady, is gambling. Unfortunately, he is neither a wise nor a skillful gambler. I did hear, from him, that he owns part of the *Santa Maria Nunciada,* and is expecting to recoup a fortune when she returns. Perhaps if he had a fortune, he would cease gambling."

"Does the leopard change his spots?" asked Johana dryly. "Or what is more important, would he be willing to go outside the law to gain that fortune?"

"Only if he were sure he would not be caught."

"And yet he is still a friend of yours."

"Oh, yes. I find him infinitely amusing, although when he complains too much, he can become wearisome. Why do you ask?"

"I think he is a husband one could do without," said Johana.

"I think he would be an amusing but expensive husband," said Bonshom. "But I never had to deal with him longer than a day or two at a time. He may grow wearisome on longer acquaintance. But I must take my leave, my lady. Other, less pleasant, duties call me away." He rose, bowing courteously, and left.

Unsettled and unsure, Johana left her chair and began to walk around the orchard, back and forth, in the shade of the trees, many of which were still heavy with fruit. Margarida's cat had given up her hunt, and was asleep under the cool greenery. As she stared unseeing into their dark leafiness, she heard a tactful shuffle of boots nearby. It was one of the Princess's grooms. "You are seeking me, Sanch?"

"My lady," he said, "there is a person who wishes to talk to you."

"Who is it, Sanch?" she asked.

"She gave her name as Jacinta, my lady."

"Show her in. I will see her."

And the composed little girl walked carefully in, curtsied, and then looked around her with great interest. "My lady," she said quietly. "I have come with a message. I cannot stay long," she added, and for a moment worry printed itself across her face. "My mistress does not know that I have left the house, except that it is the Sabbath, and so I am not to do any work."

"I understand," said Johana. "Someone might miss you and wonder where you are, but not because your work is undone. Then let us sit down over here in the shade and you can give me your message."

The little girl looked suspiciously around the orchard and then leaned closer to Lady Johana. "Your faithful servant," she whispered, "wishes me to tell you that he believes he is recovering."

"That is all that he said?"

Jacinta nodded.

"And is he?"

"Master Jacob has a friend who is a great physician, my lady. He has come to the house for a wedding. He reset the patient's bones—we are only allowed to call him the patient, my lady—and gave him tinctures that allow him to sleep and to eat. He looks much better than he did. But you must not cry, my lady," she added, in tones of great concern. "He said you must not cry."

"All the world here knows I weep for the death of my husband. A few more tears will not matter," said Johana, wiping her eyes. "What does this physician say?"

"He told Master Jacob that the smell of death had left the patient for now. And Master Jacob told the mistress that it was very good news, for Master Isaac almost always knows if a man will live or die. And, my lady, Master Isaac has an apprentice who is a ward of His Majesty, named

Yusuf. Yusuf told me that Master Isaac is the physician from Girona who cured the Crown Prince, the Infant Johan, when he was a baby and so sickly Their Majesties despaired of his life."

"Will you carry a message back to my loyal servant? Tell him that I am well, and wish him well." She leaned over and whispered in the child's ear.

"Yes, my lady. I will tell him. And now I must go or I will be missed."

"Take this," said Johana, "and don't lose it."

Jacinta looked at the heavy silver coin in her hand and quickly tucked it into a fold in the sash of her gown. "Thank you, my lady," she whispered. "And I wish you well."

<hr />

"WHO was that sweet child you were talking to?" asked a voice behind Johana.

"Margarida," she replied. "When did you come down?"

"A moment ago. The Princess is on her way." Margarida clapped her hands together and the groom appeared. "The Princess will be here in a moment," she said. "She requires her chair and cushions. As well as refreshments."

"At once, my lady," he said and disappeared.

"Who did you say she was?"

"She brought me a message about my lord's manservant. He has left to return to his family in Valencia. I can understand why he would wish to leave," said Johana. "But if he had waited until tomorrow, I would have seen that he received what he was owed."

"And what is due a servant who deserts his mistress at the first sign of trouble?"

"You are too hard, Margarida. He has not been paid his wages since last quarter day, and I am sure that Arnau would have wanted him to have more. He was very loyal to him."

"I wonder," said Margarida. "You think he was loyal, Johana. What if he weren't? The simple fact that the attack killed Arnau but spared the servant would make me suspicious of him. And why run off now?"

"I believe that he left now because he feared for his life," said Johana.

PRINCESS Constança and her ladies appeared at the entrance to the orchard a few seconds after the bustle of preparations had ceased. The Ladies Johana and Margarida rose, curtsying; the servants backed away into their unobtrusive positions. Nothing moved but the leaves rustling in the breezes. With no regard for courtly etiquette, her little spaniel came racing in and romped at her feet in an ecstasy of excitement, before dashing off in search of the tortoiseshell cat. Her mistress sat down, and the spaniel raced back, collapsing happily on the Princess's feet. "Lady Johana, come and sit by me," said Constança. "Let us talk once more."

Johana curtsied again and came over to take the most prized seat among the ladies-in-waiting, next to the Princess.

"I have taken a few steps to alleviate your condition," said Constança. "But I do not know whether they will be successful."

"Your Highness," said Johana, and tears once again started to fill her eyes. "I am deeply grateful and most humbled that you have condescended to act on my behalf. It is much more than I deserve."

The Princess looked at her curiously. "It gave me pleasure," she said. "And it will give me even greater pleasure if my efforts succeed. But, alas, in spite of all this," she added, waving her hand around at the servants, the ladies, the orchard, "I am a person of little real power, except in small things. I am dependent on the whims of others. On the other hand, I am better able than most people to approach those who do have the power to assist you. I have used that ability. We shall see what happens."

+>══ ══<+

THE physician's house seemed to curl up and fall asleep in the warmth of the afternoon sun. Raquel was sitting by the window, her needlework in her lap, doing nothing, wondering if she could run down and fetch a book before her patient awoke. The door opened quietly and Yusuf came in.

"I will watch him," he whispered. "You have been here all morning."

"Jacinta came in for a while," said Raquel softly. "She likes sitting with him, she says. But I accept your offer. Is there anything left to eat?"

"A little," he said dubiously. "Fruit, and chickpeas dressed in vinegar."

"That's all I need," she said. "Perhaps I will bring him a ripe pear. He is growing hungry."

She ran down the stairs, making almost no noise in her soft leather boots. She walked out into the silent courtyard, stretched her cramped arms and legs, and went over to the table, where the various dishes had been left out, neatly covered with linen cloths. She wrapped two pears and an apple in a napkin, spooned some chickpeas in sauce into a bowl, and poured a cup of cool mint and lemon drink. She pulled a small piece of chicken from the almost cleaned-off bones, and while she was nibbling on it, and searching for more bits of chicken, she heard hesitant footsteps from the front part of the house. Hastily wiping her greasy fingers, she moved her little cache of food over to a shady corner of the table and sat down, prepared to be interrupted.

No one came in. Suddenly it occurred to Raquel that those might be her father's steps, walking with uncharacteristic hesitation because he was in a part of the house he did not know. Stabbed with remorse that she had scarcely worried about him since they arrived, her own beloved father, a stranger, blind, in a strange house. Knowing the master for all these years mattered not at all if he did not know the house, and yet somehow she had forgotten that. She took a bite of bread, for she was terribly hungry, and hurried off to assist him.

When Raquel went in the half-open door, she was in time to see Bonafilla, walking on tiptoes, followed by Ester, just as they wrenched open the heavy front door and left.

TEN

SUNDAY morning it rained. Mistress Ruth handed her small son over to Leah, wrapped on an apron, and headed into the kitchen to help the cook and Jacinta. For in addition to breakfast, there was the wedding banquet to be prepared. The great dishes—the dozen or so whole baked fishes, the innumerable fowl, the haunches of mutton, three whole lambs—would be baked on Tuesday in the baker's oven, of course, along with the cakes and breads, but they were yet to be spiced, salted, oiled, softened in wine, and in other and various ways prepared to be carried over there. Other dishes, the several types of scented rice, peas, and lentils were to be cooked at home. Close to eighty people in addition to those who were in the house were expected at the wedding, which would be held in the hall and garden built onto the synagogue. Ruth was intent on providing a feast that would please them all.

She had already decided that Leah was better with small children than she was with helping in the kitchen, and that the morals of Jacinta's forebears were less important at that moment than her willingness to do what she could.

The rain eased off by noon, and by dinnertime it was dry enough in the courtyard to lay the table outside. The whole house, by now, was caught up in the domestic ferment. Isaac went up to sit with the patient, sending Raquel and Yusuf downstairs to help; David and Jacob were pressed into service as reluctant messengers; even Bonafilla was drafted into service in the kitchen.

Then Bonafilla, who had been grinding spices, set down the mortar and pestle and said that she had a headache.

"You certainly look terribly pale," said Raquel. "Can I get you something?"

"No, please. I want nothing, just somewhere quiet where I can lie down."

"Go to our chamber," said Raquel. "I won't disturb you, I promise."

"Thank you. I'll come back to help as soon as I can," said Bonafilla, and ran from the room.

"Oh, dear," said Ruth.

"She'll be fine in a moment," said Raquel. "Don't worry about her."

"I'm not worrying about her," said Ruth. "I'm worrying about living with a woman who gets a sick headache over grinding spices. I could wish David a bride who was more useful around the house."

"With her dowry, he won't need one," said Raquel dryly. "You'll be able to hire another servant. But won't David have a house of his own?"

"One day, perhaps," said Ruth distractedly. "Master Samiel Caracosa did offer to lend me a helper for today and tomorrow. I wonder if I should accept."

"Master Astruch's cousin?"

"Yes. The same person."

"Then why don't you?"

"I would, except that right now there is no one to send to his house with the message." •

"It can't be that far away," said Raquel.

"It's all the way out of the *call*," said Ruth. "That's where the big houses are. This is one of the largest inside the *call*, and as you can see, it's not that big. That is why Master Samiel invited Duran to stay—he has all the room he needs for guests."

"I'll take your message, mistress," said a voice from the doorway.

Ruth whirled around. "Yusuf," she said. "You're very kind, but you don't know where the house is."

"Don't believe that. Yusuf knows where everything is," said Raquel. "Don't you?"

"I walked over there with Duran," said Yusuf. "Just to see how grand the house was. I know where it is."

✦━━ ━━✦

YUSUF received a hearty welcome at the house of Samiel Caracosa. The promised servant was sent off as quickly as possible, carrying with her a message that Yusuf would stay and dine with them. "For," as Master Samiel said, "Mistress Ruth has enough people to feed today, especially with a wedding to prepare for as well."

"I shall go over tomorrow," said his comfortable and capable-looking wife. "And help."

Dinner was ample, varied, and leisurely. When he had finished, Yusuf wandered slowly back toward the *call*, not eager to throw himself into the frenzy of preparations back at Master Jacob's house. His route took him first to the south end of the city, where from the highest point of the hill he stopped to look at the palace, rising in all its splendor on an answering hill. Then he doubled back, pausing along his way to speak to his friends throwing dice under the arches at the Corn Market.

While he crouched in the dust, watching, his eye was caught by a swirl of red silk; he turned to look again and realized that it was Bonafilla, accompanied by Ester, walking westward toward the street where the taverns and eating-houses were grouped together on the south end of market. As recent as his acquaintance with the city was, he was sure that she was strolling through a very unsuitable area for a respectable young lady alone with her maid.

The attention of el Gros was caught by Yusuf's movement. "She's something to watch, isn't she?" he said.

"I wonder what she's doing down here?" asked Yusuf, as casually as he could.

"Don't know," said el Gros.

"Meeting her lover," said Roger, looking up from the game for an instant. "Are you playing?"

"Or looking for a new one," said el Gros, ignoring him. "Do you know her?" he asked, his eyes bright with curiosity.

Yusuf shook his head as casually as he could. Whatever she might be up to, he could see no point in drawing their attention to it.

"She's been around here almost as often as you have, lad," said el Gros. "Must be doing something. And always with that same woman."

"Her maid," said Yusuf, forgetting for a moment that he didn't know her.

"I reckon," said el Gros. "A woman dressed like that would have a maid, wouldn't she?"

"Different clothes every day," added Ahmed greedily. "Rich."

"Looks like it," said Yusuf and bent his eyes down on the game. Shortly afterward, however, he excused himself and headed toward the street down which she had disappeared.

HE found her in a small square not far away. Its only other inhabitant on that quiet Sunday afternoon was a thin, cream-colored dog, asleep in the sun. Bonafilla stood in the center of the square, facing the street Yusuf was on, and talking to a well-dressed man, apparently oblivious to everyone and everything but him. As Yusuf came into the square he could see the man's back in its well-tailored tunic. It was a most expressive back, speaking volumes. He looked taut, ready to flee or draw his sword in a moment, and his head never ceased the faint motions that indicated that he was watching in every direction but straight behind him.

A shutter slammed somewhere above Yusuf's head. The man turned his head with the speed of a striking snake and Yusuf captured a brief glimpse of a familiar face. Unless he was very mistaken, the man talking to Bonafilla was Felip, the stranger who had joined them for the last part of their journey into the city. The boy came out into the square and drifted from doorway to doorway in the shade until he reached the haven of a covered street from whose dark recesses he could get a better look at the side of the man's head. This time, Yusuf knew. He was Felip, his hair and beard newly trimmed, and wearing a tunic of the latest cut in wine-colored silk trimmed in gold velvet.

Ester was standing in the shade on the other side of the square, watching the two of them. She shifted from foot to foot in impatience, glancing up to the sky again and again to check the progress of the sun. Her face was a battleground in which worry and prurient interest battled for supremacy.

"I cannot," said Bonafilla clearly. "That is all. You make everything so difficult—I simply don't know."

Whatever Felip's reply was, it was spoken in such light and even tones that even Yusuf's sharp ears could not decipher it. He bowed gallantly and walked straight into the street, where Yusuf was lurking in the shadows, leaving a white-faced and miserable-looking Bonafilla alone in the middle of the square. Some minutes after she left with her maid, Yusuf let himself out of the door behind which he had been hiding.

JOHANA was at her needle when a servant appeared at the door to her little sitting room. "My lady," she said, "Her Royal Highness wishes to see you at once."

Johana dropped her work, rose, straightened her gown, pushed her unruly hair in place, and followed the maid-servant along the passage to the Princess Constança's apartments.

"If you will wait, my lady," said the maid, "I will tell Her Highness you are here." She whisked herself into the bedroom.

The atmosphere in the antechamber was tense. The Princess's ladies-in-waiting were all standing, looking uncharacteristically ruffled, or annoyed, or frightened. Margarida nodded to her, but neither smiled nor spoke. There was a long, silent pause. Johana stayed by the door, waiting for something to happen.

At last, the maid appeared again. "Princess Constança would like your ladyship to come in," she said, holding the door open for her, and then shutting it again firmly on the others.

The Princess was bending over a large basket that sat on a table. Tears poured down her cheeks. "Lady Johana," she said, "you must help me. Leave us," she snapped at the maid. "And don't listen at the door." She waited until the door closed behind her servant. "I have never asked you any details of who helped your husband when he was injured, because I know you feared that his life was in danger. But I have heard that he was treated—or I should say that his serving man, who was also badly injured—was treated by a physician here in Perpignan, with the help of the physician who cured my brother of his ailments. And that the man is so much recovered that he is able to travel."

"Yes, Your Highness, in a way that is what happened, although—"

"It is not important exactly what happened—what is important is the skill of these two physicians," she said impatiently.

"That is true, Your Highness. They are very skilled."

"They must be sent for at once and you are the only person who knows who they are and where they stay. Look, Lady Johana. Look at my poor Morena." She stood back from the basket, keeping her hand inside it.

The little brown spaniel with white spots lay in the basket, one leg held stiffly out and the fur of her head and leg stiff with blood. She whimpered when the Princess moved away from her, and then closed her eyes.

"Look at her leg," said Constança.

"It looks as if it might be broken, Your Highness," said Johana cautiously.

"It is. Those fools in there let her get away from them. She ran down the stairs into the great courtyard and was bitten by one of the guard dogs. I'll have someone's head for this if she does not recover," she said, and her voice shook with cold rage.

"I would be pleased to give you the names of the physicians, Your Highness. I only hope that they can heal a dog as well as they can heal people."

"Are dogs' bones made differently from people's bones, do you think?" she asked, looking very worried.

"I would think they mend the same way, Your Highness."

"Ring for my maid, Lady Johana," said the Princess, keeping her steady vigil by the injured animal.

The maid appeared with suspicious promptness. "Fetch my secretary," she said. "I will have a letter written at once."

As Johana walked away from the Princess's apartments, cold fear stole her breath. Almost everything that the Princess had said was known only to Johana. No one in the palace should have known who treated Arnau but herself and little Jacinta. And no one could have heard that conversation with Jacinta. No one—except loyal, honest Margarida, if she had been in the orchard, spying on her friend.

WHEN Yusuf returned to the physician's house, Masters Jacob and Isaac were waiting for him at the door. "Wash your hands and face, Yusuf," said Isaac, as soon as he heard him coming in. "We are to go to the palace to treat a very serious case." Standing behind them was Mordecai, carrying a box.

Yusuf cleaned himself up as rapidly as he could and scrambled out the door. "Who is our new patient?" he asked. "Not the Lady Johana, I hope."

"Why do you say that?"

"Because our patient upstairs could not bear it, lord."

"True enough. But the one we go to treat is dearly loved as well, Yusuf. But as far as I know, she is not acquainted with the man we have been looking after. It will still be a difficult case, though," said Isaac, "because unfortunately she is dearly beloved by the Princess."

"From what does she suffer?"

"She was in a fight, and suffers from a broken leg and dog bites."

Yusuf looked from one to the other. "One of Her Royal Highness's ladies was in a fight?"

"Before you become too confused, Yusuf," said Jacob, "I will tell you that this is a new venture. Our patient is a dog, dearly loved by her mistress, the Princess Constança."

THE two physicians and Yusuf were in the Princess's bedroom, since Constança would not consider moving the injured animal. Jacob started the investigation, going over every inch of the poor creature's body for wounds. Except for a tear on her ear, which had been bleeding profusely, the only other broken skin was on the injured leg itself. Yusuf and Jacob sponged the wounds with wine and herbs to promote healing and keep away infection, and Yusuf held a pad of cloth pressed to Morena's ear to stop the last of the bleeding.

All this time, the Princess stood across from them, her hand on Morena's shoulder, holding her still.

Then Isaac took the leg in his hand. Morena growled and the Princess hushed her. He began to feel it, very delicately. She growled again. "When I reach the break, Your Highness, she will have to be held so that I can set the bone where it belongs. That way she will heal. I am reluctant to feed her any drops for pain, Your Royal Highness, because I fear they may do her more harm than good. Perhaps Yusuf can hold her."

"I will hold her," said Constança. "When you reach the break, I will hold her head and her body. Then you may deal with the leg."

From then on, he worked quickly. Jacob sponged the broken skin thoroughly again and Isaac began moving his hands down the hindquarter. The dog trembled with pain and fear as he approached the site of the injury, but when the physician said, "Now, Your Highness," she lay still in the firm grip of the Princess and Jacob, who held the hindquarters. Morena lay helpless and stoical, making no protest as Isaac slipped the bone into place. Yusuf began immediately to bind it with splints. "I thank Your Highness for your assistance," said Isaac when it was finished.

"She would not have allowed you to touch her otherwise," said Constança, still caressing her. "There, she has stopped trembling already," she said. "Instruct my maid how she is to be cared for," said her royal mistress. "I am most grateful for your skill." And they were ushered out the door.

Neither Isaac nor Jacob was accustomed to dealing with sick and injured dogs, but they explained as clearly as they could how the highly nervous maid was to take care of the injured animal. While they were going over what she should do for the third time, a priest in the white robes of the Dominican fathers was ushered into the sitting room. "I will tell the Princess you are here," said the maid. "But I don't know if she will be able to see you."

"She had asked me to visit," he said. "If she wishes to see me, I will be pleased. Otherwise, it is of no importance."

"Thank you, Father."

The priest looked at the two physicians and the boy with a glance of curiosity, turning his head as they left the room.

ALL the way back from the palace, as Jacob and Isaac chatted over the case they had just attended to, Yusuf mulled over what he had seen near the Corn Market, coming again and again to the conclusion that he would have to tell someone about it. After rejecting her relatives and David's family, who would be likely to take it very badly, he decided that Raquel was his best choice as confidant. As they crossed the square of the Dominican house, heading toward the gate to the *call*, he turned his attention again to his master's remarks.

"I am not fond of bonesetting," Isaac was saying. "I never perform it—or almost never—at home. We had an excellent practitioner in Girona, but he died in the Black Death. For a while I did some in difficult cases, until his apprentice grew skilled enough to take over again."

"But you have such clever fingers," said Jacob.

"I prefer the mysteries of illness and health to practicing the skills of a bonesetter, that is all. In addition, few patients are as quiet and cooperative as little Morena."

"Here we are at last, Isaac," said his host. "Join me in a

cup of wine and something to eat—if there is anyone free to fetch it for us." And with a laugh the two entered the house, followed by a silent Yusuf. The house was calm and quiet. Mistress Ruth had called a halt to the frantic activity.

+‡>══ ══<‡+

HESITANT to knock on the door of Raquel's chamber in a strange house, Yusuf went up the stairs to the sick man's apartment. As he had half-expected, there she was, sitting by the window, working industriously.

"I will sit with him," she whispered. "It is no work, compared with what's going on downstairs."

"Nothing is going on downstairs," murmured Yusuf. "But I wanted to talk to you."

"What about?"

"Shall we sit outside the door? I don't want to disturb him."

"He sleeps more soundly now," said Raquel. "It shouldn't be necessary."

So Yusuf perched on the window ledge and recounted his observations of Bonafilla and Felip in the square.

" 'I cannot. You are making everything so difficult,' " repeated Raquel thoughtfully. "Is that what she said?"

"And she said she didn't know, as well," said Yusuf.

"Who is she?" asked the sick man suddenly. "This girl?"

"Señor, I am sorry that we awakened you," said Raquel.

"You didn't," he replied. "I was beginning to awaken before Yusuf here came creeping into the chamber. Who is she and what can she not do?"

"We really shouldn't gossip about her," said Raquel uncomfortably. "She is a young woman of excellent reputation."

"Do I know her?" asked the sick man. "Will I ever know her, do you think?"

"I don't think so, señor. For when you are recovered

enough, you will be going back to wherever you come from, which is not, I believe, Perpignan."

"True. So tell me who she is and what she cannot do."

"Her name is Bonafilla, and she is to be married on Tuesday," said Raquel.

"But not to the man whom she met in a square and to whom she said she could not do something."

"He wants her help for some reason," said Yusuf.

"Think, Yusuf," said Raquel impatiently. "Who in this city could want her help? He wants her. She is very pretty, señor. No—I lie. She is very beautiful."

"More beautiful than you, mistress?" he asked. "I ask that not in gallantry, but as a serious question."

"She is more strikingly beautiful," said Raquel after a moment's thought. "If she went through the streets unveiled, more heads would turn than if I did."

"I understand. She is to marry on Tuesday and you believe that this man wishes her to elope with him? Have they known each other long?"

"They met on the last day of our journey here," said Raquel. "But she has seen and spoken to him since then. She told me. And he pressed her to run off with him."

"Offering marriage?"

"I don't know what he offered her as an inducement. She didn't say. He is motivated by desire, I suppose. And since he spoke of it to her, also by her father's gold, brought here for her dowry. That must be part of his motive."

"Ah. Greed. Perhaps she does not know how she would get her father's gold from the house."

"I don't know how she could," said Raquel. "It must be locked up. And Master Astruch is not so easily hoodwinked that he would give it to her because she asked for it."

"This is stuff of a *jongleur's* romance," said the sick man. "She meets someone while traveling, they fall in love, and are desperate to elope together. Did they spend much time together in conversation?"

"No," said Yusuf. "They may have exchanged pleasantries, or complaints about the weather—it was raining—but Bonafilla was always with her father and brother, as well as her maid and Raquel."

"Not the easiest circumstances for seduction," said the sick man. "Right under a father's nose."

"I cannot believe that she would throw over family and a good marriage to someone she finds handsome, attractive, and witty so that she could run off with a perfect stranger," said Raquel.

"Unless they had met before, and he fell in with you by design," said the sick man. "Now, if I were attempting to rescue my true love from a forced marriage, I might try something that desperate at the last minute."

"But she simply glows with pleasure when she's with David," said Raquel. "I've seen it. And if she had been in love with someone else, I think her father would have listened to her. He is, at heart, a kind man."

"Not, perhaps, if the lover were a Christian," said the sick man. "Is he?"

"At the time, I supposed that he was," said Raquel. "But he does not have to be. We spoke of nothing more than the weather, our destinations, and the condition of the roads. And in traveling, anyone with sense will dress and comport himself like a Christian for safety's sake, as His Majesty allows."

"Does she go alone to meet him?" asked the sick man.

"No," said Yusuf. "She takes her maid."

"I feel we should tell someone about this," said Raquel, "except that it might cause unnecessary trouble."

"It is possible that she is amusing herself with a taste of danger for a few days before settling down as a respectable married woman," said the sick man. "After all, a few meetings in the afternoon in a public square under the watchful eye of her maid could be very exciting yet really quite safe.

I have heard that young ladies enjoy feeling wicked as long as their actions can have no consequences."

"I will ask Ester what she thinks. Or knows," said Raquel. "Because you may be right. She is annoyed at her father."

"Why?"

"He has taken a young wife, a pleasant woman whom Mistress Bonafilla dislikes. She believes her father arranged this match at the instigation of his wife because they wanted to enjoy life without Bonafilla sulking about the house, and glowering at them."

"Her little revenge," said the sick man.

"Yes. But she always seems to me to be too . . ." Raquel paused. "Too careful to risk serious consequences."

"Then go at once and ask her maid," said the sick man. "And return with whatever news you glean from her. But first, mistress, I am afflicted with hunger again. Do you think you can find me something more sustaining than broth or custard?"

"Do you think you can eat it?"

"I could eat a haunch of beef at the moment, I believe. These mysteries give one an appetite."

"I don't know what you're talking about, mistress," said Ester. "We haven't gone out anywhere."

"Your loyalty to your mistress is all very well, Ester," said Raquel. "But I've seen the two of you sneak out of the house. The cook has seen the two of you sneak out of the house. Yusuf has seen your mistress talking to the gentleman we met on the road in a public square in the middle of Perpignan. What is going on?"

Ester reddened and then looked nervously around the courtyard. "Mistress Bonafilla made me promise not to tell anyone about it," she whispered.

"If something happens, and they find out that you knew

about it and did nothing, Ester, you are going to be out in the streets, I assure you."

"I've told her that, again and again, and she pays no attention," said Ester in great distress.

"Is she in love with this man?"

"She seems to hate him," said Ester, "and yet—I don't know, mistress. I have my suspicions, but there's much I'm not sure of. I can tell you that since we came to this house I haven't let her out of my sight unless she were with you or with Master David's family. She hasn't done anything she shouldn't, I swear it, even though we did go out to meet that man."

"Ester, will you do something for me?" said Raquel, taking a heavy coin from her purse and slipping it into the maid's hand. "Will you keep watch over her, and let me know at once if you think she might run off with him?"

"But what if she doesn't tell me?"

"I don't think she'll go without at least some of her clothes and all the gold from her dowry she can carry. Do you?"

Ester paused to consider. "No, you're right, mistress. I don't know about the gold, but I can keep my eye on her best gowns and silk shifts. And I'll tell you."

And with that small reassurance, Raquel returned to her patient.

ELEVEN

MORE showers passed through the city on Monday, and Mistress Ruth, out of bed early the day before the wedding, looked up unhappily at the gloomy skies. With so many in the house and so much to be done, life would be easier if her family and guests could be encouraged to stay out in the courtyard. She did a round of the house, checking that Leah was up with the baby, routing the housemaid out of a deep sleep so that she could start her chores well before the guests were awake, and ending up in the kitchen. There, at least, all was in order. The fire was hot, Jacinta had fetched the morning's bread, and the cook and the new kitchen maid were pausing to break their fasts. Ruth sat down with them, cut a piece of cheese, broke open a roll of bread and began to eat.

"There's no point, mistress," said the cook, with the assurance of an essential retainer, "in your running about like this and risking your health. You should rest today. We can manage, can't we, Jacinta?"

"Yes, mistress," said the little girl. "The sick man is not so much work as he was."

"He's eating proper now," observed the cook. "Like the rest of us. Mistress Raquel came down yesterday and fetched him some braised chicken with lentils and bread for his supper. He ate it all."

"Excellent," said Ruth. "But before we talk of resting, what remains to be done today?"

And they bent their heads together in an intense discussion of shopping, preparation, and cooking, not forgetting meals for the guests.

+>=— =<+

SHORTLY after the bells rang for terce, the sun came out and began drying off the courtyard. Isaac and Master Astruch were in the dining room, lingering over their breakfasts; Bonafilla had just finished dressing with Ester's help; Yusuf was off at the market with Jacinta and the cook, who had a whole list of crucial purchases to make and needed help in carrying them back. Master Samiel Caracosa's wife had arrived and was already in the kitchen with Mistress Ruth, shifting the load of tasks to be done onto her own capable shoulders. Raquel was sitting peacefully in the haven of the sick man's room, looking out at the steaming roofs and watching him eat a breakfast of bread, cheese, and fruit.

The bell rang at the door of the house. Raquel wondered who would arrive at the busiest hour of the morning and was glad it had nothing to do with her. It rang again. The youthful housemaid scrambled down the stairs from straightening up the beds, opened the front door, and gulped in astonishment. On the doorstep stood a Dominican priest, resplendent in his robes, alone.

"Good morning," he said gently. "Could you tell your master that Father Miró of the Order of Preachers is here and would like to speak to the sick man? You do have a sick man in the house, I believe," said the priest.

The frightened girl nodded.

"I would like a few words with him."

"I'll tell the master," said the housemaid in a panic, slamming the door in his face and racing off to find Jacob. She delivered her message, scarcely able to breathe.

"Thank you," said Jacob. "Where did you put him?"

"On the doorstep. He's on the doorstep, sir," she replied, and rushed off to tell her mistress.

"Father Miró," said Jacob when he had opened the door again and ushered the priest inside. "You are welcome to my house. I must apologize for my housemaid," he added. "She is a raw, untrained girl, but she should have known better than to leave a visitor standing on the step in such a way."

"It is no matter, Master Jacob," said the priest, following the physician into his study. "Did she pass on my message? You have a patient staying here, I believe."

"I do," said Jacob without hesitation.

"Is he well enough for me to speak to him?"

"I think so," said the physician. "You will be able to judge that yourself when you see him. I only ask you to remember that his injuries are severe, and although he recovers well, he is still not out of danger. If you will come this way," he said, leading him out into the courtyard, "I have accommodated him in a quiet chamber away from the bustle of the house."

When the priest and the physician arrived, the sick man was peacefully finishing his breakfast of cheese and bread. Raquel jumped down from the window seat and made a quick curtsy to the stranger. "May I present Mistress Raquel?" said Jacob. "She is helping look after my patient. Father Miró would like to talk to him for a little while," he added.

"Would you like me to stay, Father?" asked Raquel.

"Thank you, mistress, but you need not stay."

"I will be in the courtyard if you require anything," said Raquel. She curtsied again and left the room. Jacob lingered a moment, as if reluctant to leave the two men alone, then bowed, and followed.

Father Miró turned to the man in the bed. "What manner of evil creature has done this to you, señor?"

"Evil?" said the patient cautiously.

"Do you dispute the existence of evil men in this world, then?" asked Father Miró with a smile.

"You speak of men," the patient replied. "I have seen too many evil men to doubt their existence, Father, but the question does not apply to my case. My injuries were the result of my own carelessness, not the malice of men. I fell from my mule."

"I think not," said Father Miró firmly. "But if, for some reason, you wish to shield the identity of the man who attacked you, you may. It is not my concern. Remember that."

"I have a habit of caution, Father, but I have no reason to shield anyone from you," said the patient, pausing to collect his forces. "The moon was bright when it happened, and although the street was somewhat shadowed, I did catch sight of the men who did this. I have spent many hours thinking about them, I assure you, and on the whole, I think that they were not evil."

"Although they came close to killing you? You are a singularly forgiving man, señor."

"I would that I were, Father," said the patient, and closed his eyes. "I saw them move and act," he said at last. "They were big men, slow-witted, poor. Someone had taught them words to shout at me that would not have come to the lips of common thieves. Someone paid them in silver or gold to do what he would not do himself. Does that make them evil?"

"You do not believe all men to be evil?"

"I believe that any man can be shaken by evil desires

from time to time," he said, pausing for breath. "It is difficult to be wholly good, but I refuse to think that we are wholly evil. The person who hired those men, and therefore did not have to raise a hand against me, he may well be evil. But those three men he hired?"

"They injured you. That is wrong."

"Tell me, Father, does God condemn from birth the untaught and slow of wit for doing what he can to feed himself and his children?"

"He could do other things than murder. He could work on the land."

"Only if he were born on the land. If those three had been born on my land, they would have been comfortably employed. They were not." He stopped, panting from the effort of so much speech. "We neglect such as these from the moment they are born. No one taught them truth and virtue. Are they to be cast into the flames for it? Was your own order not founded, in part, to teach men to go out and impart such necessary learning?"

"These are vexing questions, my son," said the priest. "Likely to lead us onto paths that are not fitting for us to travel. What do you think?"

"I tell you truthfully, Father, I do not know and it troubles me. Even lying here as I am, I trust and believe that God, knowing everyone's state in life, sees more clearly than I, or even you, Father, which man deserves mercy."

"Even your enemy, the one who hired these assassins?"

"You give me a more difficult case, Father."

"By your own statement, he too might deserve mercy. The only difference is that the victim was you and not a stranger."

"No, Father. The rich man—I assume wealth, since he was able to hire assassins . . ."

"Inefficient ones," added the priest.

"Fortunately. The rich man, who has been taught what is right and what is wrong, and yet in spite of his learning is vicious, grasping, avaricious, or uses his gold to satisfy his evil desires—he must be evil. My heart cries out for vengeance, not against the poor fools who broke my bones, but against him. Yet I cannot see into his heart, and I lack the wisdom and learning of great men. I do not know what is right."

"Are you still in great pain?"

"Not as much as before, Father. My injured limbs are swollen and uncomfortable but, I thank God with all my heart, my fever has almost gone and my appetite has returned. I am being very well cared for here," he added.

"I am glad to hear it," said the priest. "What I have to ask you may come as no surprise to you," he began, when the door suddenly opened and Mistress Ruth appeared in the doorway carrying a bowl covered with a linen cloth and a basket with bread and fruit in it.

"I am so sorry, señor," she said. "I did not know you had a visitor. Please excuse me. But our patient had said that his simple breakfast was not enough to satisfy his appetite. He must eat all he can, and so I brought him a good hearty soup." She placed the bowl on the table by the bed and took off the cover. "There," she said, "a strengthening soup of mutton, broth, and beans, with onions, garlic, and herbs. You must eat, señor, if you are to get better."

"I admit to being hungry still, mistress," he said, and looked over at the priest.

"Please, señor, eat. It smells delicious." The Dominican peered at the bowl of soup. "Surely for a man in your condition such large pieces of mutton are not to be recommended?"

"Yesterday, he ate braised chicken and vowed he could finish a haunch of beef," said Ruth in pleased tones. "I think he believes we are trying to starve him out of here," she added with a slightly forced laugh. She spread the linen cloth over his lap and set the bowl on it, along with the bread. She handed him a spoon, which he took awkwardly in his left hand, and as rapidly as she had entered the room, left it again.

"You will notice, Father, that it is a very small portion of mutton and beans," said the sick man, as he took a spoonful and started to eat with evident enjoyment. "It is a wonderful dish," he added, between mouthfuls. "But you had questions to ask me, Father. Please, start, and I will answer to the best of my knowledge and ability."

WHEN bells rang for sext, the Dominican stopped what he was saying and looked at the sick man. "You look very weary," he said. "I fear that I have greatly overtaxed your strength."

"It is unimportant, Father. I have the rest of the day and then the days after that to sleep quietly."

"Is there anything I can do—anything that is within my power, that is—to assist you?"

"You can pray for me, Father. I am much in need of prayers, and except for one, who never ceases to ask Heaven to intercede on my behalf, I doubt there are any left to do so."

"Gladly will I pray for you," he said.

"And if you should pass by the palace, there is someone there who is in need of spiritual strength and consolation."

"Who is this person?"

The sick man beckoned him near and whispered a name in his ear.

"It shall be done, my son," said the Dominican.

IN the courtyard, Jacob and his wife sat close to the staircase from the sick man's room and waited. The servants had come in from time to time and been chased away. All activity in the kitchen had stopped, although the cook, frantic at the unexpected delay, took Jacinta and Samiel Caracosa's servant, along with some pots, to a helpful neighbor's fire. Bonafilla had come down to join her new family and been sent off to Jacob's study to work on her fancy linens.

"It is because of the rumors that he is a follower of the Cathars that the priest has come, is it not?" asked Ruth, her voice trembling.

"Without a doubt," said Jacob. "Why else would they send one of his order? I am troubled by his presence in our house. These accusations are easier to make than to refute, my dear. How can he prove that he does not believe something? How can we prove that we are not assisting a heretic?"

"There must be some way," said Ruth. "Perhaps they are simply talking."

"He has been in there a long time," said Jacob.

"He could not be forcing a confession from him, could he?"

"Without witnesses, in our house? I doubt it. But they have questions that they ask—questions that will trap an unwary member of the sect."

"I don't know if I did right, Jacob," said his wife uneasily. "But when the priest came, he was eating bread and cheese for his breakfast, and I remembered that the Cathars would eat no meat or eggs or even milk and cheese. I was so frightened but I brought him a bowl of mutton and beans. Surely if he belonged to that sect, he wouldn't want to eat them and would have made some excuse for pushing them aside, wouldn't he?"

"Did he eat them?" said another voice.

"Yes, Master Isaac, he did," said Ruth, turning to acknowledge the blind man's presence. "When I left he was eating the soup with a lively appetite."

"May the Lord be thanked for that," said Isaac.

At that moment the Dominican came down the staircase

and into the courtyard. Jacob Bonjuhes rose courteously and walked with him toward the front of the house.

"I believe that we met, after a manner of speaking, yesterday," said Father Miró, pausing in the hallway in front of the study to take his farewell. "Her Royal Highness summoned me to the palace. It seems you acted most skillfully in caring for her poor little dog. She was sleeping quietly by the time I left—the dog, that is. The Princess is very happy."

"I am pleased to hear that, Father. I hope that little Morena continues to do well."

"Please convey my apologies to your wife, Master Jacob, and accept them on your own behalf for my untimely visit," said the priest. "I would not have come at such an early hour except that today I leave for Conflent."

"Today?" said the physician. "I fear you will have a late start."

"I will travel only as far as I can," said the priest. "I had hoped to visit Santa Maria de Serrabona tonight," he added.

"Is that not somewhat out of your way, Father?" asked Jacob.

"Do you know the roads well that go into the west, Master Jacob?"

"I have traveled them," said the physician. "And that is a difficult road, as I remember."

"So I have heard. If it grows too late, I shall not attempt it. It was only to see an old friend and satisfy my curiosity," he added rather wistfully, as if he seldom allowed such diversions in his life. "My greater duty calls me into Conflent. It is likely that I will stop for the night wherever I can find harborage."

"I hope you reach Santa Maria," said the physician, "and I wish you a good journey, father."

"And may all be well with you and your family," said the priest. "My visit here," he added in clear tones as the door opened, "was a waste of my time. My informant must have been mistaken."

"Such errors can happen," said Jacob easily, and ushered his unwelcome visitor out to the road.

As the Dominican turned to say farewell, Isaac and Yusuf came out of the door behind him. "Master Isaac, is it not?" asked the priest.

"I am he," said Isaac. "And you are Father Miró, I believe."

"I am," said the priest. "Are you walking toward the gate of the *call*?"

"We are. I have a message to deliver to the cathedral of Sant Johan."

"Then let us walk together at least as far as the Dominican house, which is on your way," said Father Miró. "It is inconvenient, really, that one must go north to get out of the *call* when one has business to the south or west, but such are the ways of cities. They grow oddly."

"There has been no talk of putting in another gate?" asked Isaac innocently, knowing very well that it was a constant source of irritation and much conversation in the *call*.

"Oh, yes. And His Majesty has said that he will look with favor on an application to do just that. It should happen soon, but not soon enough for my journey today." He paused to gather his robe out of the way of a large and deep puddle. "I gather that you are responsible, Master Isaac, for the setting of that unfortunate man's limbs. I admire your great skill."

"Thank you, Father Miró. But his present good condition is more a credit to the good care he has received in the household of Master Jacob. And also to his own determination to get well. All that my poor skills could do was to start him on the road to recovery," the physician said.

"Then we shall hope and pray that he continues along it. Have you had much conversation with him?"

"Yes, indeed," said Isaac. "As much as his broken rib permits. What he has said to me is of great interest but little use. He is not a man who reveals much about himself in his speech."

"I had noticed that, Master Isaac," said the Dominican, laughing. "But I hope to be able to do something about the root cause of his silence."

"That would be an excellent thing, I believe," said Isaac.

"And now we have reached my destination," said Father Miró. "Do you know the way to the cathedral, young man?" he asked Yusuf.

"I do, Father," said Yusuf.

"Then I wish you both well."

FATHER Miró was walking quickly up the steps toward the Dominican house when he was stopped by a voice issuing from the shadows created by the wall and a large tree. "Father," said the voice softly. When the priest turned to look, a man materialized out of the darkness. "I wondered—that is, I hope you had a profitable visit," said the man beside the tree.

"In no circumstances could it be said to be profitable, señor," said the priest. "I had a long conversation with a man of common sense and piety—one whom I discovered to be considerably more pious in thoughts and deeds than you are, I would judge. The conversation cost him much pain because of his illness and cost me much time that I can ill afford. It was unnecessary."

"You do not believe he is a Cathar?"

"No, I don't. He is not. It was a ridiculous assumption."

"Then if he is not a Cathar, he must be a Christian, contravening the law by living in the *call*."

"That I cannot say," said the priest. "All I can tell you is that he is not, as you aver, one of the *Perfecti*. You would have seen as much for yourself if you had accepted my invitation to come with me."

"I am sorry that other duties prevented me from taking up your kind offer, Father."

"Because of your misplaced zeal, or perhaps, your malice, I spent a good part of my morning, time I needed for other duties, watching a man I was told was not merely an adherent, but a *Perfectus*, a leader of a renewed Cathar movement, breaking his fast with bread and cheese, then eating with gusto a soup of mutton—fine, large pieces of mutton. The next time you wish to cause trouble to someone, think of a better excuse for it. You have wasted a good deal of my morning in this malicious and mean-spirited endeavor. Farewell. I intend to speak of this at greater length, but this morning I begin a journey and must leave at once."

"Where are you going?"

"I wish to see you this day next week in the evening, when I will be back. Do not fail me, sir, or I will come to seek you."

Around the corner of the Dominican house, Isaac and Yusuf, pausing at the fountain, listened with interest to the conversation. "Do you recognize the other man—the one the priest is talking to?" said Isaac.

"I cannot see him, lord, and therefore do not recognize him. His voice seems somewhat familiar."

"You are familiar with the accent of the town he is from, that is all," said the physician. But still he looked somewhat troubled.

HIS Excellency, the Bishop of Perpignan, was sitting at his desk when Isaac and Yusuf were ushered into his study. He greeted them abruptly, bade them sit, and came directly to the point. "I received Bishop Berenguer's letter, and I thank you for bringing it to my secretary in person. On Friday, I believe."

"Yes, Your Excellency. We received it on Friday," murmured his secretary.

"Are you familiar with its contents?" asked the Bishop.

"I know only that it has to do with concerns that the abbot of Sant Feliu has about certain difficulties in the city," said Isaac tactfully.

"Difficulties!" said the Bishop. "Have you been here long enough to know what they are?"

"I only know those that at the moment are centred around the sailing of the *Santa Maria Nunciada*," said Isaac.

"Ah, yes. The venture started by Don Arnau Marça. A most regrettable incident. I cannot decide whether it was an honest mercantile venture that somehow became hopelessly corrupted or whether from its inception it was part of the cauldron of sin, debauchery, and lawlessness that we seem to suffer from here."

"Is it not still possible that it is an innocent trading voyage?"

The Bishop looked carefully at the blind man's unexpressive face. "If it is, Master Isaac, then a man has died for nothing, nothing but rumors and talk. And I am bereft of words adequate to a response."

"Your Excellency feels strongly about it."

"I do. But Don Arnau was a friend, and I take his death and his apparent treachery—and I have said apparent from the beginning, because I have great difficulty believing it—very hard." The Bishop stood up and began pacing back and forth across his study floor. "I can believe that he might have rashly stumbled into such a thing before, but not now."

"I'm afraid I do not follow Your Excellency's argument."

"Of course. You do not know Don Arnau. Generous, brave, daring—often too much so—and frequently imprudent. But his lady, whom he married a few years ago—how many?" he threw at his secretary.

"Four, Your Excellency."

"Of course. Four years ago. I married them myself. His lady is the soul of prudence and virtue. Not to say wisdom. She guides him gently, and for her sake, he no longer risks his life or his fortunes on foolish ventures."

"He was most fortunate in his choice."

"Yes, and she suffers greatly now. She is with child, close to her time. Fortunately the Princess shelters her at the palace. But as unfortunate as that affair is, it is another man that causes me greater grief. One whom I suspect of much evil, without a word of proof. That is not a very useful report to send to Don Vidal de Blanes, I admit. And it is for that reason that I have not responded to his inquiries. But, when you arrived, my secretary and I were struggling over our reply. If you could wait a little longer, we will have it wrapped up in diplomatic language for you."

＊ ＊

AND in the grove on the quiet track outside the city walls, the three men met once more.

Once again the leader of the group pulled down his hood and remained on his horse, looking down at his subordinates. "Explain why we are meeting this time," he said. "It is most injudicious."

"I spoke to the priest," said the slight man. "I fear that he is angry at us for sending him into the *call*."

"At us?"

"I beg your pardon, señor. At me."

"That is better."

"Something must be done about him," said the tall man.

"What do you suggest? That we bribe him?" said the hooded man. "Somehow I do not see him as a suitable subject for bribery."

"I have various ideas in mind," said the tall one. "Where did you say he was going?"

"I don't know," said the slight man. "He would not say."

"Do you know when?"

"This afternoon. He will have left by now, I expect."

"We can catch him up," said the tall man confidently.

IN spite of his oft-repeated statement that he was in haste, Father Miró did not reach the royal palace until most had finished their dinners. He found the person to whom he was to deliver the message from the sick man with no difficulty. After an hour or two's conversation with various people, he collected his mule again and set out toward Conflent.

The sun was already in the southwest and moving toward the horizon. He urged his beast on until she broke into a rambling and uncomfortable canter that ate up the miles. His thoughts were divided evenly between his present discomfort, his concern over the man he had spent the morning with, and the situation he was going to face when he reached his destination.

He was a knowledgeable man who had spent years studying the records from the great battles, spanning some two centuries, against the heresies of the Cathars and the Waldensians. For that reason, he had been sent out to investigate charges contained in a badly written letter received by his provincial. The letter spoke darkly of witchcraft, the old heresies, and new obscene rituals that were, in the mind of the writer, corrupting the souls of his village and tearing the heart out of the diocese.

He agreed with those who were sending him that in these cases it was best to arrive quickly. It may have been years since the sands along the banks of the river Tet had seen huge fires for the burning of the accused in Perpignan, but soon enough, in the small village he was heading for, someone might take it into his head to settle the problem by hanging all the suspects and their families too, for good measure. Many in the archdiocese—although he was not one of them—believed that in addition to his learning, he possessed the God-given gift of being able to look straight into men's hearts, and to separate malicious accusations from honest suspicions.

When asked how he did it, he would say, "It is easy to see. When you talk to people, you can tell the difference between the terror an innocent man feels at being accused unjustly and the anguish of true guilt. I listen to their answers, nothing more." But no one believed it, and so his reputation clung to him.

He continued along the road, whiling away the time puzzling over the day, and contemplating tomorrow. As the sun slipped behind the mountains, without slackening his pace he murmured a prayer of thanks for the day that had been granted him and another for his sins to be forgiven.

That done, he began to consider where he would spend the night. The road had narrowed conspicuously and was rising steeply. The mule eased off to a walk, and Father Miró calculated that another hour at a moderate pace would bring him to a monastery guest house. The sky was still red and orange with the splendor of the sunset; there would be sufficient light for his mule to make her way safely to the monastery ahead.

Behind him he heard a horse galloping up the slope as if its life depended on it. Before he had time to turn and see what was happening, a ferocious blow hit the back of his head and tumbled him over the edge of the road down to the stream beneath.

TWELVE

RAQUEL was in the courtyard, her work lying idle in her lap. Jacob and his brother sat apart, deep in private talk, and Raquel turned her attention to a conversation between Bonafilla and her father. Or more accurately, she thought, to listening to Astruch talking at his daughter, for she seemed to have very little to say. "Do you not agree with me, Mistress Raquel?" asked Master Astruch. "That Bonafilla will be happier staying here? She will have a friend in Mistress Ruth, someone to talk to and advise her. Running a household of your own is a heavy responsibility when you are not used to it."

"Others do it," said Bonafilla.

"True," said her father uneasily, and turned back to the other men. "Jacob, my friend," said Astruch, "I have remembered one small thing I wished to talk over with you."

"Then let us go into my study," said Jacob. "It will be quiet there."

"Excellent," said Astruch. "We will leave the young people to amuse each other."

David walked purposefully over to his prospective bride. "There are a few things that we should talk about as well, Bonafilla. Will you join me in the corner by the lemon tree?"

Bonafilla gave Raquel a quick, panicky look and rose. "Of course," she murmured, clutching her needlework to her chest like a shield, and walked to the bench under the tree like a brave prisoner mounting the gallows.

Raquel turned her back to the pair of lovers, caught in a dilemma. Her presence in the courtyard was necessary to their conversation; if she left them alone, she knew that Bonafilla would flee after her. But in the quiet of the afternoon, by some trick of the warm air, or where she was placed, she could hear every word they spoke. To move farther away would tell them that she had heard what they were saying. She bent resolutely over her work and pretended deafness.

"Did you have a pleasant walk this afternoon?" David was asking.

"I stayed in," answered Bonafilla promptly. "I had many preparations to make for tomorrow," she added.

"Just as you have stayed in every other afternoon that you have been here?" said David in a cold voice.

"May I not leave the house from time to time?" she said defiantly. Raquel turned enough to be able to see her tossing her head as she always did when checked, and suppressed an urge to call out a warning to her. Bonafilla had elected the potentially disastrous strategy of attacking an opponent whose strength and reactions were unknown. "I never go out uncovered or alone. I need air and exercise, like anyone else."

"You seem to dislike air and exercise when the family takes it," he said, watching her closely, "or even your friend Raquel. You prefer to creep out of the house while everyone is resting. What sort of fool do you take me for, Bonafilla?"

"You have been spying on me," she said accusingly.

Raquel dropped her thimble and bent sideways to pick

it up, giving her a clear view of Bonafilla's cheeks scarlet
with anger and David's face white with rage.

"No, my beautiful Bonafilla, I have not. I do not need
to. You lack discretion as much as you lack virtue. It has
been hard to escape noticing what you are doing when all
the servants and most of the household see you." Suddenly
his voice changed, and his suppressed anger burst out in a
staccato of clipped, precise words. "I will not have a wife
who makes a fool and a cuckold of me, Bonafilla. No matter
how beautiful and no matter how rich. If you thought you
were buying a complaisant husband, you were wrong. Who
is he?" he snapped quickly.

"Who is who?" said Bonafilla, in a voice so breathless
Raquel could scarcely hear the words.

"Your lover. The man who followed you from Girona.
The man you meet every afternoon after dinner in the
square near the Corn Market. You make a poor liar, Bonafilla. Your behavior contradicts every word you speak."

"It is not what you think. I swear it, David. It is not."

"Unless you can explain yourself, Bonafilla, and provide
adequate proof of that, I promise you, that before the Lord
and in front of all the witnesses at our marriage, I will
repudiate you as a wanton. I take my leave and wish you
a pleasant evening."

He bowed stiffly and left the courtyard.

Bonafilla dropped her face into her hands and wept.

After a pause long enough to enable David to get out
of earshot, Raquel went over to Bonafilla, grasped her, not
gently, around the waist, and propelled her into the house
toward the stairs to their chamber. As they climbed, she
caught sight of the housemaid. "Go find Ester," she said,
"and tell her to bring a cup of wine to her mistress as
quickly as possible." Still steering the sobbing young
woman, she pushed Bonafilla into the chamber and down
onto a chair. "Stay there," she said. "Now, what is this
about?"

"David thinks——"

"Don't bother with all that," said Raquel. "Your conversation was so loud that I could not help but hear every embarrassing word. You said that it wasn't what he thought. I know what he thought. What was it?"

Ester opened the door, bringing with her a jug of wine, and another of cool water from the well. From under her apron she took two cups and set them down. She poured a generous amount of wine in each and filled the measure with water. She picked up one and held it to her mistress's lips. "Drink this, mistress," she said coldly. "Then you will be able to talk." She poured some in her mouth, giving her a choice of drinking it or spitting it out all over her gown. She drank, and the effort of swallowing interrupted her spasms of grief and vexation.

"Well," said Raquel. "What was it? If he is not your lover, if you did not meet him in Girona and arrange all this with him beforehand, how do you explain your behavior?"

"Is that what you think? It's not true, I swear it," said Bonafilla, looking aghast. "As far as I know, he's never been in Girona. And certainly I never saw him there."

"Then after the most trifling acquaintance on the road, a mere flirtation at best, you were willing to risk your marriage, your reputation, everything? That is worse."

"Excuse me, Mistress Raquel," said Ester. "But there was more to it than a trifling acquaintance. Is that not true, mistress?"

"I don't know what you mean, Ester," said Bonafilla, in full command of herself again. "And I won't be accused and questioned like a criminal by my own maid."

Ester ignored her mistress, directing her words to Raquel. "I wasn't with Mistress Bonafilla during that terrible storm. She found herself a place in the woods and I went back to the wagons because it was drier there. When I found her again, she was in such a state, mistress, as you couldn't believe. All wet and muddy and covered with leaves on her back and her gown all wrinkled and muddy too. And her shift covered with blood . . ."

"Of course I was muddy," snapped Bonafilla. "I had been curled up in a little space under a bough that I had to crawl into, and I scratched myself on the legs and arms getting in and out, and my face and hair . . ." Her voice was rising hysterically again.

"That wasn't what it looked like to me, mistress," said Ester, still addressing Raquel. "I wondered who was in that wood with her for all that time. But I never wondered what they were doing. I knew that."

Bonafilla's tears flowed again. She hiccupped, buried her face in a large square of linen that Ester handed her, and refused to look at the others.

Raquel picked up her cup, sat down on the bed, and stared at Bonafilla. "What do we do?"

"He cannot help but find out," said Ester. "What will *he* do?"

"I was so afraid of the storm," said Bonafilla. "I thought we were going to die and I was so afraid, I wasn't thinking . . ."

"Clearly not," said Raquel. "But that wasn't what puzzled me most. Why did you keep meeting him? Did you think he would rescue you from your problems? Were you hoping he would marry you?"

"No. It wasn't that, Raquel. You have it wrong, all wrong. He made me come to talk to him," said Bonafilla. "I wouldn't have, because truly David is the most wonderful man I have ever seen, but he said if I didn't come and if I didn't do what he wanted, he would make sure that David and everyone knew what had happened. He said he would furnish proof—"

"What proof beyond his word?"

"He took the little ring that I had from my mother. My

father will recognize it right away because he had it made for her . . ."

"You gave it to him," said Raquel.

"I wasn't thinking," wailed Bonafilla again. "I didn't know what I was doing, I was so afraid . . ."

"Then start thinking now," said Raquel, "and don't start crying again, or we'll never get anywhere."

"But what will I do tomorrow night?" she whispered in real terror.

"There are certain measures that one can take," said Ester.

"True," said Raquel. "But for anything like that, we would need help from someone here in the city, and that would be risky. Bonafilla will be living here."

"What are you talking about?" said Bonafilla, and began to cry even harder.

"I have to think, Bonafilla," said Raquel. "And I can't do it in here with you sobbing in my ear. I might ask my father. He will have ideas."

"No," said Bonafilla, covering her face again. "You can't. I'd die if you let him know."

"If someone doesn't come up with something, Bonafilla, everyone will know by Wednesday morning, I assure you."

"I will sit with her, Mistress Raquel," said Ester. "Go and consult Master Isaac."

+‡⇒ ⇐‡+

WHEN Raquel went out, she saw little Jacinta sitting on the bottom step of the flight of stairs leading up to the garrets. "*Hola,* Jacinta," she said. "What are you doing?"

"Listening," whispered the child. "Mistress Raquel, I would like to talk to you."

"Yes, Jacinta?"

"Master David gave me a penny to follow Mistress Bonafilla and find out what she did after he talked to her," said Jacinta.

"That was most unkind of him," said Raquel.

"Well, he has to know, doesn't he?" she remarked. "He's going to marry her tomorrow."

"Why are you telling me?" asked Raquel.

"Because you told her that you had to think what to do, and said you might need help, and I thought my mother could help you. She knows a lot about men," said the little girl in a matter-of-fact way. "If you want, I'll go and tell Master David that Mistress Bonafilla went to her chamber and cried until she fell asleep. It's true, almost, and he won't learn anything more from it. Then I'll fetch my mother. You can meet us in the square outside the *call*. She won't come inside the gate."

"Why?" asked Raquel.

"She never said," said Jacinta. "Just that she won't."

RAQUEL walked down the hill the short distance to the square and waited. Quick footsteps heralded the arrival of a veiled woman dressed soberly in a brown, light woolen gown, holding Jacinta by the hand. "This is my mother," said the little girl.

"Has she been helping?" the woman asked.

"She has," said Raquel. "I don't know what Mistress Ruth would have done without her."

"Well, it was not for Mistress Ruth that I sent her," observed the woman, "but I am glad that she finds her useful. I prefer to have her employed away from my house," she added. "She is old enough to know why. But Jacinta tells me that you are in need of my advice, as strange as that may seem. What can I possibly tell one like you, mistress?"

"I do not know that anyone can rescue us from our dilemma," said Raquel, "but Jacinta seemed to feel that you might be able to."

"Tell me what your dilemma is," answered the woman,

sounding amused at the situation. "And I will tell you if I have a solution."

Raquel laid it out as clearly as she could, and as briefly.

"What does the man want?"

"Money, I think," said Raquel. "She was so confused in her speech, and weeping so furiously that it was difficult to tell. At first I thought he wanted to marry her and claim her dowry, but I don't think it was that."

"I wouldn't think so," said the woman. "But gold to hold his tongue sounds more likely. So we have two problems. If it were simply a case of loss of virginity, there are ways of deceiving the most suspicious of men."

"I have heard of those," said Raquel.

"It takes a clearheaded girl to carry it off, though," said the other. "But the threat here is someone who lives in the city, wanting gold or he will tell the husband. He won't go away, you know. If she deceives her husband over her virginity, she is even more vulnerable. That man will have power over her for as long as she lives. Or at least until her husband dies."

"I have thought of that too," said Raquel. "What do we do?"

"There is a choice," she said calmly. "You can have him killed—and there are those who will do it for less gold than he wants, I suspect. Then you must try to deceive the new husband—what is his name?"

"David."

"Or you can have a serious conversation with David. Someone with a persuasive tongue must convince him that the circumstances were extraordinary, and then point out to him how lovely she is, how rich she is, and how very unlikely it is that she will ever do the same thing again."

"Which would you suggest?"

"As much as I think that vermin like her seducer would not be mourned, I prefer the second. It is cheaper and safer, since he may have told a confederate or a servant. Once the husband knows, no man will have a hold over her. The only danger is that the husband will repudiate her when he finds out."

"There is a real danger of that already," said Raquel.

"At least it cannot make the situation worse," said Jacinta's mother.

"Perhaps I could get my father to talk to him," said Raquel, quailing at the thought of doing it herself.

"I will talk to him. Send him to me at Esclarmonda's house. I will be there. And since I promised to let her know how her patient is, perhaps you would be kind enough to tell me."

DAVID did not return to the physician's house until halfway through supper, and when he appeared, he had a thoughtful look on his face. He greeted everyone with almost all his usual charm and courtesy, excused his lateness with a plea of last-minute business, and took his place beside his affianced bride.

THIRTEEN

ON the marriage day, Ruth, her sister, Dalia, who had come in from Elna, and Master Samiel Caracosa's wife took over the bride to prepare her for her wedding. With Bonafilla and Ruth, along with attendant friends and servants, at the baths, and David, Astruch, and Jacob occupied over a host of details, the house settled into a false calm. The baker's ovens had been afire all night to deal with the extra work caused by the wedding feast. The Caracosas' maid was hard at work with the cook and Jacinta, preparing dish after dish that would come from their kitchen. Leah was looking after the baby, the boy was sweeping, and Raquel, Isaac, and Yusuf were all in the sick man's chamber.

"How are the bride and groom, do you think?" asked the sick man. "I have not been able to avoid hearing the sobs and tears and angry words between them. It is like having my own traveling players to entertain me with drama and comedy, giving me something to think about besides my own small troubles."

"He greeted her with a certain affection in his voice this

morning," said the physician. "I also noted that she was at breakfast much earlier than is her custom."

"Perhaps in order to find out if she was really to be married today," said Yusuf, whose ears had also picked up the storms of yesterday. "But if you will excuse me, lord, I promised the cook to fetch some herbs from the market."

"And is she?" asked the sick man, once Yusuf had left the chamber.

"The women think so," said Isaac. "They are preparing her for a wedding. It's a great deal of work, my wife tells me, and it is effort wasted if the wedding does not take place."

"I think you're both very unkind to her," said Raquel. "Talking about her like that."

"Perhaps we are," said Isaac. "But I am pleased that he is going to marry her, no matter what she has done."

"You do not think he should repudiate her, Papa?"

"No," he said. "She has been frightened into her senses and will make a good wife once she has grown up a little."

"Did you know what happened in the woods, Papa?"

"Let us say that I knew that she did not spend that long hour during the storm alone."

"How did you know that?"

"Because when she was looking for a comfortable place in which to shelter from the rain, I heard her run right by us, pausing to notice that we were there. She is frightened by storms. If she had been alone when that first bolt of lightning struck so close to us, she would have rushed over to where we were. Therefore, she was not alone. She already had someone to reassure her. If you had listened to something besides the thunder and the rain, you would have heard them."

WHEN Yusuf returned, he delivered the basket of herbs to the kitchen, and cheerfully pointed out to the cook that he was not another kitchen lad when she tried to enlist his help again. "My master is waiting for me in the sick man's room."

"If you're going up there," she said, "you can take him something to eat. He had a very small breakfast." She handed him a bowl with spiced chickpeas in it and a small loaf, and sent him on his way.

━┼━ ━┼━

"I have brought our patient a little dinner," said Yusuf. "It is not much, but they are in a flurry in the kitchen. There will be much more later, señor, and I have instructed the lad to make sure that you get some of it."

"And where will you be, Yusuf?"

"I thought that I would go back to the market and see how my new acquaintances there are faring," said Yusuf. "If we are leaving tomorrow, it will be my last chance to see them."

"You are leaving tomorrow?" asked the sick man.

"You are in good hands here," said Isaac. "You do not need us. And you may go, Yusuf. But remember to comport yourself with caution."

"Yes, lord," he said obediently, and escaped.

As soon as the door closed behind the boy, Isaac turned to the sick man. "I had an interesting conversation with the Bishop regarding you, señor."

"And what could His Excellency the Bishop have to say about someone as unimportant as I am?"

"A great deal," said Isaac. "He had some curious misconceptions about you, but some of the things he said to me confirmed my assumptions of who you are."

"I am no one," said the sick man. "What misconceptions does he suffer from?"

"The greatest is that you are dead. Not only dead, but buried. And he is also convinced that you have a wife."

"I have no wife, I tell you. I have no wife. Please, Master Isaac, I beg you to remember that."

"Wifeless you may be, señor, but I assure you that you are not dead. You cannot deceive me on that point. I think it is time that you cast aside these masquerades and told me the truth."

"The truth can be the most difficult and dangerous weapon a man can use," said the patient. "It often destroys him who wields it more surely than it destroys his opponent."

"Nonetheless, I think I must know it."

"Can anyone hear us?"

"Except for those in the kitchen, we are almost alone," said Isaac. "Raquel, go to the foot of the stairs and watch for those who would listen to our conversation."

"Yes, Papa," said Raquel, somewhat reluctantly, and left.

"I believe that I told you in a feverish moment that I was married," said the sick man.

"You did. Married and to a rich woman. You were explaining why you owned a shirt of exquisite cloth."

"Ah, yes. That shirt. How the small things of life do betray one. Perhaps I did not mention that I married her for love and desire of her person?"

"You neglected to say that," said Isaac.

"It was just the beginning of my good fortune that not only did I win her person, but to my surprise, a substantial fortune. Her father was a licensed money-changer and a man with many investments in sound and profitable ventures. I knew that, but I also knew that he had a nephew whom he had taken into his business. I thought that most of his fortune would go to his nephew. I had not realized that he was planning to settle so much of it on his only child, both by dowry and by testament. It seemed that he approved of the match. He knew my family circumstances, and wished us to have a life as free from worry as can be in this world. I am glad the good man did not live long enough to see me now."

"I doubt if he would have cause to change his mind about you, señor. He appears to have been a man of good judgment," murmured Isaac.

"We will see," said the sick man. "Master Isaac, she is loyal and clever, as well as rich, and she loves me. We married, to the distress of those few noble relations I had left, and she has managed me and my affairs ever since. It is for her that I cannot die."

"A powerful motive, señor. But you are improving, enough to engender hope."

"There are other things that threaten my life besides my battered body. You do not know the entire history."

"Tell me, señor. We have all day."

"My wife—her name is Johana—suggested that I use some of her money to buy the fourth part of a ship's cargo, and lease one fourth of a ship from Bayonne, now at anchor at Collioure."

"The *Santa Maria Nunciada*." said Isaac.

"Did I say the name of the ship in my feverish ravings? No matter. I and my partners—there are eight others— acquired a shipload of fine linen, wool, and high-quality armor and weapons to go to the East. On her return journey, she was to bring back silks and spices."

"I have heard of this enterprise from other people," said Isaac. "It seems to be an important venture."

"That may be," said the sick man. "But because of the weapons and armor, the cargo required expensive export permits to get it out of the city and onto the ship. Otherwise it would have to be smuggled out. I was not willing to do so; it was not worth the risk, even if I had wished to defy His Majesty's edicts."

"And how did your partners think on this issue?"

"Our consortium had members from farther away who sent me instructions to negotiate legal permits, but I was the only member here in Roussillon who argued firmly against the dangerous but cheaper way. It seemed so foolish to me; the cargo we were shipping was worth a great deal. The cargo we were bringing back would be worth even more. Why risk it all for a few pieces of gold?" He stopped as if he expected an answer.

"Let me tell the next part of your story, señor," said Isaac. "Correct me if I am wrong. Your name is Arnau Marça and your ship, the *Santa Maria Nunciada*, is already well on her way to her destination."

"She has sailed?"

"More than a week ago, Don Arnau," said Isaac. "The day she sailed you were arrested and charged with attempting to smuggle weapons of war essential to the kingdom out of the county of Roussillon. A serious charge when His Majesty is at war. Do not interrupt me yet, señor, while I finish what I know of your history. These weapons and other materials were shipped without your partners' knowledge, your accusers said, under cover of an innocent shipment of cloth and foodstuffs. What you are accused of, stripped of its details, is treason, Don Arnau, a capital offense. You were about to be tried and no doubt, executed, when you attempted to break out of your prison. Am I correct so far?"

"Substantially so, Master Isaac."

"The story next asserts that you died in that attempt. Not only are you dead, Don Arnau, but apparently you are lying with your ancestors."

"That is not quite true," said Arnau. "As you can see. Could you pass the cup of water to me?"

Isaac picked up the cup of water and handed it to his patient. "How come you to be here, in Master Jacob's house?"

"To be convicted of such a crime, Master Isaac, would mean that not only would I lose my life, but also that my wife and the child she bears now would be disinherited and my estates would revert to His Majesty. My wife arranged my escape from the royal prison here in the city, most efficiently. Unfortunately one of the people she bribed told at least one other person. We were set upon and badly beaten by four ruffians."

"We?"

"Johana, my servant, Jordi, and I. Johana went for help, and after the brutes had been chased away, she and Jordi, whose injuries seemed lighter than mine, dragged me to Lo Partit, where a woman of his acquaintance took me in."

"The one who arranged that young Jacinta be sent here."

"The same. We spent two days with Esclarmonda. During that time she went off to the old clothes market and bought me everything I needed to sustain my role as an impoverished merchant from Carcassonne, but unfortunately neither she nor the drunken bonesetter she found to treat me were willing to take off my shirt, which remained to betray my origins to you and your daughter. She also managed to talk Master Jacob into taking us in. She felt that I might be safer in the *call* than anywhere else in the city."

"And your servant, Jordi?"

"To my endless grief, Jordi turned out to be in worse case than I was. Shortly after we arrived here, he died of the fever caused by a putrid infection of his wounds."

"That is difficult to guard against," said the physician, "and even more difficult to treat once it is established. I am sorry."

"Jordi had been at my side all my life. We were almost of an age, and as much friends as master and servant. It is he who lies in my place in the tomb built for my ancestors."

"But how could his body be mistaken for yours?"

"My wife took him back, declaring that he was me. Jordi bore a strong resemblance to me, Master Isaac. We could well have been brothers."

"Such resemblances do happen," said Isaac.

"True, and in our case, the resemblance was not surprising. He was the child of a Muslim slave girl, Felicitat, who belonged to my grandfather. Jordi was his child and thus, my uncle. In his will, my grandfather freed mother and child, and gave Felicitat a good dowry. She converted, married a man from the village, and had two more children. I spent my childhood with Jordi," said Arnau. "He was a friend, a companion, a teacher to me. We were a year apart in age, and Felicitat looked after both of us until I was nine. Then my grandfather died, she married, and I was sent out as a pageboy to a cousin's estate. I begged to have Jordi come with me, as a personal servant, and a year or two later, he was sent to me. We remained close friends, even after becoming master and servant."

"And he saved your life."

"Twice, Master Isaac. Once on the night we were attacked, and then again by lending me his person in death. It is most fitting that he should lie in the tomb of our ancestors, for he was the bravest of my grandfather's three sons."

"But you cannot come alive again without risking immediate death," said Isaac. "That is a difficulty. Tell me, Don Arnau, who is your enemy?"

"My enemy?"

"You know that you have an enemy. Who accused you of smuggling vital materials in time of war? And did the ship contain them or not? Who followed your progress so closely that he knew you were about to escape and tried to kill you as you did so? Who went to the trouble to discover that you were here, disguised as a Jewish merchant from Carcassonne? Who sent an agent of the Inquisitor to visit this house? You are most fortunate that Father Miró is an intelligent and thoughtful man."

"I have spent endless hours asking myself those very questions, Master Isaac, and meditating upon vengeance."

"Vengeance is a worthless dish if there is no one to eat it, Don Arnau," said Isaac.

"Someone has tried to strip me of everything—those I love, my health and strength, my possessions, and my very life. I feel I am owed a measure of vengeance, my excellent physician."

"First you must recover your health," said Isaac.

TWO of the three men accustomed to meet there rode into the quiet grove and dismounted. "Where is the hooded man?" asked the slighter of the two. "I thought he wanted us to meet him here. I must return to the city very soon. This is most inconvenient."

"He did," said the tall one. "But he too has heavy duties to fulfil that cannot be ignored. Much heavier than yours, my friend."

"Isn't he rich?" asked his companion. "What could he have to do?"

"Even rich men have people to answer to," said the tall man carelessly. "But he told me to tell you that you are needed tonight, and then, if all goes well, you will be paid off and may do what you wish."

"Do what I wish? But what will that be?" said the slight man in a panic-stricken voice. "I can do nothing here. I am afraid to slip away from the house that employs me and walk in the streets. The priest knows who I am, and as you well know there are others who can recognize me."

"I have a simple suggestion. When we have accomplished what must be done tonight, you return to wherever you came from. Our employer is a generous man; you will not be in want. But don't worry about the priest. I have taken care of him."

"What do you mean?"

"Permanently. It doesn't matter now that he knew who you were." The tall man gave him a wolfish grin.

"May God forgive us!" said the slight man, crossing himself and murmuring a prayer under his breath. "A priest! How could you do such a thing?"

"It was very simple," said the other. "Now—this is where we are to meet," he added briskly, and the two men sat down in earnest conversation on a piece of fallen log.

FOURTEEN

JOHANA moved restlessly from her sitting room out into the gallery. The stone-paved passage was deserted, but a murmur of conversation drifted up from three ladies seated below in the courtyard. Margarida was not one of them. She breathed a sigh of relief and came down the steps.

She had spent the night in hours of painful wakefulness alternating with snatches of troubled sleep. Her talk with the shrewd-eyed Dominican had been profoundly disturbing. Living in the palace had given her an illusion of safety, allowing her most of the time to ignore life outside its gates; she had erected her own inner walls to protect her from that reality, and to prevent her from dwelling on bitter losses and chaos to come. Father Miró's words, far from bringing her comfort, had destroyed her flimsy walls and left her nothing in their place.

"He is alive and not in prison," she had said stubbornly. "I have done that. I wrote to the procurator; he will not act. I have begged the Princess to intercede on our behalf.

What else can I do? I dream of fleeing the country as soon
as he can move. And perhaps we can."

"Much more can be done to protect him, my daughter,"
he had said. "What you have tried is only a beginning.
Now let me take up your burden for a while. I have already
written to one or two people who are likely to take my
plea seriously. You must not lose hope." But instead of
calming her, his words had destroyed her peace, as if hope
were a noxious tincture poisoning her mind.

And Margarida. Margarida, whom two days before she
would have trusted with her life. Except that she had allowed Margarida to believe that Arnau was dead. It was
only, she said to herself, because she feared that anyone
who knew the truth might inadvertently give him away,
let slip a word, say or do something that a suspicious observer could fasten on. And now she realized that the suspicious observer was Margarida, spying on her, lurking
behind the pillars, eavesdropping on her conversations. She
began pacing back and forth in the courtyard, unable to
think of anything else, when a groom headed purposefully
toward her.

"His Excellency, the procurator, would like to speak to
you, my lady," he said, bowing low. "If you would follow
me."

Huguet, the procurator of the region for the duration of
the King's absence while he waged war in Sardinia, had
established himself for the time being in a comfortable
apartment in His Majesty's wing of the palace. He nodded
his head when she entered, indicated that she should sit,
and waited until the groom had left.

"I received your latest petition for a review of the case
against your husband," said Huguet briskly. "Your late
husband. Allow me to say how sorry I am at your loss. But
the objections I had before have not disappeared."

"My latest petition?"

"The one I received yesterday," said Huguet.

"Yesterday," said Johana, feeling herself shrink into her chair. Either the man was mad, or she was mad. There had been no petition. She could not have written out another one, could she, and forgotten? "I had not expected it to be considered so quickly," she said, truthfully enough.

"I did not wish you to suffer long while awaiting a response," said Huguet.

"Thank you, my lord," she murmured. "Can you tell me what will happen now?"

"The other owners of the *Santa Maria Nunciada* are petitioning for a hearing into the matter. At that time the various questions of ownership and liability will be examined and decided. My secretary will be able to explain it in greater detail. I should add that your condition," he continued, "protects you for the time being from prosecution."

She walked slowly back down to the courtyard, puzzling out the interview. Who had advanced a further petition to him, now rejected? And for what reason? So that they—whoever they were—could swear that the case had been considered from every angle? Clearly Huguet's aim was to discourage her and then to terrify her with talk of prosecution. Were they hoping to chase her from the country before the child was born to prevent her from pursuing her case? Three days ago she would have laid out her arguments in front of Margarida, and listened to her friend scoff at her fears while warning her of unseen traps at her feet. Now she had no one to talk to but herself.

Father Miró had told her that she must visit her husband. In vain, she had laid out the reasons why she should stay as far away as possible from him. She had told him that she would be followed, that it would be agony for both of them, and that it would arouse the suspicions of everyone in the palace. The Dominican had shaken his head and said, "Go to him."

In her solitary confusion, she yearned to go to him, to throw all her problems into his care in spite of the terrible risk. It puzzled her Father Miró should have ignored the dangers; either he wished them both taken, or he knew, for some reason, they would not be. "Then go," she whispered to herself, "but cautiously." She could not go alone. If she took Felicitat, they would believe she was trying to run away before the baby came, heading east out of Roussillon to escape prosecution. Or worse, they would realize that she was going to her husband. She would have to leave Felicitat here as a token that she was returning quickly. She would take one of the maids. And she must slip away while Margarida sat with the Princess in her vigil over her wounded spaniel.

YUSUF drew near the Corn Market looking for his old friends the porters. When he first caught sight of them, the group of dice players seemed to have grown considerably in size and number since the day before; as he came closer, he realized that there were only two unfamiliar faces, but attached to such large bodies that they themselves were sufficient to create a crowd. It took the length of a heartbeat for him to swerve off his path, heading past the Corn Market toward the Fish Market. Years before, when a bloody uprising had cast him loose, a friendless child in a strange land, he had learned caution even before the language of the country. Now he strolled slowly by, some ten strides away from the gamblers, nodding politely in their direction as if he were thinking of more important things.

"And there is the lad I was telling you of," said el Gros to one of the newcomers. "Come over here, Yusuf. Come and meet the stupidest porter at the Corn Market."

Far from taking offense, the porter looked over at Yusuf, grinned, and nodded. Yusuf stared for a moment, coughed to cover up his confusion, and smiled cheerfully in return.

Although the new porter was almost as big as el Gros, he was a pitiful sight. One eye was swollen shut and surrounded by a rainbow of colors shading from red through purple and into yellow. Various spectacular bruises showed through his torn clothing. He was further decorated with a long scratch down his cheek, a filthy, blood-soaked bandage wrapped around his forehead, and another tied around his hand.

"Isn't he pretty?" asked Ahmed.

"Pretty," said the Englishman, and broke into gales of laughter.

"He's learned another word," said Ahmed, pointing at the Englishman, as proud as a mother with her firstborn.

"You know who did this to me?" asked the bandaged man. Yusuf shook his head. "El Gros," he said, and began to laugh almost as much as the Englishman. "El Gros did it."

"And you're not angry?" asked Yusuf.

"Why should I be angry?" asked the bandaged man. "Someone paid me very well to get these bruises, and then someone else paid him well to give them to me. He didn't know it would be me."

"Yes, he did," said Ahmed. "Didn't you, Gros?"

"Who else would it have been?" said el Gros. "It was like this," he said to Yusuf. "If you can believe it. A man came in here and offered a lot of money if three or four would help him kill someone who was escaping from jail. He approached me first—"

"That's because he's so big," said the bandaged man, "and everyone knows there's no one better in a fight, even if he doesn't like fighting much."

"He approached me first, and I asked him how he knew this man was escaping."

"When he talked to me," said Roger without looking up, "he said that he had heard about it at the fish market."

"He told me he'd heard about it from one of the jailers,"

said el Gros. "So I asked him when the escape was going to be. I mean, who wants to sit around outside the jail night after night? And you know what he said?" asked el Gros.

"No," said Yusuf.

"He told me. The day, the hour, the place. I asked him how he knew, and do you know what he said?"

"He told him it was because he had arranged the escape himself," said Ahmed, yawning.

"Clever, isn't it?" said el Gros. "Arrange an escape and kill a man as he's doing it."

"But why?" asked Yusuf.

"He said it was because the prisoner used to be his friend, and he had betrayed their friendship by seducing his wife. He wanted vengeance. And this idiot believed him."

"I never," said the bandaged man, with injured pride. "But I needed that money," he said. "He paid me a lot. And I got him and another to help. I had to pay him some of it," he added, nodding to his companion, who remained squatting on the ground, staring at the dice. "El Gros hit the other one a little too hard, so I never had to pay him."

"Did you?" asked Yusuf, turning to el Gros.

"Maybe. Maybe it was the wine he'd been drinking. Anyway, he never got up again," said el Gros.

"The man who hired us promised us more afterward," said the bandaged man, "but the cheap bastard never gave it to us."

"I told him not to do a thing until he got his money," said el Gros. "I know that kind. They never pay once they have what they want."

"I did too," said the bruised porter, looking as pleased as a man with a mangled face can.

"I understand that. What I don't understand is why you beat him and his companions," said Yusuf, turning to el Gros. "Was the prisoner a friend of yours?"

"A friend of mine? Certainly not. I never meddle in affairs between a man and his wife. Anyway, I don't mind a little squabble, but he wanted the man dead. That's serious."

"Anyway, if he'd left the prisoner in there for a few days, the executioner would have taken care of his vengeance for him," said Ahmed. "Free."

"I don't understand," said Yusuf. "Who would hire you to do something like that? Why not just leave the man in prison?"

"He didn't say. I didn't ask. Why do you want to know?" asked el Gros.

"He was a foreigner," said one of the others. "Some of them have strange ideas."

"You're a foreigner too," said another. "Do you have strange ideas?"

"Not that kind," said the first man. "I've seen him somewhere before, but he's not from the city."

"That's right," said el Gros. "You can tell from the way he talks. I didn't like him much. But it's a good thing I didn't say yes, because that night, someone—a nice lady it was—came along here and asked me to help her husband before they killed him. So I chased them away. I gave this one," he said, ruffling the bruised man's few uncovered locks of hair affectionately, "a few little knocks so he could go running off without looking bad, that's all. And she gave me a fistful of money for my help. I got paid anyway." He grinned. "I had some help too," he said. "Only I didn't have to pay mine."

"You know who helped him?" said Roger. "It was a priest."

El Gros laughed. "It was. He came along with his big preacher's voice and a cudgel. That's how my friend here got a sore head. I wouldn't have cudgeled him on the head."

"Was that the same priest they brought in this morning on a cart?" asked Ahmed.

"There are as many priests around here as fleas on a dog," said el Gros. "And unless mine grew smaller and changed his name in the last week or so, it wasn't. That carter said the one they brought in was Father Miró. Everyone knows him," he said in explanation to Yusuf. "He's a preaching friar. He's been around the city for months. He's about the same size as Ahmed here, and the one who helped me was as big as I am."

"Father Miró?" said Yusuf. "Is he dead?"

"As dead as you can get," said Ahmed. "They found his body in a stream. He'd tumbled from his mule, they said, and died from the fall."

"Trust a priest to die falling off a mule," muttered Roger.

"He didn't," said Ahmed. "The man I talked to was the farmer who found him, and he said he looked like he'd been thrown off the cathedral tower onto the stones of the square, not like he'd tumbled a few feet down a slope into a brook."

"I knew someone who died from a couple of broken bones just stumbling over a cobblestone on the street," said one of the others.

"We all knew that old fool," said Ahmed. "He was a sick old drunk, as skinny and yellow and dried up as a dead leaf. Father Miró was as strong as English here," he said, pointing at the Englishman with the unpronounceable name. "He used to move around the city like a whirlwind. Once I saw him pick up an injured man and carry him all the way up a hill into his house. Nothing frail about him."

"I helped move his body from the grain cart to a litter," said Roger. "He looked like he'd been beaten by ten men with iron cudgels."

"So did I," said another. "He's right."

"Someone murdered him," observed Roger. "Who was

he after right now?" And they all turned inquiringly toward Yusuf, except for the Englishman, who hadn't understood.

◆━━ ━━◆

WHILE Yusuf was listening to the wisdom and the gossip of the marketplace, Raquel sat on a bench near the staircase to the sick man's room and alternately daydreamed and dozed lightly in the hazy sunlight. A slight bustle in the front of the house—a door opening and closing, voices murmuring in conversation—roused her from her semi-slumber. She stood, listening carefully, and then ran halfway up the stairs. "Papa," she called softly. "There is a visitor."

The murmur of conversation from the sick room ceased immediately. Raquel went back to the courtyard and turned toward the door leading into the front of the house. The boy opened it, saying over his shoulder to someone standing behind him, "I will ask if you can see him, mistress," and ran across the courtyard to consult with Raquel. Hard on his heels came the visitor. She was dressed in mourning, heavily veiled, and heavy with child.

"Forgive my breaking in upon your peace, mistress," she said, panting slightly from her exertions. "You are Mistress Ruth, wife of Master Jacob Bonjuhes?" She took a deep breath, pressing her hand on her side. "May I sit down, Mistress Ruth?" asked the visitor. "I have walked quickly—foolishly quickly—across the city to see a patient of yours. I have been told on excellent authority that he is here. Please, Mistress Ruth, I must see him. If you will send a message to him, and take him this," she said, struggling to remove a ring from her finger, "I am sure that he will say he wishes to see me. I am his wife, Johana Marça."

"Did you understand that message?" Raquel asked the boy. He nodded. "Then take the ring. Be very careful of it, give it to the sick man, and tell him the message."

"Please, my lady, sit down," said Raquel in some confusion. "But I am not Mistress Ruth. I am Raquel, daughter of Isaac of Girona, the physician who gave some assistance to Master Jacob in caring for your husband."

"Father Miró spoke of you, Mistress Raquel, and of your father when he told me what good hands my husband had fallen into. I am most grateful for everything that you have done."

"Thank you, my lady. He is not healed yet," said Raquel, "but he improves every day."

"I fear hope like the plague," said Johana. "It kills me as surely, Mistress Raquel."

The boy came running down the stairs, jumped the last three, landed on one foot and both hands, got up, and raced over.

"My lady," said the boy carefully, "your husband bids me tell you to come up to his chamber in all haste."

"Thank you, lad," she said, slipping a penny into his scratched and dusty hand.

"Go to the kitchen and ask the cook to send up something cool to drink," said Raquel to the boy. "I will show you to his chamber, my lady," she added.

⊷ ⊷

JOHANA walked into the chamber, lifting her veil from her face and tossing it back. Raquel introduced her father quickly and retired discreetly to the far corner of the chamber where he had been sitting and joined him. Johana Marça sat down in the chair by the bed, her eyes fixed on her husband. "Arnau," she murmured, her face wet with tears.

"Johana," said the sick man. "My dearest. I cannot believe it is you. When I saw the ring, I greatly feared it had been sent by someone who had wrested it from your finger to entrap me."

She dropped her head on the cover next to his chest and

said something incomprehensible. He stroked her hair with his uninjured hand and murmured soft and comforting words. At last she raised her head, wiping the tears from her face with a piece of silk that she drew from her sleeve. "I am well," she said. "Now that I have seen you I am well. I have not dared to send a message or to make the least inquiry about you, and I have been sick with apprehension these past two weeks."

"Are there no reliable messengers at the palace?" asked her husband.

"There are, Arnau. But I begin to believe that someone watches every move I make at the palace, noting everyone I speak to and listening to all my conversations." She halted, distress in her voice, steadied herself and went on. "I felt it safe to come out today because of Father Miró. He assured me that he has written letters on your behalf to men of power and influence, but he would not tell me who they were. And then he said that I must come to visit you."

"You came across the city alone?"

"I brought a maid from the palace. She is waiting for me in the square in front of the church of the Preachers. The less she knows about my business here, the better."

"Why does she think you're here?"

"To borrow money, of course," said Johana. "What other reason could I have to come into the *call*?" she asked innocently. "I confessed that I needed to visit a moneylender and asked her for the name of a discreet one. I bribed her to stay quiet, and then, to make sure that she did not forget it, swore her most solemnly to secrecy. She is very pleased to think that she has such a weapon against me."

"How long will it take her to sell that information?" said Arnau, grinning.

"As long as it takes her to catch her breath and take off her cloak. I think she has the notion that it will go badly for me if anyone at the palace finds out that I am so poor I must haunt the moneylenders."

"Who is watching you?"

"I am not sure. I thought at first it was Puigbalador."

"Bonshom? I don't believe it. Why would he be watching you?"

"Why not?" said Johana. "Everyone now believes that you are dead; until that maid gets back to the palace with her tale of moneylenders, they also think I am mistress of a large fortune. Bonshom has already offered to lend his skills and influence to enable me to reclaim your estates from the crown."

"Has he? How very certain he must be that the judgment will go against me," said Arnau. "Because as far as I know, they are mine still. But my dearest," he said with a puzzled frown, "what good would it do him? Even if I were dead, there is his lady wife, poor creature. Unless he throws her from the tower he cannot gain our wealth through marriage."

"I grow cold to think what might be in his mind, Arnau. Sometimes he seems the soul of gallantry, and others, pure evil."

"You have been too much alone, my love," said her husband. "You should not brood on these things."

"How can I not? Arnau, the other person who seems to be watching me," said Johana, and stopped, unable to carry on.

"Yes?" said Arnau.

"I can't bear it, Arnau," she said. "I think it is Margarida. Someone overheard my conversation with Jacinta, when she came with your message on Saturday."

"Who? Margarida?"

"It was someone close to the Princess who must have been among the trees in the orchard, listening. The Princess knew everything that we said to each other. Fortunately Jacinta spoke of you only as my faithful servant."

"Which I am, my love. But I told her to call me that. It seemed safer."

"I thank heaven that you did. But Arnau, the only person in the orchard at any time that Jacinta and I were there was Margarida. She said that she had just come in at the door from the palace. Margarida, who told me to be forthcoming and friendly to Puigbalador, no matter what I thought of him. Arnau, tell me, is he your enemy? Have you quarreled with him in the past over a woman? Tell me. I won't be angry. I never thought you were a monk before you met me. I have to know."

"Bonshom? He has no reason, I swear, to be my enemy. He is something of a rogue—a gambler and a chaser of women, but at heart he's a good fellow, Johana. I have never stolen his mistress or even sold him a lame horse. The only thing I've done that affected him was to hire his man of business after he left his employ. I cannot imagine that he resented the loss."

"Not if he had any sense," said Johana. "Cassa wasn't a very good man of business, my dear."

"Cassa's a pleasant fellow, Johana."

"A pleasant fellow isn't what you want in a man of business, Arnau. You want a man with a good, clear head who tells you what is going on and what he is doing about it. That way you can be merciful from time to time and stay the hand that otherwise was planning to chase the widow and orphan off their little plot of land. It is a good thing that you dismissed him. Once all of this is straightened out, we must replace him with someone competent."

"What are you talking about? I didn't dismiss him."

"You have forgotten, perhaps," said Johana, looking at him in some alarm. "It was when you started to load the ship, he told me. He must have done something wrong and you dismissed him. He came back, packed his things, said that he had been paid off, and left."

"I too heard that tale, Don Arnau," said the physician,

still sitting quietly on the other side of the room with his daughter. "I find it an alarming one."

"Do you think my husband has lost his memory?" asked Johana.

"No. I think your husband remembers with great accuracy everything that has happened."

"Then our man of business decided to save his own neck at the expense of his master's," said Johana. "For he said nothing of it until everyone believed that Arnau was either dead or dying," said Johana. "And could not deny the tale."

"Did I not tell you she was clever, Master Isaac?" said Arnau, looking over at Isaac. "Her clear eyes look straight into every man's soul."

"Indeed. Her ladyship is a treasure of wisdom and virtue."

Johana drew a deep, sighing breath and frowned. "But Cassa's behavior, although despicable, is understandable. Bonshom's is not. He is behaving oddly. Although I still cannot imagine why Bonshom would be your enemy, my lord," she said. "I do not know enough about him."

"I have decided—and I have had little to do lying here but think about all of this—that I must have been attacked by someone seeking to attach my possessions, such as they are, onto his. Perhaps someone who covets the castle and thinks that the King, in gratitude, will pass my estates and my fortune, or at least some of it, on to himself. And not knowing much about your strength and cleverness, he might even plan to marry my wife and gain her fortune to go with it."

"And Puigbalador has a wife already," said Johana.

"Not only does he have a wife, but he has vast amounts of land—more than he needs."

"No man thinks he has enough wealth, whether in gold or in land," said Johana.

"Do not distract me, my love, with disputations. Wait until I am stronger," he added almost playfully. "The person I most strongly suspect is Pere Peyro. His wife has been dead these ten years, and so he is free to marry. He speaks softly and gently, but nothing moves him so deeply as money. Have you noticed that?"

"That could be said of most of them," said Johana. "Felicitat insists that, of the members of the syndicate who came to the meetings, Martin and Don Ramon seemed to her to be the least trustworthy."

"I love Felicitat with all my heart," said Arnau. "I would trust her with my life and with all my darkest secrets, but I do not think she knows a great deal about such things."

"She is a clever woman, Arnau," said Johana. "She understands people."

"Martin represents a viscount who does not wish his name revealed, and Don Ramon Julià is a gentleman of excellent family. As investors they were recommended by Huguet, the procurator, my dear. They are solid, wealthy, honest men."

"Unlike the procurator himself," said Johana.

"What do you mean?" asked Arnau.

"He has not been very . . ." she began and then changed her mind. "I have heard worrisome tales about him at the palace."

"My lady," said Isaac, "may I ask you a question?"

"As many as you like, Master Isaac," she said.

"Could you tell me everything that happened on the night that you and your servant helped your husband escape from prison?"

"But I have told you that already," said Arnau.

"Lady Johana saw what happened from another point of view," said Isaac. "It will be useful to hear about it."

"If you wish, Master Isaac," said Johana, and began to explain clearly and with apparent calm, the events of that night. Her voice trembled when she reached the moment of the attack, and her panic-stricken rush for help. She stopped, unable to continue. Then she drew a deep breath, and started again, completely composed. When she reached the visit to Esclarmonda's little house in Lo Partit, Isaac stopped her. "I think I know what happened from then on. But, please, Lady Johana, tell me. When you speak of bribing shopkeepers and jailers, did you do that yourself? Or send your servant?"

"I certainly didn't do it myself," she said. "It didn't seem wise. I sent my . . ." Suddenly Johana stood up and moved restlessly about the room.

"Come back here, my love," said Arnau. "Do not stand over there where I cannot see you. Are you angry that we keep going over the same things again and again? But how else are we to find the truth?"

"I am not angry at all, Arnau," she said. "I was not comfortable sitting there for a moment." She leaned, face forward, her hands clutching the windowsill, looking out at the courtyard. "It is nothing. I am a little . . ." She gasped and stood very still, grasping the edge of the stone so tightly her fingers were white.

Raquel, who had been standing silently beside her father, came over. "My lady," she said quietly, "are you ill? Or have your pains come on you?" she asked. "Please, sit down and rest."

"I am better standing," she said with effort. "At least for now." She took a deep breath and turned toward her husband. "There. It is over for the moment. Arnau, what have I done?"

"What have you done?"

"I have brought this on by walking over so quickly and then lingering for such a long time. I was a fool, but I could not bear to stay away any longer or to leave you sooner. I'm sorry."

"Do not trouble yourself," he said. "Surely children are born in the *call,* are they not? Come, sit here beside me and we will comfort each other for as long as you are able."

Lady Johana sat by her husband again; Raquel followed

and bent over toward her, talking softly. "Is this your first child, my lady?"

"No," she said. "Our first child did not live more than a few hours."

"Don't worry," said Raquel, trying to remember for how long Arnau's wife had been pretending that her pains had not started, and concluded that it had probably been ever since she had arrived. If the baby were not to be born on the floor of Arnau's chamber, it occurred to Raquel that some rapid decisions might have to be made.

"We can send you to the palace on a litter, my lady," said Raquel. "Or you may stay here. There is no difficulty. My chamber is roomy and pleasant. I can sleep elsewhere and Bonafilla will not need it any longer."

"Why?" asked Lady Johana, dragging herself back from her immediate predicament.

"Because she is being married this afternoon. If you stay, we will have two joyous occasions on one day. I shall make arrangements for the midwife and have the room prepared. And we must tell your maid, who is waiting for you."

"I wish to stay as close to Arnau as I can," said Johana firmly. "Have someone tell the maid to go to the palace and to send Felicitat with everything that is needed. You will find Felicitat useful, Mistress Raquel. She can look after Arnau or help the midwife, wherever she is needed. It was foolish of me not to bring her, but I was afraid that if people saw us going out together, they might realize we were visiting Arnau."

And thus, when the bride returned to the house to make her final preparations for her wedding, she discovered that her room was occupied by a woman in labor, a brisk and cheerful midwife, the youthful under-housemaid, and Raquel. Ruth, who was with Bonafilla, opened the door, looked around, and said without a hint of surprise, "Is there any way in which I might help?"

"We're doing nicely, mistress," said the midwife. "And

if I had any more help in here, I wouldn't be able to move."

"Where are my clothes?" asked Bonafilla. And with one accord, everyone in the room but Lady Johana combined to whisk her out of earshot.

WHEN Yusuf returned to the physician's house, the bride was ready to be taken to the synagogue for the celebration of the wedding and the subsequent feasting. It was to be held in the great hall and garden and the bride and groom were escorted by a good-humored crowd of the members of the community in Perpignan. Even those few who had no special fondness for the pleasant and skilled young physician or his brother would not willingly miss the feasting and merriment that they could expect from Mistress Ruth's household. The weather was as perfect as an October evening could be. The day had been hot and sunny; the evening breezes were carrying away just enough of the heat to make feasting outdoors a pleasure.

Yusuf raced off to wash and to change his clothing. By the time he had finished, Raquel and her father were coming out of the door into the street. Yusuf took her place beside Isaac, and she joined the women.

"I heard news in the market," said Yusuf, as soon as greetings had been exchanged with all those around them.

"What news?" asked the physician.

"Much, I thought, lord. Two of the porters whom I had not met before said that they had been hired to beat up our patient. They didn't know he was our patient, of course, or his name, but it happened on the same night, in the same place, and under the same circumstances."

"I think we can say it was our patient, then. Do we know who hired them?"

"A foreigner," said Yusuf. "That's what they said. A foreigner they don't really know but have seen from time to time in the city. And they see almost everyone from where they sit."

"A foreigner. Then it would not be the man Don Arnau thought it was, since he believes him to be someone well known from here. But it was not a foreigner that I heard talking to the priest."

"Father Miró," said Yusuf. "That is the other news I heard. And it is bad news," he said. "For him, at least," he added, stumbling over the telling. "The priest who came to see our patient yesterday," he said. "The Dominican."

"I cannot escape knowing who you mean, Yusuf. Father Miró," said Isaac. "What are you trying to tell me?"

"He was found dead not fifteen miles from the city, lord. He fell off his mule and down a slope into a brook."

"You heard this as well in the market?" asked Isaac.

"Yes. From my friends the porters."

"Why tell you? Do they know that there was a connection between Jacob's household and that priest?"

"I don't think so. It was just a piece of news. It might not even have been the Father Miró we met, except that he was a Dominican, his name was Father Miró, and he left Perpignan yesterday to ride into Conflent."

"Did they say he was riding into Conflent when the accident happened?" asked Isaac.

"They did. And in their opinion, it was no accident. Two of them helped transfer the body from the cart that brought it to a litter and carried it to the Dominican house. Father Miró was not a giant, lord, but he was a strong, lively, well-fleshed man. The porters thought that he could not possibly have sustained such injuries in a fall of no more than five or six feet. And the farmer swears that's how far down he found him from the road."

"The road to Conflent?"

"Yes, lord."

"It is an evil thing, Yusuf, if that is true. He was a man of cool and cautious intelligence, who did not seem to act unless he had excellent grounds for doing so. They are rare in this world."

"You mean among the priests?"

"I mean among everyone. And why kill him? Unless it were for his honesty."

SHORTLY afterward, a lady of some consequence rode into the *call,* followed by two servants. She inquired from the gatekeeper directions to the house of the physician, Master Jacob Bonjuhes, and having been given them, went directly up the street.

She was admitted by the little housemaid and asked for Felicitat. "She is with the Lady Johana," she added, seeing the look of confusion on the girl's face. "She is her servant."

"The lady what's having the baby?" asked the girl.

"That's the one. Her servant."

"Certainly, mistress," said the girl, and headed off.

Felicitat came down, curtsied deeply, and said, "Lady Margarida. You wished to see me?"

"Yes, Felicitat. How is Johana?"

"Doing well, I think, my lady. The midwife seems pleased."

"I have come from Her Royal Highness, who wishes me to wait until the child is born. She is very concerned about Lady Johana."

"Certainly, my lady. I will find you a comfortable place where you may wait."

"Thank you, Felicitat." She looked around the hallway. "May I sit in that courtyard?"

"Of course, my lady," said Felicitat, and moved toward the door out to the courtyard.

Margarida laid a hand on the serving woman's arm. "Felicitat, wait a moment. I do not know how to say this . . ." She stopped. "Since yesterday, Lady Johana has not spoken to me. She avoids me whenever she can. I told Her Highness that I was not the best person to come here and that she should send someone else. She refused."

"I will ask Lady Johana if she wishes to see you," said Felicitat stiffly. "She may not wish to see anyone."

"Of course. I will wait here."

Felicitat returned to her mistress's chamber. "The Lady Margarida would like to see you, my lady," she said, in tones that were not encouraging.

"Send her to me, Felicitat," said Johana. "There is something I must say to her."

When Margarida came into the room, the midwife rose from the chair by the bed where she was sitting. "I hope I am not disturbing you, mistress," said the lady-in-waiting.

"No," said the midwife. "At the moment we're waiting. Waiting for something more to happen, aren't we, my lady?"

"We are," said Johana. "Margarida, I do not feel like much conversation, so I shall be direct. Did you tell the Princess about this house and the physicians?" A pain came on her, and she held up her hand to Margarida to wait.

The midwife mopped the sweat from her face with a cool cloth, and gently rubbed her belly. "She'll do now," she said.

"No," said Margarida. "How could I? I knew nothing of them. Is this the house where they brought Arnau . . ." She stopped.

"It is," said Johana. "But why does the Princess know about it?"

"I don't know," said Margarida. "I swear, Johana, I didn't tell her. Until she sent me I had never heard of it."

Johana cried out and took a deep breath. "It's getting worse," she whispered to the midwife.

"That's fine," said the midwife. "We're almost there now. Please, my lady," she said firmly, heading toward

Margarida as if she were about to eject her bodily from the room, "she mustn't be worried. She needs all her strength."

"God be with you," murmured Margarida hastily. She rose and left the room to wait.

FIFTEEN

THE wedding guests had fallen with gusto on the platters of fish, baked with herbs and oil, or served cold, spiced and preserved in vinegar and honey, and on heaps of small grilled sardines, along with as many sauces and beans and vegetables in oil, or vinegar, or salt as the cooks could imagine. When everyone's first hunger was abated, the musicians struck up lively dance music. The young men swept up David; the young women, Bonafilla, and the dancing began.

Isaac was deep in conversation with Astruch; Raquel was dancing; Yusuf sat where he was and slowly pulled apart a roll of bread. "Except for the food," said a voice in his ear that wavered between boy and man, "weddings are boring, don't you think?"

Yusuf turned and grinned. "They are. I'm Yusuf."

"I know. Everyone knows who you are. I'm Abram Dayot, Master Jacob's apprentice."

"Why haven't I met you before? Don't you live at his house?" asked Yusuf.

"Yes. You're sleeping in my bed."

"Where have you been?"

"He sent me home."

"Why?"

"I don't know. You can't talk to the master, but I asked Mistress Ruth and she said it was because there wasn't enough room in the house with all the guests for the wedding, but there's plenty of room. They could have put me and the servants up in the garrets. It's a big house. I think it was more than that," he whispered.

"What do you think it was?" asked Yusuf just as quietly.

"I think it was because of the strange sick man they've taken in. They didn't want me seeing who he was. Have you seen him?"

"Yes," said Yusuf.

"People say he's some kind of monster. Is that true?"

"No," said Yusuf. "Not at all. He's just an ordinary man," he added, in hopes of turning the conversation elsewhere.

"What does he look like?"

"He has dark hair and a dark beard. And his eyes are dark too, I think. But since the shutters in his room are closed, it's hard to tell."

"Like someone from the south?"

"Maybe. But he's no darker than you are and you can't tell from his speech. He never says much because he's too sick. How long before there's more food?"

"Not until after the dancing. But it's worth waiting for. Three whole roasted sheep, and dishes and dishes of poultry in different sauces, and kid—I was in the kitchens over there where they're finishing off the dishes. But don't tell anyone I said that."

"Of course not," said Yusuf. "Let's go and see if it's ready yet."

Abram Dayot stood up, unfolding a tall, thin, and gangly body. He tripped on the bench as he extricated himself from it and almost knocked over a jug of wine that was rescued by the man sitting next to him. "This summer I just grew and grew," he said, apologetically. "I never seem to know where my feet are."

"I wish I were as tall as you are," said Yusuf, and the two boys headed for the kitchen.

THE cooks had finished carving the roasted sheep, and the dishes of braised, broiled, and stewed meats that had been placed out on the tables were emptying. Servants passed back and forth, filling jugs with wine and bringing them to the table, along with jugs of water and cool, mint-flavored drinks to quench the thirst induced by feasting, dancing, and conversation.

A singer mounted a step near the musicians, the instruments struck up a tune, and he began to sing a song on the joys of marriage, neatly weaving the couple's names and circumstances into his narrative. The song became bawdier and bawdier, and Bonafilla turned scarlet with embarrassment and laughter, as any bride should. Cheers from the listeners applauded her blushes, and David placed his hand over hers.

At last the songs were finished, the boards were cleared, and bowls of fruits—fresh, dried, or preserved in honey and brandy—were brought in, along with dishes of sweetmeats, and huge platters of cakes and pastries. Clusters of the most beautiful dried raisins for all the luck they brought were heaped on every dish. The dishes were set down in such abundance along the tables that no one could complain that what he fancied was not within reach.

While the guests were thus distracted, the houseman to the physician's family made his way to Master Jacob's place at the table, and murmured something in his ear.

"Mordecai," said Master Jacob cheerfully, "has a cask been broached for the kitchen? And for the musicians?"

"Yes, Master Jacob," said the servant. "But you are wanted by someone at the door. It is important, he said."

"What can be more important than my brother's wedding?" said Jacob, who by this time had had rather more wine than usual.

"Jacob," said Isaac, leaning over the table from his place, "I think you may have a patient in urgent need of your help. Would you like me to go? I have not had so much . . ." He paused tactfully. "I have not so many obligations here tonight as you do. Where is Yusuf? He can come with me."

"No, let me see who this is. Come with me, old friend. It would do us both good to stretch our legs a little, even only so far as the garden gate."

They followed the servant over to the gate. It was a slow procession, broken by much lively conversation and raucous laughter from the guests as they passed by.

"Here is the man, sir," said the servant. "If I may leave you with him, there is much to do right now."

"Master Jacob," said a man standing in the dark shadows out in the unlit street. "My master is very ill, and would like you to come at once to his house. Or as soon as you can, for he knows that you must slip away from a wedding. He is very sorry, but he feels himself like to die if he does not have assistance."

"Who is your master?" asked Jacob.

"Master Pere Peyro."

"And who are you? You do not sound like Master Pere's man."

"I am only a messenger, Master Jacob. I believe Master Pere's man is looking after Master Pere."

"Can you tell me what is he suffering from, so that I may know what to bring?"

"I was told that it was a heaviness on the chest, and gasping—he can hardly catch his breath enough with the pain of it."

"Very well," said Jacob.

"I must return to say that you are coming," said the messenger, and the black shape melted into the blackness of the night.

"Well, Isaac, my friend," said Jacob, turning, stumbling in the darkness and catching Isaac's arm. "I apologize. I fear I have drunk more than was wise. Between worrying over my patient and worrying over whether this marriage would take place . . . It was foolish of me. Hannah!" he called. "Bring me some water."

A servant girl came running over with a pitcher and a cup. She poured some and handed it to him. He drank deeply, had her refill the cup, and drank again. Then he held out his cupped hands, she poured more water in them, and he splashed it on his face. "That is better. Find Abram for me, there's a good child," he said. "Tell him he is to go to Master Pere's at once."

"Why do you not let me do this?" asked Isaac. "I will take Yusuf and a servant who knows the way. It sounds as if someone should go at once."

"Not at all," said Jacob. "That messenger is a fool. Master Pere suffers from this from time to time. It is most disturbing for him, but it comes from fatigue and distress of the mind and is easily cured. He has had many worries recently."

"What do you use?"

"You know it well, my friend Isaac. It was from you I learned the recipe when I was a boy. It is your mixture of herbs to calm the spirits and ease pain steeped in warm water."

"You use the same ones I showed you then?"

"Yes, and he has a plentiful supply; I expect that by the time Abram gets there, he will be asleep. Everyone in the house knows how to prepare it. If he suffers from something else, Abram will send for me. He is resourceful and clever when he has to be."

⊱─⊰ ⊱─⊰

ABRAM listened to the maid's whispered message and turned to Yusuf. "I must go," he said. "One of Master Jacob's patients, a Christian and an important man, is having an attack."

Yusuf watched Master Jacob and Isaac make their way back to their table and sit down. "Is your master not going?"

"Oh, no. Master Pere has these attacks all the time. I know what to do. Come with me. That way we can grab more sweetmeats from the kitchen on our way out. Or would you rather stay for the dancing again?"

"More dancing?" said Yusuf, and stood up.

"We'll take Mordecai, Master Jacob's houseman, with us. He'll be very happy to get away from clearing up after the guests. He doesn't like it at all. Let's go find him."

As Abram stood, a shout went up from all the participants. "What is that?" asked Yusuf, looking around.

"Have you never been to a wedding before?" asked Mordecai. "They're taking the bride home to be bedded. It's splendid fun, but I have to go. You can stay for it, if you like," he added gloomily.

"I'd rather come with you," said Yusuf.

⊱─⊰ ⊱─⊰

BONAFILLA shrank behind her flimsy veil and David jested with the raucous friends and neighbors who accompanied them back to the house. This was as it should be, and everyone was pleased. A swaggering groom and a shrinking bride were what the crowds wanted.

"I hate these weddings where the bride looks so pleased with herself and trades jests with the musicians and the boys," said one of the women.

"You know why *those* brides aren't nervous," said her companion maliciously. "But Bonafilla looks more than nervous, doesn't she? She looks as if she were going off to be hanged."

"Well—she has no mother. Perhaps she doesn't know exactly what to expect. You'd think Mistress Ruth would have told her."

"Or her maid. I hear she has her own maid."

"She's probably filled her head with terrible stories of what wedding nights are like. Who's going to bed the bride?"

"Ruth and her sister from Elna, and Raquel, the bride's friend. There they go." And amid encouraging cries, shouts of laughter, and an endless string of suggestive remarks, the four women went into the house and up to the chamber prepared for the bride.

And inside the house, the shouts and laughter of the crowd outside blended into Lady Johana's final triumphant scream as she delivered a son into the waiting hands of the midwife.

"He's a lovely boy, my lady," she said. "Grand and big and strong-looking."

"I want to hold him," said Johana, and the midwife laid him, just as he was, on her arm. She handed Johana a clean kerchief and Arnau's wife gently wiped his mouth, nose, and face. "You look just like your papa," she said. "Just like him." Once again that day, tears poured down her face. "I am so happy. Go, someone, at once, and tell Arnau he has a son. And fetch Margarida."

✦━━━ ━━━✦

AFTER a considerable amount of time and effort from Ester, helped, or complicated, by assistance from the other women, Bonafilla was out of her wedding clothes and into her bridal shift of embroidered silk. They helped her into bed, pulled up the bedclothes, and turned to go. "Raquel," said Bonafilla, grabbing her hand and holding her back. "What will I say?"

"I don't know," said Raquel. "I would think it depends on what he says. But you'll just have to do your best. We can't stay and help anymore."

"I'm going to pretend to be asleep," she said.

"I think that would be a very bad idea," said Raquel. "Good luck," she added and left.

When David came into the bridal chamber, only one candle of the many that had been burning remained lit. It was on the far side of the room from the bed, placed so that the bed hangings, which were pulled back most of the way, shaded Bonafilla's face. He was still dressed in his marriage robe, a flowing garment created from a whole piece of new cloth. Its old-fashioned grace suited him well; in it his handsome appearance became fiercely commanding, so that he looked like a king or an ancient prophet come to pass judgment. He picked up the candle and walked over to the bed. Bonafilla was lying on her back, looking up at him, her eyes wide with fear. He turned around, lit three more candles, set the one he held down on a table where it would light her face, and sat near the end of the bed.

"Sit up, Bonafilla," he said. "I don't like looking down at people when I'm talking to them."

Startled, she scrambled upright to a sitting position.

"It's time we spoke honestly together. We haven't been able to do that so far."

"I was always—"

"Please," he said firmly. "For now let me speak. You may have all the time you need to answer me when I finish. I went through tonight's ceremony for one reason only. I was convinced by one who knows much of the ways of the world that to repudiate you just before the wedding would be not only cruel but foolish."

"Who?" asked Bonafilla in a small voice. "Was it Raquel?"

"No. What does she know of the ways of the world?"

he said. "This woman I talked to pointed out that I would be throwing away more than I was gaining. She told me clearly and plainly and without extenuation exactly what you had done on the journey to Perpignan, and why she thought you did it."

"You know already?" said Bonafilla and began to cry.

"Don't cry," he said impatiently. "Especially when the fault was yours. It wastes time and complicates things. She explained the reasons for your strange behavior since you arrived here. Was what she said true? I would like to know that."

"What did she say?"

"She said that he was demanding gold from you to keep quiet about his deed."

Bonafilla shook her head. "No. He didn't ask me for gold. He wanted information, more information than I could give him."

"Information?" he said, surprised. "Are you sure? Never mind. Let me finish what I want to say and then you can explain what it was he wanted later. This was yesterday evening that I talked to her. I thought for a long time about the things she had said before deciding to sup with you and the family. I decided that I wanted to observe you and your behavior to other people. Then I would think about what I should do. It was most enlightening. It was clear to me then that you think only of yourself—"

"That's not true!" said Bonafilla. "I'm always thinking of other people."

"But only to wonder what they think of you. Is that not true?"

"Perhaps. Sometimes," she whispered, shrinking back into the shadows.

"I could also see how frightened and alone you are. I realized that Raquel is not even a friend, just an acquaintance, isn't she?"

"I have no friends," said Bonafilla bleakly. He could

barely hear the voice emerging from the darkness at the head of the bed. "Not anymore. Or sisters. I had two friends, but they died of the fever, and then my mother died. Now I have just my stepmother, my brothers, and my father. I have been so afraid to leave them and come to a strange place."

"That explains even more about you. After a sleepless night I concluded that the woman was right. This is not a perfect start to a marriage, but it is at least an honest one. With the fortune left me by my parents, which is good, and your dowry, which is better, we can be independent and comfortable together. That is important. She pointed out to me that instead of knowing your virtues and talents and discovering your bad side, I will start by knowing your weaknesses and will learn your strengths. Now—if you are already with child—"

"But David," said Bonafilla, her voice desperate "if I am, we will not know. Unless you want to put me aside until we do know, and then make up your mind what to do with me," she added timidly. "It is your right."

He gave her a surprised look. "That is a brave answer. But not knowing is best for us and the child," said David. "As far as I am concerned, any child you bear from now until ninemonth after my death is mine, do you understand? The incident in the forest never happened. You are a virgin. Remember that. In addition to the promises we made to each other today, you must vow to me that you will keep this as secret as the grave."

"I promise, on my life," said Bonafilla fervently. "I never knew a man could be so kind."

"It is not kindness, Bonafilla. I simply decided that I wanted you more than I was upset by what I had heard. Now—there is one last thing to do."

"What is that?"

David drew a knife from his short, soft boot.

"What are you doing? You are not going to kill me?"

she said, drawing back into the corner of the bed. "After all that you said, you wouldn't kill me, would you? Please, David."

"Don't be foolish. You *are* just a child. She said that about you too." He flung back the bedclothes, pushed up the wide embroidered sleeve on his left arm, and grinning, ran the knife swiftly over the outside of his arm.

"What are you doing?"

As the blood rose in the narrow cut, he wiped his arm against her wedding shift, then pulled it up and dabbed her thighs, and then mopped up the rest on the sheets. "In answer to your question, I am saving my wife's honor," he said. "Now let me see if you are worth all that pain and anguish." He pulled her shift over her head, held up the candle, and looked at her. "Even if the only thing you brought me was your beauty," he said in awed tones, "without your honesty and courage, that alone is worth much much more than a small cut on the arm."

"Do you really think I'm pretty?" she asked nervously.

"I have never seen a woman so beautiful," he said. "Come, wife, bind up my arm so I can get out of my boots without bloodying everything else in sight."

Bonafilla giggled, and recklessly reaching for her best silk kerchief, she washed the blood off his arm and then bound up the cut. Her husband pulled her into his arms.

"Your boots," she whispered.

"This is no time to think of boots," was his reply.

AND in the morning, in spite of the tragic events of the night before, an even more puzzled Ester draped the blood-ied sheets to air over the edge of the balcony. Those who had gathered in the street for news at least learned what none outside the house had doubted—that the lovely young Mistress Bonafilla was a pure and virtuous bride.

SIXTEEN

ABRAM, Yusuf, and Mordecai the houseman made their way out onto the street. "We can save ourselves a penny at the gate by climbing out through a garden I know of," said Abram Dayot.

"Excuse me, young master," said the houseman, "but that is not a good idea. Master Pere has summoned the physician and will not expect him to be held up because he has been caught climbing walls."

"We won't get caught," said Abram. The houseman looked straight into his eyes, holding up his torch. "Very well, we'll go by the gate and stir the gatekeeper from his bed."

"It is not so very late, young master," said the houseman. "I doubt that the gatekeeper is asleep." And so they made their way over to the gate, stirred up the keeper, who opened for them, and headed off in the direction of Master Pere Peyro's fine house.

The main entrance door to the house gave directly onto the street. When Mordecai rang the bell energetically, it was opened almost at once by a manservant who looked surprised to see them. From the back of the house, they could hear sounds of laughter and animated conversation. "We have come to see Master Pere," said Abram.

"What can I tell him you wish to see him about?"

"He sent for my master, saying that he was ill. My master sent me—uh—ahead, to find out if there was anything I could do at once."

The manservant stared at Abram as if he were mad. "Master Pere ill? Sending for the physician? Master is in the garden, entertaining guests," he said. "He appears to feel very well. But come in. It may be that I am misinformed."

Abram and Yusuf filed in and sat in a small room off the hall. Mordecai the houseman stayed outside to wait for them and the manservant hurried off to consult his master. After a considerable length of time, Master Pere Peyro, even more dapper than he had been in Collioure, came into the room.

"Abram," said Master Pere. "What brings you here? My man said some nonsense about an urgent summons."

"A messenger came and said that you were near death, Master Pere," said Abram. "My master sent us on ahead. It seems that he was mistaken. We are sorry to have disturbed you."

"Mistaken? It seems to me that someone has played an unpleasant joke on all of us. I am no closer to death than I was yesterday, or will be, I trust, tomorrow. Have a glass of wine to make up for your pains," he said hospitably. "I would stay and talk, but I have guests to entertain."

"No, no," said Abram with dignity. "You are very kind but we will not stay. My master will be pleased to hear that you are well." And with a bow, he and Yusuf headed off to the front door.

Mordecai the houseman, his torch lit against the blackness of the night, was standing three houses down the street, deep in conversation with someone. "I'll bet you have no idea where you are now," said Abram to Yusuf.

"I know my way around the city," said Yusuf. "I can learn my way around any city in a day or two. Even Barcelona. Perpignan isn't as big."

"If I weren't here to show you, you wouldn't know what direction to go in right now," said Abram.

"Of course I would. Right up there," said Yusuf.

"Yes, but when you get to that square, then where do you go?"

"I have to see it first," said Yusuf, stubbornly.

"Go and see it," said Abram, "while Mordecai finishes his conversation with whoever it is. A penny if you can get there and point in the right direction."

"Done," said Yusuf, and headed up the street.

Abram called out to the houseman.

"Are we ready?" said Mordecai. "I'll be with you in an instant," he added and turned.

The man he was talking to waited for the houseman to be a step or two away. He raised his staff and swung it down toward Mordecai's head. It hit the side and glanced off, and the houseman fell to the ground, dropping his torch. The attacker stepped back, disappearing into the darkness.

"You," yelled Abram. "Stop!" and began to run toward the place where the attacker had last been visible. Mordecai stirred, and then reached over and snatched up his torch before it could roll into a gutter and quench its flame. He scrambled to his feet, still reeling from the impact of the blow, and leaned his hand against the wall of the nearest house. As Abram passed the entrance to a narrow alleyway, a pair of arms grabbed the apprentice around the chest and dragged him, yelling fiercely, into the darkness.

At the sound of Abram's shout, Yusuf stopped in the middle of the square and peered back into the darkness. In the uncertain torchlight he saw Mordecai looking sick and dizzy. The light from the torch flared up and died down, so that the scene appeared and disappeared like shadows on a gusty day with clouds. Abram was nowhere to be seen. Mordecai straightened up, regaining his balance, and swept his torch in a semicircle, searching for the apprentice, whose cries were muffled now. In its light Yusuf saw legs and feet kicking and struggling as they disappeared into an alleyway.

Yusuf drew his sword and ran back down the street. Abram's cries had stopped. "Are you injured?" he asked Mordecai.

"Not much. It is young Abram," he said. "He dragged him in there," added the houseman, pointing to a blacker spot in the blackness.

"Give me your torch and go for help," said Yusuf.

"Where to?"

"Master Pere's. I will go in and see what I can do."

Once inside the blackness he held up the sputtering torch. There was nothing visible but pavement and walls within its pool of light. Somewhere close by he could hear the dull, sickening thud of a weapon hitting flesh. There was no other sound—no groans, no cries for help, not even an involuntary gasp made by an unconscious man. Suddenly Yusuf felt small, unprotected, and sadly lacking in skill with his sword. He backed away to the entrance just as four or five men with torches and weapons issued from Master Pere's house.

"Down here," called Yusuf and stepped back to give them room.

But the attacker had taken care to find himself a alley with a bolt-hole at the other end. As soon as the bright torchlight fell on the other end of the passage, he fled, leaving Abram where he lay.

"It's Master Jacob," said the first servant. There was a sudden silence in which no one moved.

"No," said Yusuf, who had come in with them. "It's his

apprentice, young Master Abram." He knelt over him, and placed his ear gently to his chest to listen, as he had seen his master do so many times. Abram was drawing in light, shallow, uneven breaths, but he was still alive. "He is breathing."

"Fetch a litter," said Peyro rapidly to the man standing closest to him. "And have him taken to his father's house as quickly as you can, man. And carefully."

"Yes, Master. At once," he said, and suddenly the whole scene came to life again.

"This is a terrible business," he said.

"You're not safe on the streets after dark these days," said one of the guests.

Peyro shook his head and looked gravely after the men who were carrying the young apprentice back to the *call*. "Fetch me my cloak and my sword," he said. "And I need an armed man and two torchbearers. Give my excuses to the guests," he added. "I must pay a visit to my physician. If you are to return to Master Isaac in safety, you had better come with us," he said to Yusuf. "Bring your servant with you."

MASTER Pere was shown into the physician's study, supplied with wine and a dish of dried fruits and nuts for his refreshment, and left with Yusuf. The little maid had whispered to him that Jacob was at the house of Abram's family and that the wedding celebrations had broken up. Through the open shutters on the window looking into the courtyard, Yusuf could hear the murmur of conversation in which Isaac's distinctive, deeply resonant voice formed a bass line to the mixed choir of speakers. "If you will excuse me, Master Pere," he said, "I will fetch my master. The maid said he was with the physician when the message came. He can tell you more about how things stand than I can."

"Go, lad," said Master Pere, his bright-eyed cockiness vanished. "Fetch him as quickly as you can."

In less than a minute Isaac arrived in the study. "Master Isaac," said Peyro, "have you any news of young Abram? I cannot believe that such a thing could happen on my doorstep."

"I have just come from there," said Isaac, sitting down heavily. "When I left, his parents despaired of his life, and with cause. I assure you that Master Jacob and the lad's father are doing all that they can, but some injuries are beyond the skill of man to heal. These, I think, are such injuries."

"Why should anyone attack him? A boy? A harmless apprentice. It was not a random attack, Master Isaac. This was no group of drunken rioters," added Pere. "These men lay in wait for him."

"It was not for his purse," said Isaac. "That was not touched. Why they attacked him I do not know, but I am sure they intended his death."

A bell rang at the main door and the housemaid ran to open it to her master. "Master Pere is in your study, sir," she said.

"Thank you, child," said Jacob wearily. He raised his lantern to shine it on her face. "Surely it is time you were in your bed. Off you go." He walked into the study, poured himself a cup of wine, set it down on a table, and sat next to Isaac. "Good evening, Master Pere," he said. "What brings you to my house tonight? It is clear that you are not ill."

"How is the boy?" he asked.

Jacob shook his head. "Dead. I could do nothing for him. But I grow discourteous in my shock and grief. I have not offered you anything."

"No man could have saved him, Jacob," said Isaac. "With all the skill and desire in the world, no man could have saved your apprentice."

"His father said the same, skilled physician that he is. This is a heavy blow for him. And for me," he added in somber tones.

"I came to see you, Master Jacob," said Pere, "to ask about the man who bore that false message to you. It was certainly not of my sending, but I wish to know if it came from my household."

"I can tell you nothing, Master Pere. He was a black shape outside the gate on a dark night."

"I don't suppose you recognized his voice," said Pere.

"No. I noticed nothing about him." He looked up. "But I knew he wasn't Roger, your manservant. I remember now asking him who he was, and he said he was a casual messenger hired for the occasion, or some such words. Did he not, Isaac? You were there."

"Yes," said Isaac. "He was not very precise about who he was."

"If I had not had so much wine," said Jacob grimly, "I would have gone myself at once and the lad's life would have been spared. And I might have recognized the messenger."

"I expect that he took great care that you not recognize him," said Isaac.

"I will go home and question my household. How far is it into the night?" asked Master Pere. "I feel as if the approach of dawn is near. Has the moon risen yet?"

"I do not know about the moon, for I cannot see it, but it is not that far into the night," said Isaac. "The midnight bells will not ring for an hour or two."

"And the moon will not rise above the walls for at least an hour," said Jacob. "You will have a dark walk home."

"Moon or no moon, if I can do nothing to assist you," said Pere, "I should return. I am very sorry that such a thing should have happened."

"I will show you out," said Jacob. "I have sent the servants to bed." He ushered his guest from the room.

"Lord," said Yusuf, as soon as they were alone, "there is something that I forgot to tell you."

"And what is that?"

"Something else that the porters said today. In thinking of Father Miró I forget to tell you."

"Do not tell me quite yet. Wait until Jacob has gone into the courtyard."

"What if he does not? He will want to sit and talk to you, since tomorrow at dawn we leave."

"I think he will go into the courtyard," said Isaac. "He is most distressed and weary. He does not think of the fact that we leave tomorrow."

"I must see Ruth," said Jacob when he came back to the study. A cry floated down through the still night. "What is that sound?"

"It is a newborn child, Jacob, crying as they will," said Isaac. "The Lady Johana has given birth to a fine son. Do you hear? His mother holds him and he hushes already."

"When was he born?" asked Jacob.

"According to my daughter, as the bride was brought home to bed. Go, my friend, your wife awaits you in the courtyard. I have some arrangements to discuss with my apprentice."

"Lord," said Yusuf, as soon as Jacob was out of the room, "the porters told me that the foreigner who tried to hire them to attack our patient was the same man who organized the escape."

"The same man," said Isaac. "Were they sure of that?"

"They were."

"That is most interesting. Can we find these porters now, do you think?"

"They tell me they are to be found at the Corn Market until late into the night."

"Is it far?"

"No," said Yusuf.

"Then come, lad. Fetch a lantern and we will slip quietly out the door. Introduce me to your porters."

"HIST!" said Yusuf. "Gros! Are you there?"

"Who are you?"

"Yusuf," he said.

"Then I'm here," said a familiar voice.

"I have brought my master," said Yusuf. "He wants to ask you a question or two about the foreigner."

"I knew that man would bring me trouble," said el Gros as they approached. "Ah. You did not tell me that your master is the blind physician, Yusuf. They say you can work miracles, señor."

"Then what they say is not true," said Isaac. "But I can cure some things."

"What do you seek to cure that you need information about this man?"

"I seek to restore life to a dead man."

"Then I will tell you what I can."

"Answer me one question for now," he said. "Do I, Isaac of Girona in the county of Barcelona, speak like a foreigner?"

"Of course," said the porter. "You're not from Roussillon."

"Thank you," said Isaac and felt in his purse for a coin. He held it out. "You will have to take it," he said, "for I cannot see where to hand it. There is another coin to go with it if you can answer another question as well as the first."

"Ask your question, señor."

"Tell me what you know of Esclarmonda."

Isaac could hear nothing but the heavy, regular breathing of the porter. Finally, he spoke. "That cannot be done so quickly," said el Gros. "But I will try. I know her, since everyone knows her. I have heard many fantastic tales of her history—that she is the daughter of a Moorish ruler, stolen by slavers, or that she was the favorite of a French king who grew angry at her disobedience, but her voice tells me she grew up in the city. I know that she is quietly discreet and can be trusted further than most on this earth. If you seek pleasure from her, señor, I cannot help you tonight. No one has seen her for several days now."

"I thank you, good man," said Isaac, holding out another coin. "I wish you well, and I will no longer disturb your night. Farewell."

"Did he tell you what you wished to know, lord?" asked Yusuf as they walked back to the *call*.

"I am not sure that I wished to know what I heard, but I think what he said was important. Are you weary, Yusuf?"

"No, lord," said Yusuf, speaking something less than the truth.

"Good," said Isaac. "There is much to do tonight before we sleep."

✛══ ══✛

WHEN they reached the house, Jacob, Ruth, Astruch, and Raquel were sitting in the courtyard, speaking little, but unable to go to bed. "Papa," said Raquel, "where have you been? I came in to find you and suddenly you were gone."

"I should think that you were used to your papa's sudden disappearances," said her father affectionately. "But you had no cause to worry. Yusuf took me to visit some friends he has made while here in the city."

"Friends?" said Ruth. "Where do they live?"

"In the Corn Market, as far as I can tell," said Isaac.

"*In* the Corn Market?" said Raquel, moving over to sit next to her father. "Are they mice?"

"Indeed. Very large mice," said Isaac. "They live on grain

and see and hear all, understanding only what belongs to them."

"You are becoming too philosophical and difficult for me," said Astruch. "I think I will go to bed. Expound the meaning of the mice over breakfast and I will hear it with great interest. Good night."

Astruch left them still sitting quietly.

"I am afraid that, like Master Astruch, I am too weary to sit longer," said Raquel at last. "I shall go to see that Don Arnau sleeps peacefully, and that his lady needs nothing, then I will go to bed."

"That is very kind of you, my dear," said Ruth. "You spare me from the task."

"Wait just a few minutes, will you, my dear?" said her father.

"Of course, Papa. Can I get you something?"

"Not yet."

Another voice came out of the darkness from the door by the main hall. "You are all still up," it said. "I thought I heard you speaking."

"David," said his brother. "I did not expect to see you down here."

"I am thirsty," he said. "And hot. I knew you would have something refreshing to drink down here," he said. "A jug of mint and orange! The pleasantest way to quench my thirst after all that wine."

"But your wife!" said Ruth.

"Bonafilla is fast asleep, and will not wake before my return, I think. She has had a long and tiring day. And so have you, my sister. I cannot thank you enough for all your efforts on our behalf. No couple ever had such a splendid wedding. Even in the midst of my own delight, I could see how our guests enjoyed themselves."

"Thank you," said Ruth.

"But you look almost ill with exhaustion. Jacob, you must send her to bed."

"Yes, Ruth dearest. Please. You must rest."

And Ruth said her good nights as well.

As soon as her footsteps could be heard on the stairs to her chamber, David poured himself the promised drink and spoke again. "I have been waiting until the others went to bed, Jacob, because there is something that I must tell you."

Raquel froze with anxiety.

"That man," he said, "you know the one I mean, and I'm not going into the whole story, but what that man wanted from Bonafilla was not money, as we thought, but information about your patient."

"What kind of information?"

"His name, his ailments, whether he was married, how sick he was. She told him that she did not know any of these things—that she had never seen the patient, nor spoken to him, and that all she knew was that he was from Carcassonne and was a merchant. He pressed her with many threats, told her she had to find out, to get into his chamber and see him so that she could describe him."

"What did she do?"

"She lied to him, but he did not believe her."

"What could he threaten a girl like Bonafilla with?" asked Jacob.

There was a palpable silence. "I believe," said Isaac, "from what Raquel has told me, that he convinced her that he had information that could bring disaster on her father. Is that not true, my dear?"

"Yes, Papa," said Raquel, thinking quickly. "When she finally confessed it to me last night, she was almost mad with fear and distress. But she didn't say what it was he wanted. I'm afraid I came to other conclusions."

"What a vile human being," said Jacob. "To threaten an innocent with pain to others."

"And is she reassured now?" asked Isaac.

"Having passed the burden of her worries onto shoulders

better able to carry it, she is able to sleep in peace for the first time in days," said her new husband.

"I am delighted," said Isaac.

Jacob and David fell into low-voiced conversation. After a few moments the quiet was broken by an oath. "Dead!" said David. "Who could wish Abram dead? No one could have been so harmless and gentle."

"I cannot understand it. What is happening all around us?" asked Jacob. "What have we done to have these calamities visited on us?"

"Sometimes the smallest action will bring a string of calamities behind it," said Isaac. "Sometimes they come for no reason at all. For example, why did Esclarmonda send Don Arnau to you, Jacob?"

"Why? I told you. Because she thought he would be safer in the *call*. And he is. Not many strangers enter our single gate, and each one is noticed and watched."

"But there are other physicians. Why not one of the others? Why not Abram's father, for example? Did she pick you for a reason? Any reason?"

"I do not know," said Jacob uncomfortably. "Why does a man go to one physician rather than another? Perhaps one of her clients spoke words in my praise. I say again, I do not know."

"No doubt you are right. One of her clients will be one of your patients. Does Don Arnau know why you were chosen? Did Esclarmonda not tell his lady?"

"If they did, they did not tell me. But this can have no connection with poor Abram's death. Why should he have died and so cruelly?"

"I am not sure," said Isaac. "But it must stop. This man must be taken care of. I owe it to His Excellency, and now that Abram is dead, I owe it to you, my friend, Jacob. It has caused you great suffering." He turned to Raquel and spoke quietly. "Do you know where the child Jacinta sleeps?"

"Yes, Papa. In the alcove off the kitchen."

"Make your excuses and wake her, please. If she is willing, I need her assistance tonight. It is important."

"If it is important, of course, Papa," said Raquel, puzzled.

"I will see you later. There is much to be done before we leave Perpignan."

"What did Mordecai say about what happened?" asked Isaac, turning back to Jacob.

"Mordecai? I didn't bother asking him," said Jacob. "Since Yusuf was there and could tell me."

"It's always useful to see events through as many eyes as possible," said Isaac. "I suggest we ask Mordecai what happened."

"I will wake him," said Jacob wearily. "He sleeps close by, next to the kitchen."

Mordecai looked tired and miserable but he was awake. "I could not sleep, master, for the ache in my head and for thinking of what happened," he said.

"Tell us," said Isaac.

"Well," he said, "after Master Abram went in, while I was waiting, I was talking to a man who said he was houseman to Master Pere's neighbors. We were just talking," he said defensively, "about nothing much, when Master Abram came out. He and Master Yusuf were arguing about something—if Master Yusuf could find his way back here, I think. Master Yusuf was going to prove it by going ahead. That's all I remember them saying to each other that I heard. Then Master Abram called me, I turned to go, and heard that staff swishing through the air. I ducked, but he still got me here," he said, holding the side of his head. Master Abram yelled something and came down toward us. Then he just disappeared. I didn't see what was going on because I was trying not to get killed and all I had was the torch in my hand. Then Master Yusuf came with his sword and chased off the man who was trying to kill me—and I'll always be grateful for that—and sent me to Master Pere's to get help. They came rushing out, someone screamed, 'It's the physician.' And someone else said it wasn't, it was Master Abram."

"Why did they think it was me?"

Yusuf's voice penetrated the darkness for the first time. "They went into the alley with torches and saw him lying on the ground. He was wearing your cloak, Master Jacob. His own was too short, he thought, to wear on a professional visit, because he had grown so much in the summer."

"They wanted to kill me?"

"I suspected that," said Isaac. "And now it seems clear."

"But why?"

"Because there was no reason to kill Mordecai or Abram. You knew who your patient was. The only others to know were his wife, who was safely locked up in the Princess's quarters of the palace, the priest—"

"The priest?"

"Don Arnau told the priest who he was."

"Did the priest tell anyone?"

"He had little chance," said Isaac. "He was dead by nightfall. Otherwise the assassin knew and so did Esclarmonda. I hope he does not know about Esclarmonda. I must speak to her."

"We will go at once," said Jacob.

"No. This must be done very quietly. I will slip in alone. Jacinta will show me the way there."

SEVENTEEN

JACINTA was sitting in the hall, roused from sleep and waiting patiently for Isaac to come for her. "Jacinta," he said, "I must speak to Esclarmonda."

"She will not come to the *call*," said the child.

"Then we must go to her," said Isaac. "Will you take me?"

"Now?"

"Please."

"Yes, sir. We will have to give the gatekeeper a penny."

"I have pennies for the gatekeeper," he said. "Are you warmly enough dressed? The night is becoming chilly."

"I have my shawl, Master Isaac."

"Fetch a lantern and a candle."

"We do not need it," said Jacinta. "The moon has risen and besides, I know the way."

THE child moved quickly and silently through the streets. Isaac laid his hand on her shoulder, to better follow her movements, and carried his staff well above the ground to keep it from making noise by tapping against things. From time to time he would hear footsteps in the distance. Some Jacinta ignored. For others, she tugged lightly on his tunic and stepped sideways into a doorway, pulling him after her. Each time she did that, heavy footfalls went by them. Occasionally she whispered a word of warning; otherwise, they traveled in silence.

They crested a hill and the smell of the sewage pits and knackers' yards hit his nostrils. Speaking in almost normal tones, his guide said, "We are very close, Master Isaac." Now the soundscape was enlivened by bursts of laughter, an angry exclamation, and the thud of a door slamming. Drunken voices echoed confusingly off the hills and Jacinta pulled him away from the muddy pathways every minute or two.

"I think she will be here," said Jacinta, stopping. After a considerable pause, she tapped on the door.

"It's too late," said the voice inside.

"It's Jacinta," said the child. "Is Esclarmonda there?"

"She went home, sweetheart. You'll find her there."

"This way," said Jacinta. "She sounded strange, though. And usually she lets me in."

"Perhaps she has a client," said Isaac.

"Clients are always noisy," observed Jacinta. "This is the house."

"Take me a little way from it, so that we can speak," he murmured.

She tugged him sideways until his feet reached rough foliage and pebbles. "We can whisper here," she said.

"Describe the house to me," he said. "Tell me exactly where everything is." He listened intently, occasionally interrupting to clarify a point. "Good. When I say that it is time, take me to the door, knock on it yourself, the way you would normally, and then slip away as far as you can get and still be able to hear what is going on. If there is trouble, run back for help."

"Who from?" she asked, as if her life had not held many sources of reliable help.

"The guards if you see them, but do not look for them or stop to answer their questions. Otherwise find Yusuf, or Master Jacob. Someone you can trust. Now take me to Esclarmonda's house."

THE child knocked lightly and rapidly three times, touched Isaac's arm in farewell, and was gone with no more noise than a mouse makes running across the ground. Isaac heard an indrawn breath and then a woman's voice saying, "Who is it?"

"A friend," said Isaac. "I come to visit you. I bring you a message."

Inside he heard a scuffling noise and a whisper. "What message?" she asked.

"Let me in and I will tell you."

"It is too late," she said. "I only admit friends I know after dark."

"For me, it is always after dark," said Isaac, in insinuating tones. "Blow out the candle and you will think I am a friend."

"Go away, señor," said the voice, louder this time. "You are drunk."

"I will stay here until you let me in," he replied, pushing his hand against the door. It started to creak open; at that, Isaac raised his staff, put his foot against it, and kicked hard. The door slammed against something malleable, almost soft. Someone uttered a high-pitched curse and Isaac felt the door being shoved back against him. As he had expected, someone was behind it. He pressed his left shoulder against the door to keep whoever it was trapped behind it, cleared the opening with his staff, and stepped inside.

AS he entered, the door swung back, he heard the swish of a sword through the air from his left-hand side, and ducked. He was holding his staff with both hands, crosswise in front of his head, and shifted it to take the full force of the blow. The sword bounced off and struck his forearm. "Take hold of him," said a voice he knew. "By all that's holy, get behind and take him. Leave her."

A second later the woman's voice rang out. "The candle has gone out. It is so dark in here we cannot see."

"Where are you?" murmured Isaac and heard the slam of wood striking wood.

"Where you cannot hurt me," a muffled voice answered.

"Where is he?" said another voice from the center of the room, one that Isaac had also heard before.

"Right here," said the voice he knew, from directly behind him.

Isaac took a firm grasp of his staff and whirled it around. Before it reached the man behind him, it hit something else with a softish consistency, another human being. His unintended target emitted a sharp cry and a curse. Isaac took a step sideways and turned toward the man behind him in order to have his back against the wall. But his skull collided sickeningly with something hard, and grasping his staff with both hands close together, he thrust it backward. Again, it hit something soft. He heard a breath being expelled, and then the darkness around him began to whirl. For a moment or two, the sounds through which he identified place and things combined into waves of undifferentiated sound, strange voices, doors slamming, and faraway, high-pitched laughter; in the confusion of a world without reference points, he stumbled and fell.

"Where is he?" said a voice from the void. And the void echoed back the sounds.

"On the floor. Find the candle."

"Candle," said the echo.

"I have it. Do you have flint and steel?"

"Steel, steel, steel," mocked the echoing void.

"No. But I've found him."

This time the voice sounded like that of a real person, that of the second man who had spoken.

"You've got me, you stupid fool," said the first voice, the one that Isaac recognized instantly. "Keep looking."

From the sounds, Isaac judged that both men were now in front of him. He rolled over to increase the distance between himself and them. The movement left him dizzy with pain again, sinking back into the whirling nothingness out of which he had just clawed himself. In the returning confusion, he thought, I cannot. If I go down I will never get back.

That mocking voice out of the void cried coldly, "Never get back, never, never, never."

He was sinking into suffocating blackness like a thick, sticky mud.

Another voice murmured in the void. "I will come back to you, I promise it." It was his own voice, calm and sane, and he wondered at it. Then his arm freed itself from the blackness. His fingers moved and touched something. His staff. He caught hold of it and gently, carefully, began to move.

"I have it," said the voice of the second man. It was in front of him, on his right hand, more than an arm's length away.

"What do you have?" said the first man, from somewhere close to the door. Now the whole small house re-formed itself in his mind, except that one voice was missing.

"Flint and steel," said the second. "Where's the candle?"

And from a great distance away a disembodied voice said, "Over here. Over here."

+>━━ ━━<+

YUSUF had watched Isaac leave with Jacinta with some perturbation. It was one thing that his master went fearlessly and among all kinds of men, friendly and hostile, in Girona. There he knew every house, every stone of the streets, and everyone knew him, including the efficient Bishop's Guards, and even the less efficient city guards. There, his friends outnumbered his enemies, Yusuf felt, and people looked out for him.

Here, he knew no one. The Bishop would not use his power to scour the city for him, should he not come back soon; he did not have a large number of grateful patients whose houses he could find and who would take him in if necessary. The Bishop, thought Yusuf. What had his master said about the Bishop? It was something that had struck him at the time. And suddenly he remembered. He grabbed his cloak and set out as quickly as he could.

"Gros," he said, shaking the figure lying on a heap of straw behind some barrels under the arches. "Wake up. I need you. It's Yusuf."

"All right, all right, I hear you," grumbled the porter. "What's so important you have to wake me up to tell me about it?"

"My master," Yusuf began, and stopped.

"The blind physician?"

"Yes. Jacinta's taken him to see Esclarmonda. I think he may be in trouble."

"I wouldn't be surprised. One hears that she's in trouble. Some unpleasant men left to visit her," said el Gros. He yawned. "It's time to do something, I suppose. Do you have your little sword?"

"Yes, and it's not a little sword. It's a real one, full-sized."

"Good. We may need it. Roger! Wake up! Even you might be useful."

THEY moved quickly, unconcerned for now with the amount of noise they were making, and covered the distance from the Corn Market to the slope leading down to Lo Partit in almost no time at all. The waning moon was at the quarter, but even so it lit up the streets enough for them to see their way. Suddenly ahead of them a slight figure appeared and then silently disappeared again. "*Hola,* Jacinta," said el Gros. "What's going on?"

The figure appeared again out of a patch of blackness. "I think Esclarmonda and Master Isaac are in trouble. I have come for help."

"Here we are," said el Gros. "Where are they?"

"At Esclarmonda's," said Jacinta. "Quick."

She took Yusuf by the hand and dragged them rapidly into the quarter. "Where is she staying now?" said el Gros. "They said she moved."

"It's over here," said Jacinta. "Her old house. The candles are out."

"No. Look. Someone has just lit a candle," said el Gros. "That means we don't have to use up mine," he added, patting his tunic and moving like an angry bull up to the door. He put his shoulder against it and shoved. It flew open on a scene of chaotic disorder. As soon as he stepped out of the doorway, someone from inside threw himself out of the space, encountering the edge of Yusuf's sword on the way. Instead of pausing to fight, he yelped at the contact, cursed, turned away, and fled.

"Two left," said el Gros, who was laying about him left and right with his staff. "It's hardly worth the fight. Someone has already roughed them up a bit."

A second man with drawn sword made it to the door and started outside when he came straight at Yusuf's sword. "Out of my way, you worthless pup," said the second man, turning and running in the opposite direction. He passed Roger in the pale moonlight. Roger tripped him, kicked him in the head, and went to join the others, leaving him where he was.

"I have this one," said el Gros, displaying an unhappy-looking man with his arms held firmly behind his back.

"It was the blind man who roughed them up," said a voice from a heavy chest that Jacinta was crouched on. "Oof. Let me out."

Jacinta scrambled off the chest and helped raise the lid. Out stepped Esclarmonda. "How is he?" she asked.

"If you mean me, I am well," said Isaac, who was sitting on the floor leaning against the wall. "Except for an ache in the head. I am trying to stay away from further trouble."

"Let me see what I can do," said Esclarmonda. "You need some tending, I think." She went over and gently assisted him to his feet. She righted a chair that was lying on its side and directed him into it. "I must fetch water and bandages."

"I will get the water," said Jacinta, picking up a jug and slipping out of the little house.

"What do we do with this thing?" asked el Gros, nodding in the direction of the man he was holding.

"I think we should take him back with us and present him to the Bishop tomorrow," said Isaac. "Could you and Yusuf do that? Perhaps Mistress Esclarmonda will find some rope to tie him up with."

"It never ends," said the porter. "I spend all my nights rescuing gentlemen in difficulties, when I should be out earning money."

"I would not wish that you be out-of-pocket for assisting others," said Isaac, and threw a purse in the direction of his voice. El Gros reached out and plucked it from the air with ease.

"I thank you with all my heart, Master Isaac. And I wish you a swift and safe journey home."

"Will you go with him, Yusuf, to explain to Jacob the presence of another guest in his house? I must speak to

Mistress Esclarmonda about a few important matters before I leave. I will return with Jacinta."

ESCLARMONDA lit another candle and gently washed the blood from Isaac's arm and the back of his head. She bound up the wounds and stepped back. "That looks better, Master Isaac. It will do, at least, until you return to Jacob's house."

"Tell me," said Isaac. "How long have you known Jacob?"

"For many years," said Esclarmonda.

"I knew there had to be a reason that you sent Don Arnau to him. And Jacinta."

"I thought that Don Arnau could trust him. And that Jacinta would be safe with him."

"You didn't concern yourself with any trouble that might come to Jacob because of it?"

"I thought of it," she said. "But Jacob has had a smooth and placid life until now. I thought it was time to lift him out of his settled ways."

"He is a client of yours?" asked Isaac.

"Oh, no," said Esclarmonda. "That is not how I know him. Never. As far as I know he is the most loyal and faithful of husbands. We were friends many years before I had clients."

"You knew him in the *call*," said Isaac. "Is Jacinta his child? For it is clear you are her mother."

"Jacinta Jacob's daughter?" she said, with a mirthless laugh. "Certainly not. Jacob and I were friends as children, before he left to be apprenticed. When he returned, we became more than friends. I loved him dearly, and he loved me, or so he said. Our families were pleased and a match was made. He returned to his studies, leaving me to my dreams and my needlework, very happy."

"And what happened?"

"His love was put to the test, and it broke like a rotten piece of rope. It took me down with it," she said bitterly. She rose and moved around in the little house. He heard her set a table down beside him, and then a cup. "We will have a cup of wine while we talk," she said. "I have never spoken of this before. I did not know it would be so difficult." Her voice was trembling.

"I will gladly take a cup with you," he said.

"I can still see that scene," she continued. "Our house, my parents, two counselors, the *albedín*, all standing in a circle, crowded around me, all demanding that I name my seducer."

"And did you?"

"I wouldn't speak. I couldn't. I couldn't tell anyone what had happened. And since I refused to talk, they all began, saying, 'Name him and if he does not marry you he will be punished as he deserves. You must name him.' At last I could stand it no longer and swore by everything holy that he was a Christian and that I only knew that his name was—" She stopped abruptly.

"What was your seducer's name?"

"Seducer? Master Isaac, in one sense he did not exist. I called him Johan—after all, there are so many Christians named Johan that I thought no one would be accused falsely of the crime if I did."

"Who was he?"

"The man who carried me from the *call* was the son of a neighbor. There is no point now in naming him. I knew that if I accused him they would make me marry him, and he was a man I would rather have died than marry, Master Isaac. By then, Jacob had repudiated me. I decided that banishment was better than marriage to such a man as our neighbor's son."

"A sad tale, but you should not have allowed him to seduce you, mistress."

"He didn't seduce me, Master Isaac," she said, impatiently. "He delivered me to a friend, a rich friend who paid him gold for my virginity. I was locked in a room." She stopped and picked up her wine cup. "He was a big man, this friend, and very strong." She shrugged her shoulders. "Or so he seemed to me. One should not fret over the past," she said, "and I try not to. But you asked me. I told you."

"And yet you love his child."

"Not his. That poor thing came into this miserable world before his time, and lived only a short while in it. I changed my name to Esclarmonda, and found another protector. A kind man. I had his child. He died in the Black Death and I was out on the streets. There you have my life story."

"And the neighbor?"

"He died from the Black Death as well."

"And the man who bought you from him?"

"I never knew his name or saw his face. He wore a mask. But I can tell you one thing about him. He was in this house tonight."

"Which of the three men?"

"The one who left first. I knew his voice and that laugh. I will never forget that laugh. It echoes still in my dreams."

"Tell me more about him, and then you and Jacinta must accompany me to Master Jacob's house. We are not finished yet."

EIGHTEEN

ISAAC knocked on the door of the physician's house with his staff. "It is dark inside, Master Isaac," said Esclarmonda. "The house is asleep. I should not be here. I will only disturb them unnecessarily."

"Hush, Mama," said Jacinta. "Master Isaac would not have told you to come if it weren't important."

"I cannot see why it is more important to be here in the last quarter of the night than tomorrow morning when the world is awake again."

"It is not that late," said Isaac. "The bells for the ninth hour of the night have not rung. It will not be dawn for many hours."

The argument remained unresolved with the opening of the door. Jacob Bonjuhes looked out at the three of them on the doorstep. "Come in," he said. "I have been expecting you. We were occupied in finding a secure place to put the man you sent us, Isaac, my friend. Please, Jacinta, mistress, come in. I had not realized, Isaac, that your presence in our house would make our life quite so lively."

"I apologize," said Isaac. "But I have brought an old friend to see you. She has a request to make of you."

"Papa," said a voice from the stairs. "I'm glad you're back. What is going on?"

"Nothing, my dear. Everything is settled for the moment."

"Come into my study," said Jacob. "If we sit in the courtyard we will wake Ruth up. And there is a chill in the air."

Jacob lit an abundance of candles and found chairs for everyone. "Now where is the old friend you promised me?"

Esclarmonda stepped out from behind the shadow of Isaac's broad shoulders. "Here, Jacob. Perhaps you do not remember me any longer. But that is unimportant. I came to see you to beg your kindness and generosity in respect to my daughter, Jacinta."

Jacob lifted a three-pronged candelabra to light Esclarmonda's face. In its brilliance his own face had turned deathly pale. "May the Lord forgive me," he said softly. "It is you. I had thought that you were dead. My—"

"I am called Esclarmonda now," she said. "It is neither fit nor safe for me to use the name you knew me by. And this is my Jacinta. She is not the child of my disgrace, I assure you. If you count back the years, you will be able to tell. But she deserves better than the life I lead. I am not complaining for myself, but I would like to spare her that."

"She is a good and useful child," said Jacob. "And I should have known her for her mother's daughter. There always was something very familiar in her look. My dear, whatever I can do, I will, but I am afraid that Ruth—"

"What is happening, Jacob?" said a voice. Ruth was standing in the doorway, in her shift, covered with a long shawl. "Why is everyone out of bed?"

"This is Jacinta's mother. She has come to ask us if we

are willing to employ her daughter. She is useful, and it would be a blessing to do so."

"Jacob, we have talked of this over and over again. You know how I feel. I am sorry," said Ruth, looking at Esclarmonda with a frozen expression on her face, "but we have all the servants we have room for in the house. We could not possibly take in one more."

"Ruth," said Jacob. "Listen to me."

"I have listened to you, Jacob. And you know that I keep the house in every way as you wish it. But it is also my house, and there are things I cannot live with."

"Especially now," said Raquel quickly, before Ruth could say anything more, "when the house has been so crowded that you have scarcely a place to sleep. But, Papa, remember what Mama was saying just before we left? She is desperate for a little servant girl. You remember?"

"Of course I remember," said Isaac. "And there are very few to be found in our city right now. We had even thought of buying a slave, but Judith does not like that idea at all. I don't know if you would be willing to have your daughter go from you as far as Girona, but if you would consider it, it would be a great kindness to us and to my wife, who is with child and needs more help."

"Her wage would be a set of clothes and three pounds the first year, and then if she remained satisfactory, it would be raised to five and then seven over the next four years," said Raquel briskly. "With clothes as needed. It is important to make that clear, Papa."

"What do you think, mistress?"

"Jacinta? What do you think? I would miss you, but it would be better for you."

"I think Naomi might teach you to cook," said Raquel. "And Mama will make sure that you are brought up well."

"Then I will go, Mama."

"It would be tomorrow," said Raquel.

"Then tomorrow it is," said Esclarmonda. "We need a

contract," she added with a touch of desperation in her voice. "A legal contract. I won't let her go without that."

"I will set down what I have just promised," said Raquel. "Do you know your letters?" she asked Esclarmonda.

"I do."

"Good. Then you can help me. We will sit down by the table in the corner, out of the way. Could you bring that candlestick, Mistress Esclarmonda?"

Esclarmonda picked up the candle from Jacob's desk, carried it over, and set it in the middle of the table.

"Do you have paper you could spare us, Master Jacob? Or a piece of parchment?" asked Raquel.

"Of course," said Jacob. "And pen and ink."

THE two women sat down at the table, with Jacinta on a cushion on the floor next to her mother, leaning against her. She soon fell asleep.

"Are you sure you must go tomorrow?" asked Jacob.

"I solemnly promised my wife I would return before the Sabbath began," said Isaac. "And I was most forcefully reminded of that promise earlier tonight."

"Then what do we do now?"

"What do we do about what?" David came in, neat in tunic and hose, with his boots on. He looked around, poured himself a mouthful of wine, and sat down. "I hope I do not intrude, but it is impossible to sleep in this house tonight," he added. "With people coming in and going out, running up and down stairs, opening and closing doors, and even babies crying. I did hear a baby crying in the house, did I not?"

"And Bonafilla?"

"Sleeping still. It is wonderful. But what are you plotting?"

"We have captured someone who can tell us a great deal about what has been going on, I believe," said Isaac. "I suggest we bring him in here and ask him a few questions."

"By all means," said Jacob. "David, come and give me a hand. He is not happy about being here."

"Where is he?"

"In Mordecai's room, under lock and key."

"Where is Mordecai?"

"He said not to worry. He would find himself a bed."

"He's taken over my old room, then," said David. "Sleeping peacefully."

They left, returning a few minutes later with a confused and dazed-looking man. "He was asleep, Isaac," said Jacob. "And he complains that his head is sore."

Isaac cocked his head to listen. "Is it bleeding? His head, that is."

"I see no blood on the scalp, nor is there a flux from the nose. Mostly he looks dusty."

"I believe he spent a good part of that encounter on the floor," said Isaac.

"That explains the dust. I think he'll do. Sit down. In that chair. We have questions to ask you."

"This man, who broke in upon our peace this evening," said the prisoner, "cannot see?"

"That is right, sir," said Isaac.

"I have been treated outrageously," said the man. "To set upon an innocent man who was merely accompanying a friend to visit a—a female acquaintance. To half-kill him, not even knowing who he was, and then drag him off to a private house and lock him up. I will have your head for this, my man. I have powerful friends who will gladly act to protect my interests . . ." He sneezed. "Do you have some water there?" he asked.

"Certainly, sir," said Jacob politely, filling a cup and handing it to him. "Are you finished? If you are, we will ask our questions."

"You may ask what you like," he said. "I feel no obligation to answer you."

"What is your name?" asked Isaac.

"My name is known to my friends and acquaintances, amongst whom I can name members of the court, including the royal Princesses. I do not see why I should give it to you."

"I asked you that, because even though I am blind, I was well aware that I was attacked by three men in Esclarmonda's house. And I am sure she will be glad to testify to your presence."

"I wouldn't be too sure of that," said the prisoner, his voice full of confidence.

"One I did not know," said Isaac, paying no attention. "He spoke only one or two words, but his is a voice that I believe I would recognize again. One we met on the road to Perpignan and had much conversation with. He told us that his name was Felip. One—you, sir—I recognized as the man who talked in such a fluent and persuasive fashion to Father Miró outside the Dominican house on the day of his death. You were the man who was so interested in Father Miró's movements, and so disappointed in his failure to find a nest of heretics here in the *call*."

"Those are lies," he said. "All lies and insinuations."

"Are they? I wonder if you remember your words as well as I do," said Isaac. "You asked him if he'd had a profitable visit, and when he told you it was not profitable at all, you suggested that if the man whom he visited was not a Cathar, then perhaps he was a Christian, contravening the law by living in the *call*."

The prisoner looked at him uneasily. "How did you know that?" he whispered.

"Next you asked him where he was going and instead of replying, he made a solemn engagement to meet you this day next week in the evening, when he was to be back. 'Do not fail me, sir,' he said, 'or I will come to seek you.' Do you not fear those words, señor? Do you not fear that Father Miró will come to seek you?"

"By all the saints," he said, "I do not know what you are that you can hear and remember the whispered words on our lips and the very thoughts in our hearts. But I swear I did not touch the priest. That was not me. You can't call him back after me."

"Who are you?"

"My name is Martin. I am from Valencia."

"You are the mysterious foreigner, then, Martin. The man who arranged someone's escape from prison and then hired two inefficient porters to kill him, are you not?"

"How can you know that?" said Martin. "Who tells you these things? I would never do that. Indeed, I helped a friend of a friend, by advice and counsel, to get out of prison, but then to fall upon him as he leaves—who would do that to a friend?"

"How long have you been in Roussillon?"

"Not two months."

"Who were the other two men?"

"One is Felip. Felip Cassa," he said.

"Your guest might know this man," said Esclarmonda suddenly from her corner. The prisoner jumped nervously and peered over to where the candle on the table sputtered and then died. "Jordi—my friend Jordi, who was his servant," she continued, "spoke of Felip and Martin."

"We cannot disturb him," said Jacob. "Not now, in the middle of the night. He is not well enough."

"Tell me, Martin," said David, setting a long-bladed dagger down on the table. It clattered as it landed. "Where is this Felip?"

"Where is he now, sir?" asked Martin cautiously.

"Yes, right now. You were captured, the other two are gone. Where did Felip go? You must know." His voice was quiet and menacing, and as he spoke he picked up the dagger again and examined its edge carefully. Martin shrank into the chair.

"He must be at the house," said Martin. He spoke faster

and faster, his voice rising in pitch. "But don't let them
know I told you. There is a house somewhere to the north
because Felip said that if we ran into trouble, that's where
we would go. We would be safe from anything at the
house. That must be where he went."

"How were you going to get there?" asked David, leaning forward and looking into his face.

"We were going to ride. It's a few miles out of the city.
We left the horses with a servant at the edge of Lo Partit."

"Where?" said David coldly.

"At the Vernet road," said Martin.

"Was Felip injured?" asked David.

"I don't know," said Martin. "He may have been. We
were all in the dark and it was hard to tell what was happening. But when someone lit the candle again, there was
blood on the floor. It wasn't mine. I think it came from
him."

"Good. It may have slowed him down. Now it is my
turn to leave in the middle of the night," said David, slipping the knife into a sheath in his boot. "I bid you good
night, and much enlightening conversation."

The door into the study opened and closed. His feet
clattered across the stone hallway. Then, as he opened the
front door onto the sleeping city, the bells rang out for
laud. The night was two-thirds over.

DAVID collected his mule, saddled her himself, and set
out for the road north. He started with all the speed of one
who has not thought what he should do, but as he approached the Vernet road, he slowed. For one thing, he had
no desire to warn his quarry, who was quite likely riding
a faster beast than his. For another, he wasn't quite sure
what to do. He was carrying a sword under his traveler's
cloak in addition to his dagger, and although he was angry

enough to use them, he was not foolish enough to put his life in jeopardy on his wedding night.

The road was empty as it neared the river Tet to the north of the city. Then up ahead, on the bridge, David saw in the dim moonlight three mounted figures. The man without a name, Felip, whose despicable life was owed to him, and the servant. Three against one. He slowed his mule to a bare walk, dismounted quietly, and left her by the edge of the road in the shadows. He walked on ahead, staying out of the betraying moonlight.

The three men stopped and dismounted, in order, it seemed, to carry on a heated but muted conversation. One black shadow outlined in the moonlight stood next to the horses, one stood with his arms akimbo, and one was punctuating his soft-voiced arguments with fierce, stabbing gestures. David by now was close to the bridge itself. He stopped and veered to the right. Very gently he eased himself down toward the river itself, hoping to get close enough to hear what they were saying and to see more than their outlines.

The muttering stopped. "You can't," shrieked a voice, shocking in the silence of the night, where the loudest noise to be heard was the rippling and eddying of the waters. David looked up, but could see nothing. Then, he heard a loud splash, coming from slightly upriver. He peered into the blackness under the bridge and in a moment something white bobbed up from the water. It swirled in a strong eddy and was carried onto the sandy spit at his feet. It stopped there.

"Let's get out of here. Bring his horse, for God's sake," said a voice from above. "I'm covered in blood. Hurry."

When the hoofbeats faded in the distance, David took out a lantern he had hooked onto his belt, lit the candle inside it, and held it up to look. There was the man who had met Bonafilla in the square, his throat cut from ear to ear, moving up and down in the shallow water as it whirled under him. On an impulse he never could explain to himself satisfactorily—and he was never fool enough to tell anyone else about it—he put his booted foot against the shoulder of the corpse and with a strong thrust, sent it out into the current in the deep water. "Farewell, Felip," he said. He blew out his candle and went back to collect his mule.

+>—< >—<+

"WHERE did you go?" asked Jacob. "I was worried."

"I was hoping to catch up with this Felip."

"Did you? You haven't fought with him and killed him, have you? That could bring us real trouble."

"Don't worry. We didn't fight and I certainly didn't kill him. I didn't even have a chance to confront him. But now I know that he has left the country, you might say, and will not trouble us any longer."

"What do you mean?"

"As I came up to them, his friends were convincing him to take a journey down the river to the sea. When I left, he was on his way."

"Alone?"

"Quite alone. I think I will go back to bed," said David. "After all, it is my wedding night, although never did a man spend a stranger one, I think."

"Before you go," said Raquel, "we have a contract drawn up here, and we need witnesses to it. Could you sign? You and Master Jacob?"

"Certainly," said David cheerfully. "Where?"

"Just there," said Raquel, pointing to just below where Esclarmonda had signed "Deborah, Jewess of Perpignan."

"And I think that we should go to our beds as well," said Isaac. "There are still things we must do before we leave, but I do not think I will rise too early."

"When do you think to leave?" asked Jacob.

"If it is agreeable to you, after an early dinner. Astruch sends one of his men with us, and so we shall be six."

NINETEEN

DOÑA Margarida slept badly that night. She had seen the child, waited long enough to make sure that all was as well as it had seemed at first, and then returned to the palace to deliver her joyful news. But when the birds began to chirp in the morning, she was already awake. She gave up all thoughts of trying to sleep any longer. Soon the noise of the royal household preparing itself for a new day would be added to the chattering of the birds, and would awaken her again anyway.

She got up quietly and dressed herself without help from her maid, who slept peacefully on. She was too restless to sit and work or read in the half-light, and since there was no one around to talk to, she took a cloak, for the morning was cold, and moved quietly down the steps to the little door leading out to Her Majesty's orchard. There she could walk under the trees, passing the time until breakfast.

As she wandered aimlessly under the trees, picking a piece of fruit for her breakfast and eating it with more hunger than she knew she had, a faint screech of metal drew her attention. Sudden fear gripped her and she turned rapidly in the direction it had come from. She was looking straight at a small, heavy, wooden door in the outer wall of the orchard. It was held together with broad iron bands, and altogether it was massively enough built to withstand a determined attack. Ordinarily, unless the gardeners were busy at their tasks, it was locked and barred. But at that moment, the bar had been raised, and someone outside the wall had turned a key in the rusty lock. If this were a stranger intent on evil who was penetrating this fastness, he could easily overpower her and enter the castle through the door she had left open to the sleeping house.

Then Margarida smiled at her own foolishness. Of course, the silver of the sky was turning to blue, even though the sun had not yet risen, and gardeners would be out by now, tending the orchard before the Princess was out of her bed. That was how they sustained the illusion that the order in this little paradise was a gift of nature rather than the work of man.

But the figure who came in through the door in the wall was neither a gardener nor an enemy. It was Bernard Bonshom, Lord Puigbalador. A few murmured words and the jingle of a bridle told her that his groom was with him, and had been charged, no doubt, with taking both their horses to a more orthodox entrance. He came in, quietly but not furtively, closed the door, and locked it with the heavy key he carried in his hand. He shifted the massive oak bar down into its rest, brushed off his hands, and turned around.

"Good morning, my lord," said Margarida. "It is a beautiful morning for a ride."

"It is indeed, Doña Margarida," he said with a bow. "But early. I had not expected to meet anyone at this hour. The sun wants some time still before it rises."

"I slept badly," said Margarida, "and came out to soothe

my spirits in the peace of the morning. And what are you
doing abroad at this hour?"

"Doña Margarida, I beg for your discretion," said Bonshom. "I passed the night with a friend. Rather unexpectedly, you might say. I had hoped that I might not be
observed coming in. I particularly hoped," he added, "that
my absence from the palace might not be noticed. This is
a most convenient and discreet entrance if one reaches it
early enough," he added. "And pleasanter than crawling
through the drainpipe."

"You certainly would not want to ruin that spotless linen
and those polished boots in a drainpipe," said Margarida.
"Although you do look as if you have not slept much this
night. You are as pale as a hopeless lover."

"You jest at my expense, Doña Margarida," he said,
smiling. "But I admit to deserving the cut. You know I
cannot bear to be dusty or disheveled."

"Do I know your friend, who sends you away from her
door gleaming like a pearl?"

"I do not believe so," he said casually. "She is a delicious
creature and very amusing. We played all night at cards."

"All night, my lord?"

"Most of the night, Doña Margarida." He shivered in
the cool air. "I fear I left my cloak behind me, most foolishly."

"Or perhaps it was done by design, to give yourself cause
to return. What I cannot understand, though, is your concern for your own reputation," said Margarida. "The lady's
yes, but is it not rather too late to protect yours?"

"Alas, that is too true," said Bonshom. "But the Princess
Constança has intimated that she has not been pleased with
my behavior while I am here in the palace. It seems that
someone has been telling her wild tales about me."

"Untrue tales?"

"Not necessarily, but indiscreet. And Her Royal Highness begins to think herself as powerful as her royal father

now that she has grown to a woman's height."

"It is not only in growth that she has become a woman, my lord. She bears herself with a most queenly grace and manner. Perhaps she feels that some deference is owed to her."

"She merely tests her power," said Bonshom vindictively. "It is time she were married to someone with the rank to put her in her place."

"My lord, you forget where you are and to whom you speak," said Margarida. "I am Her Royal Highness's lady and not one of your companions at the gaming table."

"You are, of course, correct. I offer you my profoundest apologies. My weariness betrays me and my jests are timed ill. If you will forgive me, Doña Margarida, I have not yet met my bed this night. Although my linen may look crisp, I am not." He bowed, and left in the direction of the palace.

Margarida observed him with interest. For she had seen him setting out the night before, looking equally elegant, in linen as white as the snow on the mountaintops, but overnight his tunic had changed from green to scarlet, his hose from gold to deep blue, and his boots from brown to black. She wondered how he had managed to establish a household and a mistress close by and keep even the slightest word of it from the tightly knit, gossiping community of the palace.

Margarida returned to the quarters where the ladies-in-waiting slept outside the Princess's chamber. She woke up her sleepy maid, washed, and donned apparel more fitting to what she had in mind for the day.

"My lady rides this morning?" asked the maid.

"Yes, I do," said Margarida. "Once I have had some breakfast and bid good morning to Her Royal Highness."

BY this time, the drawbridge had been lowered and the portcullis raised; the archers were posted in the barbican above the gates to guard the now vulnerable entrance. The heavily fortified palace was prepared to greet the rest of the world once more.

The first visitor from the outside to ride up created a considerable amount of interest. He was a royal courier, bearing letters and documents. He had left Collioure, where the royal galley had anchored, at first light that morning. To no one's surprise, one of the letters was for the Princess. Don Pedro, King of the Aragonese empire, was a most affectionate father. Although he traveled constantly, he wrote frequently to his daughters. As common an event as a letter from him was, it was still delivered to her in all haste. Nothing could have pleased her more except the fact that Morena was scampering about the chamber on three legs and beginning to show great interest in getting out the door.

When after breakfast Margarida requested a moment with her, Constança was seated at a table with the letter in front of her. "I was about to send for you, Lady Margarida," she said. "I have had a most curious letter from His Majesty, with directions that some of its contents be communicated to Lady Johana and Don Arnau. I realize that cannot be, but I wish that Lady Johana be given this," she said, handing her a piece of parchment carefully folded and sealed with her own seal. "It is important that she receive it as soon as possible."

MARGARIDA set out at once. When she arrived at the *call,* it was bustling with housewives marketing, and merchants and men of business conducting their affairs out in the pleasant warmth of the sun and bright light of morning.

The only house to remain shuttered and quiet was that of the physician Jacob Bonjuhes.

"Is all well in the house?" asked Margarida of a neighbor setting out to do her marketing.

"I have heard no different," the good woman said. "But the merriment from the wedding went on far into the night," she added. "People coming and going, back and forth, doors opening and closing. I'm not surprised they're not up. But go ahead, ring at the door. They won't mind," she said, and settled down to wait, in case something interesting happened.

The groom rang the bell and then knocked firmly at the door. After some time, the little housemaid opened the door. She stared up at the imposing figure in front of her. "Good morning, my lady," she said.

"Is all well?" asked Margarida.

"I think so," said the girl in surprise. "Except that the master and mistress were up late last night and haven't come from their bed, nor have the guests that were to leave today."

"How is the baby?"

"Crying lustily, my lady. He seems very strong."

"May I come in?" she asked, despairing of being shown into the house.

"Yes, my lady. I'm very sorry, my lady. Please come in. Do you wish to see the other lady?"

"I do," said Margarida, stifling a rising laugh. "If I may. Will you take up my name? Lady Margarida. And please tell the Lady Johana that I bear a letter for her from the Princess."

"Goodness!" said the child, wide-eyed. "From the Princess? I will, my lady."

As Margarida waited in the hall, the house gradually filled with the sound of people rising. Doors slammed, voices called out to servants and to one another. It occurred to her with a pang of conscience that after a wedding that had gone far into the night, it was her untimely arrival that was dragging them from their beds. She was preparing her excuses and apologies when the little housemaid returned and hurried her up the stairs to Lady Johana.

Johana's son, neatly swaddled in fine linen, was in her arms, at her breast. She looked up when Margarida came in the room and smiled. "He was born hungry, Margarida. He attacks me with great vigor."

"He sounds just like his poor papa," said Margarida, with tears rising all at once in her eyes. "But no more of that. I am here to see how you are, and clearly you are well, and to deliver a letter from the Princess. She was up at daybreak, I think, writing it."

"I will read it as soon as he falls asleep," she said.

"How comes it that you are alone?" said Margarida.

"Through my own choice, Margarida. I sent the midwife home to rest, and Felicitat to bed for a while. They were both asleep on their feet. I expect they will return soon. The good doctor and his wife have not yet arisen."

"I think my groom's robust hammering on the door has awakened them and everyone else in the house," said Margarida.

"They have been very kind," said Johana. "Mistress Ruth brought me her child's cradle late last night. She offered her own baby things—she is with child again, she says—but we did not need them. Felicitat brought all the clothes I have been working on. I am well looked after. And to judge from the sounds coming up from below, I hope to have some breakfast soon." She cooed gently at the baby and looked up again. "He is asleep," she said with wonderment in her voice.

"I will put him in the cradle," said Margarida.

"No, please. Leave him here with me." And she nestled him down in the crook of her arm. "Now, let us see what Her Royal Highness has to say."

Johana broke the seal and unfolded the letter. Another piece of parchment fluttered out of it and dropped down onto the baby. Johana laughed. "It must be for him," she said, holding up the letter to the light of the half-opened shutter. "The Princess is so kind," said Johana, and went back to the beginning to read it again. Then in a sudden fever, she snatched up the leaf that had dropped on her little son, and unfolded it. She read it with a frown, as if it were written in some strange and foreign tongue, and then burst into floods of tears.

"Johana, what is the matter? What does the Princess say? What is that?" Flustered, she rang the bell.

A few moments later Felicitat arrived. She picked up the sleeping baby and set him down in his cradle, and then put her arms around his sobbing mother. "There, there, my lady, it's all right," she crooned gently. "Everything is fine, my lady. You mustn't fret yourself."

"Oh, Felicitat, I'm fine too. Everything is fine. This came from His Majesty. It's a pardon."

"If only it had come earlier," said Margarida. "I'm happy for you that it came, but if we had been able—"

"Don't think about it, Margarida. Felicitat, will you take it to our friend? And bring me some breakfast? You can't know how hungry I am."

Felicitat glided rapidly out of the room, appalled that her mistress should feel hunger, but determined to deliver her news to the master as soon as possible.

"Now, Margarida," said Johana, as soon as they were alone. "Whose side are you on? I must know."

+≡══ ══≡+

WHILE Margarida was closeted with Lady Johana, the members of the physician's household and the houseguests were gathering around the table in the sunshine of the courtyard. Ruth was the first to appear, looking tired and fraught with worries.

David came in next, neatly arrayed and walking briskly over to the table. "I have left my bride sleeping," he said, "but I ordered that her breakfast be sent up to her. I think it is time she awoke."

"But David, a bride is allowed to sleep all she likes, and not come down for days if that is what she wishes. You know that," said Ruth.

"I don't want her to be bored," said David. "Or to fall into bad habits. Ah, here come the first dishes and some excellent fresh bread. I am uncommonly hungry this morning."

"You seem in cheerful temper," said his brother, coming into the courtyard.

"And why would I not be?" asked David. "I have a lovely and sweet-tempered bride, and all our little problems have been settled. Such things give a man appetite."

Jacob laughed. "And where is everyone else?"

"I am here," said Raquel. "I have been helping Leah pack our boxes. Papa and Yusuf are right behind me. They too are packed. Good morning, Papa," she said. "When are we leaving?"

"Later. We have a few things to settle, and one visit to make before we depart. Mistress Ruth has promised us a very early dinner. We shall leave after that."

"I fear it will be a simple meal," said Ruth, "put together from some extra dishes we cooked for the marriage feast. I apologize that the last dinner of your visit should be dishes from yesterday's supper. But they were left in the kitchen and so they were not eaten nor given to the poor. But the cook has been out already and found some beautiful sardines for grilling."

"Nothing could be better," said Isaac. "Now, let us have our breakfast."

"Does your head trouble you, Papa?" asked Raquel softly.

"Only very slightly, my dear. I think I have done it no real harm. There is a tender spot," he said, touching the back of his head, "that feels a trifle bruised. I would not like to have someone hit it again. Other than that, I am well, although I am hoping that we can stay someplace peaceful tonight. And what have we to break our fast with?" he asked, as Raquel filled his plate.

"Savory rice, fruit, a roll of bread, and two kinds of cheese. There is much more on the table if you wish it."

"You have given me what I most enjoy on a sunny warm morning," he said.

WHEN breakfast was finished, Ruth excused herself to attend to her domestic duties. Astruch, who had come down late and eaten quickly, also excused himself. "Since you are not leaving at once, then I wish to speak to Duran about several small things to do with business. We will return in time to bid you farewell, Master Isaac, Mistress Raquel. And you too, Yusuf.

"What visits must we make, Papa?" said Raquel, with a sigh. She had risen from her bed a very few hours after she had gone to it, in order to finish her packing and organize all she could before breakfast. She longed to be home.

"I promised His Excellency, the Bishop—"

"Which bishop, Papa?" asked Raquel.

"Both bishops," said Isaac. "His Excellency the Bishop Berenguer asked me to deliver certain messages and to bring back certain information from this city. And the Bishop of Perpignan requested that I bring him any information I may have heard to enable him to write his report."

"What report, Papa?"

"One promised to Bishop Berenguer, which is ultimately destined for His Majesty, I believe. But in order to do that, we must try to make sense of what happened last night. And since we have one of the participants locked up in Mordecai's room, I think we should bring him out again and find out more from him."

"Didn't he tell us all he knew last night?" said Raquel.

"I doubt that very much," said Isaac. "He told us all he felt he had to let us know."

The door to the courtyard from the house opened and Lady Margarida walked out. "I come with a message from Lady Johana," she said.

"Certainly," said Isaac. "For whom?"

"For you and Master Jacob, I think, Master Isaac. It concerns you both," she said. "You have both accepted risk since Master Jacob took in her husband."

"Because he had escaped from prison or because he is a Christian?" asked Isaac.

Margarida reddened with confusion. "Both, I suppose, although sheltering someone who had escaped from prison would surely be more serious for Master Jacob. Lady Johana hopes that the truth will protect you. There are certain things that she and I know that might help if they were made known. She has sent me to tell you what I can."

"That is excellent, Lady Margarida," said Isaac. "If you will sit down, we are only lacking two participants."

"And who are they?" asked Jacob.

"The man in Mordecai's chamber and your patient. If you do not object, I think he should be carried down here to join the meeting. The air and sunshine will do him much good. He has been in that room far too long."

There was a flurry of activity as a couch was carried out, piled high with pillows and made as comfortable as possible. Raquel and Yusuf prepared the patient, and Mordecai and David carried him down the stairs.

The couch was placed in the dappled shade of the lemon tree. Arnau was set gently down on it and took as deep a breath as he could. He smiled. "It hurts less to breathe, I think," he said. "And this good air is like some tincture of the gods."

Last of all they unlocked the door of Mordecai's chamber. It was a small room that had been built as a storehouse, next to the kitchen. It had been little used by Ruth or her cook, and so as soon as the houseman had been promoted out of the kitchen he took it over. Martin came out, blinking in the sudden light, and looked around him.

"Martin!" said Arnau when the prisoner stepped into view. "It is a pleasure to see you even under these strange circumstances. Why are you here? What is happening?"

Martin began to scream in terror. He backed away until he collided against the wall of the courtyard, where he slumped down to the ground, staring at Arnau.

"Who is screaming, Don Arnau?" asked Isaac. "And what is wrong with him?"

"He is terrified, Papa," said Raquel. "He cannot stand for fear."

"He is one of my investors," said Arnau. "Or perhaps I should say, the agent for one of my investors. And I cannot tell you why he should be so afraid. Martin," he called. "Come over here. I hope you are not here to bring me bad news. Do not tell me, Martin, that the ship has foundered and we have lost everything."

"You can speak," said Martin.

"Of course I can speak," said Arnau. "Why should you think . . . I understand. He has heard those rumors that I was dead and thinks I am a ghost, come back to haunt the syndicate. But ghosts don't return in the light of the morning, Martin. The sun shines, and I am quite substantial. Get up, man, and pull yourself together."

"I don't think anything has happened to the ship," said Martin, scrambling to his feet.

"Come over here," said Marça once more.

Martin looked around and then walked nervously toward Don Arnau. When he reached the couch Marça was lying on, he dropped to his knees beside it. "Señor, please believe me," he said rapidly. "I had nothing to do with all of this, nothing. I knew nothing about it until you had already been injured. I didn't know it was you in prison until I saw you, and then it was too late. I was only to go to the meetings and to vote as I was told. I didn't know. I am so sorry."

"What are you talking about?" said Arnau. "Physician, what is this man saying? When I last saw him he was a quiet, careful man, completely possessed of his senses. Now he is babbling nonsense like a madman. How long have you had him locked up?"

"From halfway through the night until this morning," said Jacob. "In a room with a small window for air and a comfortable bed. He has had both food and drink in abundance."

"Let me explain," said Isaac. "First, you should know that I was set upon last night in Esclarmonda's house by three men."

"Why should I know that? What has it to do with Martin?" asked Arnau.

"Those three men were there either to silence Esclarmonda, or to discover from her your whereabouts. Which was it, Martin?"

"To discover your whereabouts, Don Arnau," said Martin, still pale from fear. "They had been looking for her for several days, because they had heard that she knew where you were. There were rumors that you were still alive."

"Who are they?" asked Arnau. "Who are these mysterious enemies that pursue me?"

"One of them I cannot say, my lord," said Martin. "I have only seen him three times, and his face has always been hidden beneath his hood and a kerchief. The first time was right after you were arrested, the second was two weeks ago, and then last evening, I swear. He never gave his name."

"And the second one?" asked Arnau coldly. "Who was he?"

"His name was Felip," said Isaac. "But which Felip of all the Felips in the world, I have not been told. I first met

him on the road from Collioure to Elna, where he joined
our party. He rode with us as far as the road to the palace.
A personable fellow, señor, full of jests and goodwill."

"What day was that?" asked Arnau. "The day you arrived? When was that, Master Jacob?"

"It was the fifth day of your stay here, señor," said Jacob.
"A Thursday."

"What did this Felip look like?" asked Arnau.

"He was dressed in a traveling costume of great worth,"
said Raquel, "a brown tunic, the sleeves slashed with gold,
and trimmed with vair. His hair is of a light shade of
brown, and his eyes are gray. He has fleshy lips and a merry
sort of smile. His brows and the bones of his face are well-
marked. He seemed to have a scar above his ear that dis-
appears into his hair."

"You have a gift for describing people, Mistress Raquel,"
said Arnau.

."That is because I am in the habit of doing it for my
father," she said. "Also, for quite a long time, I rode
slightly behind him and to the side, giving me almost
endless opportunity to observe him."

"Was this scar above his right ear?" said Arnau.

"Yes, his right ear," said Raquel, after a second's
thought. "Do you know him, señor?"

"Oh, I know him," said Arnau. "I also know my favorite
hunting garb. His name is Felip Cassa and he is my man
of business. Who was the third?"

"The third was Martin here, whom I recognized as the
man who spoke to Father Miró, asking him where he was
going and when he would be on the road, the very day
that he was killed. He has a distinctive voice," said Isaac.
"Uncommon in Perpignan."

"Martin killed Father Miró?" said Arnau. "This miserable little treacherous worm killed him?"

"No, no, señor. Not I. It was Felip. I do not have the
nerve for murder, I swear."

"That is true," said Isaac. "For one thing, Father Miró did not tell him where he was going. For another, he was sent out to kill you, señor, and instead, hired two bumbling fools to do it for him. A foreigner, they said. And to the men he recruited, all foreigners are alike. From France, from Mallorca, from Aragon, or from Valencia, like you."

"And who killed my unfortunate apprentice?" asked Jacob.

"I did not, sir," said Martin. "I swear it. I do not know. All I know is that Felip wanted you dead because you had seen him talking to someone and could point him out."

"I have never seen him," said Jacob. "Not to my knowledge."

"I saw him," said David. "Surely he did not confuse poor Abram with me?"

"It is possible," said Isaac. "My daughter tells me you are both tall men. What did he know of the household?"

"I believe Bonafilla told him where she was staying," said David. "He knew she was about to be married. I had not thought that he noticed me when I saw him, but it is possible. Perhaps he thought I was my brother."

"Where is Felip?" asked Arnau.

"Disappeared," said David. "Not a trace of him to be found anywhere."

"How do you know?" asked Arnau.

"I went off to look for them," said David. "Martin said that the other two were probably riding north toward a house where they would be safe. I followed along the road and caught sight of two men riding very rapidly away, with a third horse following them. I saw no sign of the rider of the third horse along the road as far as I went."

"Perhaps he escaped down the river by boat," said Arnau. "He would not be the first man to do that."

"Perhaps he did," said David.

"But who is the third man?" asked Arnau.

"He is someone important, I think," said Martin. "Rich.

I never saw him clearly and I was told not to talk about him, so I never asked anyone who he might be. I never saw anyone like him in town. I looked all the time, whenever there were other rich and important people. I haven't been here long," he added. "I don't know many people."

"Who gave you your instructions?" asked Arnau. "Who told you what to say at meetings? There is no viscount, is there?"

Martin laughed nervously. "No, señor. No viscount. My instructions came from Felip."

"Felip Cassa?"

"Yes."

"My man of business?"

"Yes."

"Johana told me not to trust him," said Arnau. "And he's not clever enough to have thought all this up for himself. There is someone else's mind behind this."

"Excuse me, Don Arnau," said Margarida, "but what I have to say may explain some things."

"What is that?" asked Arnau.

"An odd thing happened to me this morning," she said. "I couldn't sleep, and was out in Her Majesty's orchard in the dawn. Bernard Bonshom came in—it seems he often creeps into the palace that way. No doubt he has some arrangement with the gardener. He had been out all night . . ."

"He was at his house near Vernet, that is all," said Arnau. "He holds lavish parties there with the most exquisite of food and drink, but the most disreputable entertainment. Fortunes are lost there in gambling; ladies of good families, bored with their husbands, come seeking amusement. I have also heard strange tales of young girls disappearing into the house and not being seen again, although those may be rumors only."

"I know about that," said Margarida impatiently. "Everyone has heard those tales. But he tried to tell me that he had spent the night elsewhere, with a mistress, playing cards. He had had too much wine, fell asleep, and was trying to creep into the palace without any of Her Royal Highness's attendants finding out. She disapproves of him."

"That sounds very like him," said Arnau. "He's been behaving like that for years. I don't know how he keeps it up."

"His health, you mean?" asked Isaac.

"I was thinking rather of his purse," said Arnau. "Everything that he enjoys in life comes at a very high price. Except that there are those who say . . . But I interrupt you, Lady Margarida."

"The odd thing was," said Margarida, "that although he claimed to have spent the night in riotous living, he had clearly just come from his bath, having dressed in fresh linen and not the same clothes he went out in."

"Did you see him go out?" asked Isaac.

"I did, Master Isaac. He and I left the palace together. I was coming here; he was going wherever he was going. He didn't head for a city gate. And he was dressed in completely different clothes for the evening."

"Perhaps he had been home," said Raquel. "And bathed and changed there."

"He certainly didn't go back to the family manor. Not just to bathe. He could not possibly have ridden all the way there and all the way back in the darkness," said Margarida. "It is too far."

"He keeps an apartment at the house near town," said Arnau. "And no doubt, clothes."

"And a woman?" asked Margarida.

"Perhaps," said Arnau. "I was never a habitué of the house, and have not been near it for years now. It is entirely possible that his habits have changed."

"Why were you so sure that he had just bathed? Does he usually appear dirty and unkempt?" asked Raquel.

"Not at all. He is very particular about his dress. It was

the smell," said Margarida. "It was so strong. He smelled freshly of sandalwood. And his hair was wet, newly washed."

"Sandalwood," said Isaac. "It was sandalwood that I smelled in Esclarmonda's little house. Does she use sandalwood?"

"Where is Jacinta?" asked Raquel. "Jacinta!"

"I am here, mistress," said the child, coming out of the kitchen.

"Does your mama use sandalwood?"

"Sandalwood?" said Jacinta. "I don't think so. She perfumes herself with jasmine oil sometimes, but nothing else. And Mistress Raquel, may I say good-bye to her? Since we are not to leave until after the bells ring for midday."

"You may. But don't be late."

"Does the important man, as you call him, smell of sandalwood?" asked Isaac.

Martin nodded. "When I met him, he did."

"And what about my other syndicate members?" asked Arnau. "Were they plotting against my life as well?"

"I don't think so," said Martin. "They didn't seem to know anything about it."

"What do we do with him?" asked Arnau.

"We take him to the Bishop," said Isaac. "He wished a report. He can get it from the man's own lips. Perhaps someone could escort him back to his room."

"And who is the beautiful vision looking down on our deliberations from the gallery?" asked Arnau, once Martin had gone. "Good morning, mistress."

"Good morning, señor," said Bonafilla. "You are welcome to the house," she added shyly.

"She does not know I have been here all this time?" said Arnau.

"She is our bride, and had so many concerns meeting her new family and preparing herself for the wedding that we merely said there was a patient up there," said Jacob.

"You are a fortunate man," said Arnau to David.

"I most truly believe so," said David, looking up. "Come down, my darling," he said.

TWENTY

"YOUR Excellency," said Isaac, "you wished to hear of anything I learned in my brief stay in your city. I am here."

"And what have you discovered?" asked the Bishop.

"A few things, Your Excellency, with the help of many good citizens of Perpignan."

"Tell what you know and my secretary will record it."

"In your palace now, under guard, is one of the three men responsible for several evil acts. He is the least culpable, by all the reports we have. I would judge that he was an underling, doing only what he had been told without full realization of what it was. His name is Martin and he is from Valencia. He knows his fellow conspirator, but has never had a close look at his master's face.

"A second man appears to have been responsible for carrying out most of the deeds. All we can say of him is that his name is Felip Cassa, and when he was last seen, he was on the bridge over the Tet. He may have escaped by boat."

"If he did, it was not far," said His Excellency. "I have

heard other reports today, Master Isaac. One was that Felip Cassa was taken from the river this morning, his throat cut."

"Then, one way or another, his deeds have caught up with him," said Isaac. "For I believe that he was responsible for the deaths of Father Miró and Abram Dayot Cohen, Jacob Bonjuhes's apprentice."

"Why? What good could that innocent man's death do him? Or the young apprentice's?"

"It all has to do with a ship, Your Excellency, and its cargo."

"The trial of Don Arnau Marça," said the Bishop. "Which did not take place. I could not believe all that was said of him, or his fate."

"Your Excellency is a most shrewd judge of men. Most of what was said of him was not true." And he explained what had happened to Marça from the time of his arrest. "This morning, Your Excellency," said Isaac, "Don Arnau received a pardon from His Majesty, given at the earnest petition of the Princess Constança."

"And all that over a ship's cargo," said the Bishop with a sigh.

"And the profits from contraband. According to Don Arnau, if the ship does not founder, and is not captured by pirates, it will return to its investors almost double their capital. If it had carried contraband and had been successful in disposing of it, it would have returned five- or sixfold. A powerful incentive. Don Arnau was against it."

"Hence the information laid against him?" said the Bishop.

"Yes. They believed it certain that he would die under the headsman's ax. They did not take his wife into account. Anxious to save him, she organized his escape. Unfortunately, she asked their man of business—"

"Felip Cassa."

"Yes, Your Excellency. She asked him to arrange the

details. He did so, and instructed poor Martin, the man now down in your cellars, to hire three layabouts to attack and kill him as he came out. Don Arnau was injured, but escaped death because of the timely arrival of a pair of rescuers."

"Who?" asked the Bishop. "Not the guard, or they would have put him back in prison."

"He was rescued by one of your own priests, Your Excellency, a big man with a booming voice who was on his way to a deathbed, and a porter. His wife was then advised to hide him in the *call,* and did so."

"I know who that must have been," said the Bishop, smiling broadly.

"His servant died as a result of the attack, and his wife buried the servant, letting it be known that it was her husband."

"But why kill Father Miró? He was not one of your meddlesome friars, Master Isaac, but a good man and a cheerful dinner companion. He will be bitterly missed."

"They wanted to make sure Arnau was dead, and went to Father Miró with a tale of a heretic concealed in the physician's house. He investigated, discovered I do not know what, and chided the informer severely for his malicious lies. Shortly after, he was thrown down a cliff."

"He told me before he left the city that he was seriously troubled by the accusations against Marça. He was going to look into them on his return."

"Apparently they believed that Jacob Bonjuhes knew something of who they were, and in trying to lure him to his death, caught his apprentice in their trap."

"And who do you believe is responsible for all this? With Martin a simple tool, and Felip Cassa dead, whom do I punish?"

"Beyond doubt, Martin is not entirely without guilt," said Isaac. "He will tell you anything he knows, I believe, but unfortunately they told him little and he witnessed less. Our only real witness is my nose, but there are suspicious circumstances," said Isaac. "Let us take the death of Felip Cassa, which may have been the only one the man you seek committed himself—possibly the only one he has ever committed himself. A man left the palace at dusk dressed elegantly in green and gold, and returned at dawn, dressed in equal elegance in scarlet and deep blue, scrubbed clean and drenched from head to foot in sandalwood, a scent he affects. One of the men abroad in the night, seeking Don Arnau, smelled strongly of sandalwood. I myself came across him and received a slight blow from him; but I noticed that scent. He, Felip Cassa, and a servant were followed north toward Vernet. At the bridge, Cassa disappeared and his horse was seen galloping after the others."

"And the name of this man, Master Isaac," said the Bishop. "Although I believe I know already who he is."

"It is Bernard Bonshom, Lord Puigbalador, Your Excellency," said Isaac.

There was a long silence. "You deduce that Bonshom cut Cassa's throat, and being covered in blood, had to ride out to his infamous house in the country to wash it away and change his clothing. You may be correct. But consider my witnesses: a man who cannot identify his master, and a blind man who could not see his attacker. And to have as my only evidence a change of clothing between dusk and dawn and a gentleman who likes the scent of sandalwood."

"There might be bloodstained clothing still in the house," said Isaac.

"That is possible," said the Bishop. "The bridge is stained with blood. Whoever cut Cassa's throat left the bridge with hands drenched in his blood. I thank you, Master Isaac. My secretary is writing up the report even now. I shall speak of my suspicions. The death of Father Miró brings the affair to some extent under my jurisdiction, and if I do nothing else, Bonshom's house will be closed down and the man ejected from the city."

"I should also mention that His Excellency the procurator went to great lengths to prevent any delay in the judgment against Don Arnau—almost as if it were to his benefit that Don Arnau should die before a proper inquiry could be made."

"I shall add that extra note to my report. When do you depart?"

"Between sext and nones, Your Excellency. We dine early and leave."

"The report will be finished and delivered to you, either at the physician's or on the road. You travel at normal speed?"

"We do, at an easy pace."

"I wish you a safe and pleasant journey."

WHEN Isaac and Yusuf returned to the physician's house, all that could be done to prepare for departure had been done. Their modest box was fastened down and tied, ready to be loaded on the cart. The cook had packed a large basket of food for the road, and each person's bundle was sitting in the hall.

Arnau was still lying under the lemon tree, dozing in the shade. He awoke at the sound of renewed activity. "*Hola,* Master Isaac," he said. "How goes the hunt?"

"Almost over," said Isaac.

"And we know everything except what is on board that wretched vessel," said Arnau.

"When do you think you will find out?" asked Raquel. "And what will happen if it is stuffed full of contraband?"

"I can assure you it won't be by the time the *Santa Maria* returns," said Arnau. "If the captain has any sense, as soon as he sees it, he'll sell it to the first available buyer and pocket the cash." He turned his head and saw a figure standing in the doorway. "*Hola,* Lady Margarida. Come and sit here in the shade." Hesitantly she started over. "He knows I didn't want it on board," said Arnau. "He'll pretend it wasn't there. But whether it was or not, we won't find out anything until the ship returns. Fortunately, His Majesty seems convinced that I was innocent in the whole affair. I don't understand why, but he does."

"You may thank your lady wife for that," said Margarida, as she came up to them. "She convinced the Princess so thoroughly that Constança convinced her papa. But, my lord, I bring you someone who desires to be made known to you. And since you cannot easily come to him, then he has to come to you." And she laid the wrapped bundle in her arms down on Arnau's left arm. "Your son, my lord," she said.

Arnau looked down at the boy and then awkwardly, carefully moved his splinted right arm over and touched him on the forehead gently. "He is as beautiful as his mother," he said.

"And as strong and determined as his father," said Margarida.

TWENTY-ONE

RUTH and her cook set out an abundant but simple dinner shortly after the sun had reached noon. Those who were to leave sat down at once. Then Astruch and Duran arrived, filled with business talk of profits and percentages; Bonafilla hurried out of the kitchen to sit with them. To the considerable agitation of the cook, she had attached herself to her sister-in-law in the kitchen for the latter part of the morning. David soon joined her at the dinner table. Jacob was the last to arrive.

"Where have you been?" asked his wife, who had regained her distraught look.

"I have been to the palace," he said. "Looking after a very special patient."

"The Princess's dog?" asked Yusuf, trying to choke back a laugh.

"I beg you, do not make fun of my husband for obliging the Princess," said Ruth, rather sharply. "She and her sister spend much time here in Perpignan, and she is an important person for the city."

"I am very sorry, Mistress Ruth," said Yusuf, abjectly. "I had not intended any lack of respect either to the Princess or your husband. How is the little dog? I know that a broken leg is a very serious thing."

"She is not a horse, Yusuf," said Raquel, "to have an arrow put through her head because she has broken a leg."

"Whatever she might be," said Jacob, "your skilled fingers seemed to have set her limb aright, Isaac. She is looking bright of eye, and spends most of her time trying to escape from the confines of her mistress's chamber. I have great hopes that she may recover. Her Royal Highness is most grateful. She asked me about a sickly lady-in-waiting while I was there."

"You are to be congratulated," said Isaac. "It is clear that the young Princess feels comfortable in your presence. Raquel, are we prepared to leave?"

"Yes, Papa. The box and our bundles are on the small cart. The mules and Yusuf's mare have been brought around from the stable. As soon as we are ready, we may leave."

"Then let us go," said Isaac. "But first I wish to say my farewells to Don Arnau and his lady."

"I will be with you in a moment, Papa," said Raquel, lingering behind to exchange a word with her hostess. "I hope that all goes well with Bonafilla and David," she whispered.

"We shall see," said Ruth quietly. "She has been down in the kitchen with me and the cook, trying to learn how we do things here. The cook looks as if she finds Bonafilla's assistance a little trying, but my new sister has already learned to prepare a rice dish that David is fond of. And David told me that he honestly believes he could not have chosen a better wife. When I asked him why, he said that she has most of the attributes a good woman should have, plus a great deal of honest humility. I would not have thought that of her, would you?"

"She seems to have learned much on the journey here," said Raquel. "She had seen nothing of the world before that, except for her father's house," she added, and fled to Don Arnau's bedside before she said any more.

THEIR farewells made, the procession, much diminished from the one that came from Girona, finally went down to the gate of the *call* and then around to the Elna gate. Astruch's manservant drove the cart to which two of the baggage mules were hitched; Leah and Jacinta rode behind him on rugs spread over a thick layer of straw to cushion them from the bumpiness of the road. Raquel led her father's mule while managing her own, and Yusuf rode his mare, now dancing with impatience from the limited exercise she had had since they arrived in the city.

Raquel's spirits rose enormously as soon as they passed the palace on their right and headed toward the thick forest of His Majesty's *devesa*. The sun was shining; nothing seemed likely to hold them back. "How far do you think will we travel today, Papa?" she asked.

"Are you impatient, my dear?" asked her father.

"I am. I want to be home."

"There is a respectable and reasonably comfortable inn some two hours' ride past Collioure. At our present pace, if all goes well, I would think we can reach it by sunset."

"That would be excellent, Papa. I do not like traveling after sunset. I do not feel safe," said Raquel.

"Then we will not travel any farther than that today. We should be quite safe on this section of the road."

The sound of galloping hoofbeats behind them made everyone edge over to the side of the road to give the overtaking rider enough room to pass by safely. Instead of profiting from their action, he slowed down. By the time he reached them, he was moving at a walking pace. "Are you Master Isaac, the physician of Girona?" he asked.

"I am, sir," said Isaac.

"I come from the Bishop of Perpignan. He bade me give you this document into your own hand." The messenger placed a roll of parchment in Isaac's outstretched fingers.

The physician ran his hand along it to check its size and length and then tucked it into his tunic. "Thank you, sir. The Bishop of Girona will be most grateful." He began to hunt in his purse for a coin to reward the messenger.

"His Excellency suggested that we ride together," said the messenger. "I go as far as Figueres. Even though I travel armed, I feel that a group is safer than a lone rider."

"Excellent. Our patient escort who drives the mule cart is also armed with a stout staff and a dagger. Between the two of you, and Yusuf, who carries his sword, we should be safe," said Isaac.

THE inn was no better and no worse than most along this well-traveled road. The women were able to get a chamber for themselves with two beds in it, so that Leah, whose proportions were ample, had one, Jacinta and Raquel had the other, and everyone was able to sleep. Isaac and Yusuf shared a room with two other travelers; the manservant and the messenger slept on the thick straw on the floor of the cart, with a heavy canvas cover over it, fastened to the four corner posts. Thus they avoided the scramble of finding a place inside, and were able to keep an eye on the animals.

There was no temptation to linger at the inn in the morning. They breakfasted on bread and cheese and were on the road before the sun rose. The day was sunny; a brisk wind blew off the water and the well-rested animals needed no urging to hurry. "How far today, Papa?" asked Raquel.

"My plan is to travel until dinner, rest for a short while, and be in Figueres well before the sun sets. Astruch's friend

Master Beniamin has urged us to spend tonight with him. I hope we shall be able to."

Raquel was lost in her thoughts for most of the day. They reached Figueres well before the bells rang for vespers, had the luxury of washing the dust of travel off in peace and comfort, and then supping magnificently.

TWENTY-TWO

IT was not long after the dinner hour, in the quietest part of the afternoon, that the travelers crossed the bridge over the river and rode up to the north gate to the city. "Oh, Papa," said Raquel. "It looks so beautiful."

"The gate, my dear?" asked her father. "As I remember it, it is a sturdy, well-built gate, but not an object of great beauty. Has it changed?"

"It's not that, Papa," said Raquel crossly. "We're home."

"We are. And I too am very glad to be here," he said.

"You're not stopping to see His Excellency, are you?" asked Raquel.

"Judging by the quiet of the city, I believe that His Excellency would not thank me if I disturbed him now. We will go straight to the house and find out how your mama is faring."

JUDITH, who had been sitting in the courtyard waiting for them, rose at the clatter of hooves on the cobbles and came over to the gate. She clasped her husband's hand in both of hers. "I had not expected you so soon, Isaac," she said. "Have you eaten?" She paused for a moment, and said, "Who is this?"

"We rode like the wind, my love. I have missed you so sorely that we scarcely dismounted from our mules when we stopped to eat," said Isaac. "But eat we did. And this, my dear, is Jacinta. You needed a clever, good, honest little serving maid. We found you one in Perpignan."

"In Perpignan?" said Judith. "But we have serving maids here in Girona. I have already looked at one or two. Where did you find her?"

"At the house of my friend Jacob Bonjuhes. Since Bonafilla brought her maid with her, they no longer needed Jacinta."

Jacinta, looking pale with fatigue, stood wary and still, like a small woodland creature. Only her eyes betrayed her interest, darting back and forth, looking at the wide courtyard, the solid stone house, the fountain, and finally at the mistress.

"She is very good in the kitchen, Mama," said Raquel, "and also good with children. And very quick."

Judith looked down at the neat little girl, who curtsied with a bob of her head. "And your parents were willing to send you so far from home?"

"My mama was, mistress," said Jacinta.

"And your papa?"

Raquel steeled herself for the revelation, knowing full well what her mother's reaction would be.

"My papa is dead, mistress," said Jacinta, and Raquel took a deep breath of relief. "My mama thought it such a good post that she was willing to let me go. But she and Mistress Raquel made a contract and signed it to make sure that I would be all right."

"That is good," said Judith. "Why did your mama think it a better post than you could get in Perpignan?"

"I'm afraid that's my fault, Mama," said Raquel, hastily interrupting. "When we were helping in the kitchen with the wedding preparations, I noticed that Jacinta was clever with her hands and so good at following instructions that I said if she came to us perhaps Naomi would teach her to cook."

"Would you like to learn to cook, Jacinta?"

"Yes, mistress. Very much," said the child earnestly.

"Well," said Judith, "Leah's not much use in the kitchen, and the boy is hopeless at anything but tending the fire. Leah!"

"Yes, mistress," said Leah, who was already on her way up to the kitchen to gossip with Naomi.

"Get Jacinta settled, and once she's washed and ready, take her in to meet Naomi. She might be able to help a bit with the preparations for tonight. Goodness knows, I don't feel much like it."

"Are you not well, Mama?" asked Raquel.

"I'm very well," said Judith, yawning. "I just seem to be very sleepy. I think I will go and rest. And I suggest that you all do the same, after your long journey."

━┿━━━ ━━━┿━

THE courtyard cleared as if a troop of soldiers had come in shouting orders at them. Raquel went to her chamber and took off her traveling clothes with a sense of relief. She washed and put on a clean shift. It was too early to visit anyone; it was even too early to send a message. She might as well do as her mother suggested and rest. She stretched out on her familiar bed.

A fly circled around her head, determined to land. Every limb she had twitched irritably. The last thing she wanted to do at the moment was have a pleasant rest.

She rose from her bed, put on her pale green gown of fine light cotton, loosened her hair and shook it out, picked up her needlework, and went back to the courtyard. It was still deserted. A murmur of conversation drifted down from the kitchen; no other sound broke the silence but the rustling of leaves in the faint breeze.

"They said you were home," said a voice at the gate. "But I grew tired of waiting for a message."

"Daniel," said Raquel, running over and struggling with the recalcitrant fastening with shaking fingers. "I came down to send you a message but there's no one to take it. Everyone's disappeared." The gate swung open and Daniel stepped inside. Raquel took a quick look around the courtyard for onlookers, and threw her arms around his neck.

After a long, long moment, Daniel gently released himself from her embrace. "You're such a welcome sight, Raquel. We have been apart too much these last months. But tell me everything that happened while you were gone."

"What happened?" said Raquel, taking his hand and pulling him over to the bench by the fountain. "A great deal, it seemed then, some of it very strange. We thought until the day of the wedding that the marriage wouldn't take place at all. First she didn't want him, and then he didn't want her, and then suddenly there were never lovers so much in love except in some poet's tale. And, of course," she added, reaching up and giving him another kiss, "us."

"So you went for a wedding and there was one. What else happened?"

"A dead man came back to life, a baby was born, I found you the most interesting pair of ladies' gloves and brought them back for you to look at, and Papa and I rescued a little serving girl from becoming what her mother is. When we marry, Daniel, would you mind if I brought her with me? You'll like her. She's quiet and very serious."

"When we marry? Raquel, if that day ever comes, you can have anything that is in my power to give you. And certainly a little serving girl. But what is her mother?"

"Shh, Daniel," whispered Raquel, "you know what I mean. I daren't say it even in the tiniest voice. If I do, I swear to you that Mama will hear it in her sleep. She'd never forgive us. Mama doesn't understand much about the world."

"Yes, she does," said Daniel. "She just doesn't approve of it. But if you and your father thought her good enough to bring back from Perpignan, she must be a good little child. Now, tell me, Raquel. When can we marry?"

+‡=⟞ ⟝=‡+

"I don't understand it, Isaac," said Judith. Her gown and shift were hanging on the pegs on the wall, and she was standing by the basin and water ewer in the semi-darkened room. Her slender body, usually so quick in its movements, was beginning to be overbalanced by her swelling belly and breasts. "Why was Jacob's wife willing to let that child go if she's as good as you say?"

"I'm afraid it is more that we stole her, Judith," said Isaac. He lay on the bed, listening to his wife washing herself and then rubbing scented oil on her body. "Ruth had taken her on only because her maid was ill. There was going to be much work for the wedding, and many visitors. Everyone spoke of how useful she was but I don't think Ruth intended to keep her. So when her mother visited, we arranged a contract that pleased them both. But enough of maids. Come here, my dearest," he said.

"What do you mean, Isaac?" said Judith in mock surprise. "I've just left my bed and I'm all washed and tidied up again."

"I want to feel how you're growing," he said. "I wish I could see you, my lovely Judith."

"I am so very happy to have you back with me, Isaac," she said, coming over to the bed.

TWENTY-THREE

ANOTHER letter arrived from Perpignan, a month after the wedding of David and Bonafilla. It was brought to the physician's house by Duran, who had happily extended his stay in the city for many weeks longer than expected. A stern summons from home had dragged him back, carrying letters and good wishes from all.

The sun was low in the sky when the letter arrived, but still warm enough that everyone had gathered in the court-yard to gossip until supper was prepared. Raquel tore her-self away from a conversation with Daniel to take the letter and break the seal. "Do you want me to read the whole thing, Papa?"

"Please do," said Isaac.

"He says, 'My dear Isaac, Master Duran, who has been in the city since Bonafilla and David were married, is re-turning to Girona tomorrow, and I take this opportunity to send you greetings. No doubt he will acquaint you with the progress of his courtship of Samiel Caracosa's daughter; I send you news of less interest to a young man in love.

" 'You will be pleased to learn that Don Arnau can walk and ride almost as well as he ever could. The leg has healed most satisfactorily. He complains of stiffness in the wrist, although he is able to use his hand well enough. Still, he tells me, his ability in the hunting field has been somewhat hampered by the injury, as well as his expertise with the sword. I tell him that time is required to heal such an injury, but he turns out to be an impatient man. Doña Johana's son is thriving. I gather that they are no longer in danger of pursuit by the courts. They have returned to Don Arnau's estate.

" 'Of equal importance for me is the gratifying fact that Morena, the Princess Constança's little spaniel, seems to have recovered completely. Since she has no voice to complain of stiffness and walks well, we assume the best. The Princess is delighted, and as a consequence I am now treating one of her ladies-in-waiting for a severe cold. I hope that I will not be asked to treat any more sick or injured beasts at the palace. I am not very confident that I know what to do with them.

" 'Bonafilla is settling in. She prods David into buying a house of their own, saying that when Ruth's child is born, we will all be very crowded. To my surprise, Ruth agrees. I had thought she enjoyed having a companion in the house.

" 'I have written out a list of medications that I know you prepare. I include it with the letter. Could you send them with Duran when he next comes to the city? He will pay you and collect the money from me. And when you send them, could you do something else for us? Bonafilla would like to know the name of the glover she visited with Raquel; in the excitement of the wedding preparations, she has forgotten which one he was. Apparently he makes very fine gloves. Raquel will know, she says.

" 'Ruth sends you her regards, as do David and Bonafilla. David would also like me to say hello to little Jacinta on his behalf, and he hopes that she is doing well. It seems she did them some service for which he is most grateful. The coin enclosed in the letter is for her.'

"And that is all, Papa," said Raquel. "He tells a great deal, but not enough."

"Perhaps someone will let us know what has happened to our various friends and acquaintances there," said Isaac. "And Jacob needs to train an apprentice in how to make herbal mixtures. When we reply, we must suggest that."

+}=== ===={+

A week later, the end of summery warm days brought cold rain and another letter to Girona from Perpignan, by way of the diocesan courier. It was accompanied by a small box. Isaac, who had been visiting the Bishop, handed it to Raquel before shaking the water from his cloak and going up to join Judith and the twins by the fire in the dining room.

"Who is this from?" asked Raquel, following him in.

"I do not know, my dear," said her father. "Open it and see."

Raquel broke it open, paused to glance through it, and looked up. "Lady Johana Marça, Papa. She writes, she says, on behalf of her husband, who is either too lazy or his hand is too stiff to write, she cannot tell which. She is very amusing, Mama."

"That is enough explanation. Read us the letter."

"Yes, Papa. She says, 'Dear Master Isaac and Mistress Raquel.' Then she explains what I just said about why she is writing. 'I have not forgotten all that you did for us. At the moment when you departed, we were not ready to thank you adequately. The box that comes with this is but a small token in recognition of your aid.

" 'Since your departure, Bernard Bonshom, Lord Puig-balador has been forced to leave the city in disgrace. I am not a vindictive woman, but when I consider what he set in motion, I can hope that he will not enjoy a peaceful old age.

" 'Rumor says that Huguet, the procurator, busies himself with packing up the gold paid him by unfortunate petitioners like me, along with the gold he was given to overlook the abundance of false coinage under his administration. He is expected to flee Roussillon, but whether he will go to France or to Castile is a matter of speculation.

" 'Most interesting to us is news of the *Santa Maria Nunciada*. I will not tell you what it is, but I copy out the letter my husband received from the master of the ship. The good man left it with the landlord of the tavern in Collioure before he sailed, with instructions to give it to no one but Arnau himself. The landlord is one who takes a man at his word. He kept it safely until we returned to the castle, when it occurred to him that he might be rewarded for delivering it.' "

"And is the letter there?"

"Yes, Papa. It is part of the letter. 'Report to Don Arnau Marça on the sailing of the *Santa Maria Nunciada*: We commenced loading Tuesday, September 30. The transfer of cargo from the warehouse to the boats was to be supervised by Felip Cassa, owner's agent, who held the master cargo list. As instructed by Don Arnau Marça, the master and his mate checked each item from the ship's copy of the list as it came off the boats and went into the hold. Nothing was loaded that was not on the list, and every item was accompanied by proper documentation.

" 'Two hours into loading, the owner's agent, Felip Cassa, visited the ship's master and suggested, with inducements, that the master facilitate the loading of all the goods in the warehouse, whether they were on the list or not. The master refused, and carried on as instructed. The said Cassa rode off, saying that he would return soon. He has not been seen since then. Ship's master took over loading from the said Cassa.

" 'On the owner receiving a message from the procurator to come at once to the city, the ship's master decided that finishing loading cargo and setting sail in an expeditious manner would be the most responsible course of action. When the loading was complete, and everything on the cargo list that was accompanied by proper export permits had been taken from the warehouse and stowed, the warehouse still contained numerous bales, crates, and barrels of goods. The ship's master informed the warehouseman that the owners had decided to ship those goods elsewhere, and that he would be paid his usual charges and no more for warehousing them until they were taken away. (Signed) Xavier Francesch, master, *Santa Maria Nunciada,* Collioure, Wednesday, October 1, 1354.'

"Doña Johana has added something at the end. She says, 'So there you have the answer to the question that worried us all. There was contraband, but since it did not leave the warehouse, it wasn't contraband. It's still there, and now the owners are disputing hotly over how it should be disposed of, and who will reap the profits, if any, from its sale. With all our most fervent best wishes, Johana Marça.' "

"What is in the box?" asked Judith.

Yusuf had been prying the top of the wooden box off. It came up with a loud popping noise. "It is something wrapped in cloth," he said.

"Let me see," said Raquel, kneeling beside him. "It is silk," she said, "a most beautiful tawny gold color. It is for me, she says, and my marriage. And here is a leather purse for Papa. Full of coins."

ON the seventeenth of August in the year 1355, Bonafilla bore her husband, David Bonjuhes, a daughter, a full ten months after her marriage day, and a week before the marriage of the daughter of Samiel Caracosa to Duran, son of

Astruch Afaman. Bonafilla named her daughter Fortunata, as her great-grandmother had also been named. Her father, who had returned to Perpignan for his grandchild's birth and his son's wedding, was puzzled.

"I thought the old lady's name was Ester," he said.

"No, Papa. It was Fortunata," said Bonafilla, giving her head a little toss, "but even if it wasn't, I like the name, and David wanted to call her that."

In the years to come, Bonafilla comported herself with modesty and becoming grace. She bore her husband two handsome sons and another daughter. Both girls were famous for their beauty, but it was a fortunate man indeed who managed to capture so much as a glimpse of them until they were safely married.

AUTHOR'S NOTE

GEORGES Huguet, procurator of the district, the high official representing royal authority in His Majesty's absence, was banished for falsifying public accounts. Pere Vidal turned out to be one of Huguet's colleagues, and a forger and embezzler.

Lord Bernard Bonshom of Puigbalador, keeper of the royal forest of Capcir, whose castle lay in the mountainous country some fifty miles northwest of Perpignan, was declared an outlaw from Perpignan for his flagrant crimes and immoral behavior.

Pere the Ceremonious's descendents and later civic administrations made various attempts to cleanse the city's reputation as a center of gambling and vice.

One of these attempts is particularly interesting. A century after the events in this book, the campaign to rid the city of its gamblers and profligates was apparently so successful that a castle outside the city walls was turned into a safe and extremely profitable casino. The castle was owned by the noble de Marça family. It became so notorious for its activities that the city couselors raised the money to buy it and close it down. It was very expensive.

But in 1357, Jacob Bonjuhes, Jewish physician from Perpignan, was elected to the council of the *call*. Then in 1371, he was appointed physician to the household of the Lord King in Perpignan—*fisichus Perpiniani de domo domini regis*.

Read all the books in this
Anthony Award-nominated series
featuring physician Isaac of Girona by

Caroline Roe

A Potion for a Widow   0-425-18365-3

Solace for a Sinner   0-425-17776-9

An Antidote for Avarice   0-425-17260-0

Cure for a Charlatan   0-425-16734-8

Remedy for Treason   0-425-16295-8

LOVE MYSTERY?

From cozy mysteries to procedurals,
we've got it all. Satisfy your cravings with our monthly
newsletters designed and edited specifically for fans of who-
dunits. With two newsletters to choose from, you'll be sure to
get it all. Be sure to check back each month or sign up for
free monthly in-box delivery at

www.penguin.com

Berkley Prime Crime

Berkley publishes the premier writers of mysteries.
Get the latest on your
favorites:
Susan Wittig Albert, Margaret Coel, Earlene
Fowler, Randy Wayne White, Simon Brett, and
many more fresh faces.

Signet

From the Grand Dame of mystery,
Agatha Christie, to debut authors,
Signet mysteries offer something for every reader.

Sign up and sleep with one eye open!